PRAISE FOR AMY CLIPSTON

"A sweet romance with an endearing heroine, this is a good wrap up of the series."

—PARKERSBURG NEWS & SENTINEL ON
A WELCOME AT OUR DOOR

"Clipston closes out this heartrending series with a thoughtful consideration of how Amish rules can tear families apart, as well as a reminder that God's path is not always what one might expect. Readers old and new will find the novel's issues intriguing and its hard-won resolution reassuring."

—HOPE BY THE BOOK, BOOKMARKED
REVIEW, ON A WELCOME AT OUR DOOR

"[A Seat by the Hearth] is a moving portrait of a disgraced woman attempting to reenter her childhood community . . . This will please Clipston's fans and also win over newcomers to Lancaster County."

—PUBLISHERS WEEKLY

"This story shares the power of forgiveness and hope and, above all, faith in God's Word and His promises."

—HOPE BY THE BOOK, BOOKMARKED
REVIEW, ON A SEAT BY THE HEARTH

"With endearing characters that readers will want to get a happily ever after, this is a story of romance and family to savor."

—PARKERSBURG NEWS AND SENTINEL
ON A SEAT BY THE HEARTH

"This story of profound loss and deep friendship will leave readers with the certain knowledge that hope exists and love grows through faith in our God of second chances."

—KELLY IRVIN, AUTHOR OF *THE BEEKEEPER'S SON* AND *UPON A SPRING BREEZE*, ON *ROOM ON THE PORCH SWING*

"This heartbreaking series continues to take a fearlessly honest look at grief, as hopelessness threatens to steal what happiness Allen has treasured within his marriage and recent fatherhood. Clipston takes these feelings seriously without sugarcoating any aspect of the mourning process, allowing her characters to make their painful but ultimately joyous journey back to love and faith. Readers who have made this tough and ongoing pilgrimage themselves will appreciate the author's realistic portrayal of coming to terms with loss in order to continue living with hope and happiness."

—*RT BOOK REVIEWS*, 4 STARS, ON *ROOM ON THE PORCH SWING*

"A tender story about heartache, healing, and hope. This is a story Amy Clipston fans will absolutely love."

—KATHLEEN FULLER, AUTHOR OF THE AMISH LETTERS SERIES, ON *A PLACE AT OUR TABLE*

"Warm and homespun as kitten tangled yarn, Amy treats the reader to hearth and table, flame and love. The invitation is open for a soul satisfying read. Come in and be blessed!"

—KELLY LONG, BESTSELLING AUTHOR ON *A PLACE AT OUR TABLE*

"From the first line in *A Place at our Table*, talented Amy Clipston plunges the reader into a gripping, fast-paced novel of hope, friendship and redemption. I loved the story and loved its heart."

—New York Times and USA Today bestselling author Shelley Shepard Gray

"*A Place at our Table* is a moving story of forgiveness and the healing power of love. Amy Clipston weaves beautiful tales of Amish life, family ties, and heartwarming romance. She has always been one of my favorite Amish authors."

—Jennifer Beckstrand, author of *Return to Huckleberry Hill*

"*Seasons of an Amish Garden* follows the year through short stories as friends create a memorial garden to celebrate a life. Revealing the underbelly of main characters, a trademark talent of Amy Clipston, makes them relatable and endearing. One story slides into the next, woven together effortlessly with the author's knowledge of the Amish life. Once started, you can't put this book down."

—Suzanne Woods Fisher, bestselling author of *The Devoted*

"Fans of Amish fiction will love Amy Clipston's latest, *The Bake Shop*. It's filled with warm and cozy moments as Jeff and Christiana find their way from strangers to friendship to love."

—Robin Lee Hatcher, bestselling author of *Who I Am with You* and *Cross My Heart*

"Clipston is well versed in Amish culture and does a good job creating the world of Lancaster County, Penn. . . . Amish fiction fans will enjoy this story—and want a taste of Veronica's raspberry pie!"

—PUBLISHERS WEEKLY ON *THE FORGOTTEN RECIPE*

"[Clipston] does an excellent job of wrapping up her story while setting the stage for the sequel."

—CBA RETAILERS + RESOURCES ON *THE FORGOTTEN RECIPE*

"Clipston brings this engaging series to an end with two emotional family reunions, a prodigal son parable, a sweet but hard-won romance and a happy ending for characters readers have grown to love. Once again, she gives us all we could possibly want from a talented storyteller."

—RT BOOK REVIEWS, 4 1/2 STARS, TOP PICK! ON *A SIMPLE PRAYER*

". . . will leave readers craving more."

—RT BOOK REVIEWS, 4 1/2 STARS, TOP PICK! ON *A MOTHER'S SECRET*

"Clipston's series starter has a compelling drama involving faith, family and romance . . . [an] absorbing series."

—RT BOOK REVIEWS, 4 1/2 STARS, TOP PICK! ON *A HOPEFUL HEART*

"Authentic characters, delectable recipes, and faith abound in Clipston's second Kauffman Amish Bakery story."

—RT BOOK REVIEWS, 4 STARS ON *A PROMISE OF HOPE*

A WELCOME AT OUR DOOR

A WELCOME AT OUR DOOR

AN AMISH HOMESTEAD NOVEL

Amy Clipston

ZONDERVAN

A Welcome at Our Door

Copyright © 2019 by Amy Clipston

This title is also available as a Zondervan e-book.

Requests for information should be addressed to:
Zondervan, *3900 Sparks Dr. SE, Grand Rapids, Michigan 49546*

ISBN 978-0-310-34912-9 (softcover)
ISBN 978-0-310-34910-5 (e-book)
ISBN 978-0-310-36388-0 (mass market)

Library of Congress Cataloging-in-Publication
CIP data is available upon request.

Printed in the United States of America

21 22 23 24 25 / LSC / 5 4 3 2 1

With love and appreciation for my wonderful Amish friend. Thank you for your precious friendship. You are a blessing in my life!

Glossary

ach: oh
aenti: aunt
appeditlich: delicious
Ausbund: Amish hymnal
bedauerlich: sad
boppli: baby
bopplin: babies
brot: bread
bruder: brother
bruderskind: niece/nephew
bruderskinner: nieces/nephews
bu: boy
buwe: boys
daadi: granddad
daed: father
danki: thank you
dat: dad
Dietsch: Pennsylvania Dutch, the Amish language (a German dialect)
dochder: daughter
dochdern: daughters
Dummle!: Hurry!
Englisher: a non-Amish person
faul: lazy
faulenzer: lazy person

fraa: wife
freind: friend
freinden: friends
froh: happy
gegisch: silly
gern gschehne: you're welcome
grossdaadi: grandfather
grossdochder: granddaughter
grossdochdern: granddaughters
grossmammi: grandmother
gross-sohn: grandson
Gude mariye: Good morning
gut: good
Gut nacht: Good night
haus: house
Hoi!: Get back here!
Ich liebe dich: I love you
kaffi: coffee
kapp: prayer covering or cap
kichli: cookie
kichlin: cookies
kind: child
kinner: children
krank: sick
kuche: cake
kumm: come
liewe: love, a term of endearment
maed: young women, girls
maedel: young woman
mamm: mom
mammi: grandma

mei: my
Meiding: shunning
mutter: mother
naerfich: nervous
narrisch: crazy
onkel: uncle
Ordnung: the oral tradition of practices required and forbidden in the Amish faith
schee: pretty
schmaert: smart
schtupp: family room
schweschder: sister
schweschdere: sisters
sohn: son
Was iss letz?: What's wrong?
Wie geht's: How do you do? or Good day!
wunderbaar: wonderful
ya: yes
zwillingbopplin: twins

AMISH HOMESTEAD
SERIES FAMILY TREES

Edna m. Yonnie Allgyer
|
Priscilla m. Mark Riehl

Marilyn m. Willie Dienner
|
Simeon (deceased)
Kayla m. James "Jamie" Riehl
Nathan

Eva m. Simeon (deceased) Dienner
|
Simeon Jr. ("Junior")

Nellie m. Walter Esh
|
Judah
Naaman

Laura m. Allen Lambert
|
Mollie Faith (mother—Savilla—deceased)
Catherine Savilla

Irma Mae m. Milton Lapp
|
Savilla (deceased)

Gertrude m. Ervin Lapp

Florence m. Vernon Riehl
|
James ("Jamie") Riehl (mother—Dorothy—deceased)
Walter Esh (father—Alphus Esh—deceased)
Mark Riehl (Laura's twin) (mother—Dorothy—deceased)
Laura (Mark's twin) m. Allen Lambert (mother—Dorothy—deceased)
Roy Esh (father—Alphus Esh—deceased)
Sarah Jane Esh (father—Alphus Esh—deceased)
Cindy Riehl (mother—Dorothy—deceased)

Kayla m. James "Jamie" Riehl
|
Calvin
Alice Dorothy

Priscilla m. Mark Riehl
|
Ethan (father—Trent Parker)
Adam (Annie's twin)
Annie (Adam's twin)

Elsie m. Noah Zook
|
Christian
Lily Rose

NOTE TO THE READER

While this novel is set against the real backdrop of Lancaster County, Pennsylvania, the characters are fictional. There is no intended resemblance between the characters in this book and any real members of the Amish and Mennonite communities. As with any work of fiction, I've taken license in some areas of research as a means of creating the necessary circumstances for my characters. My research was thorough; however, it would be impossible to be completely accurate in details and description, since each and every community differs. Therefore, any inaccuracies in the Amish and Mennonite lifestyles portrayed in this book are completely due to fictional license.

CHAPTER 1

Cindy Riehl hummed as she hung a pair of her father's trousers on the clothesline, and then she swept a lock of golden-brown hair escaping her prayer covering away from her eyes. She squinted in the bright June sunlight before pushing the line forward to make room for another pair of *Dat*'s trousers.

As she lifted them from her wicker basket, she glanced toward the fenced cow pasture just as one of the cows pushed open the gate, trotted down their short driveway, and started down the street toward the neighbor's farm.

"*Ach*, no," she groaned as she dropped the trousers into the basket.

"Jamie! Roy!" Cindy yelled for her brothers as she scurried down the porch steps. "Cucumber got out again!"

She ran toward the dairy barn, calling her brothers' names again and again. Where were they? When neither brother stepped out of the barn, she turned to the street.

Cindy raced after the cow, shouting, "Cucumber! *Hoi! Hoi!*"

On several occasions she and her siblings had retrieved wandering cows with the help of a neighbor's dog, and this afternoon she longed for both human and canine help. Corralling a cow wasn't easy as a one-person job.

Cindy dodged puddles from last night's rain as she again yelled, "Cucumber! *Hoi! Hoi!*"

The cow jogged down the street and turned into their neighbor's driveway.

Cindy followed the cow, shouting to her as she made her way over the rocks and past Gertrude and Ervin Lapp's farmhouse.

She stopped running when she saw the cow following a golden retriever toward the Lapps' barn. She cupped her hand to her forehead and groaned. Did Cucumber think she was a dog? The cow and dog sniffed each other, and then the cow trailed the dog as it walked in circles in front of the barn.

"Cucumber! *Hoi! Hoi!*" she called, at the same time trying to catch her breath. "Come on, Cucumber. I need to get you home."

The cow ignored her.

"Cucumber!" She stamped her foot. "I need to finish hanging out the laundry. Please come. *Hoi! Hoi! Kumm! Dummle!*"

When she heard someone laugh, she turned toward the little one-story house across from the barn. A tall *Englisher* stood on the porch, watching her. She tented her hand over her eyes to get a better look at him in the bright sunlight as he strolled down the porch steps and started toward her.

He looked to be in his mid-to late twenties, and his light-brown hair was short on the sides but long and messy on top, as if he'd just raked his hand through it. His chiseled cheekbones and strong jaw were covered in a few days' light-brown stubble. And he was smiling.

His smile widened as he nodded toward the cow. "Did I hear you call that cow Cucumber?"

"Yes." She fingered her black apron as she looked up into his ice-blue eyes. He was at least six inches taller than she was. She guessed he was even taller than her older brothers, who stood close to six feet. "My nephew named her. He's four and a half, and he thought it was a great name."

"It *is* a great name." He whistled, and the golden retriever bounded over to him, tongue hanging out and tail wagging. "I guess Bruce and Cucumber are friends, huh?" He leaned down and rubbed the dog's ear.

"Yes, I guess so. Cucumber learned how to open the gate, just like her mother, Sassy, used to do. I've asked my brother to fix it so she can't get out, numerous times, but you can see how well that's worked." She turned toward the cow, which had started munching on a tuft of grass. "Cucumber!" she snapped. *"Hoi! Hoi!"*

When Cucumber continued to ignore her, she harrumphed and then turned toward the man. His lips twitched as he scratched the dog's ear and looked at her.

"This is a typical Monday on your farm?" he asked, sounding . . . what? Entertained?

"No, not really." Humiliation and a little bit of anger heated her cheeks. Did he think this was funny? She needed his help, not his amusement.

"Do you happen to have a carrot?" she asked.

"A carrot?" He stood up straight.

"Yes." She pointed toward the cow. "To entice her to follow me back to our dairy farm."

"Oh. Right." He scratched his chin. "I might. If not, then I'll ask Gertrude for one. I'll go check." He looped back to the small house and disappeared inside.

"Cindy!" a voice shouted behind her.

She craned her neck to look over her shoulder. Her brother Jamie was jogging up the driveway. "It's about time," she muttered, and then pressed her lips together.

"Did Cucumber get out again?" Jamie lifted his straw hat and pushed his dark-brown hair off his forehead.

"Why else would I be over here?" She slammed her hands on her hips. "When are you going to fix that gate so she can't open it?"

He gave her two palms up. "I did fix it."

"Not well enough." She gestured toward the cow. "I asked Gertrude and Ervin's farmhand to get me a carrot."

"Ervin finally hired a new farmhand?" Jamie asked.

"*Ya*, I guess so." She pointed toward the porch where she'd first seen the *Englisher*. "He came from their farmhand's *haus*." When something that felt like wet sandpaper brushed her hand, she jumped and looked down. The golden retriever gazed up at her and panted. "Hello there, Bruce."

His tail wagged, and she scratched his ear.

"He likes you." The man had come back, and when he grinned, for some reason her cheeks heated again. He faced her brother. "Hi. I'm Drew Collins." He held out his hand, and Jamie shook it.

"Nice to meet you. I'm Jamie Riehl." Jamie gestured toward Cindy. "I guess you've already met my sister Cindy."

"Not formally." He turned his smile on her again. "Nice to meet you, Cindy."

She nodded and cleared her throat, feeling self-conscious. Why? She didn't even know the man!

Drew held up a carrot. "I found one."

"Great!" Jamie took it. "Thank you." Then he turned to the cow. "Come on, Cucumber. Let's go home."

Drew snickered. "That's such a fantastic name."

"My son came up with it." Jamie shook his head. "He's creative."

"It sounds like it." Drew crossed his arms over his middle and then nodded toward Bruce. "He really does like you, Cindy."

She looked down at the dog as he pawed the skirt of her blue dress. "I guess so." She scratched his ear again.

"Let's go, Cucumber." Jamie held out the carrot and started walking. As the cow followed him down the driveway, Jamie looked over his shoulder at Drew. "I'm sorry for the trouble."

"Yes, I am too," Cindy said. "Thank you for the carrot." She turned to follow Jamie and the cow.

"You're welcome, and it was no trouble." Drew fell into step with Cindy as they walked down the driveway. Bruce jogged beside them. What was this man doing? Didn't he have work to do?

"Do you need help with your gate, Jamie?" Drew asked.

"That's not necessary," Jamie said as he turned and walked backward, "but thanks. I'll just try again."

"I don't mind." Drew gave Cindy a sideways glance, making her uncomfortable again. "Maybe I can help you figure out a different fix to keep Cucumber from opening it."

Jamie paused for a moment before responding. "I have to admit I'm not sure what else to do," he said. "Help from someone who might have a different idea sounds great. Thank you. Are you Ervin's new farmhand?"

"Yeah." Drew jammed his thumb toward the farm behind him. "I just started last week. Their former farmhand took another job last year, and Ervin recently decided to hire a replacement."

"That's what I heard." Jamie smiled. "Welcome to Beechdale Road."

"Thanks." As they came to the end of the driveway and

turned down the street, their farm immediately came into view. Drew said, "This is your dairy farm next door?"

"Yes." Jamie pointed toward the large two-story, white clapboard farmhouse where Cindy and her brothers and sister had been born and raised. "That's our dad's house." Then he pointed to the smaller house on the other side of the pasture, also two stories and white clapboard. "That's my house."

"Oh." Drew nodded. "They're nice homes."

"Thanks." Jamie led the cow up the rock driveway and toward the dairy barn. "Let's get Cucumber situated, and then I'll grab my toolbox."

As Jamie and Drew headed for the barn, Cindy turned toward the back porch and her waiting laundry. She felt something brush her leg and looked down to see Bruce.

"Are you trying to kidnap my dog?"

Cindy looked behind her, where Drew stood grinning, his arms folded over his wide chest.

"No." She glanced down at the eager golden retriever and shook her finger at him. "I think you need to go with your dad." Then she met Drew's amused gaze. "Call him."

"I think he'd rather be with you." He laughed.

"Does he like to hang out laundry?"

Drew shrugged. "I've never asked him, but you can."

Cindy chuckled. "All right." She looked down at Bruce again. "Would you like to help me hang out the laundry?"

The dog barked, crouched, and barked again.

She turned her gaze back to Drew. "I think that means yes."

He smiled. "I do too. But I'll call him if he's bothering you."

She shook her head. "I think he'll be a great helper."

"All right." He gave her a little wave as he turned to go. "I'll call him after I finish helping Jamie."

Cindy started up the steps and then whistled for Bruce to follow. "Maybe you can hand me clothespins."

Bruce bounded up the steps and then sat beside her as she returned to the task of hanging damp clothes on the line. Bruce looked up at her, his tongue hanging out and his tail wagging.

"You're a handsome guy." She scratched his ear once more and then turned back to the basket of clothes.

As she hung a pair of her stepbrother Roy's trousers on the line, her gaze moved to the gate where Jamie and Drew worked. Drew laughed when Jamie said something before digging through his toolbox. It seemed her brother was getting acquainted with their new neighbor.

"What was all the yelling earlier?"

Cindy turned to see Florence, her stepmother, coming onto the porch from inside the house. She was holding the screen door open for her daughter, Sarah Jane.

"And who is this?" Sarah Jane asked as she came outside and gestured toward their canine guest.

"Cucumber opened the gate and took off down the lane, and I was yelling for Jamie or Roy to help me." Cindy nodded toward the dog. "She went to visit Bruce."

"Hi, Bruce." Sarah Jane leaned down to rub the dog's neck.

"Where does Bruce live?" Florence asked as she let the screen door shut.

"He belongs to Gertrude and Ervin Lapp's new farmhand." Cindy pointed toward the pasture. "His name is Drew, and he's helping Jamie fix the gate so Cucumber won't get out again."

"Isn't that nice of him?" Florence walked to the edge of the porch and looked out toward the fence. After a few moments, she turned back to Cindy. "You should invite Drew to stay for supper."

"Oh?" Cindy studied her stepmother.

"*Ya*. As a thank-you for helping Jamie." Florence looked at Sarah Jane. "Don't you think that's a *gut* idea?"

"*Ya*." Sarah Jane picked up another pair of Roy's trousers and handed them to Cindy. "I think it's a nice way to thank him."

"It's settled, then." Florence turned to Cindy. "Would you please go ask Drew to stay? I've already invited Jamie's family, and Kayla knows it will be ready in about an hour. I have two pans of broccoli, rice, cheese, and chicken casserole. That should be more than enough for everyone."

Cindy looked over at Drew and hesitated. Would inviting him to supper seem too forward?

"Go on," Sarah Jane said. "I'll finish hanging the laundry."

"All right." Cindy smoothed her hands down her black apron as she descended the porch steps and squared her shoulders.

Drew glanced over his shoulder and smiled as she approached the pasture fence. "Is Bruce proving to be a good help with the laundry?"

"Yes, he is." She looked back toward the porch, where Bruce supervised her stepsister as she hung an apron on the line. Then she met Drew's gaze again. If only she could stop blushing in front of this man!

"My stepmother would like you to stay for supper as a thank-you for your help today."

"Oh." Drew's brow pinched as if he were puzzled by the request. "That's very nice of her."

"Jamie's family is coming too. Florence said the meal will be ready in about an hour. Will you join us?"

"Yes, join us, Drew," Jamie said. "You've helped me come up with a solution that should hold this time, and we should be done soon."

"I'd like to stay." Drew nodded. "Thank you."

"You're welcome," Cindy said. As she headed back to the house, questions about Drew filled her mind. Maybe she'd learn more about him during supper.

· · ·

After their silent prayer, Cindy scooped some casserole onto her plate as conversations broke out around the long table in their kitchen. She peeked across the table at Drew and found him plucking a roll from the basket. His gaze met hers, and he nodded with a smile before dropping his eyes to cut the roll in half.

At the far end of the table, her niece Alice hummed in her high chair and chewed on a roll. Cindy smiled. Alice had grown so much during the spring. Now eighteen months old, she resembled her parents with Kayla's sun-kissed blond hair and Jamie's deep-blue eyes.

Alice's older brother, Calvin, sat on a booster seat in a chair beside her. At four and a half, he shared the same blond hair and blue eyes, making their brother-sister relationship easy to detect. Alice finished her roll and then moaned, arching her back. Calvin handed her another roll, and she squealed her thanks. Cindy smiled at the scene, hoping the siblings would always be close.

"So, Drew," Florence began, her voice rising above the other conversations filling the air, "how did you wind up working for Ervin and Gertrude?"

"My aunt who raised me recently passed away—" Florence gasped, stopping him from going on. Yet he seemed at ease despite the sadness behind his words.

"*Ach* no," Florence said, and when Cindy turned her eyes back to her stepmother, she found her dark eyes misting. "What happened to your parents?"

Cindy inwardly cringed. Her stepmother never shied away from a personal question.

"They died when I was ten." Drew picked up his glass of water and took a drink as the kitchen fell deathly quiet.

Cindy's chest squeezed as she looked into Drew's eyes and imagined the depth of his grief. He'd lost his parents and then his aunt. Like Drew, Cindy had weathered a turbulent sea of grief, ever since her mother had died from an accidental fall seven years ago.

"I'm so sorry," Florence said, and Cindy's father and siblings murmured similar words of sympathy.

Cindy opened her mouth to tell him she was sorry, too, but her words were trapped behind trembling lips.

"Thank you." Drew looked down at the mountain of casserole on his plate. "My aunt never married, and when she became too ill to continue her work as a nurse, I took care of her the best I could, taking whatever jobs I could find when I got out of high school. Then when she died, she left me a little bit of money, and I thought I'd enroll in a few college classes and look for a job I could manage at the same time. A friend told me about the part-time job at the Lapps' dairy farm, taking care of a few animals and the milkings, and I thought it might be perfect since I'd have a place to live and a small salary."

Cindy took in Drew's handsome face and thought about how kind he seemed. He appeared to be a genuine person—possibly even someone who could be an understanding friend since he, too, had experienced personal loss. But how could they be friends? He was an *Englisher.*

"How old are you, Drew?" Florence's question pulled Cindy back to the present.

"Twenty-five." Drew forked some casserole. Another personal question, but Drew didn't seem to mind.

"Really?" Florence brightened. "You're the same age as Sarah Jane."

Drew wiped his mouth with a paper napkin. "I'm one of the oldest students in my entry-level classes." He gave a sheepish smile. "But at least I'm going to school. For the past few years I've felt as if I've been searching for something. I don't know what it is, but I suppose I'll know when I find it."

Cindy stilled as his words soaked through her. He'd just expressed aloud how she'd felt inside for the past seven years. How could an *Englisher* understand her confusion? Perhaps they were more alike than she'd imagined.

"How do you like working on an Amish farm?" Jamie asked as he added another scoop of casserole to Calvin's plate.

"I like it," Drew said. "I appreciate the simplicity of your lifestyle. It's quiet and homey. And please, every word doesn't have to be in English around me. I don't know many Pennsylvania Dutch words yet, although I hear Gertrude and Ervin speak them, but you should speak any way you wish."

"Well, we'll see," Florence said, "but in our family we don't want to be rude to the *English*. Not that we encounter very many of you except in stores and such."

"Uh, where did you live before you came to Bird-in-Hand?" Kayla quickly asked.

Cindy knew her stepmother didn't mean to offend Drew with her *you* or insinuate Gertrude and Ervin should speak only English around Drew, but she almost sighed with relief. She could always count on Kayla to steer conversation in a friendly direction. She'd had practice when she worked in her family's restaurant before marrying Jamie.

"Not far from here," Drew said. "My aunt and I rented a house in Wakefield."

"How did your friend hear about the job at Ervin's farm?" *Dat* asked.

"He was at the hardware store in Bird-in-Hand while Ervin was there. He mentioned to the clerk that he needed a new farmhand since the work was getting too difficult for him alone, and my friend knew I was looking for a job. He got Ervin's number and then passed it along to me." Drew put another forkful of casserole in his mouth, and after swallowing he said, "This meal is delicious, Florence."

"Thank you," her stepmother said, obviously pleased by the compliment.

Cindy studied Drew's easy demeanor as her family members peppered him with questions during the rest of supper, including during dessert. They seemed to like him.

After everyone was finished, Cindy, Florence, and Sarah Jane gathered the serving platters while Kayla saw to her children. Then Cindy stood at the double sink and began to fill one side with hot water. She looked over her shoulder at Drew as he lifted his plate and utensils from the table.

"Drew," *Dat* said as he stood, "why don't you join us on the porch for some of my homemade root beer?"

"That sounds nice. Thank you." Drew carried his dishes to the counter and handed them to Cindy. "Thank you for inviting me to eat with you and your family. I appreciated the company."

"It was Florence's idea, but you're welcome. I'm glad you stayed." Cindy knew her voice sounded soft and unsure as she looked up into his eyes. That was because, for the first time in her life, she felt interest stirring in her heart as she looked at a man.

She watched Drew out of the corner of her eye as he thanked Florence, and then heard him leave to join the men outside. She felt confused. How could she feel a connection to someone who wasn't Amish?

CHAPTER 2

Drew, what do you think of my root beer?" Vernon asked as he sat in a rocking chair on the porch.

"It's the best root beer I've ever had." Drew angled his body toward Vernon as he relaxed on one of the porch's gliders. "It's even better than the root beer at A&W, and I always thought that was the best."

"Thank you." Vernon's face seemed to glow with pride. Drew guessed Vernon was in his late fifties, and despite the graying light-brown hair and beard, Drew could see the similarities he shared with two of his children. Both Jamie and Cindy had Vernon's striking blue eyes, and Jamie had the same nose and strong jaw. Roy and Sarah Jane, however, both had dark hair and eyes, similar to Florence's.

Cindy called Florence her stepmother when she invited Drew to stay for supper. Did that mean Roy and Sarah were her stepsiblings? He'd puzzled over that during supper, but he didn't feel comfortable asking. After all, it was none of his business.

Drew glanced back and forth between Vernon and Jamie as he took another sip of the delicious root beer. He suddenly realized that both Vernon and Ervin had beards, but Jamie, also married, was clean-shaven.

He turned to Jamie, who was sitting on the other glider beside his son. "I thought all married Amish men had beards." He pointed his mug at Jamie. "Why don't you have one?"

Jamie leaned back and rubbed Calvin's leg as his little boy snuggled into his side. "I'm a volunteer firefighter. The bishop in our district makes an exception to the rule for married volunteer firemen like me because we have to wear custom-fit facemasks."

"Huh," Drew said. "That's interesting. How long have you been volunteering?"

"Since I was a teenager. A group of friends and I all joined at the same time. I volunteer at Station 5 in Bird-in-Hand." Jamie gestured toward the street.

"That's cool." Drew looked toward Jamie's house across the pasture. It was a beautiful night filled with the warm June air and the smell of moist earth. The pasture was green and lush, reminding him of how much he loved being in the rural parts of Lancaster County.

Drew turned back to Jamie and Vernon. "I've found the work never ends on a dairy farm. Don't you agree?"

"Yes." Roy snorted as he leaned against the railing in front of Drew. "You could say that."

"Laugh all you like, little brother." Jamie grinned at him. "You think you're blessed to be abandoning me, but you'll still have work. Lots of it."

"I know." Roy sighed.

"I'm just teasing you." Jamie raised his mug toward his younger brother. "I'm going to miss you, but I'm happy for you."

Drew raised an eyebrow as he divided a look between the brothers. "You're leaving, Roy?"

"He's getting married in October," Vernon chimed in. "But he's moving to his future father-in-law's dairy farm. He's not escaping work."

"He's just leaving *me* with all the work here." Jamie looked down at Calvin. "We need to teach you how to clean the milkers."

"*Ya!*" Calvin sat up straighter. "I'm almost as tall as you, *Dat*." All the men laughed as Calvin grinned.

"You'll be working beside me before you know it." Jamie touched Calvin's nose.

Drew settled back on the glider and took another sip of root beer while he glanced around the farm. A pang of sadness rang through him as he considered his childhood. What would it have been like to have a few siblings while he was growing up? Would he have shared the same camaraderie the Riehl siblings seemed to have?

The screen door opened and then clicked shut behind Drew. He craned his neck and looked up as Cindy appeared with a plate of cookies.

"Are you going to share any of that root beer with the rest of us?" Cindy stepped forward and lifted a tray of cookies. "I brought chocolate chip."

"You can have this mug of root beer in exchange for a chocolate chip cookie." Vernon held a filled mug out to her, obviously prepared for any of the women who might join the men.

"Thanks." She took the mug her father offered, and he grabbed a cookie from her plate.

Roy took a cookie as well, and then Cindy held out her plate for Jamie and Calvin to take one. When she turned to Drew, she seemed to hesitate.

"Do you like chocolate chip cookies?" she asked.

"Are you kidding?" Drew teased her. "I love them."

A smile turned up her lips, and her pretty face lit up. Cindy was beautiful with her striking baby-blue eyes and high cheekbones. The hair peeking out from her prayer covering reminded him of sunshine. She was taller than her stepmother and Sarah Jane, and she was slender. He thought she was close to her mid-twenties, perhaps a year or two younger than his twenty-five.

She glanced down at the empty side of his glider and then looked away.

"There's room for you." Drew slid to the far side. "Join me."

She paused for a moment, but then she sank into the seat beside him and held the plate toward him.

"Thanks." He swiped a cookie and took a bite, and then he closed his eyes and smiled, enjoying the sweetness of the cookie.

"Do you like it?" Her tone sounded hopeful.

"You could say that." He took another bite and then swallowed. "I can take the rest of those cookies off your hands, if you'd like."

"I don't think so," Vernon said, and everyone laughed.

Drew turned back to Cindy, who had placed the plate of cookies on the small table beside her and was sipping her root beer. "You're a fantastic baker."

She shrugged. "Not really."

"You should see her sewing and quilting," Jamie said.

"That's the truth," Vernon chimed in. "She's very talented."

"Stop." Cindy stared down at her mug as her face flushed pink.

Drew marveled at her shyness and humility. Was she always this easily embarrassed?

Cindy set her mug on the small table, picked up the plate of cookies, and turned toward him. "Would you like another?"

"Yes, I would. Thank you." Drew took one. "These are fantastic. What else do you like to bake?"

"Anything." She shrugged again. "I make cakes, pies, breads."

"*Aenti* Cindy?" Calvin leaned toward her. "May I have another *kichli*?"

"If your father says it's okay." Cindy looked at Jamie, who nodded. "Here you go."

"*Danki*," Calvin said as he took the cookie.

"*Gern gschehne.*" Cindy turned back to Drew. "Thank you for helping my brother today."

"It was my pleasure." Drew rested back on the glider and took another drink from his mug. As he once again took in Cindy's pretty face, trying not to be obvious about it, questions swirled through his mind. What did she like to do besides sew and bake? He was already aware that members of the Amish community usually kept to themselves and rarely mingled with the outside world. Would he ever see her again after this evening?

The men had become engrossed in a conversation about their farm, but he realized Cindy wasn't listening to them. She was looking at *him*.

"What kind of classes are you taking in college?" she asked.

Drew blinked, stunned by the question.

"I'm sorry." She gave a little laugh. "Is that question too personal?"

"No, not at all. I'm just surprised you asked since the Amish don't go to school after eighth grade."

"That doesn't mean we're not curious." She shifted her body toward his.

"I didn't think about that." Drew moved his fingers over

the condensation on his mug, leaving swirled streaks in their wake. "I'm just taking introductory classes right now."

"Like what?" She seemed interested.

He shrugged. "English and math. Nothing very exciting."

"What do you want to study?"

"I'm not sure. I'm still trying to figure out what I want to do with my life." He felt his expression grow sheepish. "That sounds pretty pathetic at my age, doesn't it?"

"No." She shook her head, and then her expression became serious as she lowered her voice. "I understand exactly what you mean."

Curiosity nipped at him as he studied her gorgeous blue eyes. From what he understood about the Amish, they were expected to marry and have large families. Why would this beautiful young Amish woman doubt her future? And why was she so concerned her family might hear what she'd told him?

The screen door opened and clicked shut, and Kayla appeared, carrying her daughter, a diaper bag slung over her shoulder.

"We need to get going," Kayla said. "Alice needs a bath." She kissed the toddler's blond head and then looked at Calvin. "You need one too."

"*Ya, Mamm.*" Calvin sighed as he climbed off the glider.

Drew hid his smile by taking another sip of his root beer.

"It was nice meeting you," Kayla told Drew. She said good night to Vernon, Roy, and Cindy before looking at Jamie. "Are you ready?"

"Yes, dear." Jamie grinned as he stood. He said good night to everyone and then shook Drew's hand. "Thanks again for your help today. I think we might have actually found a fix for keeping Cucumber inside the fence."

"Let's hope so," Cindy quipped. "I'm tired of chasing her."

Everyone laughed, and Cindy joined in, her smile wide and bright.

"I'm happy to help anytime," Drew said. "Just come and get me."

Jamie and his family waved at everyone as they started down the porch steps and then continued down the path that led to his house.

"I should probably head home too." Drew picked up his empty mug and stood. "It was really nice meeting you all."

"I'll take your mug." Cindy reached for it, and when he gave it to her, she set it on the table. "Would you like some cookies to take home?"

"That would be great. I never turn down cookies," Drew admitted.

"Just give me a minute." Cindy hurried into the house.

Roy stood up and yawned. "I guess I'll go check on the animals." He shook Drew's hand. "Thanks again for your help today."

Drew nodded. "You're welcome."

"I'll help you, Roy." Vernon stood and shook Drew's hand too. "Don't be a stranger, neighbor."

"I'll try not to." Drew stood and walked to the edge of the porch. He leaned on the railing as Roy and Vernon disappeared into the largest barn.

Once again, his mind spun with questions about Cindy. Based on what she'd said, he wondered if she was unhappy living on this farm. But whatever she meant, why would she open up to him, a stranger?

When the screen door opened and clicked shut behind him, he spun around. Cindy held up a clear plastic storage container packed with cookies.

"I didn't have many of the chocolate chip left, but I hope

you like oatmeal raisin and peanut butter." Her smile seemed shy as she handed him the container.

"Thank you so much. It beats the packaged cookies I picked up at the market yesterday."

She shook her head. "My cookies are much better than the ones you can buy at the market." She gasped as her eyes rounded. "That sounded prideful. I didn't mean to sound arrogant."

"I get the feeling you don't have a prideful or arrogant bone in your body."

She hugged her arms to her chest. "But we all sin and fall short of the glory of God."

"That's true."

An awkward silence fell over the porch as they stared at each other. How he longed to get to know her better, but she was Amish, and he wasn't. Despite Vernon's invitation to not be a stranger, there was a chance he'd leave her porch and never see her again. Why did that bother him?

"Well, I should get inside." She gestured toward the door. "I need to finish a sewing project."

"Thank you for the cookies." He held up the container. "I'll bring this back for you to refill for me."

She gave a little laugh. "That works."

He held out his hand. "I hope to see you again soon."

She shook his hand and smiled. "Good night."

As Drew started down the porch steps, he couldn't imagine never seeing Cindy's smile again.

. . .

Thursday afternoon Cindy leaned over and pulled another weed as the sun warmed her back. When she thought she felt something brush against her hip, she craned her neck, alarmed. But then she smiled.

"What are you doing here, Bruce?" she asked.

The dog sat back on his haunches and looked up at her, his tongue hanging out of his mouth as if he were smiling.

"Does your *dat* know you're here?" She dropped the weed into the overflowing bucket beside her and swiped her hands down her black apron.

Bruce held up his paw, and she laughed as she shook it.

"You're a bit of a flirt, aren't you?" She wagged her finger at him. "Let's get you back home before your *dat* starts to worry about you—with a proper entry this time." She started toward her home's short driveway and whistled to Bruce. He was at her heels within seconds. "You sure are a cutie."

"Cindy!"

She spun toward Jamie as he exited the barn. *"Ya?"*

"Where are you going?" Jamie asked.

"I'm taking my unexpected visitor home." She pointed to Bruce, and Jamie chuckled. "I'll be right back."

"All right." Jamie gave a little wave. "Tell Drew hello for me."

"I will." She waved and then led Bruce down the driveway to the street before turning toward the Lapp farm.

They walked up the Lapps' driveway together, past the big farmhouse to the barn. Cindy peeked inside and then in the pasture for Drew. After scanning the property once again and finding no one, she made her way to the little house where Drew lived. She climbed the steps and then knocked on the front door.

After a few moments, the screen door swung open and Drew stood before her clad in worn blue jeans and a faded gray T-shirt. As he had the last time she saw him, he sported a sprouting light-brown beard, and his hair looked as if he had just raked his fingers through it. Although her father might have called Drew's appearance disheveled, Cindy found it to be almost endearing.

She pushed that thought away.

"Cindy." He opened the door wide. "How are you?"

"I'm well. Thank you." She pointed to the smiling dog. "Bruce just came to visit me. I thought I should bring him home in case you were frantically searching for him."

"Oh." He seemed confused as he looked down at the dog. "Were you trying to run away?"

Bruce gave a little bark and then moved past Drew into the house.

"I'm sorry." Drew rubbed the stubble on his strong jaw. "I was so focused on studying for an exam that I didn't even notice my dog was missing." He gave her a sheepish expression. "That sounds terrible. I'm really not a neglectful dog owner, so don't report me to the authorities."

Cindy laughed. "I have a cow that goes missing, so I'm not in any position to judge."

When he leaned his head against the door and seemed to study her, she shifted her weight on her feet and cleared her throat. "Have you finished the cookies I gave you?"

"I have. I suppose you want your container back."

"Only to refill it for you." The words escaped her lips without any forethought, and she suddenly felt bold. But would Drew consider her assuming he'd like more cookies from her too forward?

"That would be amazing. They help me study." He stepped

into the house and motioned for her to follow. "Come on in. My house is a mess, but I can offer you a drink."

Cindy lingered at the doorway. It was inappropriate for her to be alone with a man, but she didn't want to be rude. He wasn't a member of their community, but if Gertrude or Ervin caught her walking into his house without a chaperone, they could tell her father and—

"Do you like Coke?"

"What?" She glanced across the small family room to the kitchen area, where he held up a can of Coca-Cola.

"I also have water, iced tea, and milk." He seemed eager to share a drink with her.

"Water would be perfect."

"Coming right up." He leaned into the refrigerator and took out a bottle of water. Then he crossed to the doorway and handed it to her before making a sweeping gesture around the family room. "Come in. I'll clear off the sofa." He began moving a pile of books from the sofa to the coffee table, where he stacked them next to a laptop computer.

He looked up at her, looking first puzzled, then concerned. "Was it inappropriate for me to invite you in?"

"It's probably best if I stay here." She pointed to the threshold.

"Oh." He looked a bit embarrassed. "I'm sorry."

While remaining in the doorway, Cindy glanced around the room, taking in the television set, light switches, light fixtures, and lamps. In the kitchen she spotted a microwave, toaster, and toaster oven. "This house has electricity?"

"Yeah. Why?"

"I'm just surprised. I always thought this was a *daadihaus*."

"A what house?" His lips twitched.

"The grandfather house or the end-of-life house." She opened the bottle of water. "It's where the grandparents live when the younger couple take over the farm. It's normally an Amish house. I'm surprised Gertrude and Ervin have a home with electricity on their property."

"I hadn't really thought about it, but Ervin told me he built this house for his son to try to convince him to stay on the farm. Apparently it didn't work, because his son still moved to New Jersey. He never bothered to have the electricity removed just in case his son came back to visit."

"That makes sense. I remember when their son moved away. It was difficult for Gertrude and Ervin." Cindy took a sip from the bottle.

Bruce bounded into the room, his jowls wet and water dripping from his mouth.

"I guess he got a drink." Drew snickered as he scratched Bruce's head.

"Did you name him?"

"No, my aunt named him after her favorite action movie star, Bruce Willis."

"Oh." She had no idea who that was, but she didn't want to say anything to disrespect his aunt. "It's a great name."

"Yeah." Drew grinned down at the dog.

She pointed to his computer. "What are you studying?"

"Math." He rolled his eyes. "It's not my best subject. Did you like math when you were in school?"

"I didn't *dis*like it."

"Were you good at math?"

"I was okay."

"You're also good at baking, cooking, sewing, and quilting, according to your family."

"It's normal for Amish girls to learn how to do those things."

Cindy squeezed the bottle of water, and it crinkled in protest. She needed to steer the conversation away from herself. "What are you good at?"

He sat down on the arm of a wing chair. "I guess I'm good at fixing things."

"You proved that the other day." She pointed the bottle of water at him. "What else?"

"Hmm. I like living on this farm, and I enjoy taking care of the animals." He pointed to a table in one corner. "I also like to do puzzles. My aunt always did them, and I liked to help her. I guess that's sort of my hobby."

"That's a neat hobby."

"Who taught you how to sew and quilt?"

She stilled at the question.

"I'm sorry." He leaned forward and held up his arms. "I didn't mean to get too personal."

"That's not too personal." She looked down at her bottle. "My mom did."

"You mentioned Florence is your stepmother."

"That's right." She met his gaze and found warmth there. "My mom died seven years ago. It was an accident."

"I'm so sorry."

"It's been really tough without her," Cindy said, her voice sounding small and unsure, as if she were a child. "My father was devastated and lost. He withdrew from all of us for a time while others kept the farm and house going. Then my siblings moved on, but I still feel like I'm floating aimlessly without her." She took a long drink of water to wet her suddenly dry throat.

"All of your siblings?" He tilted his head as he studied her.

"Yes." She gripped the water bottle, and it crinkled once

again. "I have three older siblings—Jamie, Laura, and Mark. Laura and Mark are twins. They're married and have children. They don't live far from here, but I don't see them as often as I'd like."

"What about Roy and Sarah Jane? Are they your step-siblings?"

"Yes, along with Florence's son Walter. He lives with his family in Gordonville, and they come to visit frequently. But Roy is getting married in October, and I wouldn't be surprised to see Sarah Jane get married soon. She's had a couple of boyfriends, but nothing serious yet. She's so outgoing, and the young men in her youth group seem to like her." She paused. "Sometimes I feel like I don't belong in this family. I haven't even joined the church, and I—" She stopped speaking and held her breath. Why was she telling this stranger her deepest secrets? What was wrong with her?

She had to leave before she confessed every burden in her soul.

"I'm sorry." She took a step back onto the porch. "I need to go. It was very nice talking to you. Thank you for the water. Have a good day." She turned toward the porch steps.

"Cindy!" Drew called after her. "Cindy. Wait!"

She stopped at the top step and peeked over her shoulder at him.

"You forgot your container." He held it out to her. "After all, I need more fuel for studying."

She turned and took the container, nodding. "Oh, right."

"I'll do my best to not eat them all in one sitting next time."

His smile was so adorable that she laughed. "You'd better not."

"I hope to see you soon."

She nodded again, turned, and left.

As she headed home, curiosity and dread filled her in equal measure. She'd felt interest the other day, but now she found herself *longing* to know this man better. What would her father say if he knew she found it easier to talk to an *Englisher* than to any of the young Amish men in their community?

. . .

Drew leaned on the doorframe as he watched Cindy hurry down the driveway. He frowned as regret whipped through him. Why had he asked her so many questions about her life? If he hadn't been so nosy, maybe she would have stayed and talked longer.

Still, at the same time, she'd seemed to want to share with him. He could feel the sadness radiating off her as she talked about her mother and how much she missed her. He could relate to her pain. In fact, she felt like a kindred spirit, and he'd love to get to know her better.

Drew wasn't a dolt. He was aware that it was forbidden for an Amish person to have a relationship with someone who wasn't Amish. But was friendship also forbidden? How he longed for a friend who could understand the depth of his grief for his parents and aunt. Cindy seemed like she could be that friend.

Bruce appeared at his heels and gazed up at him.

"Thanks for bringing Cindy over to see me." Drew rubbed the dog's head. "Maybe you can do that again sometime soon."

Then he recalled that Gertrude and Ervin were hosting church in their barn on Sunday. He'd be helping them with the setup. Maybe he'd have a chance to see Cindy then.

CHAPTER 3

Cindy smoothed her hands down her white apron and pink dress as she walked down the street between Roy and Sarah Jane. They were on their way to Gertrude and Ervin's farm, and Jamie and his family walked in front of them while *Dat* and Florence followed behind.

When they rounded the corner and started up the Lapps' rock driveway, she looked toward the pasture. A line of buggies stretched along the fence for what seemed like a mile. Horses filled Ervin's pasture, and men dressed in their Sunday black and white stood talking by the barn.

Cindy's gaze moved to the small house across from the barn, and her insides fluttered. She'd stopped by with another batch of cookies for Drew yesterday and was disappointed to find his burgundy pickup truck missing and his home empty. She'd left the cookies on the bench by his front door before hurrying back home.

The bench was now empty, indicating that Drew had found the cookies. She'd hoped to see him today, but, like yesterday, the pickup truck was gone. Would she be able to see him before she went home?

She tried to dismiss her thoughts of Drew as she climbed Gertrude's porch steps to join the women in the congregation. Drew was an outsider, and any desire to spend time with him was inappropriate. But he was beginning to feel like her friend. How could she ignore a friend?

Cindy followed Florence and Sarah Jane into Gertrude's kitchen. When she spotted Gertrude speaking to the bishop's wife, Cindy approached them.

"*Gude mariye.*" Cindy shook their hands.

"How are you?" Naomi, the bishop's wife, asked.

"I'm well. *Danki.*" Cindy looked at Gertrude. "How are you this morning?"

"I'm *gut,*" Gertrude said.

When Naomi turned to speak to someone else, Cindy leaned in closer to Gertrude. "Did Drew go to church this morning?"

"*Ya,* he did. He attends a community church in Bird-in-Hand."

"Oh, that's nice." Cindy's heart warmed with the knowledge that Drew was a Christian. But why did that matter? They attended different churches and were from different worlds.

"He's such a nice young man." Gertrude smiled brightly. "He's been a tremendous help to Ervin and me. He cleaned out my flower beds and planted more flowers for the service today. He also repaired our barn doors, and he's working on replacing the rotten boards in the fence. I've been telling Ervin to hire someone since Darren left last year. I'm so thankful he finally did, and I'm grateful God sent Drew our way."

"That's *wunderbaar,*" Cindy said, agreeing with her.

"He told me about how your cow came over and made friends with his dog. You have the funniest cows! I remember how Sassy used to get out and come visit us sometimes." Gertrude chuckled.

"*Ya, mei dat*'s cows have always had unique personalities." Cindy smiled.

"Drew also said Florence invited him to stay for supper. He went on and on about how *gut* your *dat*'s root beer is and how *wunderbaar* your *kichlin* are. He really enjoyed spending time with your family."

Cindy's smile faded. Had Drew told Gertrude she'd visited him last week and that she'd left him cookies yesterday? If so, would Gertrude tell her father or the bishop? How could she explain her behavior or her friendship with a non-Amish man?

"*Aenti* Cindy!"

Cindy turned as her seven-year-old niece, Mollie, ran toward her with her arms open for a hug. Mollie was her sister Laura's older daughter.

She looked over at Gertrude. "Excuse me."

"Of course! It was nice talking to you," Gertrude said before turning to speak to another woman.

"Mollie! How are you?" Cindy leaned down and hugged the little girl. Cindy often thought about what a blessing it was when Laura adopted Mollie Faith after marrying her widowed father. Allen's first wife, Savilla, had been one of Laura's best friends. The whole family cherished this small version of her after she suffered a sudden and fatal illness not long after Cindy's mother died.

"I'm *gut*." Mollie pointed behind her. "*Mamm* and Catherine are coming." Her mother headed toward them, holding Mollie's eighteen-month-old sister's hand as she toddled along.

Cindy waved at them. "*Gude mariye!*"

Catherine squealed and held her arms up to Cindy.

"She's excited to see you." Laura laughed as Cindy lifted the toddler into her arms. Laura's hand immediately moved to her abdomen. She'd be a mother of three shortly before Christmas, but she didn't show any signs of pregnancy quite yet.

"It's so *gut* to see you, Catherine." Cindy kissed her niece's cheek as Catherine rested her head on Cindy's shoulder.

"Did she sleep well last night?" Cindy asked Laura as she rubbed Catherine's back.

Laura nodded. "She did. She didn't even want to get up this morning."

"How are you feeling?" Cindy nodded toward Laura's middle.

"*Gut.*" Laura sighed. "I have about six months to go. Allen keeps saying the time will go quickly, but I don't know. The months were long with Catherine."

"I'm just glad you're feeling well," Cindy said. "I can't wait to be an *aenti* again." For a brief moment, Cindy wondered if she'd ever have a family of her own, but she dismissed the thought. She needed to be happy for Laura and not think of herself.

"*Aenti* Priscilla!" Mollie took off toward the door, where Mark's wife pushed a double stroller through the doorway with her son Ethan's help.

After Priscilla had the stroller situated, Ethan disappeared through the mudroom. Cindy was certain he was hurrying to catch up with Mark and the rest of the men out by the barn. At eight, he was more interested in spending time with them than with the women.

Mollie rushed to Priscilla and gave her a hug before looking into the stroller and talking to her one-year-old twin cousins.

"Mollie is the little mother." Laura smiled as she gazed at her. "She's such a *gut* helper."

"*Ya*, she is." Cindy shifted Catherine's weight. "You'll be even more grateful for that when your new *boppli* comes."

"That's true," Laura admitted with a smile.

"Good morning." Priscilla pushed the stroller over to Cindy

and Laura. "I thought we were going to be late. These two were fussy this morning." She sighed. "I hope they're not getting summer colds."

When Catherine moaned and squirmed, Cindy set her down on the floor. She toddled to the stroller and peeked at Adam and Annie.

"See the *zwillingbopplin*?" Mollie pointed to the stroller.

A squeal erupted as Alice, Jamie and Kayla's daughter, toddled to the stroller as well. She lit up when she saw Annie and Adam.

"*Gude mariye.*" Kayla joined Laura, Priscilla, and Cindy. She seemed to study Priscilla. "You look exhausted. Did the *zwillingbopplin* keep you up last night?"

"*Ya.*" Priscilla cupped her hand to her mouth to stifle a yawn.

"And my twin didn't help you?" Laura rested her hands on her hips.

Priscilla rolled her eyes. "Mark slept right through the crying."

"That sounds like him," Laura said. "Why didn't you wake him up?"

"I thought he could use the sleep. He works so hard on the farm." Priscilla glanced down at the stroller.

"And you work hard in the *haus.*" Kayla wagged a finger at Priscilla. "Don't let him get away with it. You'll need his help when you have more *kinner.*"

Priscilla grimaced. "I'm still trying to get used to having *zwillingbopplin.*" She looked at the ceiling. "Please don't bless me with more *kinner* just yet, Lord."

"You don't mean that." Laura touched her arm. "You and Mark will have more, and it's wonderful for siblings to be close together."

Kayla gave Laura a nudge with her shoulder. "Maybe you'll have the *zwillingbopplin* next time."

"Don't be so sure, Kayla." Laura clicked her tongue. "You and Jamie could have *zwillingbopplin*. They're in the family."

Kayla groaned, and Priscilla and Laura laughed.

Cindy pressed her lips together as dejection rolled over her. When her sisters discussed their children, she always felt like an outsider, someone who didn't belong in the family because she couldn't relate to motherhood or their happiness. She longed to disappear, fade into the walls, get away from the feeling of loneliness that plagued her.

Would she ever fall in love and have a family of her own? Her father and siblings had all moved on and found happiness after *Mamm* died, but she was still drowning in grief at the loss of her best friend. How could she find someone to love when she felt so lost and alone? Everyone else lived as if everything was back to normal, but Cindy felt so left behind, struggling to make sense of God's choosing to take her sweet, loving, supportive, wonderful mother. Why didn't they feel the same grief she felt day after day?

When the clock on the wall chimed, announcing nine, she looked up.

"I'll see you after church." Laura gave Cindy a side hug.

Cindy forced a smile and then followed her sisters to the barn.

. . .

Drew steered his pickup truck into the driveway, careful to keep his speed at a minimum because of the Amish folks meandering between the main farmhouse and the barn.

After parking his truck in his usual spot next to his house, he climbed out and started for his front door. When he reached the porch, he turned, hoping to get a glimpse of Cindy with the other Amish women who were carrying trays of food from the house to the barn. Disappointment curled through him when he didn't find hers in the sea of faces.

"Drew!"

He spun and found Jamie and Roy approaching.

"Good morning." Drew shook Jamie's hand and then Roy's. "I suppose I should say good afternoon since it's noon."

"How are you?" Jamie asked.

"Great. I'm just getting back from church."

"Have you had lunch?" Roy asked.

"Not yet." Drew pointed toward his house. "I'm going to make a sandwich."

"You should join us." Roy gestured toward the barn. "We were just getting ready to sit down and eat."

"Oh, I wouldn't want to impose." Drew shook his head. "You two enjoy your time with your friends."

"Don't be silly. You're our friend, too, so you're not imposing." Jamie beckoned him. "Come and meet the rest of our family."

Drew hesitated and then shrugged. "All right."

He followed Jamie and Roy into the barn. The benches he'd helped set up yesterday had been converted into tables, where only men now sat. He glanced around for Cindy and found her in one corner, serving bowls of pretzels. She looked pretty in a pink dress with a white apron. When she said something to one of the men, her face lit up with a beautiful smile. He felt a strange and mystifying connection to her.

"Drew, this is my brother Mark."

Drew swiveled toward a man who was slightly shorter than Jamie. Mark's hair and beard were light brown, not dark brown like Jamie's. But the brothers shared the same bright-blue eyes.

"It's nice to meet you." Drew shook Mark's hand.

"I'm the better-looking brother." Mark smirked and elbowed Jamie in the ribs.

Jamie responded with an eye roll. "Mark is the comedian of the family." Then he pointed to the man beside him. "This is Allen, my sister Laura's husband."

Drew shook Allen's hand and greeted him.

"You have to meet my twin." Mark looked over his shoulder. "Hey, sis! Come here!"

A short woman with dark-brown hair and blue eyes, carrying a coffee carafe, crossed the barn floor and stood next to Mark.

"Laura," Mark began, "this is Drew. He's Ervin and Gertrude's new farmhand."

After they all greeted one another, Jamie gestured toward a long bench. "We should take a seat."

"And I'll fill your coffee cups." Laura held up the carafe.

Drew sat down between Jamie and Mark and then handed his Styrofoam cup to Laura. After she filled it, he sipped the coffee as the brothers began to chat.

"So I heard Cucumber got out again," Mark said.

"She did." Roy pointed toward Drew. "That's how we met our new neighbor."

"I think *Englishers* would buy tickets to come see the escaping cow," Mark quipped.

"That's a *gut* idea." Jamie nodded. "That would help pay for the repairs to the barn we need."

Drew laughed.

"Would you like some pretzels?"

Drew looked up as Cindy leaned over him and set a bowl of pretzels on the table.

"I'm glad you decided to join us for lunch." Cindy smiled down at him.

"It's nice to see you." Drew opened his mouth to thank her for the cookies she'd left on his porch, but before he could get out the words, she was gone, moving down the table and delivering more bowls. He would have to try to talk to her later, so he could tell her how much the cookies meant to him.

"So, Drew," Mark began, "where are you from?"

"Not far from here." Drew relaxed as he settled into a comfortable conversation with Cindy's family.

. . .

Drew headed out of the barn and ambled home. He'd enjoyed both the meal and the company, but he was ready to relax and then study for another math quiz. He just hoped to see Cindy again before disappearing into his house.

When he glanced at Ervin's house, he spotted her talking with Sarah Jane on the lawn—although he thought they might be arguing. He froze, taking in Cindy's deep frown as Sarah Jane waved her arms. Then Cindy wagged a finger at Sarah Jane, who shook her head.

His eyes followed Sarah Jane as she spun and walked toward the pasture, where some young people were gathered around a few horses and buggies. Her posture was rigid, and her expression frustrated, if not angry.

He turned his eyes back to Cindy, who had hugged her arms

to her chest and started down the driveway. Panic gripped Drew. He didn't want her to leave without talking to him.

"Cindy!" he called as he took off after her. "Cindy. Wait!"

She turned toward him and wiped at her eyes before lifting her chin.

His stomach twisted. What had her stepsister said to make her so upset?

"Are you all right?" he asked as he approached her.

"Yes." Her voice was hoarse, as if she'd been screaming all morning. Anxiety and frustration seemed to come off her in waves.

"Do you want to talk about it?"

She glanced past him and then looked up at him, her eyes misting over. "Sarah Jane keeps pressuring me to go to youth group with her, and I don't want to go. No matter what I say, she won't let up. She doesn't understand that I'm not like her. I'm not ready to date or get married, but it's all she talks about. She sounds like a teenager, not a grown woman."

She opened her mouth and then closed it as if deciding she'd already shared too much.

"I'm sorry she upset you." Once again, questions swirled in his mind. He'd thought all Amish women wanted to get married. He longed to find out more about her. Why was she so unhappy?

"I'm sorry." She pointed to the street. "I'm just going to head home."

"Wait." He held up his hand, and she stilled. "I want to thank you for the cookies. I'm sorry I missed you yesterday. I'd been home all morning helping Ervin and Gertrude get ready for today. I just ran to the market really quickly to get something for Gertrude, and when I came back, I found the cookies. They were a nice treat."

"I'm glad you liked them." Her shoulders seemed to relax slightly. "Do you like pie?"

"Who doesn't like pie?"

She smiled, and relief filtered through him. "I'll have to bring you one sometime."

"That sounds wonderful."

She glanced past him, and her smile faded. He looked over his shoulder as Laura headed toward them.

"Cindy!" Laura hurried over. "Where are you going?"

"Home to take a nap." Cindy fingered the hem of her apron as she spoke. Was she nervous? With her sister?

"Gertrude invited us all to stay and visit." Laura divided a look between Cindy and Drew, and then her gaze settled on her sister again. "I haven't seen you in two weeks. I've missed you. Please come visit with us. It would mean a lot to Mollie and Catherine too."

"Okay. I will." Cindy turned toward Drew. "It was nice seeing you."

"It was nice seeing you too." He said good-bye to Laura and then headed for his house.

As he climbed the porch steps, he realized he knew one thing about Cindy. She needed someone to talk to, and he wouldn't mind being that someone. Not at all.

CHAPTER 4

I'm so glad you stayed this afternoon," Laura told Cindy as they stood at Gertrude's sink. They were washing the dishes they'd used while eating baked goods and visiting with Gertrude and the rest of the women in the family for the past couple of hours. "It's been so long since we've been able to talk."

"I know. I'm glad I stayed too." Cindy washed a plate as she looked out the window above the sink. She'd seen Drew go into his house, but now he was visiting outside with the men in her family.

She studied him as she worked. He looked different today. His strong jaw was clean-shaven, and he was dressed in a light-blue button-down shirt that brought out the blue in his eyes, along with pressed khaki trousers. His hair was combed, and the disheveled and messy look was gone. He must have dressed up for church, and he was even more handsome than the previous two times she'd seen him.

She scolded herself at the thought. Why was she allowing herself to think about Drew's looks, as though he could ever be more than just an acquaintance? He wasn't a member of her community, and her family would never approve of their being special friends—or friends at all. But she couldn't deny the growing interest she felt swelling in her chest.

"Are you okay?" Laura's voice was close to Cindy's ear.

"What?" Cindy spun toward her.

"You just seem down today." Laura glanced past her as if to make sure they were alone.

Both Kayla and Priscilla had disappeared into Gertrude's family room to retrieve their children from the portable cribs they'd brought, and Gertrude had left the kitchen for a moment.

"*Was iss letz*?" Laura asked.

"Nothing is wrong." Cindy turned back to the sink and began scrubbing a handful of utensils.

"You seemed upset when you were talking with Drew."

Cindy rinsed off the utensils and set them in the drainboard as she considered her response. If she told Laura that Sarah Jane was once again pressuring her to go to youth group, Laura would take Sarah Jane's side. She wanted Cindy to go to youth group too. Lying was a sin, so it was best to not even share her conversation with Sarah Jane.

"I'm *gut*." Cindy picked up a mug and began to wash it. "Drew was just thanking me for *kichlin* I left for him yesterday."

Laura's forehead puckered. "Why did you make him *kichlin*?"

"Remember how I told you he helped Jamie fix the gate and then stayed for supper?"

Laura nodded.

"I gave him *kichlin* to take home, and when he returned the container he told me they helped him study for his college tests. So I made him more and left them for him yesterday." Cindy shrugged as if it weren't a big deal.

"Cindy, I don't think it's a *gut* idea for you to make *kichlin* for an *Englisher*."

"They're just *kichlin*." Cindy set the clean mug in the drainboard and started work on another.

"But he might get the wrong idea." Laura's tone held a thread of warning.

"Don't be *gegisch*." Cindy turned toward the doorway as Kayla entered the kitchen holding Alice and a diaper bag. Florence was right behind her.

"I need to get her home. She needs another nap." Kayla sighed as Alice moaned and rubbed her face against Kayla's shoulder. "It was really *gut* seeing you, Laura."

"You too." Laura dried her hands and then walked over to Kayla. "Have a *gut* nap, Alice." When Alice snuggled deeper into her mother's shoulder, she kissed her niece's head.

"Let me walk home with you," Florence offered. "I'll carry your portable crib."

"*Danki*, Florence," Kayla said, and Florence left the room to get it.

"It was so nice spending time with you," Gertrude said as she walked into the kitchen.

"*Danki* for the fun visit." Kayla gave a little wave and then headed outside, Florence following.

"I should get going too," Laura said. "But I'll finish drying the dishes first."

"You can go," Gertrude said. "I'll finish them."

Cindy helped Priscilla and Laura gather their portable cribs, then carried them outside one at a time. She said goodbye to Laura, Allen, and her nieces, then waved as their buggy started down the driveway.

"Cindy." Priscilla sidled up to her. "Is everything all right?"

"*Ya*." Cindy folded her arms over her middle. "Why do you ask?"

Priscilla glanced behind her to where Mark was loading the twins into their car seats, secured in the buggy.

"You don't look all right. No one can hear us, so you can be honest with me." Priscilla lowered her voice. "You were so supportive of me when I was struggling with returning to the church. What's wrong?"

Cindy pressed her lips together and glanced toward Drew's house, where Drew stood on the driveway talking to her father and Roy. While she longed to pour out her heart to her sister-in-law and tell her how she was tired of Sarah Jane's pressure and feeling like an outcast in her own family, it would take more time and emotion than she could spare before Mark would announce it was time to go.

"I'm *gut*," Cindy said.

Priscilla was silent for a moment as her chestnut eyes studied her. Then she leaned forward and lowered her voice again. "When you're ready to talk, you know where to find me."

"I appreciate that." And Cindy did.

"All right, you two." Mark sauntered over to them. "That's enough girl talk. It's time to get these *narrisch kinner* home."

"I'm not crazy," Ethan called from the buggy.

"That is up for debate," Mark quipped.

Priscilla laughed as she swatted his bicep. "You need to stop talking about our *kinner* that way. If they're crazy, then we made them crazy."

"And I take pride in that." Mark grinned down at Priscilla, and Cindy could feel the love sparking between her brother and his wife.

Will I ever be blessed with a love like that?

"Well, we'll see you soon." Mark touched Cindy's arm. "Be *gut*, and make sure Cucumber doesn't escape again."

"I'll do my best." Cindy gave Priscilla a hug and whispered, "*Danki*," in her ear.

"Come visit me if you want to talk," Priscilla whispered in return.

"I will." Cindy leaned into the buggy and waved at her niece and nephews.

The twins smiled and waved, and Ethan said good-bye.

Cindy stepped back as Mark guided the horse toward the street. She waved once more and then turned toward Drew's house, where her father, Roy, and Drew now sat on the bench and rocking chairs on his front porch.

Dat waved. "Are you heading home now?"

"*Ya*," Cindy called back.

"Would you please tell Florence I'll be there soon?" *Dat* asked.

"Of course." Her gaze moved to Drew, and he gave her a smile and a nod. She longed to sit next to him and talk to him. But instead of giving in to that urge, although she knew it wouldn't be the same with her father and brothers there, she continued down the driveway.

Surely Drew would finish the cookies she'd left and return the empty container soon. That container would be their key to another meaningful conversation, and possibly a deepening of their friendship—forbidden or not.

. . .

"Cindy!" Kayla's voice sounded from the back of the house as a baby wailed. "Cindy!"

Cindy dropped the broom she was using to sweep the family room and rushed into the kitchen, where Kayla stood holding a screaming Alice in her arms. Calvin stood behind her sniffing and wiping at his red, puffy eyes.

"*Was iss letz?*" Cindy touched Kayla's arm as worry slammed through her.

"It's Alice." Kayla shook her head and sighed. "She's been screaming all morning. Her temperature is up, and I can't get it down. I've tried everything, and I'm out of pain reliever. I can't reach Jamie's driver. He took Jamie, *Dat*, and Roy out to get supplies. I can't remember the phone number for *mei dat*'s driver, and I'm just so worried about her. It could be a tooth coming, but I'm just so exhausted." A tear trickled down Kayla's cheek.

Cindy's heart nearly shredded as Calvin began to cry along with his sister.

"I can help you." Cindy touched Kayla's arm again as an idea gripped her. Although she hadn't seen Drew in nearly two weeks, she was certain he would help in an emergency. "I'll ask Drew if he can take me to the store. Today is Thursday, and he mentioned he has classes on Monday, Wednesday, and Friday. I'll offer to pay him. Let me just get my purse, and I'll go ask him." She started toward the stairs.

"*Danki*," Kayla called after her.

"I'll be back soon. I promise," Cindy told Kayla when she returned.

"Where are Florence and Sarah Jane?"

"They went up the street to visit a neighbor, but they should be home soon." Cindy walked Kayla and the children out the back door. "I'll come to your *haus* as soon as I get back with the medicine." She gave Calvin a quick hug. "Don't worry. We'll get your little sister what she needs."

"*Danki*," Kayla shouted over Alice's cries as Cindy rushed away.

As she jogged up the Lapps' driveway to Drew's house, she thought about how disappointed she was that he hadn't come to her house to deliver her empty container. She didn't want to go to his house without a better reason than asking for it.

Today she had a good reason, and she prayed he would help her. Relief flooded her when she spotted his truck parked beside his house. Now she just had to convince him to give her a ride.

She knocked on his door and then turned toward the sound of barking. When she spotted Bruce standing in the doorway of the barn, she rushed over there.

"Hi, Bruce," she said. "Is your *dat* in the barn?"

Bruce barked again and wagged his tail.

"Cindy?" Drew appeared in faded jeans and a black T-shirt. He pulled gloves off his hands as he walked over to her. His jaw was again covered with light-brown stubble, and even in her panic, she noticed his eyes were bright and intelligent. "How are you?"

"I need your help." She pointed toward his pickup. "I need to get to a drugstore, and our driver isn't answering his phone. Kayla desperately needs medicine for Alice. Could I pay you to give me a ride?"

"No."

She stared at him. Had he really said no?

"I'll take you to the drugstore, but you're not going to pay me." He nodded toward his house. "Let me clean up a little, tell Ervin or Gertrude I'm leaving, and then we'll go. What's wrong with Alice?"

"She's running a fever and she's really fussy." Cindy fell into step with him as they walked toward the house. "Kayla has tried all the usual ways to bring the fever down, and nothing has worked. She needs pain reliever, but she's out of it."

Once up the steps, he opened the front door and stepped back for her to go through. "Just give me a minute."

"Thank you." She stepped inside.

"There's no need to thank me." He headed toward the kitchen. "I need to give you your empty container too. Maybe more cookies can be my payment."

"That works." She smiled as he disappeared through a doorway beyond the kitchen, and the door clicked shut.

She stood by the front door and scanned the family room, taking in the pile of books by his laptop on the coffee table and the modest furnishings. Other than the fact it had electricity, she hadn't noticed much about the place when she was here before, looking in from the doorway.

Bruce appeared at her feet and licked her hand.

"Hi there." She scratched his head, and he tilted it to give her better access. "*Danki* for getting your *dat* for me."

She spotted the table in the corner with the puzzle and walked over to it. She knew she shouldn't be in his house with him alone, but they were in separate rooms. Surely her presence was acceptable given the circumstances.

The puzzle featured a beautiful waterfall with a bright sun and rainbow above it. She touched a few puzzle pieces and imagined him sitting at the table in the evening, fitting in the pieces and thinking of his aunt.

She turned and saw a bookcase in another corner of the room, beyond the television. A couple of framed photographs sat on one shelf. With Bruce at her heels, she crossed the room and examined them.

The first one she picked up featured a young boy sitting between a man and a woman who looked to be in their early forties. The boy had to be Drew with his light-brown hair, bright

ice-blue eyes, and wide smile. Cindy guessed he was about
ten years old, and he looked so happy as he gave the camera
a toothy grin. His parents also beamed. She studied them, realizing Drew had his father's eyes and his mother's thick light-
brown hair and smile.

She set the photograph down and picked up the second one,
which looked only a few years old. Smiling, Drew stood with
his arm around an older woman who also posed for the camera with a bright grin. She looked to be in her early sixties, and
she had kind blue eyes.

"That's my aunt Shirley." Drew's voice was close to her ear.

Cindy jumped with a start, almost dropping the photograph
as she spun toward him. He had changed into clean jeans and
a green T-shirt. His hair was brushed, and a whiff of spicy co-
logne permeated her senses.

"I'm-I'm so sorry." She set the photograph down on the
shelf. "It was rude of me to touch your things. I apologize." She
stepped away from the bookcase and tried to will her cheeks
to stop burning.

"You don't have to apologize." His smile was warm as he
picked up the frame and ran his fingers over it. "She was a saint.
She put up with my moods and my temper when I was an
ornery teenager, angry at the world for what happened to my
parents."

He set the photograph down and then picked up the other
one. "These are my parents. This was taken about a month before they died." He stared at the photograph, and Cindy longed
to read his mind. Was he remembering the happy times? Or
was he thinking about how they died?

"You must still miss them," she said, her voice sounding
soft and reverent to her own ears.

"Yeah. I do." He gave her a sad smile as he set the photograph back on the shelf. "I think about my parents and my aunt every day. Sometimes I even find myself talking to them. Does that sound crazy?"

"No. I completely understand."

He met her gaze, and she was almost certain something unspoken passed between them. It was as if she truly saw him, and he saw her grief in return.

In that moment the connection she'd thought she felt suddenly became real, almost tangible, and it terrified her. How could she feel so close to someone who wasn't a member of her community?

"We should go. I need to get Alice's medicine to her." Cindy scooted past him and out the front door.

CHAPTER 5

Cindy could feel Drew's eyes watching her as she took two boxes of pain reliever off a shelf in the drugstore. A tingle of awareness shimmied up her spine.

"That should do it." She looked at him, and he smiled, making her feel off kilter. "I'll go pay."

"Are you sure you don't need anything else?" He gestured around the aisle.

"No, thank you." She hurried to the cash register and took her place at the back of the line.

When she turned toward the exit, she found Drew leaning against the wall and perusing a magazine. She felt as if her nerve endings were frayed after the strange moment they shared in his family room. She was grateful Drew had kept the conversation light during the drive to the store. He'd made small talk about the weather and his college classes, and Cindy answered his questions while peering out the window to avoid another awkward encounter. She had to dismiss her growing admiration for him before it got her into trouble with her family.

After she paid for the medication, she followed Drew out to his truck and climbed into the passenger seat.

"I appreciate your help today," she said as he steered out of the parking lot. "You really helped my family."

"It wasn't a big deal at all." He kept his eyes focused on the road. "I'm happy to help anytime. Just come and get me if you need a ride somewhere."

"Thank you." As they motored through the heart of Bird-in-Hand, she fiddled with the plastic bag containing the medication and racked her brain for something to say. The quaint business area zoomed by her window, and she watched tourists walking in and out of the quilt stores, the gift shops, the hardware store, her favorite little bookstore, the fire station where Jamie volunteered, and Dienner's Family Restaurant, which her sister-in-law Kayla's family owned.

"Remember how you asked me how Bruce got his name?"

Cindy angled her body toward him. "You said your aunt named him after her favorite movie star, right? Was it Bruce Wilson?"

"Bruce Willis." He smiled as if his mind had produced a special memory. "Besides her other health problems, my aunt had arthritis in her hands, and in her last couple of years she couldn't even do puzzles anymore. So she mostly sat in front of the television and watched movies. I adopted Bruce so she'd have company while I was at work all day. She loved action and adventure movies the best, and she'd watch her favorites over and over. When I told her she had to name her new friend, she said she wanted him to be her hero. That's why his name is Bruce."

Warmth filled her chest. "That's a great story."

Drew slowed to a stop at a red light. "I do miss her." He turned his head toward her and smiled. "But I remember the good times."

"What are your favorite memories?"

"Hmm." He rubbed at the stubble on his chin. "I would guess

popping popcorn and watching movies with her. I think of her every time one of her favorites comes on television."

"That's wonderful. Her memory can live on with her favorite movies, right?"

"Right." He looked at her again. "Have you ever seen a movie?"

She shook her head. "I once went to visit an *English* neighbor, and she had the television on. I had to wait for her to give me something for my mom, and I saw a few minutes of the television program. But I'm not sure what it was."

"Do you remember what the program was about?"

She bit her lower lip and tried to recall the details. "I think it was about police officers investigating a murder. It seemed like a mystery program."

"A lot of those are on television. What did you think of it?"

She shrugged. "I don't know. I didn't see enough of it to form an opinion."

He turned his attention to the light, and when it turned green he eased through the intersection. "What are your favorite happy memories?"

Cindy stilled as his question barreled over her. Memories of her mother echoed through her mind, and she tried to swallow against the messy knot of emotion that threatened to strangle her. She opened her mouth, but words refused to come as grief descended like a bank of dark clouds.

He peeked over at her, and his pleasant expression faded. "I'm sorry. I crossed a line, didn't I?"

She turned toward the window to avoid the regret that seemed to flicker on his face.

An awkward silence floated inside the cab of the truck like a rude, uninvited guest. As much as Cindy wanted to open her heart to Drew and share all her guilt, regret, and sadness over her mother's death, she couldn't. Those feelings had been trapped inside of her, locked up for seven years.

"My aunt used to say God sends us friends when we need them most."

Cindy's gaze snapped to his. "She did?"

He nodded. "I think that's why he led me to the job at the Lapps' farm."

She studied his eyes and searched for clues to the hidden meaning of his statement. Was he referring to her friendship or her entire family? Did he also feel a bond growing between them?

Of course he was referring to her entire family, but also the Lapps. Why would he want a close relationship with her when they were from different worlds? She was kidding herself by thinking she might be special to him.

She turned her thoughts back to Kayla and Alice and looked out the windshield as her father's farm came into view.

Drew parked in the driveway and Cindy leapt out of the truck before hurrying down the path to her brother's house. She rushed up the porch steps and wrenched open the screen door. Kayla was rocking Alice in the family room.

Cindy opened the bag and pulled out the medication. "I got you two boxes of pain reliever."

"*Danki.*" Kayla's expression eased slightly. "What do I owe you?"

"Nothing." Cindy took the bottle from its box and opened it. She read the dosage instructions and then helped Kayla give it to Alice. "I hope this helps her quickly."

"*Danki* so much." Kayla stroked her daughter's hair.

"Can I do anything?" Cindy pointed toward the kitchen.

"Would you like me to make supper or clean? Do you need me to take Calvin for the afternoon?"

"No." Kayla shook her head. "I can handle them both."

"Are you sure?" Cindy asked.

"*Ya*, but *danki*." Kayla looked past Cindy and smiled. "Thank you for taking Cindy to the store for me. You saved the day."

Cindy turned to where Drew stood in the doorway. He looked solemn.

"How is she?" he asked.

Kayla pushed the rocker into motion. "Her temperature is still up, but I got her to calm down. The medication will help a lot."

"Where is Calvin?" Cindy asked.

"He's reading books in his room." Kayla leaned her head back on the rocker. "We'll be fine. I promise."

Cindy stood. "I'll come by later to check on you."

"*Danki*." Kayla waved.

Cindy met Drew at the doorway, and then they stepped outside together.

. . .

"I can't thank you enough," Cindy said as she stood beside Drew on the porch steps.

"You can stop thanking me now." Drew felt his lips turn up into a smile. "But I do seem to remember something about a pie."

Cindy snapped her fingers. "You're right. I do owe you a pie."

"You don't owe me anything, but I'll accept a pie."

Cindy seemed relieved by this. "I'll make you one."

"All right." Guilt nipped at him as he took in her face. The pain in her eyes when he'd asked her to share a happy memory was almost too much for him to bear. He had to apologize. "Listen, I'm really sorry for what I asked you in the truck—"

"Please don't worry about it." She waved off the statement. "Oh, there's *mei dat*." She hurried down the steps as a white van pulled into the driveway.

Drew frowned as he followed her. Was she angry with him for bringing up something so personal? Or was she simply avoiding a painful issue? He squelched the urge to pull her back and insist she speak to him so they could sort this out. But he had no right to force her to tell him anything. He simply cared about her feelings.

"*Dat!*" Cindy rushed over to where Vernon, Roy, and Jamie were unloading the back of the van. "Drew had to take us to the drugstore to get medicine for Alice."

"Why?" Jamie's eyes widened. "Is Alice okay?"

Cindy nodded. "She's better now, but she was inconsolable before. She's been running a fever. Nothing worked when Kayla tried to bring it down, and she needed more pain reliever." She turned to the man standing beside Vernon. "She tried to reach you, Blake, but she couldn't. So I asked Drew to help."

"She couldn't reach me?" Blake moved to the driver's side and fished around until he pulled out his phone. "My ringer was off." He frowned. "I'm so sorry."

"It's okay." Cindy looked at Drew and her expression warmed. "It all worked out."

"Thank you for helping my family, Drew," Jamie said.

"You're welcome," Drew told him.

Jamie wore a concerned expression as he started walking fast toward his house.

Drew moved to the back of the van. "Let me help you." He picked up two bags of chicken feed.

"Oh, no, no." Vernon shook his head. "I'm sure you have chores of your own to do on Ervin's farm."

"I don't mind helping." Drew turned to Cindy. "Where does the chicken feed go?"

Cindy opened her mouth to respond, but she was cut off by her stepmother's loud voice.

"Vernon!" Florence called as she and Sarah Jane walked up the driveway. "You're back. How was your trip to town?"

"*Gut*, but Alice is *krank*." Vernon motioned toward Jamie's house. "Drew took Cindy to get medication for her."

Florence's dark eyes widened. "Alice is sick?" She hurried up the path toward Jamie's house with Sarah Jane following close behind her.

"I'll take that." Roy took the chicken feed from Drew. "We can handle this. *Danki* for helping Cindy."

"You're welcome." Drew turned to Cindy. "See you soon."

She gave him a little smile. "Thank you again."

"Don't forget about my pie," he whispered, and then gave her a wink and sauntered over to his truck.

After he climbed into the driver's seat, he lingered for a moment, watching the Riehl family interact as they unloaded the van. His heart suddenly felt heavy, and envy was like a snake twisting his insides. Would he ever have a loving family of his own?

. . .

Drew was reading the instructions on the back of a frozen pizza when a knock sounded on the door. After setting the box on the counter, he crossed to the front door and found Gertrude on the other side of his screen door. In her mid-seventies, she was several inches shorter than he was, and she reminded him of his aunt with her graying brown hair, kind brown eyes, and welcoming smile.

"Gertrude, hi." Drew unlatched the screen door and opened it. "What can I do for you?"

"You can join us for supper." She motioned toward the house. "I made chicken and dumplings, and we have plenty to share."

"Oh, no." Drew shook his head. "I don't want to impose."

"Impose?" She craned her neck to peer into his kitchen. "Is that a frozen pizza on your counter?"

"Yeah." Drew almost felt ashamed.

"Put that away and come join Ervin and me. I insist." Gertrude lifted her chin.

"All right. Let me turn off the oven and put the pizza back in the freezer."

A few minutes later, Drew took a seat at the Lapps' long kitchen table. They all bowed their heads for a silent prayer and then began filling their plates with chicken, dumplings, and green beans. The delicious aroma of a homemade meal made Drew's stomach gurgle with delight.

"This is fantastic," Drew told Gertrude after he took a bite. "Thank you for saving me from that frozen pizza."

Ervin's loud, boisterous laughter filled the kitchen, and Drew and Gertrude joined in.

"My Gertrude's cooking can beat frozen food any day." Ervin wiped his eyes with a napkin as he continued to smile. Like Gertrude, he was in his mid-seventies. His hair and long beard were completely gray, but his bright brown eyes and big smile told he had many years left in him.

"You were busy today, weren't you?" Gertrude asked Drew.

Drew nodded while he finished chewing, then said, "I

worked on repairing that bench in the barn, and I also had to run Cindy Riehl to the drugstore."

"Oh?" Gertrude's eyebrows lifted. "Why did she ask you instead of her driver?"

"It was an emergency for Kayla." Drew explained how Alice had been ill and Kayla couldn't reach their driver. "I took her to the store to get some pain reliever. By the time we got back, Alice had settled down some."

"That's a shame that their driver had his ringer off. I still say those cell phones aren't as reliable as an old-fashioned phone." Ervin emphasized his words with a swish of his fork through the air.

Drew bit back a smile at the older man's comments.

"I hope Kayla isn't too worn out," Gertrude said. "It can be scary when a baby has a fever."

Drew looked down at his plate as he mentally replayed how Cindy had shut down when he asked her to share happy memories. Once again, he worried he had hurt her feelings. But her warm smile before he left her farm told him they were still friends. Maybe talking about her mother was still too painful, especially with someone she barely knew. He'd have to give her time and space to feel comfortable enough to talk about her with him.

He looked at Gertrude and recalled how close the members of the Amish community seemed during their lunch that Sunday he joined them. She would probably know the details of what happened to Cindy's mom.

"What happened to Cindy's mom?" he asked.

Gertrude's pleasant expression faltered, and Drew braced himself for an emotional story.

"Oh my. It was so tragic." Gertrude looked at her husband,

who frowned and shook his head. "Dorothy and Cindy were canning vegetables. Dorothy was carrying some jars down to the basement and apparently lost her footing and grabbed the banister, which gave way. She fell over the side and broke her neck, passing away instantly."

Drew gasped. "That's terrible."

"*Ya*, it is." Gertrude's eyes misted. "The family was devastated."

"Was Cindy there when it happened?"

Gertrude gave a somber nod. "She was in the kitchen and heard her mother scream. She found her, and then she had to run for her father and Mark. They were in the barn."

"I can't even fathom how she must have felt," Drew said, his voice shaky as he imagined the depth of her grief. Did Cindy blame herself for her mother's fall? He hoped not, but for years he blamed himself for his parents' car accident. He understood the complexity of survivor's guilt. He prayed Cindy had worked through any self-blame, just as he had with God's help.

"Jamie was on duty with the fire department that night," Ervin added. "He got the call and rushed to the house only to find his mother already gone."

Drew cringed. "That had to be heartbreaking for him."

"I believe it was." Gertrude sighed. "That family has faced a lot of challenges, but they've made it through with God's help."

"*Ya*, that's the truth," Ervin agreed.

Drew nodded. Would Cindy confide in him someday, tell him how she felt about her mother's accident? He wasn't sure what more he could do to earn her trust, but he knew he wanted to try.

CHAPTER 6

Drew pushed his grocery cart toward the end of the cereal aisle, but then he halted when he spotted a young Amish woman standing at the meat counter. He took in her tall and thin stature, and his thoughts immediately turned to Cindy.

It had been two weeks since he'd taken her to the drugstore, and he'd thought of her every day. He'd been disappointed when Roy stopped by with a strawberry pie from Cindy. While the pie had been delicious, he'd hoped to see her in person.

The story of her mother's death had invaded his thoughts. Of course, he would never bring up the subject, but if Cindy mentioned it, he'd be ready to listen and offer his sympathy and encouragement.

The young woman at the counter paid for her items and set them in her cart. When she turned to go, Drew caught a glimpse of her face and then hurried down the aisle.

"Cindy!" he called.

Cindy turned toward him, and a beautiful smile broke out on her face. She looked so pretty in a purple dress with a black apron, but he knew she'd look pretty in a burlap sack. "Drew. Hi."

"How are you?" He stopped his cart beside hers.

"I'm well. How are you?"

"I'm great." *Especially now!* "Thank you for the delicious pie. I need to return the pie plate."

"You're welcome. I'm sorry I couldn't deliver it, but it's been a busy couple of weeks."

"How's Alice?"

Her expression warmed. "She's fine. Her fever broke soon after we brought her the medicine. Thank you for asking."

"I almost stopped by to see how she was, but I wasn't sure if that would be appropriate."

"That's so kind of you. Thank you for thinking of her."

"Of course." He studied her, and an awkward silence fell over them. Had she truly been busy all this time? Or had she deliberately avoided him? Was he kidding himself that they could ever truly be friends?

"Well, I should go." She gave him a shy smile. "Take care."

As she started to walk away, he racked his brain for something to say to make her stay. Then an idea floated into his mind.

"Cindy!" he called again, and she turned toward him. "What are you doing tonight?"

Her brow furrowed, and she looked adorable. "What do you mean?"

"It's the Fourth of July." He pushed his cart over to hers again. "Do you have any plans?"

She shook her head. "No."

"Would you like to go see fireworks with me?"

She hesitated. "I don't know."

"Have you ever seen fireworks?"

"I saw them from afar when I was at a friend's farm once."

"You have to be in the park to see them up close. I'll take you."

"I'm not sure that's a good idea." She grimaced. "I don't think my dad would let me."

"It'll be so fun." He held his breath. *Please say yes!*

Her expression relaxed slightly. "What time would we have to leave?"

"Probably around seven."

"I'll ask my father, and if he says yes, I'll walk down to your house at seven."

"Great." Hope lit in his chest.

"Maybe I'll see you later, then." She gave him a little wave and then pushed her cart down another aisle.

Drew was sorry none of his friends were there to give him a high five, not that he'd socialized much since Aunt Shirley died. If he were honest, he'd have to admit he'd had only superficial friendships since high school, when his close friends all left for college. He hadn't even dated beyond a few first dates.

After a week of wishing he could spend more time with Cindy, though, he just might have the chance tonight. If only her father would say yes . . .

. . .

Cindy set the last plate in the drainboard and then turned toward where her father and Roy sat at the table as Florence wiped it down. Sudden nervousness blossomed in her belly as the question she'd longed to ask him all afternoon echoed in her mind. She'd waited for the perfect opportunity to talk to *Dat* alone, but it never came.

Her gaze moved to the clock, and her chest tightened. It was six thirty. She had to ask him now, or she'd never make it to Drew's house on time.

"Let's go take care of the animals," *Dat* told Roy before pushing back his chair and standing.

"*Dat*," Cindy said, "I need to ask you something."

"What is it?" *Dat* turned toward her, a pleasant expression on his handsome face.

"Could I please go with Drew to see fireworks tonight?" The words escaped her lips and then hung in the air as her father froze.

Florence looked up, her brow furrowed. "With Drew?"

"Did Drew ask you out on a date?" Sarah Jane looked as if the words tasted sour as she dried a pot.

"No, it's not a date." Cindy's cheeks burned, and she tried to bury her irritation with Florence and Sarah Jane behind a shaky smile. "I saw Drew at the market today, and he asked me if I'd ever seen fireworks. When I told him I hadn't, he invited me to go with him. May I go, please?" She kept her eyes focused on her father even though she could feel the others' stares burning into her skin.

"Why would you want to see fireworks?" *Dat*'s words were simple but held an edge of anger. Or was it worry?

"Why not?" Cindy shrugged. "It's the Fourth of July, and the *Englishers* go to see fireworks."

"You're not *English*." A frown twisted her father's face.

Frustration swept into every tense muscle. "I'm not baptized either." She heard Florence gasp at her bold statement, and her anger flared.

Dat's eyes widened for a moment, and she was almost certain she found pain and sadness there. Guilt chewed on her insides, but she tried to dismiss it. Yes, her father wanted nothing more than for her to join the church, but it was her decision when—*if*—she would. *Dat* had no right to make that decision for her.

"It's inappropriate for you to date when you haven't been baptized," *Dat* barked, his voice bouncing off the cabinets.

"We're only *freinden*." Cindy heard the hint of a whine in her voice. "You have no reason not to trust me. You and Jamie invited him to join you for lunch after church. You seem to trust him."

Dat studied her. "Why would you want to spend time with Drew?"

Cindy shrugged. "He's nice. I like talking to him." She folded her hands as if to pray. "I've never given you a reason not to trust me, and I don't plan to start now. Please let me go. Drew is a *freind* of the family, and you know him. You know he's a *gut*, Christian man."

Dat looked down at the floor and then fingered his beard. Cindy could almost hear his conflicting thoughts.

When he looked up, his lips made a thin line, but he looked resigned. "Come home right after the fireworks end," he finally said.

Cindy's heart did a little dance. "*Danki, Dat*. I promise I will."

Dat and Roy headed outside as Cindy turned her attention back to the frothy water in the sink. She began to quickly wash the last of the dishes and set them in the drainboard. She was aware of Sarah Jane's dark eyes watching her. She tried her best to finish before her stepsister could start berating her.

Cindy set the last glass in the drainboard and then dried her hands. "I need to get ready," she muttered before starting for the stairs.

"Cindy," Sarah Jane called. "Wait. I have a question for you."

Cindy turned to face her stepsister's hard gaze.

"Why do you want to go see fireworks with an *Englisher*,

but you refuse to go to youth group with the members of your community?" Sarah Jane motioned around the kitchen as if for emphasis.

Cindy's throat thickened as Florence came to stand beside her daughter, wearing the same judgmental expression. Cindy could feel the disappointment rolling off her stepmother. Cindy would never live up to Sarah Jane's perfection.

"Drew is *mei freind*." Cindy couldn't control the quaver in her voice.

"What are the members of our community, then?" Sarah Jane said, challenge in her tone.

Cindy looked at Florence in search of understanding, but found nothing but chagrin in her dark eyes. She looked past them toward the clock, and her heartbeat jumped. She had only ten minutes to get changed and down to Drew's house.

"I have to go." She rushed up the stairs and changed into her favorite blue dress. Then after checking her prayer covering in the mirror, she hurried down the steps, through the kitchen and mudroom, and out the back door.

She was grateful Florence and Sarah Jane didn't speak to her as she left, but she was certain they were discussing her at length now. She swatted that thought away as she hurried to the Lapps' farm.

Her heart rate spiked at the thought of seeing Drew again, just like it had at the market that morning. Had he missed her as much as she'd missed him this past week? He'd seemed glad to see her, and then this invitation . . .

When she baked the strawberry pie, she told Florence it was to thank Drew for helping her get the medicine for Alice. Florence had Roy take the pie to Drew so fast she'd had no time to protest. Still, she didn't want to appear too forward.

That's why she was thrilled when Drew approached her, sparing her from chasing after him like one of the young women who used to pursue her brother Mark before he married Priscilla.

Why were her feelings for Drew so complicated?

Her shoes crunched on the rock driveway as she made her way to his house. When her feet hit the porch steps the door swung open, revealing both Drew and Bruce.

"You made it!" Drew's smile was bright as he opened the screen door and Bruce bounded out to see her.

"Hi, Bruce." She gave a little laugh as she rubbed his neck. "I missed you, too, buddy."

"I'm so glad your dad said yes."

"I am too." She looked up at him, taking in his khaki shorts and crisp green T-shirt. "I didn't bring any food or anything. Did I need to?"

"No." He shook his head. "I just have to grab a couple of things from inside. I'll be right back."

"Okay." Cindy continued to pet Bruce while she waited for Drew to return.

A few minutes later, Drew appeared with a cooler and a quilt.

"Oh no." She cringed. "I *was* supposed to bring food."

"No, you weren't. I just grabbed a few drinks for us. I thought we'd go out for ice cream afterward, if you have time."

"That sounds great." She thrust away her father's insistence that she come home right after the fireworks and reached for the quilt. "Let me carry something."

"Thanks." Drew set the cooler on the porch floor and held the screen door open. "Go on inside, boy. I'll see you later."

Bruce whined as he looked at Cindy and then at Drew.

"Aww." Cindy laughed. "He doesn't want to go inside."

"I know, buddy, but hopefully we'll see her again soon." Drew whistled and motioned toward the house. "Go on now."

Bruce reluctantly walked into the house, and Drew closed and locked the front door. Then he picked up the cooler. "Let's go. I want to find you a good seat."

Cindy followed him down the steps and to the truck. She climbed into the passenger seat and set the quilt at her feet as he took his spot on the driver's side.

She tried to forget the conversation she'd had with her father, Sarah Jane, and Florence as Drew drove toward the main road. Guilt and irritation warred in her gut as she recalled the disappointment and accusation in her family members' eyes. Why couldn't they see that Drew was just a good friend?

Because a relationship with an Englisher *is forbidden.*

She squeezed her eyes shut as the words echoed from the back of her mind. Yes, this relationship was forbidden, but how could an innocent friendship be sinful?

When Drew stopped the truck at a red light, he looked over at her. "Penny for your thoughts?"

She bit her lower lip. She didn't want to ruin their pleasant evening by telling him she'd shared heated words with her family members over him. Besides, if she admitted to Drew that her father wasn't happy about their friendship, he might take her home out of respect for *Dat*. She didn't want that.

"How's your math class going?" The question leapt from her lips.

"Well enough. I got a B on my last test."

"That's great." She clapped her hands.

"Do you want to know my secret?"

"Sure."

He leaned over and whispered in her ear. "Your cookies and pie were my good luck charms."

She waved off the statement with a chuckle. "That's not true."

"It's the truth." He crossed his finger over his chest as if crossing his heart.

She shook her head. "You did it all yourself. You studied, and you earned the good grade."

"No, I think it's your baking for sure." He steered the truck through the intersection.

"How's your English class?"

"Good. We're reading a pretty interesting novel right now."

"What's the book about?"

Drew spent the rest of the drive telling her the book's premise and plot, and she enjoyed listening to his assessment of the symbolism in it. She studied the line of his jaw and enjoyed the sound of his voice as he spoke too. He was the most handsome, appealing man she'd ever met.

The thought caught her off guard, and she swallowed a gasp. Was she developing feelings for Drew? But she hadn't known him very long. Was it even possible to develop feelings for someone she hardly knew?

When they arrived at the city park, he found a parking spot not far from their destination. Then they walked together into the park's big open area. Cindy was aware of curious stares as they crossed the grassy venue. Brushing off sudden self-consciousness, she quickened her pace. Drew led her to a spot away from trees, and after spreading the quilt, they sat down.

"Would you like a drink now?" He opened the small cooler and pointed to bottles of water and cans of soda.

"I'll take a bottle of water," she said.

He handed her the bottle, and then she surveyed the crowd, taking in families gathered on quilts and young couples sitting beside each other on beach chairs. The early evening sky was beautiful with shades of orange and yellow as the sun began to set, and the air smelled like moist earth. She breathed in the sweet air and felt her shoulders relax.

Drew gave her a wide smile. "You look like you're having fun already."

"I am having fun."

"Just you wait. It's going to get better." He nudged her shoulder with his.

She smiled at the familiarity in the gesture, and happiness bubbled inside of her.

They talked comfortably about everyday things until darkness shrouded the park.

"The fireworks are going to start soon," Drew told her as he leaned in closer. His breath was warm on her cheek, sending shivers of awareness over her skin. "Are you ready for this?"

For a moment, she couldn't respond. Was she ready for any of this? She wasn't sure.

Suddenly, a tremendous boom thundered through the sky, followed by a shimmering explosion of reds, purples, and blues.

Cindy blew out a puff of air and grabbed Drew's arm. The contact sent heat zinging up her arm. She released his arm and shifted away from him.

"I'm sorry," she muttered.

"It's okay." He gave a little laugh. "Are you all right?"

His question was interrupted by more thundering booms and glorious colors erupting across the sky. Cindy stared up in wonder, her mouth slightly open. She'd never seen anything so beautiful.

"You like it?" His voice rumbled close to her ear, and his nearness stole her breath for a moment.

She nodded with emphasis. "I do."

"Good." He remained close to her, his arm and leg resting against hers.

When a boom shook the ground, she grabbed his hand, her fingers instinctively entwining with his.

"It's okay," he whispered in her ear.

More booms and blasts of color followed, and Cindy didn't let go.

She closed her eyes for a moment, relishing the comfort of his touch. Why did being so close to him feel so right? And what would her father say if he saw her right now?

Cindy released his hand, but she didn't shift away from him. Having Drew by her side brought a comfort she'd never known—one she already knew her family would never understand.

As the two of them sat together beneath the dark, sparkling sky, she quietly feared what the future held for the two of them, while at the same time she was eager to find out.

CHAPTER 7

"What did you think of the fireworks?" Drew asked Cindy as they sat in an ice-cream parlor later that evening.

"It was breathtaking." Cindy dug her spoon into her butterscotch sundae. "It was fantastic. Thank you for taking me."

"Thank you for going with me." Drew scooped a spoonful of his chocolate sundae into his mouth. "I'm still surprised your father let you go with me."

"Why would you say that?" She hoped her tone didn't give away her concern.

"I'm not Amish." He dug his spoon into the tall glass again. "I didn't think Amish were permitted to be friends with non-Amish."

Cindy took another bite to avoid responding to his statement. She didn't want to lie to him, but she also didn't want to share what her father and Sarah Jane said.

"Could I ask you something?" he asked.

Cindy's stomach seemed to drop as she nodded. "Of course."

"The day of the service, when you were upset with Sarah Jane . . . Why don't you want to go to the youth group gatherings with her?"

Cindy gritted her teeth. She suddenly longed for him to ask about her conversation with her father instead.

"Never mind. Forget I asked." He held up his spoon. "You don't have to tell me if it's too personal."

"No, it's not too personal." She studied her half-eaten sundae while considering where to start. Her heart pounded as she searched for the courage to share her deepest and most vulnerable emotions. "It's complicated. When my mother died, I was shattered. It's hard to explain, but it wasn't just about losing her. I also felt guilty for many reasons, and I felt lost."

She peeked up at him, and the compassion in his eyes sent warmth and confidence spiraling through her, giving her the strength to continue.

"When I say I felt lost, it was more than that. I felt disconnected from my family and my community. Before she died, I was certain I would join the church like my siblings had, and then I would date, fall in love, get married, and have a family. But after she died, I wasn't even certain I wanted to join the church.

"My sister Laura told me she felt God's call before she joined the church. She said it was as if God had called her heart, and she knew to the depth of her bones that she was supposed to be a member of the Amish church. Jamie and Mark told me something similar. I've never felt that. Ever."

She sniffed. "But it was more than that. I also have doubts and questions that the church can't answer for me. I don't understand why God chose to take my mother. In my religion, it's a sin to doubt God's will, but I just don't understand it. Why did God take my mother so early? We still needed her. I still needed her.

"I live like an Amish person, but I've felt myself floating since she died—not in the Amish world, yet not in the *Englisher* world either. For seven years I've tried to figure out where I belong, while my siblings moved on with their lives, marrying and starting families. I could never understand how they were able to just move on with life after we lost our mother. I'm still so sad and broken after losing her. She was more than my mother. She was my best friend." She took a deep breath before continuing.

"My stepsiblings are comfortable with their lives too. Roy will be married in October, and then Sarah Jane will probably meet the man she'll marry. I'll be left at home alone when they move on too. I'll be the only sibling who isn't settled."

She paused, her throat constricting against her words as if her deepest and most painful emotions were rising to pour out of her. She felt emotionally naked, completely unprotected. She studied Drew, looking for any signs of judgment or ridicule, but she found none. All she could see was steadfast compassion and caring.

"So I haven't joined the church," she said. "That means I can't date or marry."

"And that's unusual for someone your age, right?" he asked.

"*Ya.* My siblings joined when they were teenagers." She looked down at her sundae and moved her spoon to create swirls of butterscotch in her lake of vanilla. "They've all moved on so fast that I wonder if they miss her as much as I do. Even my dad moved on. He met Florence five years ago and then married her. I was so hurt and surprised. It never made sense to me."

Her eyes snapped to his as renewed guilt bubbled up inside her. "Is it terrible that I was hurt when my dad remarried so quickly?"

"No." He shook his head. "It had to be a difficult adjustment for your father to bring a new wife and siblings into your home."

"It was. I felt as if I was trapped in the past while everyone else moved on without me. I still feel that way." She lifted her spoon and let melted ice cream drip from its tip. "When Laura left, I was crushed. I was happy she'd found love, and she and Allen have a wonderful marriage. But she and I always had each other. We shared a room from when we were children until Jamie got married. After *Mamm* died, we would cry ourselves to sleep in the same room. Laura was always there, and then she left."

Cindy shook her head. "But when Mark got married two years ago, it got even worse. Then I was the last Riehl sibling left in the house." She stared at the middle of their table. "Sometimes I feel like my dad and Florence are disappointed in me."

"Why would they be disappointed in you?"

"Because I'm not like everyone else in the family. Because I'm not like Sarah Jane." She dropped her shoulders. "Because I haven't joined the church."

"It's your choice when you join, right?"

"*Ya*, it is." She set her bent elbow on the table and rested her chin on her palm.

"And aren't Amish people supposed to be nonjudgmental?"

"That's right."

"So then why would they be disappointed in you?"

Cindy sighed. "It's expected that we join when we're teenagers, and we're called to marry and have children. We're supposed to be active in youth group because that's where we meet our future spouse. That's when the dating starts. Well, I can't date until after I join the church, but I'm still supposed to be a member of my youth group."

"Did you go to youth group before your mother passed away?"

She shook her head. "I've never gone."

"Why?" He leaned forward on the table as if he were riveted by the discussion.

"I've never felt a pull from my youth group either. I've always been shy. When my mom was alive, my older siblings would have their friends come and visit, and I would stay home with them instead of going to youth group. I've always been close to my family."

He nodded slowly. "Are you close to them now?"

"I think so." She looked down at her melting sundae. "But I don't relate to them like I used to. Laura and my sisters-in-law talk about their children when we get together, and I can't relate to that. I love all my sisters and my nieces and nephews. I just don't know if I'll ever have the life they do. I believe in God, and I feel his presence in my life daily, but like I said, I have unresolved questions about why he took my mom. I can't share that with my family since we're not supposed to question God's will." She gave a nervous laugh. "Does that make any sense?"

"Yes, it does."

"So what about you?"

"What do you mean?" He scooped more ice cream into his mouth.

"I understood what you meant when you said you were searching for something, but you didn't know what. I felt as if I had met someone who might actually understand me." Her eyes widened, and embarrassment pressed down on her shoulders when she realized what she'd revealed. She'd said too much, but she couldn't take it back.

"I felt the same when you said you understood what I meant." His words were simple, but their meaning was a song to her heart.

"How did you lose your parents?" She held her hands up. "You don't have to tell me if you don't want to."

"I don't mind." His smile was easy. "I'll tell you. I was ten years old, and I had been in a fight with a bully at school. My parents had to come up to the school to meet with the principal and me. My dad left work early and picked up my mom at her job. They were hit head-on by a wrong-way driver on a road not far from the school. They died instantly."

"I'm so sorry." Her heart ached at the grief she found in his eyes.

"Thanks." He licked his spoon dry before he spoke. "For many years I blamed myself. If I hadn't been in a fight, they wouldn't have driven to the school, and they'd still be alive. I beat myself up over that for a long time, but I can't change what happened."

"You can't change God's will, but sometimes it's difficult to swallow."

"Exactly." He pointed his spoon at her, and something softened in his face.

"Drew, how did you accept God's will when you lost your parents?"

He pressed his lips together and looked down at the table as if contemplating his response. "I guess I accepted it when I realized God was there guiding me all along. He sent me my aunt, and I rebuilt my life with her."

Cindy nodded, trying to understand.

They sat in silence for a time, and then Drew asked, "Do you have any guilt about how your mom passed away?"

She blinked as she studied him. "I do. How did you know that?"

"Just a feeling." He studied her. "Do you want to talk about it?"

Tears pricked at her eyes as she stared at the wall past Drew's shoulder. "She and I were canning the day she died. She said she was going to take some of the jars down the basement stairs. We think she lost her balance, and when I heard her scream, I ran to her."

She pressed her eyelids closed with her fingers, hoping to stop the tears. "I was too late. She had grabbed on to the banister to try to stop herself and it shattered. I had asked Jamie to fix the banister that morning, and he promised he would. I blamed myself because I felt like I should have been the one who carried the jars down the stairs. But I did the worst thing possible."

"What was that?" Drew's voice was soft.

"I told Jamie I blamed him. I said it was his fault she was dead." She looked up as the tears escaped her eyes. "I told him he killed her, and I didn't talk to him for weeks. I punished him to deal with my own guilt, and I know it was a sin. I was terrible to him, and I still feel horrible about it all these years later." She wiped at her tears, and Drew handed her a paper napkin from the holder at the end of the table.

"I know he forgave you," he said. "I could tell you were close when I met him."

"He has forgiven me, but I still feel bad. And I still feel horrible for not carrying those jars downstairs myself. If I had, she would still be here." She wiped her eyes and then her nose.

"Don't say that. You shouldn't blame yourself." Drew reached across the table and touched her hand. "A therapist once told me my parents might have died another day, in a different accident. We don't know, and we can't change what happened. And like you said, it's God's will. Sometimes loss is in his plan."

"I know it was his will, but I still don't understand it. And perhaps I never will." She heaved a deep sigh. "It feels good to talk about this."

"I'm glad. I feel the same way." He pointed his spoon at her sundae. "Your sundae is melting. That's not allowed. You must finish it. Ice cream is not to be wasted." He grinned before spooning more of his own melting sundae into his mouth.

"You're right." She ate another spoonful. "Tell me more about your aunt Shirley."

"What do you want to know?"

"You said she liked movies with an actor named Bruce Willis. What else did she like?"

"Hmm. I already told you she liked to do puzzles." He looked up at the ceiling as if the fluorescent lights held the answers. Then he looked back at Cindy. "She liked to bake. She wasn't as good as you are, but she was good."

"What was your favorite thing she baked?"

"Chocolate pie. It was fantastic."

"Interesting." Cindy made a mental note as she scooped more ice cream. "Tell me more."

Soon their ice-cream sundaes were gone, and they climbed back into the truck and headed home. They talked about the fireworks, and disappointment crept in the closer they came to her farm. She didn't want this night to end. She longed to stay in the cab of the truck and drive around with Drew all night long.

When he steered into her driveway, Cindy's heart grew heavy.

"I had a fantastic time," she told him as he brought the truck to a stop.

"I did too." He turned toward her. "May I see you again?"

"*Ya.*" She nodded. "I'd like that."

"I would too."

They studied each other for a moment. "Well, good night," she said.

"May I walk you to the door?"

"I . . . No, that's okay. I'm fine."

"Good night, then."

"Tell Bruce I said good night to him too."

He chuckled. "I sure will. Sleep well, Cindy."

She wrenched open the door and then climbed out of the truck. She felt as if she were floating on air as she started up the path to the house. She spun and waved at the truck as it turned around and headed down the driveway, and then she hugged her arms to her chest and grinned as she made her way to the house.

When she looked up at the porch, she stopped dead in her tracks. Her father was sitting in his favorite rocking chair, and the lantern at his feet illuminated his scowl. The disapproval radiating off him filled her belly with dread.

"*Dat,*" she said, her voice thin. "You startled me."

"Do you know how late it is?" His tone resembled a growl.

"No." She shook her head.

"It's midnight, Cindy." He stood. "Do you think it's appropriate for you to be out until midnight—with an *Englisher*?"

Her hot temper swept through her. "He's *mei freind*, and nothing inappropriate happened between us."

"You shouldn't be out with an *Englisher* at all!" He pointed at her face for emphasis. "You shouldn't be dating any man until you're baptized, and *Englishers* are off limits."

"I'm not dating, and I'm not breaking any rules." She enunciated the words so there'd be no mistaking her stand.

"*Ya*, you are!" His sharp words ripped through her. She hadn't seen him this angry since before *Mamm* died. "You should be baptized and dating like Sarah Jane is. Why are you being so difficult?"

"Difficult?" She winced as if he'd slapped her. "You think I'm difficult?" She took a step back as a twisty pang lit in her chest—a mixture of fury and hurt. "I'm not Sarah Jane. You need to accept that." Now her voice was shaky, but she was so angry.

"Cindy." He'd somehow calmed, and he scrubbed his hand down his face. "It's just that—"

"*Gut nacht.*" Before her father could respond, she raced into the house and up to her room, where she flipped on the lantern on her dresser, closed the door, and sank down onto one corner of her bed.

Emotions raged through her like a tornado—anger, sadness, guilt, happiness, excitement, and grief. She felt guilty for talking back to her father and angry that he compared her to Sarah Jane instead of listening to her or trusting her. She couldn't allow him to force her to be baptized, and she refused to agree that her friendship with Drew was sinful. She cared about Drew, and she enjoyed his company. How could she ever believe that God would disapprove of an innocent friendship?

She closed her eyes as her lower lip trembled. Oh, how she missed her mother. If *Mamm* were here, she would listen to her. She would understand what Cindy was feeling, and she would never compare her to Sarah Jane.

But her mother was gone.

She hugged a pillow to her chest as a torrent of tears threatened to drown her. She needed guidance. She needed to know her feelings were valid.

Lowering the pillow and folding her hands, she began to pray.

God, I'm so confused, and I need your guidance. Please send me a sign so I'll know if my friendship with Drew is sinful or if you bless it. I can't deny how I feel about him, but I also can't shake this guilt that my family is trying to push on me. Please show me your will.

Then she changed into her nightgown, turned off the lantern, and climbed into bed. As she stared up at the ceiling through the dark, she contemplated her wonderful evening with Drew. She smiled as she recalled holding on to him during the fireworks and then pouring out her heart to him at the ice-cream parlor.

Drew was important to her, and he was quickly becoming her best friend. How could their friendship be wrong if it felt so right?

CHAPTER 8

Drew sang along with the radio as he steered his truck toward Beechdale Road the following afternoon. He couldn't get Cindy's beautiful face or her laughter out of his mind, making it difficult to concentrate in his classes today. He couldn't stop smiling either.

He recalled how soft her skin was when she'd allowed him to hold her hand during the fireworks, and how her hair had smelled like flowers. He kept replaying their conversation in the ice-cream parlor when she'd opened up to him. When he'd invited her to the fireworks, he'd hoped they would spend some time talking and laughing, but he'd never imagined he'd break through her wall of secrecy.

His heart warmed as he recalled the way she seemed to trust him. He felt as if he'd known her for years instead of only a few weeks. And now he craved more time with her. He wanted to know everything about her.

He slowed his truck as he passed her father's farm, hoping to get a glimpse of her outside, but he didn't.

Disappointment settled over him. He didn't want to wait another week before seeing her again. He hoped God planned for their friendship to grow and blossom like the flowers Drew planted in Gertrude's garden. He would water and nourish their friendship just as he cared for the flowers. He just needed

Cindy to continue to open her heart to him and trust him the way she'd trusted him last night.

But he had to be careful too. They could never be more than friends.

. . .

"I made a chocolate pie for dessert," Cindy announced as she carried the pie to the table after supper. "I made two of them."

She pointed to the fridge, where she'd stowed the pie she planned to take to Drew later—if she could get away. Her pulse fluttered at the thought of seeing him again tonight. Spending time with him two evenings in a row would be a dream come true if she could!

Sarah Jane gave Cindy a strange expression as she set a pile of dessert plates and forks on the table beside the pie.

Cindy turned to her father. "Would you please slice the pie?"

Dat gave a curt nod and then began the task.

Cindy sat down beside him and chewed her lower lip. By morning her anger had dissipated, and she'd hoped he wouldn't still be angry with her. It would be best if they could work things out. But how could she find the right words to apologize or ask for his forgiveness? Why would she when she didn't believe her friendship with Drew was wrong?

Maybe it didn't matter. While he hadn't brought up their disagreement when she found him alone on the porch earlier, he'd seemed distant, and he only politely answered the questions she asked him. Perhaps it was better not to talk about it.

Dat finished slicing the pie, and Cindy distributed the pieces. After a silent prayer, she dug into her portion and nodded with satisfaction at the sweet flavor.

"This is *appeditlich*," Roy said.

"*Danki.*" Cindy sat up a little taller. "I'm glad you like it."

"Oh *ya*," Florence agreed. "Very *gut*."

Sarah Jane nodded from across the table. "Fantastic."

"*Danki.*" Cindy turned to *Dat* and awaited his approval.

He nodded and then took another bite, but he remained silent.

The disappointment she'd been fighting expanded in her chest. Was *Dat* going to continue to treat her with polite silence? Her heart ached at the possibility. She didn't want to be at odds with him.

When they'd finished their dessert, the women gathered the dirty dishes and carried them to the counter. *Dat* and Roy headed outside.

Cindy turned on the faucet to fill up one side of the sink with soapy water. She added the plates and utensils and hummed as she washed them.

When she realized Sarah Jane and Florence were quiet, she looked up and found Sarah Jane studying her with pursed lips.

"What?" Cindy asked.

"Why did you make two pies?" Sarah Jane leaned forward on the counter as if Cindy's response would be as juicy as the gossip she and Florence traded with the other women at their quilting bees.

Cindy shrugged off the question and returned to washing the dishes.

"You made it for Drew, didn't you?" Sarah Jane's voice held an edge of accusation.

"*Ya*, I did." Cindy pivoted toward her. "He told me last night that his aunt used to make him chocolate pies, and he enjoyed them. So I thought I'd make one for us and one for him."

"Are you planning on taking that pie to him tonight?" Florence sidled up to Sarah Jane, and Cindy suddenly felt as if they were ganging up on her.

Cindy lifted her chin and hoped it illustrated confidence. "I'm going to take it to him after we finish cleaning the kitchen."

When Florence and Sarah Jane shared a concerned look, Cindy turned back toward the sink and tried to ignore the muscles tightening in her neck.

They worked in silence for several minutes while Cindy washed, Sarah Jane dried, and Florence wiped off the table. Cindy hoped to finish the chores and then leave without another confrontation.

When she'd finished rinsing the last washed utensil, she went to the refrigerator and pulled out the pie. She smiled down at her creation and imagined Drew's handsome face when he saw the surprise she'd planned for him. She hoped he would enjoy eating it as much as she'd enjoyed making it for him.

"I'm concerned about your relationship with Drew." Florence's words crashed through Cindy's happy thoughts and slammed her back to the present. "If word gets around that you're spending time with an *Englisher*, the bishop might make a visit to our *haus*. I don't think you want that, and I know for sure your *dat* doesn't want it."

Although anger boiled in Cindy, she looked at her stepmother and fixed a smile on her face that felt brittle—and probably looked as phony as it felt.

"My friendship with Drew is just that—a friendship." Cindy divided a look between her stepmother and stepsister. "And as far as the bishop is concerned, he has nothing to say to me because I haven't joined the church." Gripping the pie in her hands, she moved past them toward the mudroom. "I won't be out late."

She hurried out of the house, down the porch steps, and toward the street in hopes of avoiding her father and brothers. She picked up her pace and did her best to leave her anger and frustration back home in the kitchen. She was going to enjoy the rest of her evening, despite her family's growing disapproval.

When she reached Drew's back door, she knocked and then took a deep breath and squared her shoulders as she shook off her irritation. The door swung open and her pulse galloped as she took in Drew's handsome face.

"Cindy." His smile widened. "What an awesome surprise."

"I have another surprise for you." She held out the pie. "Chocolate is your favorite, right?"

"Wow." He pushed open the screen door. "Am I dreaming right now or are you really standing in front of me with a chocolate pie?"

"You're not dreaming." She craned her neck to look into his kitchen. "Do you have a coffeepot?"

"I do, and guess what." He held up a finger. "I have mugs too."

She laughed. "That sounds perfect."

"Would you like to come in?"

Her stepmother's warning about the bishop rang through her mind, and she looked at the rocking chairs on his back porch. They matched the ones Ervin had provided in the front. "Why don't we sit out here and enjoy the beautiful night air?"

"Sure." He pointed toward the house. "Let me get a little table for us."

"Perfect." Cindy stepped inside and gathered plates, utensils, and mugs while Drew started the coffee and found what he called a folding TV tray.

Soon they were sitting side by side in the rockers and enjoying coffee and the pie. Bruce lay on the porch between them, softly snoring.

"How do you like it?" she asked after he'd taken a bite. "Although I'm sure it doesn't compare to your aunt Shirley's."

"It's exquisite, and I'm sure my aunt would have said the same. You can keep making these for me." He lifted his mug as if to toast her. "Thank you very much."

"You're welcome." She sipped her coffee and breathed in the night air as bliss settled over her. For a moment, everything was perfect. If only she could keep this feeling when she returned home to her disappointed family.

"Tell me about your mother."

Cindy looked at Drew. "What do you want to know?"

"Do you look like her?"

She considered the question. "Yes and no. She had dark-brown hair, like Jamie and Laura, but my eyes are like hers. I'm also about her height. She was beautiful too. I think Laura looks more like her."

Drew's smile was soft. "I find that hard to believe."

"What do you mean?"

"If she was beautiful, then *you* look like her."

Cindy's chest swelled with warmth as embarrassment heated her cheeks. She looked down at her coffee to avoid his eyes.

"You don't like compliments, do you?"

She shook her head while keeping her eyes focused on her mug.

"I'm sorry," he said. "I didn't mean to make you feel uncomfortable."

"I know." She looked at him again. "What else do you want to know about her?"

"Is it okay if I ask about your favorite memories of her?"

Cindy considered the question, and memories flooded her mind. She smiled as happy ones bubbled to the surface. "My best memories are when we sewed and quilted together. She taught me everything I know about sewing and quilting. I'm able to do seamstress work because of her."

"Really?" He moved his chair so he was facing her. "I knew you sewed and quilted, but I didn't know you worked as a seamstress. When do you work? And where?"

Cindy shrugged. "Every day, from home. I usually work in the afternoons after my chores are done. Customers bring projects to the house for me."

"Like what?"

"Well, sometimes I do little jobs, such as repair a quilt or hem a dress. Other times I get more complicated projects, such as tailoring a wedding gown to fit a woman's granddaughter."

"That takes talent." He lifted his mug to her again.

"Thank you." Cindy looked down at her mug. "I miss her so much. When she first passed away, I would cry while I sewed because it was just too painful to do it without her. Now I think of her and try to remember the advice she gave me." She looked up at the gorgeous splashes of orange and yellow in the sky. "Look at that. It's just as pretty as last night's sunset."

"It is."

She turned to him and found him watching her instead of the sky. Was he thinking she was as beautiful as the sunset? No, he couldn't be. She had to change the subject.

"Tell me about your parents," she said. "What are your favorite memories of them?"

He rubbed at the stubble on his chin. "Well, we used to play board games one night every week. My mom insisted we have at least one night when we turned off the television, and I wasn't allowed to play video games. Instead, we would sit at the kitchen table and play games like Monopoly or Scrabble, and the three of us would laugh and talk all evening. It was great."

"That's a wonderful memory."

"Yeah, it is." He rested his chin on his palm. "We used to take vacations too. We'd go to the beach in Maryland or drive down to Florida. My mom loved the ocean."

"Where did your dad like to go on vacation?"

"He didn't care where we went. He just wanted to make my mom happy." Drew set his mug on the little table. "They had a really good, solid marriage. They would argue sometimes like all couples do, but they truly loved and cherished each other. At least, that's what I remember."

"My parents did too." Cindy set her chair into motion as more memories came to her. "My dad had some regrets after she died. He told Jamie he was sorry he never took her to Florida. Some Amish folks rent a van and go down in the fall, and she really wanted to go. He always told her he had to stay home to make sure the farm ran well, but after she died, he realized Jamie and Mark had been able to run the farm by themselves for several years. He was angry at himself for not giving her that memory."

He shook his head. "He can't beat himself up over that. He had no idea what God had planned for your parents."

"I know." Cindy looked out toward a stand of trees.

"Are you close to Florence?"

Her gaze snapped to his, and his eyes widened.

"I didn't mean you shouldn't be," he said. "I was just wondering what kind of relationship you had with her."

"I was just surprised by the question." She took a sip of coffee while considering how much to share. "We get along, and I appreciate that she makes my father happy. She'll never replace my mother, though. I can't talk to her the way I could talk to *Mamm*."

"I understand that." He rocked back and forth in the chair. "I adored my aunt. She was a wonderful woman, and she did the best she could for me. She gave me love, along with a safe home and everything I needed, but she wasn't my mother."

They rocked in amiable silence for several minutes, and Cindy appreciated how comfortable she felt with Drew. It was as if they could sit together for hours, either talking or just silently enjoying each other's company. The only sounds around them were singing cicadas, soft snores from Bruce, the swishing of their rocking chairs, and the hum of cars and *clip-clop* of buggy horses in the distance.

"I'm glad I didn't have to wait a week to see you again," he said.

She looked at him, and a wave of warmth traveled from her head to the tips of her toes as she took in the intensity in his eyes. "I'm glad too."

"The week apart was torture. Let's not do that again."

She smiled. "I agree," she said, then, "I should get going." She stood and began to gather their plates and mugs.

"Stop." He placed his hand on hers, and her skin tingled at his touch. "I can clean this up."

"Are you sure?"

"Yes." He touched her arm. "It was really great seeing you. Please stop by again soon."

"I will." She glanced up at him, and her heart hammered in her chest.

"Would you like me to walk you home?"

"No." She shook her head as she imagined her father waiting for her on the porch again tonight. It would be a disaster if he confronted her with Drew at her side. "I'll be fine."

"Hang on." He reached under a bench and pulled out a small flashlight. "Use this. I don't want you to fall. You can return it when you see me."

"Thank you." She took the flashlight and then pointed to the pie plate. "And you can return that when you finish what's in it. I'll make you another."

"I promise I will." He gave her a dazzling smile, and then he walked her around the house to the driveway. "Good night."

She leaned down and gave Bruce a good-bye rub on his head, and then, with happiness fluttering through her like a honeybee, she ambled down the driveway toward home.

. . .

Drew leaned against the railing on the front porch and grinned as he watched Cindy leave. Elation had spilled through him when he opened the door and found her standing on his back porch with a pie in her hands. She'd hijacked his thoughts all day long, so when he saw her, he was certain he was dreaming and praying that he wasn't.

Their visit had been just as magical as their time together last night. He'd cherished every minute with her, and he'd been captivated by her smile and the sweet sound of her laughter.

Tonight she'd shared more of her memories of her mother, and he'd learned that she didn't enjoy compliments or talking about herself. She was humble, and it was clear she had no idea how beautiful and special she was, which made her even more attractive.

When the beam of the flashlight bounced out of sight, he returned to the back porch, gathered the dishes and mugs, and then whistled as he carried them into the kitchen. After storing the remaining pie in the refrigerator, and the TV tray back in the family room, he washed the plates, forks, and mugs.

When he turned toward the hallway, he found Bruce sitting there, staring at him. "She's pretty special, isn't she, Bruce?"

His dog gave a woof in response.

"I think so too." Drew grinned as he headed to his bedroom.

. . .

A soft knock sounded on Cindy's door as she climbed into bed.

"Come in," she said as she pulled her sheet over her night-gown.

When Sarah Jane opened the door and stepped inside, dread pooled in the pit of Cindy's stomach. She hoped her stepsister wasn't here to argue. She was too tired and too happy after her visit with Drew for another disagreement.

But then hope swept through her. Maybe Sarah Jane had come to apologize.

"Did you have a *gut* visit with Drew?" Sarah Jane stood at the foot of Cindy's bed.

"*Ya*, I did." Cindy leaned back against the headboard. "He loved the pie."

"*Gut.*" Sarah Jane pushed her waist-length medium-brown hair over her slight shoulder. "Do you have feelings for him?"

Cindy clenched her jaw. Sarah Jane was *not* here to apologize. "No, I don't. We're just *freinden*."

"I just don't understand why you need him as a *freind* when we have plenty of young folks our age in our church district. If you came to youth group, you'd meet more of them, and you'd feel like a part of our community."

"It's more complicated than that. Drew and I can relate to each other." Cindy shrugged. "He understands me, because he lost his parents and aunt, just like I lost *Mamm*. He knows what it's like to grieve someone. I don't feel like I fit in at youth group because the other members haven't had to navigate through the depth of grief I have. When I'm with Drew, I can be completely honest. We have a special connection I don't have with any other *freinden*. I feel like he's the only person who truly understands what I've gone through."

Sarah Jane's eyes widened, and then something like hurt flickered over her pretty face. "Cindy, I've lost *mei dat*. That's why we're stepsisters." She pointed at her own chest. "Why can't you talk to *me*?"

Guilt, hot and sharp, sliced through Cindy. But how could she believe Sarah Jane understood the depth of her grief? After all, she'd readily accepted their parents' marriage and never seemed to doubt how quickly they'd moved on with their lives. It was as if Cindy was the only member of the family who still felt the great void *Mamm*'s loss had left behind.

But she didn't want to be unkind.

"I'm sorry, Sarah Jane. I hadn't thought about it that way."

Sarah Jane shook her head. "I really don't understand you. We have everything we need in our community. *Gut*, solid Christian men in our youth group would love to get to know you, but you insist upon walling yourself off."

The fight fizzled out of Cindy, and her shoulders sagged. "Sarah Jane, I'm too tired to have this discussion again. Can we talk tomorrow?"

"If that's what you want," Sarah Jane snapped. "Just remember that *Mamm* and I warned you. If you get into trouble for spending time with Drew, it's your fault." Then she spun on her heel and marched out of Cindy's room, the door clicking shut behind her.

Cindy flipped off her lantern and rolled onto her side as Sarah Jane's words echoed in her mind. Surely her stepsister was being overly concerned. It might take some time for everyone to understand her friendship with Drew, but no trouble would come from it. They weren't doing anything wrong. She was enjoying getting to know him better, and he seemed to enjoy her company. She looked forward to delivering more chocolate pies to him if it meant more evenings like this one.

CHAPTER 9

Drew swiped at the sweat gathering on his forehead and then picked up his pitchfork to continue mucking a stall in Ervin's barn. The barn was humid, and the air was stale and still as the scent of animals filled his nose, but he smiled to himself as his mind replayed his evening on the porch with Cindy the night before.

He'd fallen asleep thinking of her beautiful smile and their easy conversation. It had been the perfect evening as they'd eaten the delicious pie and drunk coffee, and he hoped to share many more like it with her.

He was finishing the first stall when he heard someone call his name. He looked over his shoulder to find Ervin standing behind him. After leaning the pitchfork against the wall, Drew turned toward him and wiped his forehead with the sleeve of his T-shirt. "I didn't hear you come in."

"How's it going?" Ervin pointed toward the stall.

"Slowly." Drew blew out a deep breath. "It's hot today."

"Well, it's July, *sohn*." Ervin touched his beard and looked around the barn as if contemplating something.

Drew leaned back against the stall wall and wiped his hands down his jeans. "Is everything all right?"

"*Ya.*" Ervin nodded. "I want to ask you something, though. Did I see Cindy Riehl leaving your *haus* last night?"

Drew stood up straight, alarm suddenly gripping him. He couldn't allow Ervin to get the wrong idea about his friendship with Cindy. "Yes and no. She came to visit, but we sat on the back porch while we talked. She wasn't inside my house."

"Uh-huh." Ervin's expression hardened. "I need you to realize that it's inappropriate for an Amish woman to date an *Englisher*. We believe only baptized Amish folks can date and marry."

"We're not dating." Drew kept his words measured. "We're just friends, and she insisted that she's permitted to be my friend."

"You may be only friends, but others in the community might misinterpret your friendship, and that would damage her reputation."

Drew stilled as a knot of unease formed in his chest. "But we haven't done anything inappropriate. All we've done is talk." He ignored a flash of memory, how it had felt to hold her hand during the fireworks.

"I believe you, but if the bishop finds out Cindy has been spending time with you, he might visit her house and talk to her and her father. She could get into quite a bit of trouble."

"What do you mean? She told me she hasn't joined the church."

"That's true, but unfortunately, some people in the community talk. Gossip is sinful, but it exists, even among the Amish."

Drew gulped as trepidation crept up his neck. "So if I see her, people in the community might get the wrong impression, damaging her reputation."

"Exactly." Ervin's expression was grave. "You're a *gut* man, and I know you'd never want to hurt her."

"Never." Drew's response was louder than he'd intended.

"But I had to warn you before she got into trouble."

"I don't understand why she didn't tell me."

Ervin suddenly smiled. "Perhaps she enjoys your company as much as you enjoy hers, but the fact is she can't see you because you aren't Amish, not without risking her reputation."

"Can she be shunned if she spends time with me?"

"Not exactly. We can't shun someone who isn't a member of the church." Ervin pointed toward the barn entrance. "That's why *mei sohn* lived in that house for a short while but was never shunned. He never joined the church. But that doesn't mean community members won't treat Cindy differently because of her actions."

Confusion swarmed Drew's mind. He craved a relationship with Cindy, but he didn't want to hurt her. If he continued to see her, she could face judgment in her community, even though it would be unfair. How could he allow that to happen?

The answer was simple—he couldn't. He cared about her too much to take that risk. He had to stay away from her to protect her.

"I understand." Drew nodded as reality struck him. He couldn't see Cindy. The thought sent a torrent of emotions raging through him—anger, disappointment, confusion, grief, and loneliness. He'd finally found someone who understood him and made him happy. How could he let her go?

"I'm sorry, *sohn*." Ervin sighed. "I had a feeling you weren't aware of what it could mean if you continued to see her."

"I appreciate that." Despair weighed down on Drew's shoulders as he picked up the pitchfork. "I'm going to get back to work now."

As Ervin walked away, Drew returned to mucking the stall,

slamming the tool through the hay to ease the wrath that bit into his back and shoulders.

Drew had no idea how to move on without Cindy in his life. All he could do was bury his feelings the best way he knew how—by working his muscles until his body went numb.

· · ·

Cindy leaned back against her headboard as she read the Christian novel she'd started last night when she couldn't sleep. Her thoughts had been wrapped around Drew since leaving his house Friday night.

It was now Sunday afternoon, and despite her fervent prayers for relief at church this morning, her heart still ached to see him again. She'd hoped reading would both distract her and pass the time.

She turned a page, even though she couldn't recall what she'd just read. She tried to concentrate on the printed words, but it was no use. All she could see in her mind's eye was Drew's handsome face and breathtaking smile. What was happening to her?

A soft knock sounded on her door.

"Cindy?" Florence's voice sounded from the hallway. "May I please come in?"

"*Ya.*" Cindy set the book on her nightstand as Florence came in, and then she looked up as her stepmother sat down on the edge of her bed. She looked serious.

"I want to speak with you."

"What do you want to talk about?"

Florence folded her hands as her expression became even

more concerning. "This is difficult for me to say." She paused again. "Your *dat* is very upset. He didn't ask me to come speak with you. I offered to try to help fix things between you."

Cindy pulled in a deep breath as her back stiffened. *This has to be about Drew.*

"Your *dat* is concerned about your friendship with Drew, and I have to admit I am too."

"I've already told you we're just *freinden*." Cindy fought to keep her boiling temper in check. "There's nothing to be concerned about."

"I don't think that's true." Florence began to count on her fingers. "You've gone out with him alone, you've gone to visit him at his *haus*, you've baked for him, and you've delivered food to him. Those are things young people do when they're dating. It's not appropriate, and you realize that if the bishop finds out about it, he'll visit us. He'll talk to you and your *dat*. Do you want to disappoint your *dat* that way?"

Cindy felt her nostrils flare. "I'm not baptized. That means the bishop can't tell me what to do."

"No, but he can still embarrass your *dat*. Do you want him to be embarrassed?"

"No." Cindy's voice was soft as guilt began to invade her.

Florence tilted her head as her expression softened. "I don't understand why you don't want to go to youth group with Sarah Jane."

Cindy resisted the urge to roll her eyes. How many times did she have to explain her feelings about youth group? She worked to keep her expression neutral. Disrespecting Florence wouldn't help her case, nor gain her stepmother's understanding and empathy.

"Sarah Jane told me you feel like you don't belong in youth group and the community. Why is that?"

Although Cindy wasn't surprised to learn Sarah Jane and Florence talked about her, her stepmother's admission still sent a hot shaft of irritation through her.

"I've felt disconnected from the community since *mei mamm* died." Cindy's voice sounded rough to her own ears. "I don't fit in because I don't think anyone can relate to my grief. I've felt alone ever since my siblings moved on so easily . . . almost as if we never lost our *mamm*. Yet I'll never be the same because she's gone."

"We all still grieve for our loved ones. I'm certain your siblings miss your *mamm*, and you're not alone in your grief. Walter, Sarah Jane, and Roy miss their *dat*, and I miss him too." Florence paused, and her expression warmed. "I know I'm not your *mamm*, and I would never try to replace her." Florence's brown eyes seemed to search hers. "But I love you, Cindy. I truly care about you. You can always talk to me if you need someone."

The guilt gnawing away at Cindy became stronger, but she could never talk to Florence the way she could talk to her mother. It would never be the same!

"*Danki*," Cindy whispered as wetness filled her eyes.

"Your family and community love you. Why would you look elsewhere for acceptance?"

Cindy felt her eyes narrow. "I didn't plan to look elsewhere. Drew and I just connected when we met. He understands me."

Florence pointed to the floor. "You belong in this community and in the Amish church. God loves you too. And he will forgive your sins if you confess."

"Confess?" Cindy sat up straight as if steel had been poured down her spine. "I haven't done anything wrong. Making a *freind* is not a sin."

"You were born and raised Amish. It's wrong for you to look for love with an *Englisher*."

"I'm not looking for love." But wasn't she? Weren't her feelings for Drew growing daily? She ignored the questions twirling through her mind. "I have nothing to confess."

Florence pressed her lips together before going on. "You need to follow your *dat*'s rules, and that means following the rules of the church. You must promise me you'll stay away from Drew."

Cindy's lower lip trembled. "I can't do that."

"It's what your *dat* wants, and this is his *haus*." Florence pointed to the floor again. "Your behavior is hurting your *dat*. Is that what you want?"

Cindy shook her head. "No."

"Then promise me." Florence folded her arms over her apron. "If you're going to be a dutiful *dochder*, then you need to promise me."

Florence's words sent a knife through Cindy's heart. How could she not promise to be a dutiful daughter? It's what her mother would have expected, and she could never disrespect her mother's memory.

"Okay," Cindy croaked. "I promise." But the words sent the knife thrusting deeper into her heart.

"*Danki*." Florence gently squeezed Cindy's hand. "Your *dat* will be *froh* to hear it." She stood, a smile spreading across her face. "Come down in a little bit. I'm going to pull out a chocolate cake I made yesterday."

Cindy nodded and sniffed as tears stung her eyes. Florence disappeared from her room, the door clicking shut behind her.

With her chest aching, Cindy rolled over onto her side and dissolved into tears as the thought of breaking her friendship with Drew tore at her soul. How could she let go of the one person who understood her? How could their friendship be a sin if it felt so natural and pure?

Cindy had no idea how she'd go on without Drew. The grief was so intense she was certain it might smother her.

Once again, she was lost and all alone—a stranger in her own home.

. . .

"*Danki*," Cindy told Franey Herschberger as she paid for her fabric and supplies. Then she carried her large bag out of Herschberger's Fabrics and headed down the street.

It had been nearly three weeks since she'd seen Drew, and when the ache didn't dull, Cindy started pouring herself into sewing projects.

Each day after she finished her chores, she would sew or quilt for hours, asking God to give her solace from her heartache as she worked. She'd not only taken on more sewing jobs from customers, but started making a log cabin quilt featuring blocks with different shades of blue and gray. She wasn't certain what she was going to do with the quilt when she finished it. She'd briefly considered selling it, but she could decide after she'd completed the project.

She had hoped Drew would stop by with her pie plate and give her the opportunity to speak to him one last time, but as the days had worn on, she'd started wondering if her father had spoken to Drew and warned him to stay away from her. Or perhaps Cindy had come on too strong and she'd managed to scare him off with her gifts of baked goods or the confessions of her deepest and darkest emotions.

All Cindy knew for certain was that she missed Drew, and the loneliness was starting to eat away at her soul.

When she reached the corner, she stopped to let a car drive past. She stepped off the curb and then heard someone call her name.

Turning, she gasped when she spotted Drew jogging down the street toward her. Was she hallucinating? Had her heartache caused her to lose her mind?

"Cindy!" Drew's grin was wide as he hurried toward her, a bag with Lancaster Hardware Store printed on it dangling from his hand. "I thought that was you!"

"Hi." She worked to keep her expression blank to hold back any hint of the pain his absence had caused her.

Something that looked like confusion flickered over his face before his brow furrowed.

"How are you?" he asked.

"I'm fine." She lifted her chin.

"I haven't seen or heard from you in almost three weeks." His eyes seemed to search hers. "I've missed you."

A strangled sob escaped Cindy's throat, and she worked to stop the tears that threatened to follow. "You've missed me?"

"Yes. Tremendously." He reached for her hand, but then pulled his hand back. "We need to talk."

"I have to go." She crossed the street.

"Wait!" Drew came after her. "Have lunch with me."

"I can't." She whirled toward him.

"Please." He held up his hands. "It's just lunch, not a marriage proposal."

She hesitated as Florence's words about being a dutiful

daughter surfaced in her mind. But didn't Cindy have the right to talk to Drew one last time and explain why she'd stayed away from him?

"Fine," she said. "But I need to call my driver to ask him to give me more time."

"I can give you a ride home. Just tell him you ran into a friend." Drew pulled his phone from his pocket, and his expression seemed hopeful.

Had he missed her as much as she'd missed him? The thought sent a ray of hope spilling through her battered soul.

After calling her driver and telling him she'd found another way home, Cindy walked with Drew to the Bird-in-Hand Family Restaurant.

She sat in a booth across from him as confusion swirled in her chest. He said he'd missed her, but he'd also stayed away. Was he toying with her emotions?

"What's wrong?" he asked after the server had taken their order.

Her gaze snapped to his, and she found the familiar empathy there.

"Talk to me, Cindy." He leaned forward on the table, his eyes seeming to plead with hers for answers.

"If you missed me"—her voice nearly failed her—"Why did you stay away from me for so long?"

He settled back in the seat and raked his hand through his thick hair. The motion left his hair an endearing mess. "Ervin told me our relationship could cause trouble for you in your community. He said if I kept seeing you, you could be branded with a bad reputation." His expression became pained. "I was afraid I was hurting you, and I wanted to explain. I kept hoping you'd stop by so I could at least talk to you one more time."

She gasped as he said the words she'd repeated in her prayers over and over for weeks.

"I'm sorry." He frowned. "If I see you, I hurt you, but if I stay away from you, I hurt both of us. I feel like I'm losing my mind."

"I know," she whispered. "I kept hoping you'd come see me."

"Why didn't you come see me?"

She looked down at the table and began to trace circles with her fingers. "Florence said I was embarrassing my father by seeing you and breaking the rules of the community. She made me promise not to see you. She said that if I were a dutiful daughter, I'd do what was right. I've missed you so much I've felt like I can't breathe. I've been sewing and quilting to distract myself, but nothing works."

She looked up at him, and the intensity in his eyes sent a jolt of heat zipping through her veins. Her breath was trapped in her lungs, and then goose bumps tripped down her arms.

Just then, the server appeared at the table with their food, and Cindy's trance was broken. She thanked the server and stared down at her club sandwich, but her appetite had evaporated.

"I'm sorry."

Cindy looked over at him. "Why?"

"I'm sorry for causing so much trouble." He shook his head as his attractive face wrinkled into a frown. "If I hadn't asked you to go see the fireworks with me, we wouldn't be in this predicament."

"You believe that?" She leaned forward.

"No, I suppose not." He gave a little laugh. "I think our friendship would still be going strong even if I hadn't invited you to see the fireworks."

"What do we do now?" She held her breath, praying he'd

have a solution that would solve all their problems and keep their relationship afloat.

"I don't know." He looked down at his Salisbury steak and then back at her. "What if I talk to your father? He seems like a reasonable man. Maybe if I explain how much you mean to me, he'll allow us to remain friends. Do you think that would work?"

"Maybe." Cindy nodded as a tiny seed of hope took root in her soul. "It's definitely worth a try."

"I agree." Drew's radiant smile was back. "Let's enjoy our lunch, and then I'll take you home and ask your father to talk to me."

CHAPTER 10

Cindy's heart pounded against her rib cage as Drew steered his pickup truck toward where *Dat* stood at the top of the driveway. A deep frown twisted his face. A sinking feeling of foreboding slithered up her spine and dug its claws into her shoulders.

"Hey." Drew's voice was close to her ear as he placed his hand on top of hers. "Everything is going to be all right. I'll talk to your dad and explain that I would never do anything to disrespect you or him. Does that sound like a good plan?"

She nodded, but she couldn't ignore the feeling that this would be the last time she spoke to Drew.

When he wrenched open his door, she grabbed his arm. "Wait," she said.

"What?" He turned toward her, his brow puckering.

"If it doesn't go well, just remember that I care about you." She spoke slowly. "No matter what he says, it won't change how much your friendship means to me."

He entwined his fingers with hers. "I know that. And I care about you too."

She peered out the windshield and took in the fury on her father's reddening face. Her stomach tied itself into a knot as she climbed out of the truck, retrieved her bag from the floorboard, and started up the driveway.

"Where have you been?" *Dat* bellowed. "You told me you were running to the fabric store for supplies for your quilt, but you've been gone for hours! Do you think I'm a moron? Do you think I don't know what sneaking off to meet someone is?"

"I didn't sneak off to meet Drew." She worked to keep her voice steady despite her raging emotions. "I went to the fabric store, but then I ran into Drew on the street." She pointed to Drew as he walked up behind her. "He was at the hardware store. He asked me to have lunch with him and offered to drive me home. None of this was planned, so please don't accuse me of lying or sneaking around. I wasn't."

Dat shook his head. "Go into the *haus* while I have a talk with Drew."

Cindy peeked over her shoulder at Drew, and he gave her an encouraging look and a nod.

As she hurried up the path, she sent a quick prayer up to God. *Please soften* Dat's *heart toward Drew and help him understand how special our friendship is. We need your help.*

She rushed into the house and up to her sewing room, where she looked at her log cabin quilt and prayed quilting would bring her solace until she saw Drew again.

Then she moved to the window, sat down on a chair, and watched as Drew spoke to her father. She hugged her arms to her chest and begged God to keep Drew in her life.

. . .

"Vernon, please listen to me." Drew held up his trembling hands as he searched his mind for the right words to convince the man to trust him. "Cindy is telling you the truth. I didn't plan to run into her today. I went to the hardware store, and when

I walked out, I spotted her on the street. I suggested we have lunch and get caught up, so please don't punish her for seeing me. It was my idea."

Vernon took a step toward Drew, and his eyes seemed to smolder with fury. "You need to stay away from my daughter. You're not a member of our community, and you're forbidden to be her friend."

Vernon's words punched Drew in the chest, and he rubbed at the tightness there.

Brushing off the barb, Drew lifted his chin. "I respect you, and I respect your daughter. I would never do anything to break your trust in me, and I also—"

"If you have *any* respect for her or for me, you'll stay away from her for good." Vernon nearly spat the words at Drew. "Stay away from all of us." Then he pivoted and marched toward the barn.

Drew slammed his hands on his hips and took deep breaths as his body shook like a leaf in a tornado. He'd ruined his chances of winning Vernon's blessing, and he had broken his promise to Cindy to fix this. Disappointment and grief nearly overcame him.

When Drew saw movement out of the corner of his eye, he turned and saw Jamie standing on the other side of the driveway. While Jamie wasn't smiling, he also wasn't glaring at Drew with hatred in his eyes as Vernon had.

"I didn't see you there," Drew said as Jamie walked over to him. "How long have you been standing there?"

"Long enough." Jamie crossed his arms over his chest.

"Do you hate me too?" Drew gave a sardonic laugh, despite his crumbling hope.

"*Mei dat* doesn't hate you." Jamie glanced toward the barn

and then back at Drew. "It's just that you and Cindy can't be together. Your relationship with her is putting my sister in a terrible spot. You have to accept that this is just how it is in our culture, and it's not going to change just because you tell my father you respect him and you'll never do anything to break his trust."

Something inside of Drew snapped, and he felt his emotions rage. "Jamie, I don't know how I can stay away from her. These past three weeks have been torture. I care about her."

Jamie's eyes widened, and he shook his head. "You need to find a way to get over it. You can't be with her. It's just not possible."

"Why not?" Drew's voice rose. "We're all people."

"It's more complicated than that." Jamie jammed a finger in Drew's chest. "You're not Amish, and she can't be with you unless you're both baptized into the Amish church. You need to accept this."

And just like that, Drew's hope crashed. He could do nothing to make his relationship with Cindy work.

Would he really have to go on without her in his life? Would he have to suffer more loss?

. . .

Cindy fought back threatening tears as she watched Drew hang his head and then walk to his truck after talking to Jamie. It had been apparent by the way *Dat* had stomped off that Drew's discussion with him hadn't gone well either.

Nothing had changed despite Drew's effort to reason with her father. She'd lost Drew once again, just as she had nearly three weeks ago when she agreed to be a dutiful daughter and not see him. Her heart crumbled at the thought of never seeing him again. How she would miss him! He was the only person who truly understood her. She was alone once more. She took a trembling breath as tears spilled down her hot cheeks.

Heavy footsteps echoing in the stairwell outside the sewing room alerted her that either Roy or her father was coming upstairs. She swiped at her tears and lifted the log cabin quilt from the table to busy herself, suppressing the grief that had taken hold of her.

"I never expected that you'd be the one I'd lose to the *English* world."

Cindy looked up as her father hovered in the doorway, a pained expression twisting his face. "What?"

"When your *mamm* died, I expected all *mei kinner* would cling to our beliefs. You were the one who always seemed to be closest to your *mamm*. You never left her side to spend time with *freinden*, and you always seemed to have a strong faith." He stepped into the room. "It puzzles me that now that she's gone, you're not the same person. I never thought you would try to find love outside of our community."

Love?

"I didn't plan this. It just happened." She was grateful her voice sounded more confident than she felt.

"You should be clinging to your beliefs without your *mamm* here." His voice became more urgent and sterner. "You should have been baptized already. You should be married, like Laura. You should be planning a family now, not spending time with an *Englisher*."

"I'm not Laura." She gritted her teeth. "I'm not Mark or Jamie either. I'm Cindy." She pointed to her chest. "When *Mamm* died, you all moved on as if everything was just fine, but it wasn't fine." She dropped the quilt into her lap and balled her hands into fists. "Nothing will ever be fine without her."

Dat rubbed at his shoulder as if a cluster of tension had sprouted there. "You make it sound as if we don't miss her. We all miss her. I still love your *mamm*, and I will never stop loving her. But God provides our comfort. He is the great healer, and he will heal your heart if you allow him to."

"I have asked him for healing. I've prayed thousands upon thousands of times since *Mamm* died." Her voice fractured as her own tension coiled around her chest. "I've asked him to lead me since I've been so lost. I thought you would understand how lost I've felt, but you haven't, and it's obvious you still don't. No one does. You, Jamie, Mark, and Laura just moved on and left me in the dust, all alone."

"No one left you, Cindy." *Dat* crossed the room and then sank into a chair across from her as his expression and tone warmed. "We're all still here. We've all tried to reach out to you, but you just keep rejecting us."

"That's not true." She sniffed and swiped her hand over her eyes. "I've never pushed anyone away from me."

"*Ya*, you have." He wiped away her tears with the tip of his finger. "We're all here for you, and God is too. You just need to join the church. Open your heart to God and let him lead you to baptism. Then you can find a husband suitable for you."

"Suitable for me?" She shook her head. "Why do I need to join the church to find a suitable husband?"

He blew out a sigh as if she were the most frustrating person he'd ever met. "You need to find an Amish man. That's what your *mamm* would want."

She flinched as if he'd slapped her. "How dare you bring

Mamm into this? How do you know she would have disapproved of Drew?"

"Because she would want you to be Amish, Cindy," he said. "We both wanted our *kinner* to stay in the church and raise families in the faith. That's what we're called to do."

Dat stood, and his expression clouded. "You're forbidden from seeing him. I've already told him to stay away. I expect you to respect my wishes."

Cindy stared up at him, her words trapped in her throat. She clenched her teeth against the pain, and as her father exited her room, she felt as if a hole had been punched in her chest. She had lost Drew forever, and nothing she could do would fix this.

Closing her eyes, she hugged the quilt to her chest and sobbed.

CHAPTER 11

Cindy ran her fingers over the log cabin quilt as the humid August breeze swept in from the window next to her sewing table. For weeks—a little more than a month—she'd spent at least an hour each evening working on this quilt before she went to bed. And now it was finally finished.

She moved her fingers over the intricate stitches and blocks of different shades of gray and blue. The quilt was beautiful, possibly even the best she'd ever made, but that did nothing to weaken the permanent frown on her face.

She'd tried to move on after losing Drew. She'd thrown herself into her chores and then her sewing projects, but nothing helped to heal her shattered heart. She still cried herself to sleep every night and begged God to help her convince her father that Drew was a worthy friend. Not that she ever discussed Drew with her family. She kept her feelings locked away in her heart, away from the critical eyes of her family members.

"Cindy?"

Cindy turned toward the doorway as her older sister walked in. "Laura. What are you doing here?"

"We haven't had much time to talk at church for too long, so I wanted to visit with you." Laura sat down in a chair beside her and rested her hands on her protruding belly, which had, of course, grown larger.

"Where are Mollie and Alice?" Cindy asked.

Laura pointed toward the window. "They're playing at Kayla's. I thought maybe we could go over there when we're done here."

Cindy studied Laura's pretty face in search of a lie. It was Tuesday, and Cindy rarely saw her sisters during the week, unless they were planning a sisters' day, which would consist of working on a big sewing or baking project together. Most likely Laura had an ulterior motive for this visit. It wasn't just a friendly chat.

"Why are you looking at me like that?" Laura's laugh made her sound nervous.

"Why are you really here?"

"Just to see you." Laura crossed her ankles and settled back in the chair. "Florence invited me to stay for supper, so Allen is going to join us later."

"Florence invited you?" Cindy leaned forward. "Why would Florence invite you over?"

"Because she wanted to see me, I suppose." Laura's eyes moved to the quilt in Cindy's lap, and she gasped. "Did you make that?"

"*Ya.*" Cindy looked down and ran her fingers over her creation once again.

"May I see it?" Laura reached for it, and Cindy gave it to her. Her sister moved one finger over the stitches and her blue eyes widened. "This is exquisite. I think it's your best work."

Cindy shrugged.

"How long did it take you to make it?"

Cindy rubbed her chin and considered it. She had started a couple of weeks before she met Drew in town and had lunch with him—the last time she'd seen him. Her throat felt full and she tried to clear past the messy knot of emotion gathering there.

"I guess it took about six weeks." Her voice sounded like sandpaper.

"Wow." Laura clicked her tongue. "*Mamm* would be so proud of you."

"Would she?" Cindy snorted as all the resentment toward her family members came to the surface.

"What does that mean?" Laura's expression transformed into a frown.

"Why are you really here, Laura?" Cindy took the quilt back and folded it. "Did Florence tell you I have feelings for an *Englisher*? Did she ask you to come over and explain to me why my life is so much better now that Drew isn't a part of it? Is that why you're really sitting here with me?" Her words felt so tight that she had to force them out. "Tell me the truth, Laura."

Laura's mouth worked, but nothing escaped past her lips.

"I knew it." Ice and fire burned in Cindy's chest. "If you're here to tell me I should be *froh*, then you can leave." She pointed to the door. "Just go."

"Wait." Laura quietly reached over and touched Cindy's hand. "Talk to me. I'm your *schweschder*. You used to tell me everything. Why did you stop talking to me? Why haven't you told me what you've been going through? When I see you at church, you say you're all right, but I can tell you aren't."

Cindy looked down at the quilt. "You'd never understand how I feel." Her words came out harsher than she intended.

"Why don't you give me a chance to try?"

Cindy sighed and then looked up. "I have feelings for Drew Collins, the farmhand who works for the Lapps. We have a connection you would never grasp. *Dat* has forbidden me from seeing him. It's been more than a month, and I feel like my heart breaks more every day that passes."

Laura studied her and shook her head. "How could you have feelings for an *Englisher* when we're so different from them?"

"We're not really different from them. He's a Christian, too, and he's suffered similar losses to mine. We have a connection. I can tell him how I feel, and he understands me."

"An Amish man would understand you just as well, and you wouldn't have to leave your family to be with him." Laura's eyes widened as if an idea had suddenly gripped her. "Does this mean you would leave our community for him? You want to be *English*?"

"I don't know." Cindy shrugged. "I'm not sure how I feel about that. I just know how *bedauerlich* I am now that I can't see him. Not seeing him is like suffering through another loss."

Laura reached over and took Cindy's hand in hers, in what looked like a near panic. "You can't do this to me. You can't leave the church. I need *mei schweschder* in my life."

"What about what *I* need?" A rock of guilt weighed in her gut. When had she ever put her own feelings before her family members' feelings? Who had she become during the past month? But she was being honest at last.

"Your family should come first." Laura jammed a finger on her opposite palm as if to drive home her point. "You should be thinking about your family. *Dat* would be devastated. What would—"

"Don't do it." Cindy seethed her warning. "Don't you dare bring *Mamm* into this! This has nothing to do with *Mamm*. She's gone, and I'll never get over losing her." Her voice broke, and she fought tears. "You've all moved on with your lives, but I can't. Drew understands how I feel. He knows what it's like to have doubts and to feel stuck. The rest of you can't relate to me."

"That's not true, Cindy. I miss *Mamm* every day." Contrition seemed to flicker over Laura's face. "We all relate to how you feel. You don't have to leave the faith to find someone who understands you. Don't do this. Don't leave the faith for him."

"I'm still here, aren't I? I'm trapped in this *haus* with nothing but chores and sewing. He lives less than a block from here, but I can't see him because the church forbids me. Why would I want to join a church that forbids me from having a relationship with someone special just because he isn't a member?"

Laura's lips pinched. "But if you left us for him, wouldn't you miss us? We'd miss you terribly. I could cry just thinking of having to say good-bye to you."

"How could you judge me when you fell in love with Allen so soon after Savilla died?" Cindy snapped.

Laura gaped at her.

"You married him only eighteen months later. You never expected to fall in love with your best friend's husband, but you did." Cindy's body shook with anger. "Love can be unexpected. We never know when God is going to send us the person we're going to spend the rest of our lives with and build a family with. How can you sit there and act like I'm sinning when Drew could be the one God has chosen for me?"

"You're really in love with him?" Laura's eyes were round.

"I don't know, but I know I miss him so much my heart feels like it's breaking apart."

Laura clicked her tongue. "You've fallen in love with an *Englisher*." She shook her head. "You never planned to join the church, did you? You were just waiting for an opportunity to leave it."

"That's not true. Stop putting words in my mouth!"

Laura sniffed as her eyes misted over. "I'm losing *mei*

schweschder." She ripped a tissue from the box on the sewing table and dabbed at her eyes.

Cindy gulped as her own tears scorched her cheeks. "I think you should leave."

Laura shook her head. "I'm not leaving. We need to talk this out. I have to convince you to just join the church and go to youth group with Sarah Jane. You'll find happiness there, and you'll find the perfect husband."

"Now you sound like Sarah Jane and Florence," Cindy grumbled.

"Maybe that's because they're right, and they want you to be *froh.*"

"Please leave." Cindy grabbed a tissue and dabbed her eyes before wiping her nose. "I've heard enough."

Laura hesitated.

"Please go," Cindy repeated.

Laura stood. "I'm not going to give up on you. You're *mei schweschder*, and *ich liebe dich*. No matter what."

Then Laura walked out of the room, leaving Cindy alone in the stifling silence.

She studied the quilt in her lap as shame did a slow, prickly walk on spider's legs up her spine. How could Cindy allow a great chasm to divide her only sister and her?

She slammed her eyes shut as a painful headache stabbed at the back of her eyes. If only life could go back to normal.

But nothing would ever be normal again.

· · ·

Cindy swept the kitchen floor after supper while Laura washed the dishes, Mollie dried, and Sarah Jane wiped down the table.

The windows at the far end of the kitchen were open, and Florence's voice floated in from the porch as she talked with the men and rocked Catherine.

During supper, Cindy had found herself trying to imagine Drew sitting beside her as they enjoyed a meal with her family. But she knew that was a pipe dream. By no chance would Drew ever be accepted by her family unless he were Amish, and how could she even imagine asking him to join the church for her when she wasn't sure she wanted to be Amish herself?

She had remained silent during the meal while conversations floated around her. She couldn't bring herself to participate, even though the guilt of telling her sister to leave her sewing room remained heavy on her heart. The idea of losing Laura nearly broke her in two, but she couldn't allow her to criticize her the same way *Dat*, Florence, and Sarah Jane had.

"*Aenti* Cindy?"

"*Ya?*" Cindy turned to where Mollie stood drying a plate beside Laura.

"Are you *krank*?" Her little niece's pretty face crumpled with something that looked like concern.

"No." Cindy felt her lips turn up into a smile. "*Danki* for asking, though."

Mollie tilted her head as she continued to study Cindy. "You look so *bedauerlich*. Are you sure you're okay?"

"I'm *gut, mei liewe*, but it means a lot to me that you asked." Cindy noticed a look pass between Laura and Sarah Jane, and renewed anger surged through her. She couldn't stand another minute with her family, despite her sweet niece.

As soon as she finished sweeping, she excused herself and went upstairs, where she worked on a customer's project to pass the time until she was ready for bed.

When she heard the *clip-clop* of horse hooves and the whir of buggy wheels, she peered out the window as Allen's horse and buggy headed down the driveway, and another thread of guilt tangled through her middle. If only she and Laura could see eye-to-eye, but how could she convince her sister her feelings were valid when Laura had already made up her mind about Drew?

Cindy returned to her sewing and worked until she couldn't see straight. Then she took a shower and dressed in her nightgown.

She climbed into bed, where she tossed and turned and then stared at the ceiling for what felt like hours. Her conversation with Laura echoed in her mind, and she cried into her pillow. She missed her sister. She missed their close relationship, but it was gone, ruined by her unexpected feelings for Drew.

Finally, at eleven thirty, she sat up and looked out the window. The pasture was flooded in darkness. She stared out in the direction of Drew's house and wondered what he was doing. Was he asleep in bed? Was he sitting on the porch?

Was he thinking about her?

That last question brought more tears to her eyes, and she hugged her arms to her chest.

Suddenly, something inside of her shattered. She couldn't take it any longer. She had to see him, and she had to see him *now*!

Cindy quickly pulled on a blue dress and put her hair up before covering it with a matching blue kerchief. Then she slipped on her shoes, grabbed the small flashlight Drew had given her, and tiptoed out into the hallway.

She knew what she had to do. She stopped outside the sewing room and quietly opened the door, and then she shined the flashlight into the room as she slipped inside. She grabbed the log cabin quilt and then made her way downstairs and out of the house.

She hurried down the same path Cucumber had taken that day in June, her heart thumping and her pulse pounding as she approached the Lapps' driveway. The sky was dark, and the air smelled sweet with the threat of rain.

When Cindy reached Drew's front porch, she froze as if her shoes were cemented to the ground. Sudden fear and anxiety warred inside of her. What if Drew didn't want to see her? What if he asked her to leave?

She flicked away that thought and pushed herself toward the light glowing next to his front door. That light was a beacon, an invitation to climb the steps and knock. She had to see Drew, even if it was truly the last time she ever would.

. . .

Drew sat on the edge of his bed and looked down at Bruce as he whined. "I know, buddy." He sighed. "I miss Cindy too."

And it was the truth. He missed Cindy with every breath, every second of every day. She was his first thought in the morning and his last thought at night, but he could do nothing to bring his crushed heart back to life. Her father and brother had made it crystal clear that Drew had no place in her life, but that did nothing to change his feelings for her.

"Maybe we can walk by her farm tomorrow," Drew told his dog as he rubbed his head.

Walking by the farm wasn't exactly smart, but just seeing a glimpse of Cindy would let him know she was okay. He prayed for her every night before he went to sleep and every Sunday at church, begging God to keep her happy and safe.

"Well, it's bedtime," Drew said. "Let's get some sleep." He stripped down to his boxers and climbed into bed.

As he turned out the light, he was almost certain he heard footsteps on his front porch. Was he imagining them?

When Bruce barked, Drew jumped into action. He pulled on his jeans and a T-shirt and headed to the door just as someone knocked. Bruce barked again. Who would come to his house at midnight? Did Ervin have an emergency? Did he need Drew to take him or Gertrude to the hospital?

Drew wrenched open his door, and his heart swelled when he found Cindy standing on the porch.

He pushed open the screen door and drank in the sight of her. She was stunning, clad in a blue dress with a matching headscarf that made her eyes even bluer. Oh, how he'd missed her. Happiness surged through him, sending warmth cascading through his veins.

Behind her, rain began to fall, filling the air with its sweet scent. The raindrops started to drum on the roof above them.

"Cindy. Are you all right?"

"I had to see you." She seemed short of breath. So was he.

When Bruce whined, Drew pushed him back. "Stay inside, boy," Drew told him as he slipped through the door and closed it behind him. "How have you been?" he asked her.

"Miserable without you." She held out a quilt draped over her arms. "I've been working on this quilt for six weeks, and I want you to have it."

He blew out a puff of air as he took the quilt from her and ran his fingers over the intricate stitching. It was the most gorgeous quilt he'd ever seen.

"This is beautiful, Cindy. I love it."

"I need to tell you what it means." Her voice seemed to

thicken as she touched the quilt. "It's a log cabin pattern, and it has significance. This block pattern is very old and is symbolic of life." She opened the quilt and pointed. "The center square used to be red to represent the heart or hearth of the home. The strips around the center are said to represent the logs of the cabin." She continued pointing to the different shades of gray and blue.

"The light side of the block represents the sun in front of the cabin, such as babies, weddings, family, and friends. The dark side represents the shadow behind the cabin, such as death or disaster. The dark moments are supposed to remind us how wonderful the light moments really are."

She looked up at him, and her eyes sparkled with unshed tears. "I hope you'll always keep this quilt and remember your friendship with me as a light time in your life." Her lower lip trembled. "I'll always care about you, Drew, and I'll always miss you." She took a deep breath. "I should go."

Then she turned and walked down his porch steps, out of his life.

CHAPTER 12

Panic ripped through Drew as Cindy slipped away from him. He dropped the cherished quilt onto the rocker beside him and rushed after her, running down the porch steps and into the rain. When he reached her, he grabbed her arm and gently pulled her back.

"*You* are my light," he told her. "You've been the only light in my life since I lost my parents and my aunt. You're everything to me. Please don't go. Don't leave me again."

She spun to face him and then launched herself into his arms, wrapping her own arms around his neck and pulling him close. Her warmth permeated through his shirt, his skin, his bones, and his heart, sending happiness curling through him. Slowly he felt his broken spirit start to repair itself. Cindy was everything his soul needed and craved.

"Oh, I've missed you so much," he whispered into her headscarf as he breathed in the scent of flowers mixed with sunshine. "You have no idea how much I've missed you."

"*Ya*, I do." She spoke into his neck. "I've missed you too."

The cool rain sprayed down on them, soaking his hair, his shirt, and his jeans as they stood in the driveway hugging each other.

"Should we get out of the rain?" he finally asked.

She gave a little laugh. "*Ya*, I guess so."

He entwined his fingers with hers and guided her up the steps to the bench. "Would you like a towel?"

She pointed to the quilt. "We can use that."

"Are you sure? I hate to get it wet."

"You're so silly." She chuckled. "It's meant to get wet. It's washable." She picked up the quilt. "Let's try it." She sank down onto the bench and patted the space beside her.

He sat down next to her, and she spread the quilt across their laps.

"I'm so glad you're here," he said. "You've been in my thoughts and prayers constantly."

"You've been in mine too." She snuggled closer to him and rested her head on his shoulder. "It's been terrible without you. I had an argument with my sister today. My family members can't accept I have feelings for someone who isn't a member of our community. They're all pressuring me to join the church and find an Amish man."

"Are you sure that's not what you want?"

"I'm sure." She looked up at him. "I want to be with you."

His heart seemed to trip over itself as her words went through him and heated him from the inside. He placed his palm on her cheek and felt an invisible magnet pulling him to her, linking their souls. He moved closer, her warm breath tickling his mouth and jaw.

Just as his lips were about to brush hers, he stilled. Her father's and brother's warnings echoed in his mind.

He pulled back, and she stared up at him, her eyes round and shiny, her breath coming in short bursts.

"I don't want to hurt you," he said, struggling to keep his voice steady.

"Being away from you is hurting me."

He leaned back on the bench and rubbed at his eyes. "What can we do, then? If we're together, it causes problems between you and your family and it can potentially earn you an unfair reputation. But being apart is too hard. I don't know how to be a part of your life without hurting you."

His thoughts suddenly returned to what Jamie had said to him. "What if I joined the church with you?"

"What?" She spun toward him. "You want to be Amish?"

"I would do it if it meant we could be together."

"Do you realize what you'd have to give up?" She gestured around the farm, his home. "Your truck, your schooling, your laptop, your electricity." She pointed at him. "Your clothes, your music, your *Englisher* life."

"So?" He took her hand in his. "I'd give all that up for you."

"That's not the reason to join the church. You only join when you feel it in here." She touched her chest. "It has to be a pure and honest commitment to the Amish life and to God. It's not something you do so you can marry someone." Her lower lip trembled. "And how can you join the church when I feel so disconnected to my own religion? It wouldn't make sense. I'm having doubts about God's will, so I'm not even ready to join the church myself. That's not a solution for us."

She stared out toward the rain, and he tried his best to memorize her beautiful profile, the curve of her neck, and the smell of her shampoo.

Drew shook his head. He considered Cindy's big family and their community's focus on God and on one another. He could see himself assimilating into the Amish life. After all, he craved a family so deeply, but Cindy was right about his reasons. Who was he to know when it was time to be baptized into the Amish faith?

When she turned back toward him, he found determination in her gorgeous eyes. "Why don't we meet in secret until we figure out how we can get around my family?"

"Is that what you want?"

She nodded.

"Are you absolutely sure?" he challenged her.

"Why wouldn't I be?"

"Because we'd be defying your father. You said Florence made you promise not to see me, to be a dutiful daughter."

She pressed her lips together and then said, "But I'm here now, aren't I?"

"Yes, you are." *And I'm so very grateful.* "I want you to be sure. If your father finds out we're still meeting, I don't know what he'll do. Do you think he'll kick you out of his house?"

"I don't know." She entwined her fingers with his. "All I know is that I want to be with you, and I can't let them keep us apart anymore."

"I feel the same way." He settled back on the seat, and she snuggled against him before resting her head on his shoulder. When she released his hand, he looped his arm around her and rubbed her arm. He listened to the steady cadence of the rain tapping on the roof above them.

Cindy shifted closer to him and let out a happy sigh that sent a flutter through his chest. Elation like a balloon lifted him, but then guilt slashed through him. What would happen if her father found out they were seeing each other in secret?

. . .

Guilt rained down on Cindy as she sat beside Sarah Jane in church on Sunday. She bowed her head to pray, but her mind kept replaying the events of the week. After she'd visited Drew Tuesday night, they fell into a daily routine. She would wait until her siblings and her parents were asleep and then sneak out to visit with Drew on his porch until nearly midnight.

They would talk and hold hands on the bench, and sometimes she would rest her head on his shoulder. She wanted to freeze time during their visits since they always passed so quickly. Then she would head back home and into her bed, where she'd sleep and dream of their future visits.

Now she sat in church with the rest of her community and worshipped God as if she weren't a sinner. She felt like a fraud, an imposter, but she'd never been so happy.

The service ended with the benediction, and she walked with Sarah Jane as they headed for the barn exit. When she spotted Laura and Kayla in front of her, she caught up with them. She had tried to make small talk with Laura before the service, but her sister had been cold, offering only curt answers to Cindy's questions about her daughters. She longed to apologize to Laura, but she had to find the right words.

"*Aenti* Cindy!" Mollie ran to her and opened her arms.

"Hi, Mollie." Cindy leaned down and hugged her before hugging Catherine, Calvin, and Alice. "It's so *gut* to see all of you." Then she turned to Laura. "Could we please talk?"

Laura gave her a brief nod, then looked at Kayla. "Could you please take Catherine and Mollie to the kitchen?"

"*Ya*," Kayla said. "I'll give them lunch."

"*Danki*." Laura pointed to the barn's exit. "Do you want to walk outside?"

"*Ya*. Please." Cindy followed her to a secluded spot, and her insides twisted as she searched for the right words to repair the distance between them. "Laura, I'm sorry for what I said to you last Tuesday. You're *mei schweschder*, and I love you. Can we work this out?"

Laura eyed her with something that resembled suspicion. "Why are you suddenly so determined to work things out with me? You told me to leave your sewing room, and then you refused to talk to me during or after supper. What changed?"

"I've realized how much I miss you. I want you to be a part of my life as much as you want to be part of mine." Cindy folded her hands as if she were praying. "Please, let's try to get along."

Laura rested her hands on her hips. "Have you decided to stay in the church?"

"I'm not leaving the church," Cindy said. It wasn't exactly a lie. She still worshipped with her community, and she didn't plan to stop doing that.

"Does that mean you're going to join the church?" Laura raised an eyebrow.

"I don't know." Cindy lifted one hand. "That doesn't mean I won't join someday. Right now, I just want to make sure I still have my family. Can you support me while I try to figure out where I belong in the community?"

Laura hesitated and then sighed. "*Ya*, I can do that."

"*Danki.*" Cindy hugged her and breathed a sigh of relief despite the guilt that continued to plague her. While she felt bad for not telling Laura the whole truth, she was grateful to still have her sister in her life.

Cindy helped the other women in the congregation serve the meal to the men. When the men were finished, she sat with her sisters and ate lunch. She tried to make conversation with them, but they talked about their children and their husbands and once again she felt like a stranger who didn't belong.

She wanted to talk about Drew and how excited she was that their relationship was growing deeper and more meaningful with each day, but she couldn't share any of her deepest secrets. She had to smile and nod instead, as though she were fully engaged in her sisters' lives without regard to her own.

After lunch, Cindy helped the rest of the women clean up and then walked with Sarah Jane toward the line of horses and buggies awaiting their trip home. She spotted Priscilla and Mark loading their family into their buggy, and she waved.

Priscilla gave her a strange look, and then she said something to Mark before walking over to her.

"I'm going to talk to Priscilla," Cindy told Sarah Jane. "I'll see you at the buggy in a minute."

"Okay." Sarah Jane waved to Priscilla, and then she continued on to meet her mother and *Dat*.

"Do you have a minute?" Priscilla asked Cindy.

"Of course." Cindy folded her arms over her white apron and peach-colored dress.

"How are you?" Priscilla's chestnut eyes studied hers. "You seem different than the last time I saw you."

"What do you mean?" Cindy braced herself for her sister-in-law's assessment.

Priscilla touched her finger to her lips. "It's hard to explain. You seem happier, but you're still quiet."

"I'm fine." Cindy tried to keep her words even.

Priscilla touched her hand. "Just remember you can talk to me anytime."

Cindy gave her a hug. "I might take you up on that soon."

"*Gut*." Priscilla squeezed her hand. "See you then."

Cindy turned toward her father's buggy, but then stopped when she saw Gertrude and Ervin. "Hello!" she said, waving to them.

"How are you?" Gertrude said as she walked to meet her.

As they exchanged greetings, Gertrude gave her a strange look that sent tingles of worry through Cindy. Did Gertrude know Cindy was visiting Drew every night? If so, would she tell anyone?

"Cindy!" Sarah Jane called from the buggy. "It's time to go!"

"Take care," Cindy told Gertrude before hurrying off.

. . .

Later that afternoon, *Dat* stepped out onto the porch, where Cindy sat on the glider while reading her Christian novel.

"Do you have a moment to talk?" *Dat* asked, settling into the rocker beside her.

"*Ya*, of course." Cindy closed the book and turned toward her father, trying to feign composure. Did *Dat* know she'd been sneaking out all week? She worked to keep her expression blank, but inside she was trembling.

"I can't believe today is the first day of September. Where has the summer gone?"

"I don't know." Cindy shrugged and held her breath, waiting for the bomb to explode, exposing her as a liar and a sneak.

"I've noticed you've been happier this week, and I wanted to say that it's *gut* to have you back. I've missed you." His blue eyes were warm and genuine, and they sent shame plunging through her.

She nodded and tried to clear her throat.

"I'm sorry for being so hard on you." He frowned and rubbed

his beard. "I know your *mamm*'s death was toughest on you since you were there. I should have kept that in mind when I talked to you. I apologize for not being more mindful of what you've gone through during these past seven years."

"It's okay." Cindy gripped her book with such force her fingers ached.

"It's just that I can't imagine losing any of *mei kinner* after losing your *mamm*. It would be just too devastating. My biggest fear is that you'll leave us, and I'll never see you again." He gave her a sheepish smile. "Would you please forgive me for being so tough on you? I did it out of love, and I hope you know that. But I could have been more understanding."

"Of course," Cindy said. "It's all forgiven."

"*Danki.*" *Dat* leaned over and kissed her forehead before standing and disappearing into the house.

Cindy buried her face in her hands. Her father believed she was still a dutiful daughter. How long could she live this lie? She didn't know, but she knew for certain she couldn't give up Drew without giving up her heart.

. . .

Drew sipped his can of root beer and stared toward the end of the Lapps' driveway, awaiting the bouncing flashlight beam that would announce Cindy's arrival. The warm September air brushed his face, and he sighed.

His stomach had been tied up in knots all day as he'd worked on the farm. Shame had been his constant companion for more than a week now as he and Cindy had continued their late-night rendezvous.

While he enjoyed every second he spent with her, he couldn't erase the memory of his painful conversations with Vernon and Jamie and the warnings their words held. What he and Cindy were doing wasn't right, and as much as he dreaded the idea of breaking up with her, he couldn't justify the problems their relationship could potentially cause her.

But how could he let her go? She had become an integral part of his life, and she'd carved out a piece of his heart. She was part of him now, and he didn't have the strength to let her go.

The flashlight beam bounced up the driveway, and Drew sat up straight on the bench.

"Good evening," Cindy said softly as she approached the porch. "I brought oatmeal raisin cookies."

"Fantastic." He rubbed his hands together. "Thank you. I have root beer, but it's not nearly as good as your dad's."

"That's all right. I like all root beer." She sank down beside him and handed him the container of cookies. "Try one."

"I'm sure they're delicious." He opened the lid and took a cookie from the top. He bit into it and savored the sweet, delicious taste. "Fantastic." He handed her a cold can of root beer.

"*Danki.*" She flipped open the can, which popped and fizzed in response, and then took a sip. "You're right. It's not as *gut* as *mei dat*'s, but it's still *gut*." She smiled up at him, and then her smile faded. "What's wrong?"

"Nothing." He tried to wave off her question by biting into the cookie again. "How was your day?"

"It was like most Thursdays, but don't try to deflect my question." She turned toward him. "Tell me what's wrong. I can tell when you're upset." She pointed to his face. "I can see it in your eyes. And your forehead is furrowed." Her eyes widened. "Are you upset with me? Did I do something wrong?"

He snorted and touched her arm. "What could you ever do wrong, Cindy? You're the sweetest person I know."

Her mouth worked as if she were struggling for words. "If it's not me, then what is it?"

He looked out toward the street as he tried to gather his thoughts. A heaviness gathered in his chest. How could he tell her that he felt their relationship was wrong? The words would break her heart, along with his own.

"Drew." She placed her arm on his bicep. "Please talk to me. I can't stand this silence between us."

He turned toward her, taking in the face of the woman he'd come to care for more than he'd ever thought possible. "What we're doing, Cindy . . . It's not right." He rested his arm on the back of the bench behind her. "I can't get over the shame. I'm worried about what will happen to you when your father finds out. I also keep thinking that my parents and aunt would be so disappointed in me if they knew I was sneaking around with an Amish woman. What kind of man would they think I am if they knew I'm putting your reputation in jeopardy?"

Something that sounded like a strangled sob escaped her throat before tears streamed down her pink cheeks. His heart squeezed.

"Hey, hey." He wiped her tears away with the tip of his finger. "Please don't cry."

"You want to break up with me?" Her voice was tiny, as if she were a young child.

"No, no." He shook his head. "I don't want to break up with you, but I don't know what to do." He wiped away more of her tears. "I just feel like this is so unfair to you."

"Losing you would be worse."

"I feel the same way about losing you." He anchored a tendril of hair that had escaped her prayer covering behind her ear.

As Drew stared into her eyes, he suddenly felt as if the air around them was electrified, and then without thinking he leaned down and swept his lips across her cheek. She sucked in a breath at the contact.

"Please tell me you won't stop seeing me," she whispered.

He blew out a puff of air. "I don't want to stop seeing you, but I wish we didn't have to sneak around. What if your *dat* is waiting for you when you get home tonight? How would he react after he's told you more than once to stay away from me?"

"Everything is all right at home. I promise you." She held up her hands as if to calm him. "He apologized for yelling at me."

"He did?"

She nodded. "Last Sunday he told me he was glad to see me so happy again, and he said he was sorry for being so tough on me. No one knows I'm here, and they all think I'm happy because I'm not seeing you anymore." She rested her hand on his chest. "But I'm happy because I *am* seeing you. How can our relationship be wrong if it feels so right?"

Cindy scooted closer to him and rested her head on his shoulder.

Drew rubbed her arm as he looked up at the stars and listened to the sound of the cicadas serenading them in the night. He desperately wanted to believe their relationship wouldn't cause any problems, but he couldn't stop the niggling worry that taunted him constantly.

For the next hour, they finished the container of oatmeal raisin cookies, and the time passed quickly as their conversation shifted to their favorite books, ignoring the tension he'd caused. Drew longed to keep her next to him forever.

Suddenly, Cindy stood. "I need to get going. I'll see you tomorrow, right?"

"Right." He stood and pulled her in for a hug. "You be careful." He whispered the words into her prayer covering.

"I will." Then she stood on her tiptoes and kissed his cheek. Her lips touching his skin sent a current sizzling through him. "Good night."

"Good night." He stood at the edge of the porch and watched her disappear into the night.

When he glanced at the Lapps' house, he was almost certain he saw a lantern glowing in their kitchen, and a foreboding fear of discovery plagued him once again.

CHAPTER 13

C indy sipped her cup of tea and tried to stop her face from twisting into a frown as she sat surrounded by her female family members the following Sunday.

Since it was an off Sunday and there wasn't a church service, Florence had invited the entire family to visit. Cindy had spent all day with her brothers, sister, and their spouses and children, as well as Florence's family, and she couldn't stop wondering what it would have been like if she could have asked Drew to join them. Would he have sat on the porch and visited with the men?

She looked at Karen, Roy's fiancée, who was talking about their upcoming wedding. Trying to breathe past the jealousy burning in her throat, she wondered why she couldn't be the one talking about her wedding. Why couldn't she be the one planning a future with a man she loved? Why did she have to suffer this hollow feeling overtaking her chest?

"I can't believe it's a little over a month away," Karen said. "It seems like Roy just asked me to marry him yesterday. I finished the dress for *mei schweschder.* I'm so excited."

"Have you finished the table decorations?" Florence asked.

"*Ya.*"

"What do they look like?" Kayla asked, holding Alice against her shoulder and gently bouncing her to sleep.

"Well, we're having a little purple candle and then some purple flowers." Karen tapped her chin. "What was the name of that flower?"

"A lilac?" Nellie, Walter's wife, asked. "I know you can find silk ones."

Cindy couldn't take it anymore. She needed a break from this conversation. She stood and crossed to the sink, where she deposited her mug. Then she started for the stairs.

"Cindy," Florence called after her.

She stilled and pressed her lips together, her back to the kitchen. Why couldn't Florence just allow her to quietly disappear? It wasn't as if anyone had been talking to her anyway.

"Where are you going, *mei liewe*?" Florence asked.

Cindy squared her shoulders and then turned around. Everyone's curious eyes were focused on her. "I'm going to take a nap." She touched her temple. "I have a headache."

"*Ach*, I'm so sorry." Florence shook her head. "Would you like some pain reliever?"

"No, *danki*." As Cindy turned to go, her gaze entangled with Priscilla's, and from the look on Priscilla's face, Cindy knew she'd been caught in the lie. Sometimes she wondered if her sister-in-law could read her emotions.

Priscilla had endured a painful time when she returned to the community with her son three years ago after escaping her abusive boyfriend. She'd struggled with her decision to confess her sins and rejoin the church, and Cindy had spoken to her more than once about the gravity of that decision. Although Cindy's reasons for struggling to join the church were different from Priscilla's, she still felt a special kinship with her.

Cindy quickly climbed the stairs and entered her room, and then climbed onto her bed. She hugged a pillow to her chest as she stared out her open window and contemplated the past few days. She had sneaked out to see Drew each night since he'd confessed he was having a hard time with their decision to see each other secretly, and their time together had still been wonderful. He hugged her when she arrived at his house, and then he kissed her cheek before she left. They shared their secrets and talked until after midnight.

Why couldn't she tell the world about their special relationship? Why did she have to hide her feelings for Drew?

"Cindy?"

She sat up straight and looked toward the doorway, where Priscilla stood. "*Ya?*"

"Can we talk?"

Cindy grimaced. "Did Florence send you?"

"No." Priscilla stepped into the room and closed the door behind her. "Everyone thinks I just went to use the bathroom, but I wanted to come find you too." She crossed the room and sat on a chair across from Cindy's bed. "You told me at church that you would talk to me soon. How about now?"

"If I tell you, you must promise me you'll never tell anyone."

Priscilla hesitated, but then nodded. "I promise."

"I mean it, Priscilla. You can't even tell Mark. Do you understand?"

"*Ya,* I do."

As Cindy looked into Priscilla's sympathetic eyes, she felt her heart crack open, and all her emotions poured out. She needed someone she trusted to listen to her, and Priscilla was just the person.

Cindy told Priscilla everything—starting with the day she met Drew and ending with her visit with him the night before. With tears dripping down her cheeks, she shared how she'd disagreed with her father and Laura about Drew. She even shared that she had hugged Drew, and that he'd kissed her cheek.

Priscilla's chestnut eyes rounded, and her mouth dropped open several times as Cindy spoke. When Cindy finished her story, she held her breath, awaiting her sister-in-law's assessment of her secret.

"Cindy," Priscilla began, "I'm not sure what to say." She leaned forward and rested her elbows on her thighs. "You've been meeting him in secret for a couple of weeks now?"

"Right." Cindy sniffed and wiped her eyes. "I almost came undone sitting downstairs listening to Karen's wedding plans when I can't even invite Drew here for supper. He can't be a part of our family like you are. I won't ever be able to attend church with him or have Thanksgiving dinner with him. We can't be together, and it's slowly ripping me apart."

Priscilla gasped. "You love him."

Cindy opened her mouth and closed it as confusion swamped her. "I'm not sure, but I might. Laura accused me of it."

Priscilla rubbed at her forehead. "Cindy, do you know what this means? If you choose him over the church, you'll lose your family. This will crush your *dat* and your siblings."

"I know that." Cindy's voice sounded thick to her own ears as more tears filled her eyes and then spilled over.

Priscilla handed her a tissue from the box on the nightstand. "Cindy, do you want to be Amish?"

"I don't know." Cindy wiped her eyes and then her nose. "I feel so lost. I've felt this way since I lost *mei mamm*. I love my family, but I'm not sure I belong here. Isn't that how you felt when you came back?"

Priscilla sighed. "*Ya*, it is."

"But you still confessed and came back to the church."

"Well, I had Ethan to consider," Priscilla said, referring to her eight-and-a-half-year-old son from her previous relationship. "I had no choice if I wanted to stay in *mei dat's haus*. And then the bishop forced me to marry your *bruder*, we fell in love, and it all worked out. But my situation was so different from yours." She paused. "Why have you not joined the church yet?"

Cindy shook her head. "I don't know. I wasn't ready before *mei mamm* died. Then when she passed, I felt so lost and confused." She opened her mouth to say that she didn't understand God's will, but she couldn't admit she had questions about God's decision to take *Mamm*. That was sinful and against her religion, and she didn't want Priscilla to know, at least not now. She could share that secret only with Drew.

"What is God telling you?"

Cindy looked down at her quilt and ran her fingers over the stitching as she considered her recent prayers. "I feel God's presence in my life. I've been praying and begging him to show me a sign. All I know is that I care about Drew, and I can't let him go. When I stayed away from him, I was miserable."

"You're definitely in love." Priscilla cringed. "Keep asking God to guide your path. This is a huge decision."

"I know that." She took a deep, shuddering breath. "And I've been praying harder and harder every night. If he's answering me, I'm not hearing it."

"Why Drew? Why not someone in our community?"

"Do you think I planned this?" Irritation bubbled to the surface in Cindy. "I never in a million years would have thought I'd have feelings for an *Englisher*. None of this was intentional."

"I understand." Priscilla's expression warmed slightly. "I didn't think I'd ever meet anyone who would love me after I came back to the community with Ethan. Your *bruder* was the last man I ever would have considered marrying, but then the bishop forced us to marry, and it was the best thing that could have happened to Ethan and me. God's plans are never our plans, and his path for us isn't always one we would consider. But I've never been happier in my life."

"I know." Cindy nodded and wiped at fresh tears. "And that's what I want. I want the happiness you and Mark have. I want what Jamie and Kayla have and what Laura and Allen have. But I don't see that happening for me unless I can be with Drew."

Priscilla's expression hardened again. "You have to realize that life isn't always better on the outside. I know, because I've been there. I've experienced what it's like to leave."

"But I'll have Drew in my life. I need him."

"Cindy," Priscilla began, "listen to me. When I left the church, I was certain it was for *gut*. I said I'd never come back. But when I did, I realized how much I missed my mother, the community, and the faith. If you leave and marry him, it will be much more difficult for you to come back. I had *mei mamm*, but I wasn't close to *mei dat*. Your family is much bigger than mine, and this is a much bigger sacrifice. You're close to your siblings and your nieces and nephews. Are you prepared to leave all of us behind for Drew?"

Cindy stared at Priscilla as a sob gripped her and then spilled out. Her heart fractured into a million pieces as Priscilla pulled her into her arms.

"*Ach, mei liewe.* Shh. We'll figure this out somehow." Priscilla's voice was soft next to her ear. "God will get you through this."

She drew back and handed Cindy another tissue from the box beside her.

"*Danki.*" Cindy dabbed the tears on her cheeks. "Please don't tell Mark about this."

"Don't worry, Cindy. You can trust me." Priscilla squeezed her hand. "I need to get going before someone comes looking for me. You need to think about everything I said. Don't make any decisions you might regret later. I left the community in search of a better life and someone who loved me, and I went through some really, really tough spots. I don't regret having Ethan, but I suffered with his *dat*. You might think leaving the community will solve all your problems, but sometimes it creates ones much worse."

An ice-cold disquiet filled Cindy's chest.

Priscilla crossed to the door and then looked back at her. "Why don't you come downstairs? It might cheer you up to spend some time with Adam and Annie."

Cindy nodded. "I'll be down in a bit."

After Priscilla left, she lay back on her pillow as her sister-in-law's advice filtered through her mind. She wanted to believe leaving was the wrong choice, but deep in her heart she felt certain that Drew should be part of her life, no matter how she'd have to make that possible.

. . .

Later that afternoon, Cindy sat with Annie curled up on her chest while she rocked her on the porch. Soft noises came from the baby's mouth as she sucked her thumb and hummed to herself. While her family continued to discuss Roy and Karen's wedding at length, Cindy closed her eyes and lost herself in the warm September air, coupled with the sounds coming from her sweet niece.

"Hey, Cindy." Mark's voice brought her back to reality. "Would you please carry Annie to the buggy for me? Priscilla has Adam, and I'm carrying all our gear." He had a diaper bag over his arm and gripped a double stroller with a portable crib balanced on top.

Everyone had assumed Mark would be a bachelor until he was at least forty, but Cindy couldn't help but think how well fatherhood suited her formerly flirtatious brother.

"*Ya*, of course." She looked behind him. "Where *is* Priscilla?"

"She and Ethan are saying good-bye to everyone inside." Mark's expression became more serious. "I thought you and I could talk at the buggy for a minute."

"Oh." Despite the warm weather, Cindy felt a shiver climbing up her back. Had Priscilla shared their earlier conversation with Mark? If so, would Mark threaten to tell *Dat* unless she promised to stay away from Drew?

Her worries continued as she followed Mark to the waiting horse and buggy. She tapped her foot and chewed her lower lip while he loaded all his burdens into the back of the buggy.

"Sometimes I wonder if the bishop would allow parents of *zwillingbopplin* to drive pickup trucks," Mark quipped. "Or maybe I just need to put a trailer on the buggy when we travel."

Cindy tried to force a laugh, but it sounded more like a squeak. Annie sighed and adjusted herself in her arms.

Mark leaned back against the buggy and faced her. "You looked upset earlier, and Priscilla said she talked to you. How are you feeling?"

She held back a wince. Why had she trusted Priscilla with her deepest secrets? Priscilla was a dutiful wife, so she probably felt obligated to tell Mark what she and Cindy had discussed. Now Cindy had to face the consequences of her actions. She should have known it would come to this.

She forced her voice to remain casual. "I'm all right."

He rubbed his light-brown beard. "Do you want to talk about it?"

"I feel better now. I got it all out earlier. Priscilla is a great listener." She looked down at Annie and kissed her little head.

"I know it's been hard for you since we lost *Mamm*. It's been hard for all of us, but you can always talk to me. Like I told you the night before I moved out, I'll still be here whenever you need me. I live a few miles away, but you can always call the horse farm or come by to visit me." His blue eyes seemed to plead with her, begging her to allow him to be a part of her life.

And then it hit her—Priscilla *hadn't* betrayed her trust, at least not yet. Mark believed Cindy was crying because she missed *Mamm*. Cindy didn't know if she should laugh or cry. Relief washed over her, but then shame raised its ugly head. She was using her mother to deflect the truth. She was a sinner.

"You should know Jamie, Laura, and I will always help you when you need us. You're still our baby sister, and you always will be," he continued, oblivious to her inner turmoil.

"*Danki*." She looked over her shoulder as Priscilla headed their way carrying Adam. Ethan ambled beside her.

"There you are, Cindy," Priscilla said. "I was looking for you so I could say good-bye."

As Mark took Annie from Cindy's arms to snap her into her car seat, Cindy turned to Priscilla.

"Everything will work out," Priscilla said softly after Ethan had climbed into the buggy. "And your secrets are safe with me."

"I'm so glad you're *mei schweschder*," Cindy told her.

Priscilla's expression grew serious. "Just remember to pray and think about what I said. Don't make any quick decisions you might regret for the rest of your life."

"Okay." Cindy waited until Mark and his family were all in the buggy, and then she waved as they drove away.

As she walked back to the house, she tried to calm her thrashing heartbeat. She believed Priscilla would do her best to keep her promise. But she was worried Mark and his usual uncanny intuition would eventually convince Priscilla to share everything Cindy had told her about Drew. That would be only the beginning of the trouble she'd face, but she didn't know how to prevent it without giving up Drew, and she couldn't do that.

· · ·

"We had a lovely visit today, didn't we?" Florence asked as Cindy entered the kitchen after saying good-bye to everyone.

"*Ya*, we did." Cindy gathered the mugs from the table and carried them to the sink. She was washing the last one and Florence was wiping down the table when Sarah Jane waltzed in.

"Sarah Jane!" Florence exclaimed. "How was youth group?"

"*Wunderbaar*." Sarah Jane danced around the kitchen before coming to a stop next to Cindy. "I have exciting news. Remember how I told you I like Anthony Zook?"

"*Ya*." Florence's eyes lit up as she folded her hands together.

"He wants to ask Vernon if he can date me!" Sarah Jane squealed as she twirled again.

"Oh, that is so fantastic!" Florence gushed. "I can't wait to meet him."

"I'm thrilled! He's so handsome and kind. He works for his

dat's plumbing business. He's really tall too." She sighed and then looked at Cindy. "You should come to youth group with me! Anthony has a younger *bruder* your age. You would like him. He's a plumber too!"

Cindy swallowed, and her throat felt like sandpaper. Were they really going to have this argument again?

"Oh, this is the best news!" Florence dropped her dishcloth on the table and hugged Sarah Jane. "Maybe we'll be planning your wedding next."

Bile rose in Cindy's throat as she turned back to the sink. She was tired of being the odd person out, the misfit in the Riehl family. She was ready to have her own life. Priscilla had warned her that she might regret leaving the community, but at this very moment, that sounded like the best solution of all.

Then she recalled the worry and empathy in Mark's eyes when he spoke to her earlier. How could she abandon her siblings? They cared about her.

She barely restrained a sigh. When would she finally know where she truly belonged? She couldn't go on like this much longer.

CHAPTER 14

Cindy knocked on Drew's door a few minutes before midnight. When she didn't receive a response, she knocked again. She turned toward the Lapps' house, and something caught her eye in one of the second-floor windows. Was that a light? No, it couldn't be. Gertrude and Ervin must be asleep by now.

Hugging her arms to her middle, Cindy lifted her hand to knock again. It was late, too late to wake Drew, but as much as she'd tried to stay away from him tonight, just to see if she could do it for the sake of her family, she couldn't stop herself.

When Cindy knocked a third time, Bruce barked twice, and then footfalls sounded beyond the door. The door opened, and Drew stood there, his light-brown hair tousled and his ice-blue eyes hooded.

"Hi." He smiled as he rubbed his eyes and yawned. "I was wondering if you were going to come. I fell asleep on the sofa while I was waiting for you."

"I'm sorry for waking you up." She made a sweeping gesture toward the street. "I should go."

"No, no, no." He opened the screen door and grabbed her hand, nudging her inside the house. "Come in." He tilted his head. "What's wrong?"

"Nothing." She shook her head. "We can talk another time."

"Cindy." He touched her cheek. "You're here now. Talk to me."

Closing her eyes, Cindy leaned into his touch. If only she could enjoy his company and affection in the open for the rest of the world to see.

"Did something happen today?" His voice seemed to hold a thread of worry.

She nodded.

"Let's sit and talk."

She stepped over the threshold, and Drew closed the door behind him. She allowed him to steer her to the sofa, where they sat angled toward each other.

"Now, please tell me what happened," he said.

She took a deep breath and then recounted listening to Karen's wedding plans, her conversation with Priscilla in her bedroom, and then her conversation with Mark. Drew listened, his eyes sympathetic as she worked to keep her wits about her.

"To make matters worse, Sarah Jane came home and told us she met someone at youth group, and that he's going to ask *mei dat*'s permission to date her. She said I should come to youth group and meet his brother." She sighed. "She thinks I should join the church and then date this man. Why would I do that? Why would I want to date the brother of her future boyfriend?"

Something flickered over Drew's face. Was it jealousy? Or maybe disgust?

"I just kept thinking about how unfair it is that I can't invite you to join our family gatherings," she continued. "You'll never sit with me at *mei dat*'s table. We'll never attend church together. You can never be a true part of my family, and it's not fair. I feel like I'm trapped, and I don't know what to do."

"Have you prayed about it?"

She nodded. "I pray all the time, and God keeps leading me back to you. When I pray for his guidance, I feel this overwhelming need to see you."

He studied her, and then something new flashed over his expression. Was it understanding? Or maybe angst? She wasn't certain.

And then, like a pinprick to her heart, Cindy realized Laura and Priscilla were right. As she looked into Drew's kind, gleaming eyes, she knew she *was* in love with him. For the first time in her life, she'd fallen in love—and she was helpless to change her heart or circumstances. Drew would never be anything more than a secret friend and confidant unless Cindy left the community for him.

Drew trailed his fingers down her cheek, and she shivered at his touch. "I feel God leading me to you as well."

He leaned forward, and her breath hitched in her lungs. His lips moved closer to hers, and she closed her eyes, her heart pounding as she prepared for her first kiss.

Just as Drew's lips were about to make contact, a knock sounded on the door.

Cindy's heart galloped as an icy fear gripped her.

"Hide," Drew whispered, his eyes wide as he pointed to the room beyond the kitchen. "Go now!"

She leapt to her feet and rushed to the room he'd indicated. Bruce trotted beside her, his tongue hanging out as if this were a game. She stepped into his bedroom, leaving the door slightly ajar as she pressed herself against a wall.

Bruce leaned his rump against her legs as he gazed up at her, his big eyes begging for her attention. She held her finger to her lips to ask him to stay quiet as she heard the front door open.

Cindy's pulse pounded in her ears. She squeezed her eyes shut as she waited to hear the voice of the late visitor, panic rising in her throat.

Please don't let it be Dat!

"Ervin, hi." Drew's voice sounded strained. "Is everything all right?"

"*Ya.* Everything is fine." Ervin cleared his throat. "Gertrude thought she saw a flashlight beam coming up the driveway, and she said she heard voices outside. Do you have company?"

"Oh, well, I was just—" Drew's words were interrupted when Bruce gave a happy woof and then pushed the bedroom door open wide as he trotted into the hallway.

Cindy cupped her hand over her mouth to hold back a squeal and pressed her body flatter against the wall. Tears stung her eyes as she tried to calm her zooming heartbeat. *This is it. We're going to be caught.*

"Hi, Bruce," Ervin said.

Silence filled the air, and Cindy imagined Ervin petting Bruce while Drew nervously raked his fingers through his adorable hair.

"What were you saying, Drew?" Ervin asked.

"I was just standing out on my porch and talking to Bruce," Drew said. "He woke me up, and I had to let him out. Then he saw a cat and I had to chase him to get him to come back inside. I'm so sorry if all the commotion woke up you and Gertrude."

"It's no problem. I just wanted to make sure you were okay."

When the screen door creaked open, Cindy held her breath. A beat of silence passed. Did Ervin doubt Drew's explanation?

"I'll see you in the morning," Ervin said.

"Thank you for checking on me," Drew said. "Have a restful night."

The screen door clicked shut, followed by the front door's firm catch.

Drew appeared in the bedroom doorway, his shoulders sagging as his face seemed to fill with contrition. "I'm so sorry."

"Did he seem to believe you?" Her whole body trembled.

Bruce bounded into the room and pushed his nose against her hand.

"Yeah, I think so." Drew lowered himself onto one corner of his bed.

"We were so close to getting caught, Drew—too close." She shook her head as more anxiety grabbed her by her shoulders. "If the front door had been open he would have seen me on the sofa." She pointed toward the doorway. "He could have told *mei dat* or the bishop."

The room felt as if it were closing in on her, and she struggled to breathe.

She left the room and started for the front door. "I need to get out of here."

"Wait a minute." Drew grabbed her arm and gently pulled her back. "You can't just run out there. Ervin could be walking up his back steps right now. If he turns around, he'll see you for sure."

She stilled and then shook her head. "I can't come over here late at night anymore. We can't take this risk."

He heaved a deep sigh and released her arm. "I'm sorry this happened, and I don't want to lie to Ervin. We'll have to come up with another way to see each other."

"But how?" Her voice cracked. "You can't visit with me on

my back porch the way other young Amish couples do. You can't come anywhere near my house."

Determination seemed to reflect in his bright eyes. "I'll come up with something. Have some faith in me."

"I'm sorry, Drew," she whispered, her throat thickening as tears filled her eyes. "I'm so sorry, but I can't do this. I can't risk losing my family or having the bishop come to my house. We have to end it."

A frown overtook his handsome face. "Wait here." He opened both doors and stepped out to the porch.

Cindy leaned against the kitchen counter and dabbed at her eyes with a corner of her apron. Bruce sat at her feet and lifted his paw.

"Hi, buddy." She shook his paw as a half-hearted laugh escaped her lips. If only life were as simple as Bruce seemed to think it was. "*Danki* for the shake."

Drew stepped back into the house a few minutes later. "The lanterns went out in the upstairs bedroom. I think it's safe for you to leave."

"Thank you." She started past him.

"Cindy." He gently took her arm again. "Don't give up on me yet. I'll come up with a way for us to safely see each other. I'll protect you." He swept his lips over her cheek, and the contact warmed her, though it did not calm her. "Promise me you'll give me another chance," he whispered into her ear.

"I promise." She stepped away from him before she allowed herself to change her mind and stay. "I have to go. Good night."

"Good night."

Cindy rushed out the door, her heart pounding so hard she thought it could explode out of her chest. She jogged down the driveway and up the street to her father's farm, her flashlight beam bouncing off the asphalt and then the rocks in his drive-way. As she made her way to the house, she spotted a light glowing in Jamie's master bedroom on the second floor of his home. She sucked in a breath and hurried along the path, pray-ing that Jamie or Kayla didn't see her. Her nerves couldn't take another close call!

When she finally reached her bedroom, she flopped onto her bed and hugged a pillow to her chest as she prayed.

Please, God, I need your help. I'm so confused, and I feel stuck between two worlds. I feel you leading me to Drew, but I can't have him in my life and keep my family. Why would you lead me to Drew if that would mean losing the people I love most in the world? None of this makes sense. Please help me, God. Please guide my heart on the path you've chosen for me.

Then she buried her face in the pillow, and for what seemed like the millionth time since her mother died, she cried until she ran out of tears.

· · ·

Drew pushed both of his hands through his hair and stared up at the stars. They twinkled in response as if to tease him.

When he looked back at the driveway, he found it empty. He took a deep breath, trying to calm his beating heart. When Ervin arrived at his door, he'd been certain he and Cindy were caught. He was grateful Ervin had believed his story about Bruce chasing a stray cat, but reality hit him when he saw Cindy's terrified face after Ervin left. What if Ervin hadn't be-lieved him? What if the front door had been open, and Ervin had found Drew kissing Cindy?

He groaned and scrubbed one hand down his face. He

couldn't allow another close call like this, and he felt terrible for lying to Ervin. Now he had to keep his promise and protect his precious Cindy. She had become too important to him— almost *everything* to him. And now that she'd left him and hurried home, he felt as if someone had grabbed his heart and twisted it, leaving him with nothing but the sound of the singing cicadas to comfort him.

"God," he whispered as he looked up at the sky, "thank you for bringing Cindy into my life. Now that I've come to know her, I can't imagine my life without her. She's everything to me. She's my light in the darkness of my loss. She is the beacon that led me back after losing my aunt. Please help me find a way to keep her in my life without hurting her or risking her place in her family and community. I can't lose her, God. I just can't."

He sucked in a ragged breath as tears pricked his eyes. And then it hit him like a punch to his heart—he *loved* her. The knowledge settled into his bones and warmed him from the inside out. He was in love with Cindy Riehl.

Just as quickly as the warmth filled him, it turned to ice. How could he possibly love an Amish woman when she was bound by the beliefs of her community?

He looked up at the dark sky again. "Help me, God. Help me find a way to show Cindy how much I love her and that I'd do anything to keep her in my life."

CHAPTER 15

Cindy sat up in bed the following evening when a noise came from outside her window. It sounded like the hum of an engine. She blinked, rubbed her eyes, and looked at the clock on her bedside table. It was eleven forty-five. Who would idle outside her house this late at night?

Could it be Drew?

She jumped out of bed and then ran to the window and pulled up the green shade. By the dim light of the moon she could make out a pickup truck parked at the end of their short driveway. The engine died, and the truck sat there as if waiting for someone. The dome light flipped on inside, illuminating Drew in the warm yellow glow.

"He came for me." With excitement pulsing through her veins, she pushed up her window and leaned out. When his head turned toward her, she waved.

He returned the gesture, and then the light extinguished, shrouding the cab of the truck in darkness.

Cindy quickly pulled on a purple dress, matching headscarf, and shoes before tiptoeing down the steps and out the back door. She rushed down the driveway and hopped into the truck.

"Hi." She pulled the truck door closed as quietly as she could. "This was unexpected. I didn't think I'd see you again."

"I was hoping you'd hear the truck." He leaned over and kissed her cheek. "I realized it would be safer if we went somewhere else to talk since we could get caught at my house." He put the truck in reverse and let it roll out of the driveway. Then he started the engine and steered down Beechdale Road.

"Where are we going?" She rubbed her hands together as happiness rolled over her.

"It's a surprise." He gave her a smile before turning his attention back to the road ahead.

She looked down on the floorboard and found the quilt they'd sat on during the fireworks, along with a basket, a battery lantern, and a dark-blue backpack. "Are we going to have a midnight picnic?"

"Maybe." He winked at her, and her heartbeat sped up. "I thought since it's been so unseasonably warm that we could enjoy this beautiful weather.

"I'm sorry you left so upset last night." He glanced over at her. "I want to make it up to you, and this idea popped into my head while I was milking the cows today."

"You don't need to apologize."

"Actually, I do. And I hope you'll enjoy this apology."

"I'm sure I will." She scooted closer to him and touched his arm.

Soon he turned onto a dirt road that led to a small cabin.

"Where did you find this?" she asked.

Drew parked the truck and then turned to her. "This is my former boss's fishing cabin. He said we could use it tonight. I thought we'd sit out on the deck and have a little picnic." He picked up the backpack and basket. "Are you ready?"

"*Ya.*" She grabbed the lantern and quilt and then climbed out of the truck.

With the lantern guiding their way, they walked to the back of the cabin and climbed the steps leading to a deck that overlooked the lake.

She took in the moon reflecting off the water. "This view is beautiful."

"I'm so glad you like it." Drew spread out the quilt.

Cindy took a seat beside him, and she was grateful no mosquitoes had joined them.

"You asked me about my aunt's favorite movies the other night," he began as he unzipped the backpack. "I thought it might be fun for you to see one of them. It's a movie Bruce Willis starred in more than twenty years ago." He pulled his laptop from the backpack and set it on the quilt.

"You have a movie on your laptop?"

"I do." Drew pushed a button, and the laptop came to life with a little song. "I also brought popcorn and sodas, so we can pretend we're at the movie theater."

Cindy laughed. "How fun!"

Then Drew began pushing buttons on the keyboard.

"You can pull out the food while I get the movie started. It's a long movie, but I thought you might enjoy seeing who Bruce Willis is."

"What's the movie about?" Cindy fished out a bag of popcorn and two cans of Coke.

"It's called *Armageddon*. It's about the end of the world."

"Like in the book of Revelation?"

"Uh, not exactly. It's more about outer space and asteroids."

She tilted her head and furrowed her brow.

He laughed. "You're so adorable when you look confused." He touched the tip of her nose. "Just give it a chance. It's exciting." He pushed another button, and soon the movie began.

Cindy sat closer to him, resting her side against his as she opened the bag of popcorn. She sipped her soda and nibbled on the popcorn throughout the movie. Her mind raced with questions as she tried to comprehend the plot about traveling into outer space. She also wrestled with some of the characters' harsh language.

When the movie was over, she sat up straight and stared at the computer screen as the credits rolled, naming the actors and crew members who had worked on the film.

"What did you think?" Drew's expression seemed tentative.

"I'm not sure." She tapped her chin, trying to give what she'd just seen a fair assessment. "Are all of Bruce Willis's movies like this, with the inappropriate behavior?"

"Ha. Well." Drew rubbed at a spot on the back of his neck. "Not really. Some of them are worse." He gave a little laugh that sounded forced. "But not all of them take place in outer space. In probably his most famous movie, he saves people from an office building that's been taken over by terrorists. It's called *Die Hard*, but that one is a little worse. That's why I chose this movie instead." He cleared his throat. "I guess this was a bad idea."

"No, it wasn't." She leaned over and kissed his cheek. "I'm glad you wanted to share something of your life with your aunt."

He glanced at his laptop screen. "Oh no. It's after two. I need to get you home." He turned off the computer and closed it while Cindy gathered the cans and empty bag of popcorn.

When they stood, she folded the quilt and picked up the lantern.

Soon they were hurrying back to the truck and driving home. Cindy cupped her mouth to stifle a few yawns as they drove through the dark, empty streets. She glanced at Drew's handsome profile and smiled.

"Thank you for a wonderful second date." She touched his arm. "I had so much fun."

"Really? I didn't offend you with the movie?"

"No." She shook her head. "It was fun to see what Bruce Willis looks like. He truly is a hero, saving the earth from that pesky asteroid."

He chuckled. "Yeah, I guess he did."

She settled back in the seat and yawned again. She would be tired tomorrow as she took care of her chores, but it was worth it to spend a couple of hours with Drew.

"Do you like to swim?" he asked as they turned onto Beechdale Road.

"*Ya*, I do."

"Could you bring your bathing suit with you tomorrow night?"

"Tomorrow night?" She was suddenly wide awake. "Are you taking me swimming tomorrow night?"

"I will if you'd like to go. We can swim in the lake at that same cabin. I thought that would be fun since it's been so warm." He stopped the truck near the bottom of her driveway and cut the engine before turning toward her. "You don't have to sneak out with me again if you don't want to."

"I'll be ready at eleven forty-five. I'll bring my bathing suit, towels, and a picnic basket." She slid over to him and wrapped her arms around his neck. "Thank you."

"You're welcome." He kissed her cheek. "I'll see you tomorrow night."

"I can't wait." Cindy climbed out of the truck and closed the door before hurrying up the driveway.

She gingerly entered the back door and locked it before tip-toeing up to her room. As she changed for bed, she felt as if she were floating on a cloud and made a mental note of what she'd pack for them to eat tomorrow night.

. . .

The next night, as they sat barefoot at the edge of the lake, Cindy opened the picnic basket. "I hope you like chocolate whoopie pies and lemon bars. I made them this morning. I'm so glad my family didn't see me pack this picnic basket. I hid it after I put the food in it."

"Oh, that sounds amazing." Drew shifted closer to her on the quilt. She looked like an angel with the warm yellow glow of the lantern illuminating her gorgeous ivory skin and stunning blue eyes.

The evening couldn't have been more perfect. The air was warm and smelled of moist earth, and the stars twinkled above them in the sky as if they, too, were happy that Cindy had agreed to come out with Drew again tonight. No teasing from them tonight.

"Are you going to try a whoopie pie?" She held one out to him.

"Why don't we eat after we swim?"

"Sure." She put it back into the basket and stood, and then turning her back to him, she slipped off her dress, revealing a modest black bathing suit with a skirt that hung to her midthigh. She dropped the dress onto the quilt before removing her headscarf and letting it drop onto her dress. Her hair was pulled back in a tight bun, and he found himself wondering how long and thick it would be if she allowed it to fall past her shoulders. He must have stared too long, because she shifted her weight on her feet and hugged her arms over her chest.

"I'm hoping the water is warm." Drew pulled off his gray T-shirt and tossed it onto the quilt before holding out his hand to her. "Ready to take a plunge?"

She hesitated, but then grasped his hand with a certainty that seemed to tell him she was in this for the long haul. How he hoped she wouldn't give up on him.

They walked down to the lake's edge together, and Drew stuck his toe in the water, grateful to find it lukewarm.

"It's not too bad." He gave her a nudge, and they waded in together. "Have you gone swimming much?"

"*Ya.*" She shrugged. "We used to go every summer to a lake in Maryland with *mei mamm.* I like to swim."

Soon they were in the water waist deep. Drew released her hand and leaned back, allowing himself to be pulled under, drenching his body. Then he stood up and found her grinning at him.

She splashed him and then squealed as she moved away.

"Oh yeah?" He chased after her, the water swishing around his legs.

She laughed and squealed again as he gained on her. He splashed her, and she sputtered as she stumbled backward and then righted herself. When she splashed him again, he closed the distance between them. She grinned up at him as he pulled her into his arms.

"I haven't had this much fun in months." She wrapped her arms around his neck.

"I haven't either." He shook his head. "Actually, that's not true. I don't think I've ever had this much fun."

She narrowed her eyes. "I don't believe you."

"I'll prove it." Then he leaned down and pressed his lips against hers, savoring her sweet taste as her warmth wrapped around him like a comfortable blanket. Her nearness sent his senses spinning. And in that moment, he knew they were supposed to be together—as if God had blessed their relationship.

When he broke the kiss, she gazed up at him, her eyes wide and intense in the moonlight. A smile curved her lips, and she took a step back and splashed him in the face before giggling and trying to run away in the waist-deep water.

"I'm going to get you for that!" He laughed as he dove after her.

They chased and splashed each other and swam near the shoreline until Cindy began to shiver. Then they returned to the quilt and wrapped themselves in towels.

"Try one of my whoopie pies," she insisted, handing him one.

"Thank you." He removed the plastic wrap and enjoyed the sweet taste of chocolate and delicious cream filling. "Wow. This is amazing. Can you bring me one of these every day for the rest of my life?"

"That's kind of a tall order." She bit into one and then looked out over the lake.

"No, I think you can do it." He leaned back and studied her. "What's on your mind?"

"I was just thinking about how much fun I've had the past two nights. I want to do this for the rest of my life."

"Lose sleep?"

"If it means being with you."

He smiled. "Did you like the movie night or the swimming better?"

She met his gaze. "I don't want to choose."

"That's fair." He took another bite of the whoopie pie and looked out at the moonlight sparkling on the lake, trying to think of a location for their next date.

"Drew, thank you for making me so happy."

His eyes snapped to hers. "I think I need to thank *you*."

She set the remaining piece of her whoopie pie on a napkin and scooted over to him. As she kissed him, he closed his eyes and smiled against her lips. His heart swelled with happiness and love.

CHAPTER 16

"I appreciate your taking me shopping today," Gertrude told Drew as he loaded her groceries into his pickup truck Thursday morning.

"You know I don't mind." Drew put the last bag into the back seat and then turned toward her. "Do you need to go anywhere else?"

"Hmm." She turned toward the street and then looked back at him. "I am craving some ham loaf. Would you like to go to lunch? It'll be my treat."

"Oh, no. I can't let you buy me lunch."

"*Ya*, you can and you will. I'm your employer, and you have to do what I say." Her smile widened into a grin.

"Yes, ma'am. I am not one to argue with my boss."

"That's right." She chuckled as she walked to the passenger side and climbed in. "The groceries will be fine. I didn't buy anything perishable."

Drew scrambled into the driver's seat and started the engine. "Where are we headed?"

"How about the Bird-in-Hand Family Restaurant?"

Drew suppressed a smile as his thoughts meandered back to Cindy. He'd enjoyed the past three evenings spent on secret dates with her. The night before, they'd driven around for two hours. He'd taken her past the house where he lived with his aunt. They shared more of their favorite childhood memories and she talked more about her mother, telling him about special moments that had made her growing-up years happy and full. He felt as if they had reached a more meaningful depth in their relationship, his love for her growing each day.

But at the back of his mind, he still wondered how they could sustain their secret meetings and lack of sleep in the long term. If they continued to meet well into the middle of the night, not only would they be stuck in a dead-end relationship, but they'd continue to run the risk of getting caught.

"Do you like the Bird-in-Hand Family Restaurant?" Gertrude's question slammed him back to reality.

"Yes, I do." He forced a smile. "It sounds perfect."

"*Gut.*"

Drew drove to the restaurant, where they were seated in a booth by the window, next to the booth where he and Cindy had eaten lunch a little more than six weeks ago. How their relationship had transformed since that day!

When the server arrived to take their order, Drew chose the first item he saw on the menu. Then he picked up his glass of water and took a drink.

Gertrude looked at him, and her expression grew serious. "Ervin and I have noticed you've gone out late every night this week. Your truck leaves the driveway around midnight and then returns after two in the morning. Where have you been going?"

Drew froze, his glass suspended in his still hand in front of him. Alarm writhed in him as he stared at Gertrude.

"Drew, I need you to tell me the truth." Gertrude's words were slow and steady. "Have you been sneaking out to see Cindy Riehl?"

The air seized in his lungs as he debated how to respond. But the truth was the only option. How could he lie to his generous employer and friend?

"Yes, I have." Drew leaned forward on the table as panic screamed through him. "Who else knows? Does her family know? Did her father ask you to speak to me? Has the bishop found out?" His words tumbled out of his mouth at a fast clip.

Gertrude held up her hands. "Calm down. Ervin and I have discussed this only with each other. I haven't spoken to Florence since I saw her at church. No one asked me to speak to you. Talking to you today was my idea."

Drew felt his body relax slightly, yet worry held on. "How long have you known?"

"We've had a feeling for a while." Gertrude took a breath. "Ervin told me he spoke to you about Cindy, and he was hoping you would stop the relationship. When he checked on you late Sunday night, I was certain I had heard two people talking outside—but then you told him you were talking to Bruce. Ervin had a feeling you hadn't told the truth and you were protecting Cindy. When we noticed you taking late-night trips in your truck this week, we put it all together. Since we're concerned about you and Cindy, I thought I should talk to you myself."

Shame rested heavily on Drew's shoulders. "I'm sorry. I didn't tell Ervin the truth Sunday night. Cindy had come to visit me. I never should have lied. You and Ervin are important to me, and I don't want to lose your trust." He paused and sucked in a deep breath. "I never meant to disrespect your community. It just sort of happened." He held up his hand. "Please don't get the wrong impression. Nothing inappropriate has happened between us."

"I believe you," Gertrude said. "You're a *gut* man."

"Are you going to fire me?" He held his breath. While he'd recover from losing his job, he'd miss the farm and his life there.

"No, of course not." Gertrude studied him for a moment, and he shifted his weight. "Do you love her?"

"Yes." Drew slumped back on the bench seat and rubbed at a throbbing in his temple.

"You do realize that if she chooses you over the church, she'll lose her family. Do you want to be responsible for pulling her away from them?"

"No." His voice quaked. "I'd give anything to have my parents and my aunt back. I'd never expect anyone to lose their family for me."

"I know. You're not a selfish person."

"I've felt bad about seeing Cindy ever since Ervin told me what could happen to her. But I don't know what to do. We've built a wonderful relationship, and I can't imagine my life without her now. I'm in so deep that letting her go would be painful. But at the same time, I realize we can't sneak around forever. A relationship can't grow if it's based only on secret moments spent together in private. We're stuck."

Gertrude looked down at the table and then back up at him. "You know you have to end it, right?"

Drew nodded as his heart seemed to shrink.

"It will take only one of Cindy's family members seeing her climbing into your truck and sneaking off with you for everything to come crashing down on her."

"The last thing I want is for her to suffer because of me." He moved his hand over the stubble on his chin. "But I can't let her go without talking to her one last time. I need to tell her I care about her, but I can't risk hurting her. I'll pick her up for one last date, and then I'll tell her I can't see her anymore."

Gertrude shook her head. "I don't think that's a *gut* idea. You need to stop the midnight meetings now. Ervin and I have heard your truck leave the driveway and return. It's a wonder her family hasn't heard your truck too. I'm surprised Kayla or Jamie hasn't heard you when they're up in the middle of the night with one of the children, especially baby Alice. Do you really want to risk Jamie seeing his younger sister sneaking home at two in the morning?"

Drew wanted to hide under the table. Why hadn't he considered that Jamie and Kayla could have caught Cindy? He'd been so focused on seeing Cindy that he hadn't truly considered the risk they'd been taking, even at such late hours. He rubbed at his temple as his headache flared.

"You're right. I can't see her again, but I don't know how I can explain my concerns and intentions to her, then." He clenched his jaw as despondency made his very bones seem to ache. "If I don't pick her up tonight, then I don't know how to get in touch with her. Her father would run me off his property if I showed up there. I have no way to talk to her unless I run into her by accident."

"I can help you with that."

"What do you mean?"

"I can find an excuse to deliver a letter to her. You write the letter, and I'll take care of the rest."

"Thank you." Drew nodded. "I'll do that." But how could he possibly put all his feelings into writing?

• • •

Drew stared at the blank piece of paper and rested his head in his hands. He'd been staring at it for nearly an hour, but he couldn't seem to form the right words to tell Cindy he cared for her, even though he had to end their relationship. He didn't want to break it off with her, but it was the right thing to do. He had to save her from losing her family.

When he heard a whine, he looked over at his dog. Bruce was sitting by the front door.

"I know. I miss her too."

Bruce whined again and then hunkered down on his belly and sighed.

"I feel the same way, buddy."

Drew looked down at the paper and finally began writing.

Dear Cindy,

This is the most difficult letter I've ever had to write. I've sat here staring at the paper for an hour, trying to figure out how to tell you how much you mean to me. How can I describe the light and happiness you've brought into my life since that day you ran up the driveway yelling for Cucumber? It seems impossible to put it into words, but I'll do my best.

I told you that you were my light when you gave me the beautiful quilt, and I meant it. You've been a beacon to me when I thought I would never find anyone I could consider my family.

When my aunt died, I felt alone once again—an orphan in a cold world. It sounds ridiculous to say I'm an orphan at my age, but that's how it feels when you lose the last of your family.

You've become my best friend, my closest confidante. Our

late-night talks and special dates have been the highlight of my days, and I've enjoyed sharing so much time with you. I'd never do anything to deliberately hurt you, and I hope you already know that. But that's also why I'm writing to you.

Gertrude told me she and Ervin knew I lied to Ervin the night you hid in my bedroom. She also admitted she and Ervin have heard my truck leaving late at night. She warned me that we need to stop sneaking out before you get into trouble. She made me realize your family could easily catch you slipping into my truck, and I can't run the risk of your losing them.

As much as it hurts me to say good-bye, we have to stop meeting. Please understand I'm not breaking off our friendship to hurt you. I'm doing this to protect you. I don't want to cause you any more problems with your family.

You mentioned Sarah Jane encouraged you to go with her to youth group, join the church, and find an Amish man who will love you and take care of you. You said she even knows a man who might be good for you. I think she's correct. I can't be a part of your community, so it only makes sense that you find someone who is, someone who will love you openly for the rest of your life.

I will always cherish our friendship, and I'll never stop caring about you. The quilt you gave me will remind me of the time we spent together and how your light gave me back the hope I lost when I lost my parents and aunt. Please don't forget me.

Always,
Drew

With tears in his eyes, Drew folded the letter, sealed it into an envelope, and carried it over to the Lapps' house. When

Gertrude opened the back door, his gut soured as he handed her the letter.

She gave him a sad smile. "This is for the best, you know."

"Right," he said.

But did Gertrude know his heart had never felt so broken?

CHAPTER 17

"Gertrude! Hello." Cindy opened the back door the following morning. *"Wie geht's?"*

"I'm doing well. And you?" Gertrude adjusted a quilt slung over her arm.

"I'm *gut.* What brings you here today?" Cindy searched Gertrude's face. Did her visit have something to do with Drew? Her heart fluttered at the thought. She'd waited at her window for Drew's truck last night, but she'd been disappointed. He never appeared through the darkness.

At first she was worried, but then she decided Drew must have fallen asleep. After all, they had met at midnight three nights in a row, and the lack of sleep had to have caught up with him. Hopefully, Drew had rested up and would resume their midnight rendezvous tonight.

"I want to know if you can repair this." Gertrude gestured toward the quilt. "It has a tear in it, and it's special to me. My favorite *aenti* gave it to me many years ago when I was around your age."

"I'd be *froh* to fix it for you." Cindy touched the quilt. "May I see the tear?"

"Could we go up to your sewing room?"

"Of course." Cindy nodded slowly as she studied Gertrude's expression. Was there a hidden message in the request? Or was

Cindy imagining it? She gestured for Gertrude to follow her through the mudroom and into the kitchen.

"Gertrude," Florence exclaimed when they stepped into the kitchen. "How nice to see you."

"It's nice to see you as well." Gertrude gave Florence a generous smile. "I stopped by to see if Cindy has a few spare minutes to repair my quilt."

"Oh." Florence gestured toward the counter, where potato salad and a basket of rolls sat. "You must stay for lunch. We can get caught up."

"Ervin's gone to town, so that would be *wunderbaar. Danki.*" Gertrude looked at Cindy. "Could you please look at my quilt before lunch?"

"*Ya.*" Cindy led Gertrude up to her sewing room, where she sat down at the machine and waved to the chair beside her. "Let's have a look at that tear."

Gertrude unfolded the quilt and pointed to a small split in the hem. "Can you fix this?"

Cindy looked down at the hem and then up at Gertrude. "*Ya*, but this is an easy repair. Don't you sew?"

"I do." Gertrude pulled an envelope out of her apron. "This is what I actually came to bring you."

Cindy stared at the envelope and her name written on the front. "I don't understand."

Gertrude leaned in closer. "I know you've been sneaking out to see Drew at night." She pointed to the envelope. "Drew wrote you a letter."

"He did?" Her pulse tripped and trotted.

"*Ya.*" Gertrude stood. "I'll go downstairs and keep Florence busy. You read his letter and then write a response. You can hide the letter in the quilt, and I'll make sure Drew gets it."

Appreciation filled Cindy's chest as she reached over and touched Gertrude's arm. "*Danki* for doing this."

Gertrude gave her a sad smile. "I know it's difficult to let go, but don't risk your family for an *Englisher. Mei schweschder* did." She shook her head. "She left the community and even married him, and they wound up divorced. My parents never forgave her. Don't do that to your *dat.*"

Fear squeezed the air from her lungs. For a moment she'd thought Gertrude was an ally, but she wasn't.

"Take your time reading it and responding. I'll be downstairs with Florence."

"*Danki.*" Cindy's hands trembled as she gingerly opened the envelope. She unfolded the letter and took in Drew's slanted handwriting. She ran her fingers over the ink, imagining Drew sitting at his kitchen table as he wrote.

She took a deep breath and then read the letter, letting his words fill her mind as she imagined his voice saying them aloud.

When she reached the end of the letter, tears were already rolling down her cheeks. Drew had ended their relationship. She would never see him again. How was she going to cope without him in her life?

Grabbing a handful of tissues from the box on the table, she wiped her eyes and nose. Then she stared at the letter. She had to compose a reply, but how?

Closing her eyes, she opened her heart to God.

God, I don't want to let Drew go, but like him, right now I don't see how we can ever be together. Please give me the words to tell him how much he means to me, and help me encourage him to keep asking you to find a way, just as I'm asking you now . . . if it's your will.

Cindy brought a notepad, pen, and envelope from her room and then began writing at her sewing table, a tear escaping her eyes with nearly every word she put to the paper.

When she was done, she patted her cheeks dry and quickly repaired the quilt. Then she folded the quilt before depositing it into a large shopping bag from the fabric store. She slipped her letter into the envelope and shoved it to the bottom of the bag, where it was safely hidden from curious eyes.

Cindy walked downstairs to the kitchen, a smile plastered on her face. Then she placed the bag with the quilt on the floor near the mudroom before sitting down across from Gertrude. She said a silent prayer and then busied herself with building a ham and cheese sandwich while Florence droned on about how perfect Roy's wedding would be.

When Florence took a breath, Gertrude said, "Cindy, were you able to fix the quilt?"

"*Ya.*" Cindy nodded. "It was no trouble at all."

Gertrude seemed to study her. "It's all fixed, then?"

Cindy could read between the lines. "*Ya*, it is. It's safely stowed in the shopping bag for you."

Gertrude smiled. "I know the quilt will be just perfect now, and everything will be as it should."

Cindy's response turned to sawdust in her mouth. Perfect? No, nothing would be even close to perfect again.

. . .

Cindy retreated to her sewing room after Gertrude left. She sat down at her table and touched the pocket of her apron, where Drew's letter hid. She planned to keep the letter with her as a reminder of him. She stared at the pile of customers' projects she had to complete, but she'd lost her ambition when she read Drew's letter. All she wanted to do was curl up into a ball on her bed and cry.

She looked out the window at the beautiful September sunshine and listened to the birds singing in the trees. They all seemed to ridicule her and her bleak mood. She needed someone to talk to, someone to listen and sympathize with her.

Cindy considered borrowing Roy's horse and buggy to visit Priscilla, but she didn't want to tell her sister-in-law too much. If she did, Priscilla might finally feel obligated to tell Mark, and that would lead to disaster.

Instead, Cindy hugged her arms to her chest and tried to keep the tears at bay. She looked back out the window and noticed a bird sitting on a branch and singing, as though it were trying to give her solace.

"Is that you, God?" she whispered. "Are you trying to tell me everything will be all right? Gertrude insisted I had to let Drew go, but it hurts so much that I don't know how to make it through another day. I'm still here with my family, but I feel like I've already left them because I can't talk to them. I can't be honest. I'm surrounded by people who love me, but I'm all alone. Please send me a sign, God. Please show me your will and where I belong."

Her thoughts turned to Drew, and she dabbed at a tear that escaped her eye. "Please comfort Drew as he reads my letter. Help him remember I'll always care for him. And help us both figure out how to move on without our friendship. You are the great comforter. Please comfort us both."

With a shaky breath, she picked up the first sewing project and tried to shove away her memories of Drew and the wonderful times they'd spent together.

. . .

Drew climbed out of his pickup truck and grabbed his backpack before closing the driver's side door. He looked toward the Lapps' house and spotted Gertrude coming down the back steps. He wasn't surprised to see her making her way toward him.

He'd struggled to pay attention in his classes this morning, wondering about Cindy's reaction to his letter. Now Gertrude approached him with an envelope in her hand, and a queasy fear filled him. This was it. Gertrude held the letter that would officially end his relationship with Cindy. And he wasn't ready to face it.

"I have this for you." Gertrude held out the envelope. "I saw her earlier today. She read your letter and then responded."

"Thanks." The word was barely a whisper.

"As I told Cindy, this is for the best." Gertrude's tone was firm, yet also held a thread of empathy. "Now everything will be as it should. You'll go on with your *English* life, and she'll stay Amish. Trust me. You made the right decision."

Drew wanted to nod, but he couldn't convince his neck to move. No, this didn't feel right. It didn't feel right at all.

But he had been taught to respect his elders, and he couldn't disagree with her. At least, not aloud.

Gertrude patted his arm. "I'll see you later." Then she pivoted and headed back to the house.

Drew was left alone in the driveway, staring at the envelope. His name was written in beautiful handwriting with a flourish at the end. He gripped the envelope as he headed up the porch and then unlocked the door.

Bruce met him with a happy bark and the smack of a paw.

"Hi, buddy," Drew said. "I bet you need to go out."

He let the dog out, set his backpack on the floor, and then stepped back out onto the porch before sinking onto the bench where he and Cindy had sat together so many times. This was where their friendship had formed, and this was where it would end as he read this letter.

Drew's chest rose with an unsteady breath as he opened the envelope and pulled out the light-blue paper. As he unfolded it, a dull thump started at the back of his eyes. Mustering all his emotional strength, he read the letter.

Dearest Drew,

I'm not even sure how to start this letter. I'm so overwhelmed and confused by your words. So many emotions are rolling around in my chest that I don't know how to begin to tell you how I feel. However, Gertrude is downstairs waiting for my response, so I don't have time to find the perfect words.

First, I need to tell you that I'm honored that you said I am a beacon of light to you. You're the same to me. You're also my best friend and confidant, and it's killing me that I can no longer be with you or talk to you. I've never felt so alone while living in a house with four other family members.

I'm sorry Gertrude and Ervin found out about us. As of today, my family still doesn't know, but I've been tempted to tell them the truth. I know I can't, but I want to. I want the world to know about us, but you're right. It's just not possible to continue our relationship.

I'll miss our talks and our middle-of-the-night meetings. I had such a wonderful time with you—watching the movie, then swimming, and then driving around in your truck while learning more about your childhood and family. While I'm tempted to keep visiting you at the Lapps' farm, I'm afraid Gertrude or Ervin will tell my father or the bishop about us. I can't risk hurting my family, but my heart still craves your presence. I miss your smile and your laugh. I also miss Bruce. Please give him a hug for me.

You said I should take Sarah Jane up on her offer to introduce me to her future boyfriend's brother. I hope you know I'm not interested in meeting anyone else. And I'm not ready to join the Amish church. I'm still floating aimlessly between two worlds.

I hope you will cherish our friendship and the quilt I gave you. I'll always miss you, and I'll continue to think of you and pray for you daily. You're important to me, and I will carry you in my broken heart forever.

Always,
Cindy

Drew read and reread the letter until he had nearly committed it to memory.

It was over. Cindy was no longer a part of his life, and he had no idea how he would face another day without her.

"God," he whispered. "Give me strength. I can't face another loss without you. This is too much for me to bear alone. Help me through this."

Covering his face with his hands, he shielded his eyes as tears poured down his cheeks.

CHAPTER 18

Cindy folded her arms over her chest as she sat next to Sarah Jane on the backless bench in Karen's father's barn. The cool October weather did little to stir the stuffy, humid air in the barn packed that afternoon with close to three hundred community members. They'd all come to celebrate Roy and Karen's wedding.

While Sarah Jane smiled and wiped her eyes during the service, Cindy had to try her best to keep a pleasant expression on her face. It had been a month since she'd sent her letter to Drew, and she couldn't recall the last time she'd smiled or laughed. Her frown felt as if it had been etched on her face.

Cindy had followed along with the service as if she were in a fog. The ceremony had begun with Karen and Roy's meeting with the minister while the congregation sang hymns from the *Ausbund*.

When the hymns had been sung, Karen and Roy returned to the congregation and sat with their attendants, Karen facing her sister, Lena, and Roy facing his brother, Walter. The two men wore their traditional Sunday black and white clothes, and both Karen and Lena were clad in the purple dresses Karen had made for the wedding.

As Cindy studied those beautiful dresses, she couldn't help but imagine what she would wear if she were to get married.

Since she'd been a young girl, she'd imagined sitting at the front of her father's barn with Laura as they wore the peacock-colored dresses she'd sewn.

But that would never happen. The man she loved wasn't welcome in their community, and she couldn't marry him unless she walked away from the Amish church, leaving her family behind. The only other solution was for Drew to join the church with her—but Cindy still wasn't even sure about joining the church herself. And how could she ask him to give up the only life he'd ever known for her?

Once again, she felt the same empty spot inside her expand into a dark, lonely cave filled with sorrow that threatened to swallow her whole. She tried for the thousandth time in the past month to shove Drew out of her mind. But it was too late. He had burrowed in, dug in deep, and stolen a piece of her heart. He was a permanent fixture in her mind, and no amount of prayer seemed to erase him from her mind or soul.

After another hymn, the minister delivered a thirty-minute sermon based on Old Testament stories of marriages. Cindy glanced around the barn as he spoke, taking in the familiar faces of her congregation as well as those of strangers she assumed were members of Florence's former congregation, the one she'd been a part of before she married *Dat*.

Cindy's gaze moved to the married women's section, and she studied her older sister. Laura was beautiful in her blue dress and black apron as she listened to the minister. She fanned her face with one hand while resting her other hand on her expanding abdomen. She was now seven months pregnant and looked radiant. Her baby should arrive on time, shortly before Christmas.

While Cindy was thrilled for Laura and her growing family,

jealousy slithered through her like a snake. The thought of living her days as a spinster, like several of the older women in their community were, made her slump down even farther on the uncomfortable wooden bench. She couldn't imagine a lonelier life.

Kayla and Priscilla sat on either side of Laura, and they each wore a serene expression as their eyes remained fixed on the minister. They also seemed to enjoy happy marriages. It wasn't fair to be prevented from having a happy marriage too. Even Sarah Jane had started dating Anthony Zook a month ago, and she seemed content. Why couldn't Cindy have what her sisters had? Why did the community have the right to dictate whom she loved?

Cindy bit her lower lip and turned her focus to holding her hands still. She ran her fingers over her white apron and sighed.

Sarah Jane turned and nudged Cindy with her elbow. "Cindy?" she whispered. "Are you all right? Do you need a tissue? You look like you're about to cry."

"I'm fine." Cindy looked down at her lap.

"Weddings always make me cry. You don't have to hide your tears." She handed Cindy a wad of tissues.

"*Danki*," Cindy muttered before pressing her lips together.

Sarah Jane was too clueless to comprehend how Cindy felt. She'd spent the past month nagging Cindy to join the church so she could date her boyfriend's brother. She'd never understand the depth of her grief over losing Drew.

Cindy kept her head down and squeezed her eyes shut as she joined the rest of the congregation in kneeling for the silent prayer. Then she opened her heart to God and poured out her sorrow.

Lord, I'm trying to understand how my pain is your will. Do

you truly prefer that I live in grief and sadness instead of find-
ing joy with Drew? Am I truly supposed to watch my siblings'
families grow while I stay at home and try to drown my misery
with the chatter of my sewing machine, with nothing but loneli-
ness in front of me? I don't believe that's true. My alternative is
to join the church and search for a man who will love me despite
my broken heart after losing Drew, but how would that be right
for me or that man?

I can't fathom that being trapped in a marriage with a man I
don't love back is your will. You call us to bear fruit, but I don't
want to bear fruit without marrying my true love. I believed—I
still believe—Drew is the man you've chosen for me. It makes no
sense to me, then, that you would allow us to meet and become
attracted to each other. If we can't be together, though, then what
is the holy purpose of our special friendship? Please lead me on
the path you want for me. Lead Drew. Show us your will. Help
me understand.

As she finished praying, everyone rose for the minister's reading of Matthew 19:1–12.

Bishop John Smucker then stood and began to preach the main sermon, continuing with Genesis, including the story of Abraham and the other patriarchs in that book. While the bishop spoke, Cindy kept her gaze focused on the edge of her apron and thought of nothing but Drew.

Sarah Jane leaned over to Cindy again and tapped her arm, yanking her from her thoughts. "I can't believe Roy is getting married," she whispered.

Cindy smiled as bittersweet joy filled her. How could she be angry about someone else's happiness? "I know," she whispered back. "I'm glad Roy and Karen are so *froh* together. I'm sure they'll have a *wunderbaar* life." And she was.

"I hope I'm next." Sarah Jane rubbed her hands together. "Anthony is amazing. I'd love to marry him and raise a family with him."

Cindy nodded.

"You really need to meet his *bruder* Neil. You'd like him."

Cindy bit back the urge to ask Sarah Jane how she could possibly know what Cindy looked for in a man. Did Sarah Jane know her at all? Did any of her family members truly know her? Was that the real root of all their problems with Drew? They just didn't understand what she needed in her life? Whom she needed?

"Just think about it," Sarah Jane whispered. "Maybe you can come to youth group with me on Sunday."

Cindy looked toward the soon-to-be newlyweds. Karen beamed at her groom, whose eyes shone with love for her. Then her eyes moved to the sea of young, unmarried men at the other side of the room, and she tried to envision Drew sitting there, despite her reservations about asking him to join the church— that is, if she decided joining was what she wanted too. Would he blend in with her community? Would the other young men welcome him?

But how could she ever expect him to give up the *Englisher* life into which he'd been born? It was presumptuous and self-ish for her to even entertain the notion. If only they could find happiness together despite the rules and traditions that separated them . . .

With a trembling breath, she turned back to the bride and groom, who seemed to be listening intently to the bishop's lecture about the apostle Paul's instructions for marriage in 1 Corinthians and Ephesians.

After instructing Karen and Roy on how to run a godly

household, he moved on to a forty-five-minute sermon on the story of Sarah and Tobias from the intertestamental book of Tobit.

When his sermon was over, the bishop looked back and forth between Karen and Roy. "Now here are two in one faith, Karen Rose Miller and Roy Sylvan Esh." He looked out at the congregation. "Does anyone here know of any scriptural reason for this couple to not be married?" He paused for a moment, and when the congregation remained silent, he continued. "If it is your desire to be married, you may in the name of the Lord come forth."

Roy took Karen's hand in his, and they stood, coming before the bishop to take their vows.

While the couple responded to the bishop's questions, Cindy wiped at the wetness now gathering under her eyes. Despite longing for a different outcome, she had to accept that she could never celebrate a marriage with Drew. But how could she convince her heart not to hold fast to hope? He still haunted her thoughts during the day and her dreams at night.

Oh God, please either help me accept what I must or show me a way to be with Drew. I can't go on like this.

Cindy dabbed her nose as the bishop read "A Prayer for Those About to Be Married" from an Amish prayer book called the *Christenpflict*.

Once the bishop returned to his sermon, Cindy slipped her hand into the pocket of her apron and touched Drew's month-old letter. She had carried it around with her every day, and even though it was only a piece of paper, Cindy felt as if it represented a piece of Drew's heart.

She ran her fingers over it and silently recited the words, which she had memorized weeks ago. Although she wasn't allowed to speak to Drew, she doubted her feelings for him could ever evaporate.

When the sermon ended, the congregation knelt as the bishop again read from the *Christenpflict*. After he recited the Lord's Prayer, they all stood, and the three-hour service ended with another hymn.

Then the men began rearranging furniture while most of the women, including Cindy, headed to the kitchen in the house to prepare to serve the wedding dinner. Cindy had been hearing about the menu for months. They'd be having chicken with stuffing, mashed potatoes with gravy, pepper cabbage, and cooked cream of celery. The bountiful desserts included cookies, pie, fruit, and Jell-O salad.

Cindy followed Sarah Jane out the barn door and was relieved to be greeted by the cool October air. She started toward the house, but when she felt a hand on her arm, she stopped and spun. It was Priscilla.

"Can we please talk in private?" Priscilla adjusted Annie in her arms and nodded toward one corner of the barn.

"*Ya.*" Cindy walked with her toward that spot, away from the groups of people leaving the barn. When they reached it, Annie squealed and reached for Cindy. Unable to resist her sweet niece, Cindy took Annie into her arms, and the baby snuggled down on her shoulder. Cindy sighed as she began to pat Annie's back.

"*Was iss letz?*" Priscilla's chestnut-colored eyes seemed to plead with Cindy. "I watched you during the wedding, and the expression on your face. I've never seen you this *bedauerlich*. Please tell me what's going on with you. Is this about Drew? I can't stand to see you this unhappy."

Cindy kissed Annie's head as she considered her answer.

She could avoid the conversation and tell Priscilla she was just exhausted, but she was tired of lying, tired of hiding her feelings, and tired of the loneliness.

"I haven't spoken to Drew in a month. I miss him so much that sometimes I have trouble breathing." Cindy looked down at Annie, who was now sucking her thumb.

Cindy explained how Gertrude had helped them exchange letters, and that they had ended their relationship. "I think about him all the time. And though the wedding was lovely, it only reminded me that I'll never have a chance to build a life with him."

Priscilla leaned toward her and lowered her voice. "Cindy, leaving the community doesn't mean you'll find happiness." She pointed to her chest. "I should know. I've had more support here in this community than I ever had in the *English* world."

"It's different for me, Priscilla."

"What's different?" Laura walked up behind Cindy and divided a look between her and Priscilla. "What are you talking about?"

Cindy glanced over to where Mollie carried Catherine as she walked toward the house with Kayla. Then Cindy looked at Priscilla, who continued to stare at her as if she'd just said she'd booked a trip to the moon.

Laura turned to Cindy. "I want to apologize for being so cold to you. I've missed you, and I want to work things out." She touched her abdomen. "I want to be close again. You can trust me."

Cindy took a deep breath and then repeated what she had just told Priscilla. Laura's eyes widened, and she cupped her hand to her mouth before exchanging a look with Priscilla.

"I love Drew and I miss him," Cindy said. "I can't let him go."

"Are you going to leave the community?" Laura grabbed Cindy's arm. "No! Tell me you'll stay."

Cindy shook her head. "I don't know. All I know for sure is that I'm miserable."

"Are you still praying about this?" Priscilla looked so grave Cindy felt sorry for her.

"Every day, at least once a day." Cindy looked down at Annie again. "I want to have a life like yours. I want to be married, have *kinner*, and build a life with the man I love." She looked back and forth between Priscilla and Laura. "Didn't you dream of that when you fell in love?" She focused on Laura. "Didn't you want that with Allen when you realized you loved him?"

Laura wiped at her eyes. "*Ya*, but Allen is Amish. It's not the same."

"It *is* the same," Cindy snapped. "It's exactly the same. We're all human, whether we're Amish or *English*. We're all sinners created in God's own image."

Priscilla touched Cindy's arm. "Don't do this, Cindy. Don't leave. It's difficult to come back."

Laura cleared her throat and nodded toward the women carrying food into the barn. "Why don't we talk about this later? We're going to start attracting a crowd. We'll continue this conversation later, when we can talk alone."

"That's a *gut* idea." Priscilla took Annie from Cindy's arms. "I need to change her and feed her. *Mei mamm* is probably waiting for me to come and get Adam from her."

Laura nudged Cindy. "Let's go help serve the meal. Don't do anything until we talk. Promise me."

Cindy nodded, but deep in her soul, she knew she already had a plan in place—a plan she believed would let her know if she was meant to leave the community.

. . .

Cindy had managed to avoid speaking to Laura and Priscilla for the rest of the afternoon. She couldn't allow her sisters to talk her out of her plan, but she was also tired of deciding what to tell them and what to keep to herself, so she might have blurted her secret if cornered. It was easier not to talk at all.

She'd found a notepad and envelope in a desk in their hosts' family room, and then with a silent apology to Karen and her family, she'd written a short note. Then to make everyone in her family happy for once, she spent time with Sarah Jane and a few of her youth group friends.

Now was the moment she'd been anticipating all afternoon. Her hands shook as a tiny seed of hope took root deep in her soul.

"Gertrude," Cindy called as she caught up with the older woman just as most of the wedding guests were climbing into their buggies for home. Cindy picked up her pace.

Gertrude spun toward Cindy. "Hello there. How are you?"

"*Gut. Danki.*" Cindy glanced behind her and was relieved to find they were alone. "I want to ask you how Drew is doing."

"Oh." Gertrude's smile wobbled. "He's been quiet. I think he's *bedauerlich* and he misses you, but that's to be expected. You had forged a nice friendship, and he'll need some time to get over you."

Cindy fought against the tears that pricked the back of her eyes and squared her shoulders. "Would you do me a favor and give him one last note from me?"

Gertrude hesitated. "I don't know if that's a *gut* idea."

Cindy peeked over her shoulder once more before she pulled the envelope out of her apron pocket and slipped it into

Gertrude's. "Please, Gertrude. Just one more message. I promise this is the last one."

Gertrude pursed her lips and sighed. "Fine, but I can't be responsible for what might happen after he receives it." She held up her hand. "And I will not deliver any message back. I could get into trouble with the bishop if he finds out I already delivered letters for you both."

"*Danki.*" Cindy hugged her as excitement bubbled through her. "*Danki* so much. I promise I won't ask again."

As Cindy hurried to her father's buggy, she touched the letter in her apron pocket and smiled. Maybe, just maybe, there was still a chance she and Drew could make their relationship work. She just had to know if he thought so too.

. . .

Drew opened his front door later that evening and was surprised to find Gertrude standing on his porch. He swung open the storm door. "Hi. How are you?"

"*Gut.*" Gertrude lifted her chin. "Ervin and I were at Roy Esh's wedding today."

"Oh. That's nice." Drew motioned inside. "Would you like to come in?"

"No, thank you." Gertrude frowned. "I saw Cindy today, and she asked me to deliver a message to you."

Drew's heart slowed and then jumped into hyperspeed. "What did she say?"

Gertrude shook her head and took a step back. "This isn't right. I shouldn't be doing this. If the bishop knew . . ." Her voice trailed off as if she were internally battling through a dilemma: what option to choose—bad or worse.

"Gertrude." He stepped onto the porch, let the storm door shut behind him, and lowered his voice. "Please tell me. You can't come over here and tell me you have a message from Cindy and then not share it. That's just cruel."

Gertrude sighed. "I know. I just don't want to cause more problems. I've already become too involved."

"Please just tell me. No one holds you responsible."

"Cindy asked me to give you one last note from her." She pulled an envelope from her apron and handed it to him. "I need to go." She huffed and then turned and marched down the porch steps.

Drew opened the envelope and removed the note as a quiver began in his hands and traveled down to his feet. The paper trembled as he held it.

> Dear Drew,
>   I love you and I miss you.
>
> > Forever,
> > Cindy

Drew blew out a deep breath and wilted. He grasped one side of the porch bench and sat down so he wouldn't hit the floor.

In the last month he'd convinced himself Cindy didn't want him in her life after all. That he was too much of a risk for her. *That she didn't love him.*

But this message, this short message, changed everything.

"She does love me," he whispered.

An almost maniacal laugh escaped from deep in this throat as he stood and turned toward Bruce, who was sitting on the other side of the storm door, watching him with his head tilted.

"She loves me, Bruce! She loves me!" Drew went inside, picked up his dog, and spun around with him. "Cindy still cares about me. She loves me!"

Then he set Bruce on the floor and flopped onto his sofa. His grin faded as reality crashed over him. Cindy loved him, but they still had a problem—he wasn't Amish.

He scrubbed his hand over the stubble on his chin as he contemplated what to do. He needed help. He needed to pray.

"God," he whispered. "Help me figure out what to do. I love Cindy, and she still loves me. But how can we be together? If she sent me this message, it means she still wants me in her life. How can I make that happen? How can I build a future with her without ruining her life? Help me see the right path for us."

Drew stood and paced, and then he turned to his dog, who was still sitting on the floor, staring at him.

"I know what I'm going to do, Bruce. It's the only way."

CHAPTER 19

Cindy pulled another weed from her garden and then dropped it into her bucket with a *plunk*. She looked up and found dark clouds had started to clog the blue sky as the faint scent of rain filled the air.

When she saw movement out of the corner of her eye, she looked up and gasped, dropping the bucket as Drew walked up the path toward the house.

"Drew," she whispered, her heart pounding. *He got my message!*

Her heart took on wings as she drank in his appearance. He was clean-shaven and wearing khaki trousers and a blue button-down shirt. It was as if he had dressed up for this visit.

She wiped her hands down her apron as she ran to the path to intercept him. "Drew! What are you doing here?"

He turned toward her with a look of surprise, and then a smile. "I got your note." He placed his hand on her cheek and she leaned into his touch. "I love you." His voice was raspy. "I can't live without you, Cindy. I have to be with you, and I want to work this out. We have to find a way to make it work."

"I love you too." Her lungs clenched as she craned her neck to look back at the barn. "*Mei dat* is home. We should really talk about this another time. Should I come and meet you tonight?"

"No." He shook his head. "I can't wait any longer."

"But I don't think—"

Drew dropped to one knee. "Cindy—"

"What are you doing?" She motioned for him to stand. "Get up."

"I've spent the past month wondering if I'd lost you forever." He reached for her hand and took it in his. "I've prayed again and again, begging God to find a way for us to be together. Then I had myself convinced you'd decided I wasn't worth having in your life. When I got your note yesterday, I nearly fell down with relief. I'm so grateful you still care for me. I'm so honored, and I can't stand being away from you one more day."

Cindy's heart squeezed as tears filled her eyes and then spilled over. Warmth hummed through her entire body. These were the words she'd dreamt of hearing. Was she dreaming now? Could this be real?

"I know we're from different worlds," he continued, his voice sounding thick with emotion. "But that doesn't change how I feel about you. I love you. I want to spend the rest of my life with you. I don't have much to offer, but if you give me a chance, I'll do my best to make you happy."

Cindy wiped at her eyes as her knees shook.

"What I'm asking is . . . Will you marry me?"

"Drew, I . . . I . . ." Cindy's head swam. "I don't know what to say."

"Say yes." His eyes searched hers. "Please. We'll build a life together. We can have a future, a family. I want to grow old with you."

Cindy opened her mouth to speak, and a sob escaped. She cupped her hands to her face as all her emotions came forth, as though they were exploding from a dam that had been holding them back. These were the words she'd always wanted to hear. Drew was in front of her and he wanted to spend the rest of his life with her. Her prayers had been answered.

"I'm sorry." Drew stood and pulled her into his arms. "I didn't mean to make you cry."

She wrapped her arms around his neck and cried into his shoulder.

"What's going on here?" *Dat*'s voice boomed.

Cindy released Drew and then spun to face her father, Florence, Jamie, and Sarah Jane as they all walked toward her, their expressions a mixture of confusion and anger. Panic weighed heavy on Cindy's shoulders as she focused her gaze on her father and wiped her face of tears.

"I said, what is going on here?" *Dat*'s eyes narrowed as a red flush crept up his neck.

Cindy swallowed against her suddenly dry throat. She hadn't seen her father this angry since Jamie and Mark had raced buggies when they were teenagers.

A light mist of cool rain began to sweep over them, filling the air with a sweet aroma.

Drew took a step closer to her father and lifted his chin. "I came here to propose to Cindy. I love her, and I want to spend the rest of my life with her."

"How dare you?" *Dat* seethed as he took a step toward Drew. He shook a finger just millimeters from his nose. "I've already told you to stay away from my daughter, and now you have the nerve to come here and propose marriage? You're not welcome here. Get off my property!" He pointed to the street. "Now!"

Drew opened his mouth to speak, but Cindy placed her hand on his chest to stop him.

"He's welcome here, *Dat*—because I say he is." Cindy's words were steady and even, although her body was vibrating with a mixture of excitement and angst.

The rain fell steadier, bouncing off her shoulders.

Dat's eyes widened as he studied her. "He's not one of us. You can't possibly be considering accepting his proposal."

A strange and sudden sense of calm came over Cindy as she looked into Drew's eyes. She knew at that moment that she belonged with him. He was her future.

She turned back to her father. "I am accepting his proposal."

Dat's mouth opened and closed a few times as Florence and Sarah Jane gaped at each other.

"Cindy." Jamie stepped to her and touched her arm. "You need to think this through. This is a huge decision."

"If you choose Drew, you'll lose us." *Dat*'s blue eyes seemed to shine with pain, stabbing at her heart.

Cindy nodded. "I know."

"Have you prayed about this?" Florence asked, her expression challenging her.

"I have." Cindy looked up at Drew as she threaded her fingers with his. "I feel God has led me to Drew." Her heart pounded again, and her legs wobbled, but she was going to stand firm. This was her future, and she needed Drew in it.

Drew smiled at her and squeezed her hand. "I've prayed too."

The rain began to soak through Cindy's dress and apron, but she didn't care.

Dat shook his head, and renewed anger seemed to grip him as his expression twisted into a frown. "I forbid this." He pointed to the ground. "I will not allow you to marry him."

"It's my decision," she told her father. "This is my life and my future." Then she looked up at Drew. "May I come to your house for supper tonight?"

"Of course." He squeezed her hand again.

"*Gut*," Cindy said. "I'll be there at six o'clock, and we can talk about this more."

Drew nodded.

Then she released his hand and hurried toward the house.

"Cindy!" *Dat* called after her. "Cindy! We need to talk about this."

"You're making a mistake!" Florence chimed in.

Ignoring them, Cindy entered the house, leaving her family behind her in the rain.

. . .

Drew rubbed his hand over his stiff neck as he watched Cindy rush into the house with her father and stepmother close behind her, calling her name. A mixture of confusion and elation poured through him.

The rain had soaked his hair and his clothing, but he wasn't worried about that. He smiled and blew out a breath that seemed to bubble up from his toes.

She's going to marry me!

Jamie stepped into his view, his eyes narrowing. "Do you realize what you're doing? You're breaking up our family." His voice wavered. "We already lost my mother, and now my sister is going to leave us? Don't you have a conscience?"

Drew fought the guilt that dug its talons into his back. "It shouldn't be that way. Cindy and I are in love. We should be permitted to build a future together just like you and Kayla have."

"It's not the same," Sarah Jane protested. "You're not a member of our community. If you marry her, you'll destroy our family. Doesn't that mean anything to you?"

"Yes, it does." Drew jammed a finger into his chest. "I've lost my family—my *entire* family. Do you know what that feels like?" He nearly spat the words at her.

Sarah Jane shook her head as she took a step back from him, her dark eyes widening.

"It hurts so badly that sometimes you wonder how you'll face the next day." Drew glanced toward the house. "But then I found Cindy, and I felt like I could move past the grief. I felt like I could have a life worth living. I realized I could be happy again."

Drew divided a look between Jamie and Sarah Jane as his frustration simmered. "I love Cindy. I will take care of her and cherish her. It's not your place to decide her future. That's her decision, and you need to respect that."

With his muscles burning as if they were on fire, he turned and started down the driveway.

"Wait!" Jamie ran after him. "Please, Drew. Wait."

Drew balled his hands into fists and kept walking. He needed to get away from Cindy's family before he said something he would regret later.

"If you really love my sister, then you should convert," Jamie called after him. "If you were Amish, then you could be together, and she wouldn't lose her family."

Drew spun toward Jamie as white-hot anger boiled his blood. "Cindy isn't even sure she wants to be Amish, so why would I convert?" He gestured widely with his arms. "Why can't we be together anyway? Why can't you Riehls accept me as I am?"

Jamie shook his head, his face stony. "This is our culture. This is how we live."

Drew gave a sardonic laugh. "Your culture makes no sense

to me. You call yourselves Christians, but you refuse to accept someone who isn't a member of your church. You think Cindy is leaving, but the truth is you're pushing her away by not accepting her love for me. Why don't you think about *that*?"

Drew turned and continued down the driveway, sure Jamie was staring.

As Drew dodged puddles, he looked up at the sky. The rain had stopped, and the sun peeked out from behind a gray cloud. The sunshine almost felt like a promise from God that everything would somehow make sense in time.

Drew made his way to his house, where he opened the front door and allowed Bruce to run out. Then he grabbed his laptop, returned to the porch, and sat down in a rocker. He switched on his laptop, and a spark of renewed excitement rolled through him as he began researching how to get a marriage license.

Tonight, he and Cindy would plan their future. He just had to make sure she was certain she would leave her church and family for him, that she hadn't said yes in the heat of the moment, in defiance of her father.

And if she changed her mind, he would have to find a way to move on with a broken heart.

. . .

"Cindy!" *Dat*'s voice echoed off the kitchen walls. "Cindy! Don't you run away from me. We're going to talk *now*."

Cindy spun toward him, her knees jiggling at the pace of hummingbird wings. She lifted her chin and tried to muster all the confidence she could dig up.

"You're making a mistake." *Dat*'s words were measured. "Right now you think you're in love, but you're wrong. You're just confused. I know your *mamm*'s death was tough on you, but that's not a reason to leave the church."

"Don't do that! Don't blame this on *Mamm*!" Anger exploded from Cindy as hot tears welled up in her eyes. "I've felt like a stranger in this *haus* for years. When I met Drew, I finally felt whole again."

"You're rushing into this." Florence's brown eyes were empathetic. "You don't really know how you feel yet. You're so young, and you think you're in love—"

"Really?" Cindy wiped away tears that had begun to trickle down her face. "How old were you when you married Alphus?"

"Well, I was . . . um . . ." Florence blinked.

"How old?" Cindy asked again.

"I was twenty-five." Florence and *Dat* exchanged a look.

"I'm twenty-four. So how can I be too young to know how I feel? Would you say the same thing to Sarah Jane?" Cindy shook her head. "You two just don't understand me. That's the whole problem."

"We don't understand why you would choose to leave the only community you've known your entire life," *Dat* said. "How can you just abandon your church? It's part of you. It's in your heart. How can that be so easy for you?"

"It's not easy." Cindy took a shaky breath. "It's difficult, but I feel God is leading me to Drew. How can I ignore God's call?"

"You're breaking my heart." *Dat*'s eyes misted over, and then he wiped them with his fingers.

Cindy closed her eyes as memories of her mother's death swamped her. Her father had cried so many times in the days following *Mamm*'s accident. How could Cindy inflict the same pain on him?

No! I can't let him stop me from seeking my own happiness!

She opened her eyes. "This is my decision, and I need you to support me."

"I can't bless this," *Dat* said. "If you do this, you're on your own."

Cindy nodded. "I understand." She started toward the stairs, and as she ascended, her heart cracked with each step.

"I never had this problem with Laura," *Dat* called after her from the bottom of the stairwell. "She never even hinted at the idea of leaving the church. She was baptized with the rest of her *freinden* when she was a teenager."

Cindy spun, her blood pressure spiking. "Stop comparing me to Laura! I'm not Laura, and I never will be." She looked at Florence, standing beside *Dat*. "I'm not Sarah Jane either." A sob caught her breath, but she went on. "I'm sorry I'm not the perfect *dochder*!"

Before they could respond, she ran up the remaining stairs.

When Cindy reached her room, she fell onto her bed and turned on her side. She looked out the window at the sun peeking from behind the clouds, and her thoughts turned to her mother's beautiful face.

"*Mamm*," she whispered. "I miss you. If only you were here to listen to me and offer your sound advice. I'm sorry for disrespecting *Dat*. I'm sorry for hurting everyone. I just want to find the happiness Jamie, Mark, and Laura have. I just want to be *froh* again. If only they understood."

Closing her eyes, Cindy prayed her father would forgive her someday and let her and Drew be a part of the family.

CHAPTER 20

Cindy's heart kicked as she knocked on Drew's door later that evening. She held the crumbly peach pie she'd baked that morning in her hands, and her stomach growled as she breathed in the sweet aroma.

Somewhere inside the house, Bruce barked.

The door opened, and Drew appeared, now dressed in jeans and a light pullover sweater, his hair slightly damp as though he'd just taken a shower. He looked handsome, but then, he always did.

"Hi," he said as he swung his storm door wide.

"Hi." She handed him the pie. "I made this earlier today, and I thought you might like it."

"It smells amazing. Come in. I'll put the pie on the table."

Cindy stepped in and smiled at Bruce as he sat erect and seemed to smile at her.

"Hi, Bruce." She patted his head as tears welled in her eyes. She'd spent all afternoon sewing and crying while trying to convince her soul that she could go on without her family. Would Drew's love be enough to comfort her for the rest of her life?

The question sent a flood of tears pouring down her face.

"Cindy." Drew appeared beside her. "You all right?"

Cindy wrapped her arms around him and rested her cheek on his shoulder as she tried to control the tears.

He rubbed her back. "I promise it's all going to work out."

She closed her eyes and inhaled his fresh scent. She felt as if she'd come home. This was where she belonged. This man was her future, her heart. She sighed deeply and relaxed into him.

She looked up at his handsome face and took in his gorgeous ice-blue eyes. She imagined her future—a home, children, a life with him. Yes, this was what she'd prayed for.

His brow furrowed. "Have you changed your mind? I thought maybe—"

"What?" She stepped back and stared up at him.

He took her hands and led her to the sofa, where they sat down beside each other. Then he angled his body toward her.

"I've done a lot of thinking this afternoon." He rubbed his chin. "I realize what you're giving up for me. It's okay if you change your mind. I know what it's like to lose your entire family, and I hate to see you go through that pain for me."

"No." She touched his cheek. "I want this. I want to be your wife and build a life with you. I'm certain God led me to you, and I don't plan to walk away."

He gestured around the room. "I don't have much to offer. As long as they'll let me, I'll keep working part-time for the Lapps, and we can live here until I finish school. Then we can find a bigger place when I get a full-time job."

"This is perfect." She whistled to Bruce, and he came to sit at her feet. "We have Bruce. What else could we need?"

He laughed, and warmth surged through her.

"I'll keep sewing too." She pointed to the doorways beyond the family room. "Could I set up my sewing machine in one of your extra bedrooms?"

"Of course." He touched her hand. "This will be your house too. You can do whatever you want." He stood and lifted her to her feet. "Why don't we eat while we make our plans?"

She walked to the small dining area and gaped when she found the table set for two with beautiful white dishes decorated with little blue flowers. Two white candles burned in the center of the table, and a pan of lasagna sat in the center of the table next to a basket of garlic bread.

"This is beautiful." She touched his chest. "You cook?"

"Yeah." He shrugged. "My aunt taught me soon after I came to live with her. It was sort of our bonding time, when we'd get to know each other. Cooking was a neutral subject we could discuss without all the emotions of what I had been through. She left me these dishes, and she taught me how to set a table too." He pulled her chair back and then motioned for her to sit. "Please."

"Thank you." She sat down.

"I also got a special drink to celebrate the occasion." He stepped into the kitchen and then returned with two wineglasses and a bottle of sparkling grape juice. "I hope you like grape."

"I do." She folded her hands in her lap as he poured the juice.

Then he sat down beside her and poured himself a glass.

Cindy bowed her head for a silent prayer and then looked up at him. "Everything smells delicious."

He served her a piece of lasagna and a piece of bread before serving himself. They ate in silence for a few minutes, and she glanced around the house, trying to imagine it as her home.

"What happened after I left today? You were upset when you got here." His tone seemed strained.

"My father lectured me for a while, and we argued. I spent the afternoon working in my sewing room. He and Florence didn't speak to me when I left to come here."

"Are you okay with that?"

"Yes and no. I sort of expected it." She sighed. "At least he's not yelling at me anymore." She looked down at her plate. "This is so good."

"I'll teach you how to make it."

"I can't wait." She imagined standing in the kitchen with Drew while he taught her to cook, and happiness coursed through her.

"I researched how to get a marriage license."

"Oh?"

"I thought maybe we could go next week." He explained they had to go to the county courthouse and would need to bring certain documents with them. "I also thought we could talk to my pastor about a small wedding. Would you like that?"

"*Ya*, that would be nice." Excitement simmered through her. They were going to do this! They were going to be married. She was finally going to have the full life her siblings had, and she couldn't wait to begin it with Drew.

"I have something for you." He pulled a small pouch from his pocket. "I know you don't believe in wearing jewelry, but I want to give you something special that belonged to my mother." He took out a small gold cross on a chain. "My mother never took this off."

Cindy touched the necklace and love swept over her, leaving her speechless.

His expression clouded with what looked like disappointment. "Oh, maybe you can't wear it. I understand." He went to slip the necklace back into the pouch.

"Wait." She reached for the necklace. "I love it. I would be honored to wear it."

"Are you sure?" He held it up again.

"*Ya*, I am. Would you please put it on me?"

He stood and slipped behind her chair. Then he put the necklace around her neck and fastened the chain.

She ran her fingers over the cross and smiled up at him. "It's beautiful."

"You deserve so much more." He sank back into his chair.

"All I want is your heart," she whispered.

His expression grew intense, stealing the air from her lungs. When his lips swept over hers, she closed her eyes and savored the feeling. How she loved kissing her fiancé!

When he broke the kiss, he traced her cheek with the tip of his finger. "I promise I will cherish you forever."

She nodded, her heart racing, overcome by the bittersweet feel of the moment.

. . .

Cindy hugged her sweater against her chest as she walked up her father's driveway later that evening. She reached up and touched the cross necklace, then smiled. She and Drew had talked about their future for hours. She could hardly wait to start the rest of her life with him, to change her last name and move into her new home.

Her gaze moved to her father's house, and she felt her lips collapse into a flat line. While she looked forward to her new life with Drew, she would miss her family and the house where she'd been born and raised. Releasing her old life would leave a scar on her heart.

She dismissed the sad thoughts for the moment. She was finally going to live the happy life she'd always dreamt of having. She couldn't allow her family to steal her newfound happiness and hope. She tucked the necklace beneath her dress and then touched her collarbone. Although she would hide the necklace when she stepped into her father's house, she would keep it close to her heart. The necklace was a reminder not only of Drew's love for her, but of God's comfort and love. He had brought Drew into her life, and she was so grateful.

"Cindy!"

She turned toward her brother's house and spotted Jamie standing on his porch, where three lanterns illuminated all three of her siblings. She clenched her fists as she pivoted back toward her father's house and started down the path, away from Jamie, Mark, and Laura.

"Cindy!" Jamie bellowed. "Please come here."

"We just want to talk to you," Mark chimed in.

"Please, Cindy," Laura added.

Cindy stilled and closed her eyes. Should she go and talk to them? She was done debating her decisions, but maybe she should listen to what her siblings had to say. After all, they did care about her.

She pivoted again and made her way down the path leading to Jamie's house, lightly touching where the cross lay beneath her dress as she walked. She stopped when she reached the bottom step of Jamie's porch.

"What do you want?" She fingered her apron as she looked at each of her siblings.

The twins exchanged a look, and then Laura met her gaze.

"Tell me it's not true." Laura pushed her rocker into motion and rubbed her belly. "Tell me you're not leaving the community for that *Englisher*."

Glaring at her sister, Cindy crossed her arms over her chest as if to protect her heart. "His name is Drew, and *ya*, I'm going to marry him."

Laura stood. "Why would you choose to leave us all behind?"

"Have you really thought this through?" Mark asked.

Cindy held up her hands. "I didn't come over here for the three of you to gang up on me." She took a step back. "*Gut nacht.*"

"Wait." Mark started down the steps after her. "Don't leave. We just want to talk to you. We're trying to understand why you made this decision. We care about you, and we don't want to lose you. You're our baby sister. Of course we're upset to hear you plan to leave us. Why wouldn't you expect us to be concerned? If we weren't, it would mean we didn't care about you."

Cindy's heart twisted. Mark was right. She would be hurt if her siblings didn't care, but she also didn't want to argue with them. Why was all of this so confusing?

"Who called you?" she asked Mark.

Mark pointed at Jamie. "He did."

"*Dat* was upset when you left to meet Drew for supper." Jamie sank down onto a rocking chair. "I thought maybe the three of us could talk you out of leaving." He leaned forward, resting his palms on his thighs. "You're our family, Cindy. How can you expect us to just let you go?"

"Exactly." Laura's voice sounded nearly strangled with emotion. "I want *mei kinner* to know you. How can you leave all your *bruderskinner*? They love you so much."

Cindy pressed at an ache in the center of her chest, feeling the cross. "I'm not deliberately leaving you. These are just the rules of our community." She pointed to each of them. "Didn't you each fall in love and marry the person you chose for the rest of your life?"

Mark held up his hands. "Priscilla and I were forced to get married."

"But it worked out, didn't it?" Cindy asked.

Mark gave her a sarcastic laugh. "I don't think this comparison is fair. You're going to leave the life you've known since birth for a man you've barely known four months, right?" He looked over at Jamie. "Didn't you say they met in June?"

Jamie nodded.

"How can you marry someone you hardly know?" Laura asked.

Cindy's eyes narrowed at her sister. "I know him well enough. I know his heart."

"Four months, Cindy. You're leaving your family for a man you've known for four months." Mark held up four fingers. "Don't you think you might regret this decision?"

"No, I don't think I'll regret it at all." Cindy shook her head as a heavy feeling in the pit of her stomach overtook her. It felt like an iron bar. "He makes me *froh*. Doesn't that count for something? Why shouldn't I have the right to marry the person I've chosen?"

"If you leave, it will be difficult to come back," Jamie said. "Especially if you're married."

"What if you and Drew have *kinner*?" Laura added. "Don't you want your *kinner* to know your family? Since Drew doesn't have any family, your *kinner* won't have any relatives. Have you even considered that?"

The notion of her children never knowing her family had not yet dawned on her. She placed her hand on her forehead as her world spun out of control. She couldn't allow her older siblings to see how much they were hurting her. She had to stay strong. She may be the youngest, but she was stronger than they thought.

"Look, Cindy." Jamie stood and walked down the steps,

coming to a stop next to Mark. "We just want you to think about this. Don't make any decisions until you've really thought through the consequences."

"I have thought them through." Cindy lifted her chin. "I may be younger than you, but I'm not a *kind*. And this is *my* life." She pointed to her chest.

Jamie held up his hands as if to calm her. "But you're killing *Dat*."

"I'm killing *Dat*? What about *me*?" Her voice scraped out of her throat, betraying the emotions she'd tried to suppress. "This is my choice, not his."

"Come on, Cindy." Laura stood as her voice rose. "You can't do this to us. We've already lost *Mamm*. We can't lose you too. Don't rip our family apart." She sniffed and wiped at her eyes.

"Don't throw *Mamm* in my face!" Her voice shook as her tears broke free. "My decisions are my own!"

"Please don't do this." Laura folded her hands as if praying. *"Please."*

"I hope you all can understand my decision someday." Cindy turned and ran to her father's house, ignoring her siblings' calls to come back.

She hurried into the house, relieved to find the kitchen empty. She made her way up to her room, where she sat down on her chair and closed her eyes. A myriad of emotions ran over her like a team of horses plowing one of her father's cornfields.

While she appreciated her siblings' concern, she also longed for their blessing. But how could they bless her decision to leave the community?

She pulled the necklace from under her dress and ran her fingers over the cross as she opened her heart to God.

Please, God. Help my family accept my decision, and help me

find a way to keep them in my life. While I believe you led me to
Drew, I also believe there's a way for me to keep my family, and
only you can show me what that way is.

When she climbed into bed a few minutes later, she waited
for sleep to send her to a land of sweet dreams.

CHAPTER 21

Cindy hurried down the stairs Sunday morning. At the kitchen counter, she bowed her head in silent prayer, then grabbed a roll from a basket. As she cut it open and buttered it, she heard footsteps behind her.

"Where are you going?" Sarah Jane asked as Cindy took a bite.

She held up one finger as she chewed and then swallowed. "Church."

"Church?" Florence walked over to her. "But it's an off Sunday."

"I'm going to church with Drew and then spending the day with him." Cindy headed for the mudroom door and waved at the two women over her shoulder. "I'll see you this evening."

Then she rushed out the back door and down the steps, eating the roll as she walked. She had planned to be up early, but she'd sewed late into the night and lost track of time. Then she had forgotten to set her alarm and woke up just in time to get dressed and dash to Drew's.

She found Drew standing in her driveway next to his pickup truck. Her heart stuttered. He looked so handsome in khakis and a gray collared shirt. His face was clean-shaven, and his eyes were as bright as the blue sky above him.

He waved, and she increased her pace as she finished the

roll. Out of the corner of her eye, she spotted her father coming from the barn, and her smile faded.

"Where are you going?" *Dat* asked.

Cindy halted and tried to ignore the angry narrowing of his eyes. "Drew is taking me to his church."

Dat flicked his glare at Drew and then looked back at her.

"Good morning, Vernon." Drew's smile seemed forced.

Dat grunted and then started for the house.

"I'll be home this evening," Cindy called to *Dat*, but he kept walking with his back to her. She shook off her frustration and rushed over to Drew. "Good morning."

"Hi." He smiled at her. "Are you ready?"

"I am." She climbed into the passenger seat and ran her hands over her yellow dress and white apron.

Drew climbed in next to her. "You know, you don't have to go to church with me if you don't want to."

"Why would you think I wouldn't want to go?"

He pointed toward the house and raised an eyebrow. "Even after your siblings grilled you Friday night?"

She had filled him in on her siblings' lecture when she visited him yesterday afternoon.

"*Ya*. I think they've given up, but that's all right. I'd rather they just accept my decision than keep questioning me." She looked at the clock on the dashboard. "We need to go or we're going to be late for the service."

"Right." He studied her and then smiled.

"What?" She touched her dress and then her prayer covering to make sure nothing was out of place.

"You're beautiful."

She laughed as heat infused her cheeks. "Thank you. And you're handsome." She pointed to the clock. "We need to go."

He turned the key, and when the engine roared to life he backed out of the driveway to Beechdale Road.

Cindy settled back into the seat and smiled as a calmness rolled over her. She'd been nervous about attending a church outside of her own, but she was also curious to see how other Christians worshipped God.

"Did I see you eating something when you were walking out of the house?" Drew looked over at her as he slowed to a stop at a red light.

"*Ya.*" She laughed. "I accidentally slept in. I only had enough time to get dressed and then run out the door. I grabbed a roll on my way through the kitchen."

"I'll have to take you out to lunch after church, then."

"You don't need to do that." She waved off the suggestion.

"I want to." He turned toward her and cupped one side of her face in his hand. "I want to spend as much time with you as I can." He ran his finger over her cheek, and the contact sent tiny shivers across her skin.

A horn tooted behind them, informing them that the light had turned green.

Cindy nodded toward the traffic signal. "You'd better go. The people behind us are in a hurry to get to church too."

Drew negotiated a turn and then pulled into the parking lot of the Bird-in-Hand Community Church.

Cindy looked up at the white church and admired the bell tower and stained-glass window. It looked like several churches she'd seen from the outside. Her chest tightened with apprehension at the idea of walking inside. She'd never stepped foot in a church before, but the possibility of worshipping a different way was exciting too.

"Are you ready?" Drew's smile was hesitant. "Remember,

we don't have to do this. If you're uncomfortable, I can take you home. I don't want you to feel like I'm forcing you to go to church with me."

"This was my idea." She angled her body toward him. "I told you. When we're married, I want to worship with you. This is our first step toward our new life together. Don't feel as if you're forcing me to do anything."

He touched her cheek again. "I love you." His voice was a little rough, as if the words came from deep in his soul.

"I love you too." She opened the truck door. "I'm ready."

They walked across the parking lot holding hands, and Drew entwined his fingers with hers. With his free hand, he waved and smiled at members of the congregation who greeted him by name. Cindy nodded in response to their curious smiles and waves to her.

"How long have you been attending this church?" she asked.

"I think it's been almost a year." He smiled at a man in a suit. "This congregation is warm and welcoming."

"Do you think they'll welcome me?" The nerves in her stomach tied themselves into a knot.

"Are you kidding?" His tone was like an audible eye roll. "They'll love you."

"Even though I dress Amish?"

"You can dress any way you want. They'll just be happy you decided to come today." He gave her hand a reassuring squeeze as they reached the front steps.

"Thank you."

He winked, and the gesture scrambled her insides with happiness.

A man in a suit and tie held open the large wooden door as Cindy and Drew entered the church. Another well-dressed man standing at the entrance to the sanctuary handed Cindy a folded booklet with a beautiful image of a mountain scene and a Scripture verse under it.

"Thank you." Cindy took the booklet and glanced up at Drew as they moved toward the pews. "What do I do with it?"

"It's called a bulletin." His words were soft in her ear, sending a tremor through her. "It's sort of like a guide for the service. It lists the order of the service, hymn numbers, and the schedule of church meetings and events for the upcoming weeks."

"Oh." Cindy followed him to a row near the back and sat beside him on an aisle. She glanced through the bulletin, taking in the order of the service as well as the page numbers and names of the hymns. She also found Scripture verses printed, along with the prayer of the day. It felt strange to have the service printed out in her hand, in a sanctuary, sitting in a pew. She was used to sitting on a backless bench in the home or barn of a community member every other week.

She looked toward the front of the room and found an altar with two large vases, each filled with a spray of orange and white daylilies and chrysanthemums. Although they were beautiful flowers, they seemed out of place to her. Neither an altar nor flowers were part of the Amish church tradition. She was accustomed to sitting in a barn or in a home that had movable walls to make room for the congregation. While couples and families sat together in these church pews, Cindy was used to sitting in a segregated congregation, divided by married men, married women, unmarried men, and unmarried women. It felt strange to have Drew sitting beside her instead of other women.

Cindy turned her gaze toward the large stained-glass window at the front of the sanctuary and the wooden cross hanging in front of it. She tilted her head and studied the display. What would her siblings think of this church?

She closed her eyes and tried to shove away the image of her siblings' disapproving expressions on Friday night. They'd bothered her more than she'd wanted Drew to know. When she opened her eyes once again, she focused on the cross. It gave the large room a warm feeling. She could feel God's presence all around her. Yes, God was here with her, no matter what her family said about her relationship with Drew.

"Good morning." A man leaned down and shook Drew's hand. He looked at Cindy and smiled. His smile felt warm and genuine. "Good morning."

"Hi, Wayne." Drew gestured toward Cindy. "This is Cindy. She wanted to come to worship with me today. Cindy, this is Wayne."

"It's nice to meet you." Wayne shook her hand. "Welcome to the Bird-in-Hand Community Church. We're happy to see you here."

"Thank you." Cindy pushed the ribbons from her prayer covering behind her shoulders. She smiled at a few members of the congregation who made their way past Wayne and nodded a greeting to her.

Were they wondering what a woman dressed like an Amish person was doing in the church? Would they stare at her throughout the service? She inwardly groaned at the thought. Hopefully, they would focus their thoughts on God and not the person who seemed out of place in their sanctuary.

Wayne and Drew chatted about the weather for a moment as Cindy turned her attention back to the bulletin. She read a lengthy prayer request list that warmed her heart. It was comforting to see that members of the congregation prayed for others' family members and friends who were struggling with illness, unemployment, or other challenges. She perused a list of the weekly events, taking in the different church committees and organizations.

Suddenly the organ sounded, and Cindy jumped. Music was another foreign element to her, because no instruments were ever played during Amish services. The voices swirling around Cindy faded to a murmur as if on cue, and the knot of people loitering in the aisle filed into pews.

Drew leaned over, and Cindy enjoyed the familiar scent of his aftershave. "Are you all right?" He rested his arm on the back of the pew behind her and ran his thumb over her shoulder, sending contentment zipping through her.

"*Ya.*" She nodded. "I was startled by the organ, but it's beautiful. I'm enjoying the music. It's different from what I'm used to, but I like it."

When the music stopped, a woman dressed in a robe took her place behind the pulpit.

Cindy leaned over to Drew and touched his arm. "Is she your minister?"

"Yes," he whispered. "That's Pastor Ellen. You'll enjoy her sermon."

"Oh." Cindy was surprised. She had never seen a female minister. Women weren't permitted to serve as bishop, minister, or deacon in the Amish church.

Pastor Ellen looked to be medium height and had a warm voice and pleasant smile. Cindy guessed she was in her mid-forties, and her dark-brown hair and deep-brown eyes reminded Cindy of the color of coffee. Although she was used to hearing Pennsylvania *Dietsch* and German during her community's services, she felt at ease listening to English.

She glanced around and found the other members of the congregation nodding and smiling as the minister spoke. Cindy marveled at how comfortable she felt. It was as if God had sent her to this service today.

The organ began playing again, and the congregation stood. Drew handed Cindy a hymnal and she flipped through it to find the appropriate hymn listed in the bulletin and on the board at the front of the sanctuary. The congregation began to sing, and Cindy listened for a few moments, enjoying the warm, rich sound of Drew's voice beside her. She smiled up at him and he winked, causing her pulse to quicken. She joined in with the hymn singing, enjoying the opportunity to worship the Lord with a new song.

When the hymn concluded, the congregation sat down, and a man dressed in a suit approached the pulpit and read the lessons for the day. Cindy folded her hands and concentrated on taking in God's Word. Proverbs 3, verses 5 and 6, struck a chord in her: *Trust in the LORD with all your heart and lean not on your own understanding; in all your ways submit to him, and he will make your paths straight.*

The verses echoed through her mind while the reader finished the lessons, and their message continued to float through her thoughts during the minister's sermon. It was as if God had chosen those verses for her today. He was ministering to her in her confusion.

Pastor Ellen's message of hope and trust through adversity spoke to her heart, just as the Scripture verses had. Cindy wondered if God was blessing her through this small church. Still, she missed the familiarity of the Amish services, including the hymns, the congregation in which she grew up, and the Pennsylvania *Dietsch* language.

Once the sermon was over, Cindy followed along with the remainder of the service, singing the hymns and reciting the prayers.

When the members of the church lined up to go to the front of the sanctuary for communion, Cindy's chest seized with anxiety. She touched Drew's arm. "I'd like to stay here. I'm not comfortable taking communion."

"I understand." Drew patted her hand. "Only do what feels right to you."

"Thank you." She sat with her hands folded while Drew went up to receive communion. She was grateful he didn't insist she accompany him.

After one last hymn, the service ended, and Cindy followed Drew into the aisle. Then they stood in line to greet Pastor Ellen. A few people walked over to greet Drew, and he introduced Cindy to them. Each person welcomed her to the church and invited her to come back. She smiled and thanked them for their kindness.

They reached the front of the line, and Drew shook the minister's hand. "Pastor Ellen, this is Cindy Riehl. Cindy, this is Pastor Ellen."

"Hello." Cindy shook her hand. "I enjoyed your service."

"It's very nice to meet you, Cindy." Pastor Ellen's smile was warm and inviting, putting Cindy at ease. "Welcome to our church. I imagine this was a very different service than what you're used to."

"Yes," Cindy said. "But I truly enjoyed it. Your church has a homey feel. I can see why Drew enjoys coming here."

"That's very true," Drew said.

"We hope to see you again, Cindy." The minister smiled. "May God bless you."

"Thank you." Cindy followed Drew to the exit. "This was nice. I really enjoyed the service."

"I did, too, and I enjoyed having you beside me in the pew." His eyes were full of tenderness that caused her heart to dance. "May I take you to lunch?"

"That would be lovely." Cindy looked up at him and wished the day would never end.

CHAPTER 22

Drew sat across from Cindy at a small sandwich shop and watched her while she studied the menu. Her blond hair and deep-blue eyes captivated him. She looked so beautiful in her yellow dress that she seemed to glow.

He was grateful to have her next to him in church today. It felt as if they were a couple—a true couple, not two people who met in secret at his house. They were truly together, and she was going to be his wife. The thought sent such warmth and happiness surging through him. How he loved her!

"I think the club sandwich sounds good." She glanced up, and her mouth tipped up on one side. "Why are you staring at me?"

"I'm sorry." He lifted his glass of Coke. "I was lost in my thoughts."

"Have you decided what you're going to order?" She placed her menu on the table.

"I think I'll have a BLT." He sipped the Coke and then put the menu back by the napkin dispenser. "Did you really like the service?"

Cindy settled back on the bench seat. "I loved the music, and the sermon touched me. I think your minister is wonderful."

"Do non-Amish ever attend your services?"

"It's rare to see them at a regular Sunday service, but I've seen *Englishers* at weddings." She swirled the straw in her glass of water. "I assume they don't enjoy it much since they can't understand what the ministers are saying."

Drew studied her ivory complexion. He longed to read her true thoughts about leaving her family. She seemed too accepting of the confrontation with her siblings. The guilt he still felt for ripping her away from them haunted him day and night. Would she tell him if she still had doubts?

A young woman appeared at the table with a notepad. "What would you like today?"

When the woman left, Cindy leaned forward on the table and studied his eyes. "If you don't tell me what's on your mind, I'm going to keep asking until you do."

He ran his fingers over the condensation on his glass and considered his thoughts. "I just want to be sure you're ready to walk away from your life in the community and your family for me. I don't want you to regret your decision to marry me."

"Drew." She leaned across the table and took his hands in hers, and the tender feel of her skin sent heat pouring through him. "Look at me."

His gaze tangled with hers and he drank in her beautiful face.

"Like I told my siblings Friday night, you're the one I want to spend the rest of my life with, and I deserve the same happiness they have." Her expression grew fierce. "I plan to continue asking God to find a way to keep my family in my life, but you're my future. I'll miss them, but I need you, and I'm here as long as you'll have me."

He smiled. "I just wanted to make sure."

"I don't plan on giving up on you, and I hope you feel the same way about me."

"Always." He lifted his Coke glass to toast her. "Here's to our future."

"*Ya.*" She touched her glass to his and then took a drink.

He silently thanked God for leading him to Bird-in-Hand and bringing Cindy into his life. Whatever they had to endure would be worth it to be together.

. . .

Cindy stood on Drew's porch later that evening and hugged his zippered sweatshirt to her chest. She gazed at the Lapps' white farmhouse and the rolling fields across the road. Fall had settled on Lancaster County, and the fields were yellow and brown. But they would be lush and green again in the spring. Cindy smiled as she considered her future here as Drew's wife.

"Thank you for loaning me your jacket," she said. "I didn't think to bring a sweater with me."

"You're welcome." He touched her shoulder. "I had a wonderful day with you."

"And I enjoyed going to church and lunch with you." She grinned. "And then you cooked for me tonight. I'm going to like being married to you if I get to eat your pork chops and mashed potatoes."

He wagged a finger at her. "Don't get used to it. I'm going to let you cook sometimes too."

"If you insist." She clicked her tongue with feigned chagrin.

"I'd still like to walk you home, just like I've wanted to every time you've been here at night. But I don't want to upset your family any more than necessary." He stepped closer to her. "It's getting late, though. Are you sure you'll be safe?"

"Yes. You're sweet, but I'll be fine." But then she sighed as disappointment washed over her. If only the day hadn't flown by so quickly!

He leaned down and pressed his lips on hers, sending her pulse into a wild swirl.

"Will I see you soon?" He whispered the question against her ear, sending a rush of heat through her.

"Of course. You know I can't stay away from you for long." She grinned, and he laughed.

"I'll be waiting for you." He kissed her cheek.

"Good night." She flipped on her flashlight and started down the driveway.

As Cindy walked past the Lapps' house, she looked up into the kitchen window and found Gertrude watching her.

Unease spread through Cindy like a choking weed, but she gave Gertrude a little wave. What would the rest of the community say about Cindy when they learned she was engaged to an *Englisher*? Did they already know?

Cindy continued down the driveway as reality grabbed her by the throat. Her life was about to change, and she prayed for the confidence and strength to stay strong through the adversity ahead.

. . .

The back door clicked shut as Cindy dried the last breakfast dish and set it into a cabinet the following morning.

"*Gude mariye*," Laura sang as she stepped into the kitchen with Kayla and Priscilla close behind her.

"*Gude mariye!*" Sarah Jane's welcome was a little too chipper as she walked over, took a tote bag from Laura, and then set it on the kitchen counter.

Cindy looked from Laura to Kayla to Priscilla. "What's everyone doing here today?"

"We're here for a sisters' day." Priscilla set her own tote bag on the counter.

"We're going to bake," Kayla added.

"*Gude mariye!*" Florence announced as she stepped into the kitchen. "I'm so *froh* you're all here."

"You know we never miss a sisters' day." Laura opened her tote bag and started pulling out baking supplies.

"Is it a special occasion?" Cindy spun to face Florence. "Did you plan this?"

"I thought it would be *gut* for you to spend a day with your sisters." Florence patted Cindy on the shoulder and walked over to Laura, Kayla, and Priscilla. "Are you going to make *kichlin*?"

Cindy set her jaw as a hot rush of frustration roared through her. She looked around the kitchen as Laura and Florence happily made room on the counter and table. So this was their new tactic to try to convince her to stay in the community.

While they continued to talk about cookies, Cindy turned and walked toward the stairs.

"Cindy!" Laura called after her. "We can't have a sisters' day without our youngest sister."

"*Ya*, that's right!" Sarah Jane chimed in.

"Please join us," Priscilla added.

"We haven't had time to just be together and bake for quite a while," Kayla said.

"I have sewing projects to finish for customers." Cindy pointed toward the stairs.

"Your sewing projects can wait." Laura beckoned to her. "Please, come here." She held up a cookbook. "I brought *Mamm*'s cookbook. We can make one of her favorite cookie recipes."

Cindy pursed her lips. If she continued upstairs, she was certain Laura would nag her until she came down. It was easier to do what they wanted than try to fight them. She crossed to the counter and peered over Laura's shoulder as she flipped through the cookbook.

Laura and Florence were discussing brownie cookies when *Dat* walked into the kitchen.

"Gude mariye!" Priscilla and Kayla called to him in unison as he crossed the kitchen.

Dat nodded hellos and then shared a meaningful look with Florence before heading out the back door.

Cindy moved to the window as *Dat* bypassed the barn and continued down the driveway. "Florence," she said over her shoulder, "where is *Dat* going?"

"He's just working in the barn." Florence kept her eyes focused on the cookbook. "Where else would he go?"

Apprehension pooled in the pit of Cindy's stomach as *Dat* disappeared down the driveway. He wasn't going to the barn, and her family was still intent on stopping her wedding. *Dat* must be going to see Drew.

Please, God. Keep Drew strong. I can't lose him.

"Cindy," Sarah Jane sang, "come help us pick out a recipe."

Cindy took a deep breath and squared her shoulders. All her sisters had come to see her, and she was happy to see them. Perhaps she could enjoy this day. After all, it might be the last time she had to spend with them before she married Drew.

She turned, and a smile overtook her lips. "Why don't we make *Mamm*'s carrot *kuche*, along with the cream cheese icing?"

. . .

Drew saw movement out of the corner of his eye as he tossed his backpack into his pickup truck. He looked up and then froze, his shoes cemented to the rock driveway. Vernon was walking toward him.

"I need to have a word with you," Vernon called, a deep glare twisting his face.

A big, heavy ball of dread settled on Drew's chest as he shut the driver's side door. "Would you like to come inside?" He motioned toward his front porch. "It will give us some privacy."

Vernon glanced back at Ervin's house and then nodded. "*Ya*, that's a *gut* idea."

Drew made a sweeping gesture toward the house. "After you." Then he followed Vernon up the steps, where he unlocked the door and let him inside. Bruce greeted them with a happy bark and wagging tail.

"Sit," Drew told his dog, and he obeyed.

Vernon glanced around the house.

"Would you like some coffee?" Drew offered.

"No." Vernon pinned him with a furious look. "I've told you to stay away from my daughter, but you haven't listened. You have no business destroying our family. You need to find a young woman in your community and leave ours alone!"

"Vernon." Drew held up his hands. "I love Cindy, and I'll take good care of her. I don't see why you have to disown her if she marries me. Why can't we all just be a family?"

"You don't seem to understand our culture." Vernon's glare continued to challenge Drew. "You need to respect how we live."

"I do respect it, but shouldn't family be more important than rules?" Drew gestured around the house. "Why should it matter that I'm not Amish?"

"Because that's what we believe. We live separate from the world, and our children are supposed to do the same. They're supposed to stay in the faith and pass our traditions along to their children." Vernon suddenly sank down onto the sofa and fingered his beard, as though the fire had just gone out of him.

Drew sat down on the chair across from him, confusion plaguing him. Why had Vernon's mood suddenly shifted?

"I lost my wife seven years ago." Vernon's demeanor reminded Drew of a wilting plant, desperate for water. "She had an accident. She fell down the basement stairs and broke her neck." His blue eyes shimmered as he stared past Drew at a wall.

"Cindy has told me the story. I'm so sorry for your loss."

"It was a complete shock." Vernon met Drew's gaze. "And I can't bear to lose another family member."

"I understand how you feel." Drew's throat suddenly felt like sandpaper. "I lost my parents and then the aunt who raised me. I have no family members left, so I know that pain all too well. But it doesn't have to be this way when Cindy marries me. That's what I'm trying to tell you."

"I know my Cindy is special. She has a big heart, and she's very giving." Vernon's eyes narrowed. "But you can't take her from us. I can't allow you to steal her from our community."

Drew felt as though he were one of the old, scratched records his mother used to play. The needle would skip and play the same musical phrase over and over. Was Vernon truly not listening? Or did he refuse to understand Drew's meaning?

"I'm not forcing her to marry me." Drew's words were slow and measured. "This is *her* choice. I've asked her several times if she's sure she wants to do this, and she keeps telling me yes."

"It's wrong." Vernon pointed to the floor. "Her leaving our community is unacceptable in my eyes *and* the bishop's."

Irritation spread over Drew's skin like static. He was tired of having the same argument over and over. He leaned forward. "I understand what you're saying, but I have a question for you."

"What?"

"Have you noticed that she hasn't joined the church yet?"

Vernon's mouth moved, but no sounds escaped.

"I think you need to take a step back and think about your daughter." Drew's body vibrated. "Maybe this is what she wants, and maybe this is what God has called her to do. Has that thought ever occurred to you?"

Vernon stood, his face flushing as red as a ripe tomato. His eyes narrowed. "I hope you can live with yourself after breaking up my family."

"She's still your family!" Drew exclaimed. "Just her last name will change, like Laura's last name changed when she married Allen."

"It's not the same!" Vernon snapped.

"It should be the same. She'll still be your daughter. She'll still have your blood running through her veins."

With the shake of his head, Vernon stood and marched out of Drew's house, the storm door slamming behind him.

Drew threw his keys across the room, where they smashed against the Sheetrock and left a dent before falling to the floor in a heap. Then he leaned forward and shoved both hands into his hair.

When a knock sounded, he stood and found Gertrude and Ervin on his porch.

"Hi." Drew pushed open the door. "Come in."

"Shouldn't you be at school?" Gertrude stepped into the house and rubbed Bruce's ear.

"Yeah, but Vernon came to talk to me." Drew gestured toward the kitchen. "Would you like some coffee?"

"No, thanks." Ervin pointed toward the porch. "We just saw Vernon leave, and he looked upset. We were wondering if everything is okay."

"Did Vernon find out about you and Cindy?" Gertrude looked concerned.

"You could say that." Drew folded his arms over his chest and leaned back on the wall. "Cindy and I are getting married, and Vernon is upset."

"What?" Gertrude asked.

"Are you joining the church?" Ervin asked.

"No." Drew motioned toward the sofa. "Would you like to have a seat, and I'll fill you in?"

Gertrude and Ervin sat down on the sofa, and Drew sat across from them while he shared how he had received Cindy's note from Gertrude and then proposed. He explained Cindy's family was anything but supportive, but Cindy insisted she wanted to move forward with their plans. Both Gertrude and Ervin listened with their eyes wide and their mouths slightly open.

"You do realize her family will basically disown her?" Ervin asked, and Drew nodded. "Life will be complicated, and you won't have her family as a support system."

"I know." Drew blew out a puff of air. "But she thinks I'm worth the risk, and I know she's worth the risk to me. I love her very much."

With God's help, their love would have to get them through this. Cindy's family wasn't giving up.

CHAPTER 23

"These brownie *kichlin* are the best," Sarah Jane gushed as they sat around the kitchen table later that morning. "You really outdid yourself, Laura." Then she turned to Cindy. "And this carrot *kuche* is *wunderbaar*. I love this recipe."

"*Danki*. I'm glad you like it." Cindy sipped her tea and then looked down at her mug. She'd enjoyed the time with her sisters while they baked, but thoughts of Drew lingered at the back of her mind.

She'd peeked out the window just as *Dat* had stalked up the driveway and into the barn, and her shoulders had tightened with a mixture of worry and dread. Had he gone to see Drew and forced him to change his mind about marrying her? The thought sent despair spiraling through her. What would she do if she lost Drew? But surely *Dat* would look happier if he had changed Drew's mind.

"Do you like the *kichlin*, Cindy?" Sarah Jane asked.

"*Ya*." Cindy's head popped up and she found her sisters and Florence studying her. "They're *appeditlich*."

"I hope you've had fun today, Cindy," Florence said. "Don't you enjoy spending time with your *schweschdere*?"

"Of course I do." Cindy moved her fingers over the edge of the table as everyone's eyes seemed to bore into her. This was it. Now they were going to take turns trying to convince her to not marry Drew.

"You haven't mentioned Drew today." Sarah Jane looked around the table. "Have you considered how much your life will change after you marry him? We won't be able to have days like this. Won't you miss our sisters' days?"

"What about church?" Florence added. "You won't be able to attend church with us unless you sit in the back with the visitors." She tapped her chin. "You went to that *Englisher* church yesterday. Wasn't the service very different from ours? Won't you miss our services?"

Cindy worked to keep a casual expression on her face as well as keep her surging frustration at bay. If she let them harangue her for a while, maybe they'd eventually give up and let her go upstairs to do her sewing. She'd rather be alone with her thoughts and prayers.

"It's not just about us, Cindy," Kayla said. "Our *kinner* need their *aenti*. Calvin and Alice want you in their lives. And if Jamie and I have more *kinner*, we'll want you to be there for them too."

"I won't be far." Cindy pointed to the window. "You're all talking like I'm moving to Florida or California. You can walk down the street to visit me anytime, Kayla. I can come and see you too. It's your choice if you disown me."

"You know that's not true," Florence said. "It's more complicated if you're an outsider. We can't include you the way we can now."

Cindy rubbed at the back of her neck as tension set into her muscles. How long before they stopped with the lecture? She was tired of their interventions. Couldn't they just accept her decision and let her move on?

"It won't be the same without you." Laura's lips trembled, and Cindy took a deep breath to hold back her own emotions.

"I need you in my life. How can I just let you leave the community without fighting for you to stay?"

"Because this is what I want." Cindy's voice sounded confident despite her sister's emotions. "You should respect my decision."

"But it's breaking my heart." Laura sniffed, and Kayla handed her a napkin to wipe her eyes and nose.

"I'll still be your *schweschder*," Cindy said. "You know that." She pushed her chair back and stood. "I know you all thought this whole sisters' day of baking and fellowship would convince me to change my mind, but it hasn't. I had fun with all of you, but I'm tired of being lectured. I need you to be *froh* for Drew and me."

Cindy lifted her mug and then pushed her plate of cookies to the middle of the table. "I have sewing I need to finish." She looked at Priscilla and Laura. "Be safe going home."

Then she set her mug in the sink and headed up the stairs, where she sat down at her sewing table and stared at her machine. Her sisters' words rolled over her, but she felt only resolve. She was going to marry Drew, and her family couldn't stop her.

"Cindy."

She spun to see Priscilla standing in her doorway. She pressed her hand to her chest and worked to slow her breathing.

"I'm sorry for startling you." Priscilla held up her hand. "I'm not here to lecture you. You've heard enough from everyone else." She stepped into the room. "I just want to tell you I don't want you to leave the community, but I know what it's like when love takes you by surprise. When I fell in love with your *bruder*, I had tried to put a cover over my heart and keep everyone out. Your *bruder* was the last man I ever wanted to trust, but he turned out to be one of God's greatest gifts to me."

Cindy nodded. "I know you two love each other very much."

Priscilla sat down on the chair across from her. "I just want you to really think about what it means to marry outside of the community. The *Englisher* world is much colder and lonelier than our community. You won't have the support system we have now. You won't have people looking after you the way you're used to. If you need help, you can't just go next door and ask your neighbor to help you." She paused and took a deep breath. "You know Ethan's *dat* abused me. You've seen my scars from his violence. When I was going through that, I had nowhere to turn for help. Is that the world where you want to raise your *kinner*?"

"Drew and I have each other. It won't be that way for us."

Priscilla looked down at the lap of her red dress and then back at Cindy. "Mark is really upset. He blames himself."

"Why would he blame himself for my decision?"

"He's one of your older *bruders*, and he feels like he wasn't as supportive as he should have been when your *mamm* died."

Cindy shook her head. "Tell him this has nothing to do with him."

"I will." Priscilla reached over and touched Cindy's hand. "I know everyone is angry, and they're all blaming Drew. But I can see the love in your eyes when you talk about him, and Mark can too. Just know you and Drew will always receive a welcome at our door."

Cindy smiled with appreciation, and she leaned forward and hugged her sister-in-law. "*Danki*, Priscilla."

"*Ich liebe dich*," Priscilla whispered.

"*Ich liebe dich, mei schweschder.*" Cindy closed her eyes as she hugged Priscilla. At least one of her sisters was on her side.

. . .

Cindy held Drew's hand as they walked through the church parking lot the following afternoon. Her head spun with all the events of the past twenty-four hours.

After her sisters left yesterday, she'd hidden in her sewing room and poured herself into her projects. When she came down for supper, *Dat* studied his plate while Florence and Sarah Jane talked on and on about the day.

After supper, Cindy helped clean up the kitchen before heading to Drew's house. Drew confirmed that *Dat had* visited him, and she was grateful that her father's words hadn't changed Drew's mind about their plans. She told Drew about her sisters' day and assured him that she, too, was still certain about their marriage.

That was when she told him she was tired of waiting and was ready to move forward, and that was how they'd wound up at the county courthouse to apply for a marriage license this morning. Now they were going to visit Pastor Ellen to ask her to marry them on Saturday. Excitement and nerves both buzzed all the way to her toes as they climbed the church steps.

"Don't be nervous, Cindy. You've already met Pastor Ellen."

"It's not that."

Drew stopped and faced her. "What is it? Have you changed your mind?"

"No." Cindy shook her head. "I'm just nervous about taking this step with you. Will you regret it?"

"Are you kidding?" He pressed a kiss to her cheek. "We've been all through this. You're my family. You're my future. This is what I want. I can feel how right it is in my bones."

Relief filled her. "That's how I feel."

"Good." He threaded his fingers with hers. "Let's go ask Pastor Ellen if she'll marry us."

Once inside, they walked down a hallway and stopped at a door that had Pastor Ellen Moore engraved on a plaque attached to it.

Drew knocked on the door.

"Come in."

They stepped inside. "Hello."

"Hi, Drew. Cindy." Pastor Ellen stood from behind a desk and beckoned them in. "Welcome. It's so good to see you again, Cindy. Have a seat." She pointed to the two chairs in front of the desk.

Cindy glanced around the office, taking in the shelves of books, decorative crosses adorning the walls, family photos, and a beautiful, colorful quilt sewn in a block pattern of reds, oranges, yellows, and pinks.

"How can I help?" Pastor Ellen asked.

"We want to know if you'll marry us." Drew looked at Cindy and smiled.

"Really?" Pastor Ellen leaned back in her chair as a smile turned up her lips.

"We applied for our marriage license today," Drew said, "and we'd like to know if we could have a small wedding here on Saturday, with you officiating."

Pastor Ellen focused her kind brown eyes on Cindy. "What does your family think about your plans to marry Drew?"

"They're not happy," Cindy said. "They've been trying to talk me out of it."

"Won't you be shunned if you marry an outsider?" Pastor Ellen's question was gentle.

Cindy shook her head. "I'm not a baptized member of the Amish church, so I won't be shunned. But my family won't include me in family functions anymore. I'll be treated as an outsider, which is almost like being shunned."

Pastor Ellen nodded slowly as if contemplating Cindy's words. "How do you feel about that?"

Cindy folded her hands in her lap and waited for words to come. "It hurts that they could just dismiss me, as if my feelings and my dreams don't matter." Her voice was strong as confidence surged through her. "I've tried to explain that I love Drew, and that he's my future. But all they've done is try to convince me to stay, to join the church and find an Amish man to marry me and take care of me. That's not what I want. I want true love like my siblings have found with their spouses." She turned to Drew and smiled. "And I've found that in Drew. This is what I want. I want a life and a future with the man I love." She turned back to the pastor. "And that's why we're here today."

"How old are you?" Pastor Ellen asked.

"Twenty-four," Cindy said.

"Don't most join the Amish church when they're teenagers?" Pastor Ellen asked.

Cindy nodded. "Yes, that's true. My siblings did."

"May I ask why you didn't?"

Cindy paused, trying to sift through her swirling thoughts. "When all my friends were baptized, I realized I wasn't ready to join the church. Then my mother died unexpectedly when I was seventeen, and I felt even more disconnected from the church and my community. I witnessed her death and blamed myself for a long time. I also found myself doubting God's will when he took her, and that's a sin in our religion."

She paused again to take a deep breath. "I couldn't admit my doubt to my siblings or my father. I've also wrestled with confusion for a long time because my father and siblings moved on so easily when I couldn't. When my father remarried quickly, and then my siblings married as well, I felt as if they'd all left me behind. I've felt like an outsider in my own home and my own congregation."

Cindy looked at Drew beside her. "I didn't feel like I'd found my home until I met Drew." She turned back to Pastor Ellen. "We're ready to start a life together, and we'd like you to help us begin that journey."

"I do have one more question," Pastor Ellen said. "You say you feel disconnected from your community and you're not ready to be baptized into the Amish church. Still, you dress like an Amish person. Are you certain you want to break from that community?"

Cindy shrugged. "I'm just comfortable in these clothes. I've never worn anything else."

"That makes sense." Pastor Ellen nodded. "Will your family come to the wedding?"

Cindy shook her head. "I doubt it."

"It will most likely just be us and you." Drew leaned forward in his chair. "Will that work?"

"Of course. We'll need a witness, but my husband will be glad to stand with you." Pastor Ellen seemed to study Cindy. "You feel confident that this is the decision you want to make? I just want to be certain this church feels enough like home to you. A wedding is one of the special moments in any woman's life. Choosing a place to worship is important too."

"I've prayed over and over, and when I ask God if marrying Drew is the path he wants me to follow, my feelings for Drew have become stronger. I want to be wherever Drew is, and I felt comfortable visiting your service here. So yes, you can be certain."

Cindy took Drew's hand in hers as they smiled at each other. "I believe in my heart that God chose you for me, Drew. That's why I'll always pray my family will someday accept you."

Drew leaned over and kissed Cindy's forehead. "I love you," he whispered.

Cindy turned back to Pastor Ellen. "Will you marry us?"

The pastor nodded. "I will, but first I want you both to truly think about this. Consider the impact it will have on Cindy's family." The pastor focused on Cindy once again. "You sound like you're close to your family. Just consider how you'll feel when they pull away from you. I know you love Drew, but will that love be enough to sustain you when you lose your siblings and your father?"

"Yes. With God's help, it will." Her throat felt so tight with emotion that she almost couldn't smile as she nodded.

"All right. I'll see you Saturday. We have your phone number here, Drew, and I'll call you tomorrow about details." Pastor Ellen stood and shook their hands before they walked out of her office.

Cindy stared out the window of the pickup truck as they drove back to Drew's house. Pastor Ellen's words twirled through her mind.

I know you love Drew, but will that love be enough to sustain you when you lose your siblings and your father?

Cindy pushed her fingers against her forehead as the words echoed again and again.

But no, she couldn't allow anyone or anything to stop her from marrying Drew! This was her future. This was the path God had chosen for her.

"Cindy." Drew turned toward her. "We don't have to do this so quickly. We can continue to get to know each other, and you can talk more to your family."

"No." Cindy shook her head as renewed conviction surged through her. "This is what I want."

"How will you break the news to them?"

"I'll tell them tonight at supper. I'll let Florence, Sarah Jane, and *Dat* know we're getting married on Saturday and that we'd like them to come. Maybe I can change their minds."

She put her hand in his and gave a gentle squeeze. "We're in this together—with or without my family or anyone else."

He nodded. "Right."

"Look at me." She ran her thumb along his jawline. "You believe in us, right?"

His blue eyes suddenly grew fierce. "Yes, I do. I'll always believe in us."

"Then stop doubting me when I say this is what I want." She touched her chest. "You have my heart. You're the person I want to spend the rest of my life with. I want to build a life with you, have a home with you, and raise a family with you. That's what you want with me, right?"

Drew pulled to the side of the road, then turned off the engine and in one fluid motion reached his arms around her, leaned over, and kissed her. She melted into him, closing her eyes and savoring the feeling of his lips against hers, losing herself in him.

When he shifted away from her, she shivered at the loss of his touch.

"I love you, Cindy," he whispered. "No matter what."

• • •

Conversation swirled around the kitchen table as Cindy stared at her plate filled with pot roast and carrots. She mentally practiced her announcement on a loop. Now was the time to speak the words, but was she strong enough to utter them?

Yes. Yes, she was. This was her decision, and her family should support her.

"I'm getting married on Saturday," she blurted, and all the conversation stopped. *Dat*, Florence, and Sarah Jane focused their shocked stares on her. "Drew and I went down to the county courthouse today and applied for our marriage license. After that, we met with Drew's pastor at the Bird-in-Hand Community Church. She's really sweet. Her name is Pastor Ellen. I was surprised to meet a female pastor, but I really like her. Anyway, Pastor Ellen is going to marry us on Saturday." The words flew out of her mouth like a horse galloping in the back pasture. "We'd be honored if you joined us."

She stopped speaking as her breath came in short bursts. As she waited for her family to respond, a suffocating silence hung over the kitchen. All three of them continued to stare at her, their judgmental eyes causing her to squirm in her chair.

Then *Dat*'s face twisted into an angry frown, and suddenly he pushed his chair back, stood, and marched into the mudroom. The back door slammed shut.

Florence jumped up, and then footfalls sounded through the mudroom before the back door opened again. "Vernon! Wait!" Cindy heard the door close behind her.

Cindy looked at Sarah Jane, who glared and shook her head as a furious scowl marred her face. "You're ruining this family. I hope you're *froh*." Then she stood and gathered the plates filled with their uneaten supper. But she only set them on the counter before stalking up the stairs and slamming the door to her room.

A lump the size of a walnut swelled in Cindy's throat as her hopes of convincing her family to bless her marriage crumbled. Not only had they not done so, but she'd finally lost them.

The sound of shutting doors echoed in her heart.

CHAPTER 24

Cindy surveyed the sea of boxes she'd packed during the past four evenings. All her favorite possessions were ready to be transported to Drew's house for her new life.

Tomorrow she would be married and then sleep in a new bed. She would become a wife and leave the Amish world behind her. Everything would change, including her name. Heat traveled in slow waves across her face and chest.

"I cannot believe you're going through with this."

Cindy turned toward Florence as she stood in the doorway and frowned. "Did you think I would change my mind?"

"I hoped and prayed you would." Florence shook her head and folded her arms over her middle. "Your *dat* did too. He's been positively crushed. He keeps telling me he let down your *mamm* by not stopping you from seeing that *Englisher*. He blames himself."

Anger sparked in Cindy. "Why does everybody think it's their fault that I made this decision? It's no one's fault. This is what I chose all by myself, and I'm not going to change my mind. What hurts the most is that none of you will support me or be happy for me."

Florence shook her head. "I can't give you my support or my blessing, and neither can your *dat*."

"How about your love?" Cindy heard her voice wobble.

"You'll always have my love, but you won't have my blessing until you—and Drew, if you've married him—join the church." Florence glanced down at the boxes and then back up at Cindy. "I don't understand how you can just leave your community and all your Amish values behind as if they mean nothing."

Cindy gasped as Florence's words stabbed her heart.

With the shake of her head, Florence turned and started down the hallway, and then her footsteps echoed in the stairwell.

Cindy sat down on her bed, reached into the closest box, and pulled out a beautiful lap quilt. It was the last quilt *Mamm* had made for her before she passed away. She'd been sixteen. The quilt featured a gorgeous star in the center, fashioned out of stunning shades of pink and gray, Cindy's favorite color combination.

She ran her fingers over the stitches as memories washed over her. She tried to recall her mother's sweet voice, her contagious laugh, her gorgeous smile, and her sage advice.

Closing her eyes, she conjured an image of her mother. She could see *Mamm* standing at the kitchen counter, talking and smiling while they washed dishes together. *Mamm* would listen as Cindy and Laura shared a story about one of their friends. She would offer advice if they had a problem they couldn't solve on their own.

But would *Mamm* have accepted Drew into their family? Would she bless Cindy's marriage? Would she have agreed to come to the church tomorrow to witness the ceremony?

Probably not.

"I miss you," Cindy whispered as her heart twisted. "I miss you so much, *Mamm*." She sniffed and ran her fingers over the fabric, so lovingly pieced by her mother. "If only you were

here to listen to me. I know you'd try to understand how I feel
about Drew. Maybe you'd even agree to have a civil conversation with him. If you were here, I know it wouldn't be quite
so painful. I miss you, *Mamm*," she repeated. "I miss you so
much it hurts."

Cindy hugged the quilt to her chest and then flopped back
on her bed as she opened her heart to God.

*Please, God, help me navigate my new life with Drew. Bless our
marriage, and keep me strong as my family turns against me.
Please soften their hearts toward my decision, as well as toward
Drew.*

Rolling to her side, Cindy touched the cross Drew had given
her, and then she closed her eyes as still more tears began to
fall.

. . .

Happiness exploded through Drew as he stood clad in his only
suit at the front of the church the following morning. All his
dreams were coming true at this moment, and he felt as if he
were dreaming. But he wasn't. He was marrying the love of his
life!

Cindy was stunningly beautiful as she held the bouquet of
pink roses he'd picked up for her yesterday. The roses just happened to match the pink dress she wore along with a white
apron and her prayer covering. She gave him another shy smile,
and her blue eyes sparkled as her cheeks flushed pink as well.

When the pastor began to speak, Drew forced his attention
away from his bride and back to her.

"Do you, Drew Taylor Collins, take Cindy Emma Riehl to be
your lawfully wedded wife, to have and to hold, from this day

forward, for better, for worse, for richer, for poorer, in sickness and in health, until death do you part? If so, answer 'I do,'" Pastor Ellen said.

"I do." Drew's words sounded as confident as he felt as they echoed throughout the empty sanctuary.

Pastor Ellen smiled and then turned to Cindy. "And do you, Cindy Emma Riehl, take Drew Taylor Collins to be your lawfully wedded husband, to have and to hold, from this day forward, for better, for worse, for richer, for poorer, in sickness and in health, until death do you part? If so, answer 'I do.'"

"I do." Cindy seemed to tremble as she said the words.

"Then by the power vested in me by the Commonwealth of Pennsylvania, I now pronounce you husband and wife." Pastor Ellen turned to Drew. "You may now kiss your bride."

Drew pulled Cindy to him and brushed his lips over hers. The contact sent liquid heat shooting from his head to his toes.

Claps sounded from the pews behind them. Drew had almost forgotten Pastor Ellen's husband, Grayson, had joined them as a witness to their ceremony. He was their only attendee, which had nearly crushed Drew's heart. He had prayed Cindy's family would change their minds and surprise Cindy by appearing at the church today, but they'd stuck to their word and refused to bless their marriage.

"I'd like to offer one last prayer before we start our celebration," Pastor Ellen said, and Drew turned his attention back to her. "Let us pray."

Drew entwined his fingers with Cindy's, bowed his head, and closed his eyes.

"Dear Lord," Pastor Ellen began, "we ask you to bless Drew and Cindy as they begin their journey together as husband and wife. Be there with them as they face the challenges of their new life, and guide them as they work to build their future. In Jesus's holy name. Amen."

Drew opened his eyes and glanced over at Cindy as she stared up in the direction of the cross. He longed to read her thoughts.

"So, Mr. and Mrs. Collins," Pastor Ellen began, "Grayson and I have a surprise for you."

"A surprise?" Cindy's eyes seemed to sparkle with curiosity.

"Yes." Pastor Ellen set down the little book she'd held during the ceremony and rubbed her hands together. "We planned a little party for you. We have a cake and some sparkling cider for you in the fellowship hall."

"You do?" Cindy grinned as she turned to Drew. "This is so kind of you."

"It is." Drew nodded at Pastor Ellen. "Thank you."

"You're welcome." Pastor Ellen made a sweeping gesture toward the door. "Let's go celebrate."

Drew held Cindy's hand as they made their way down the hallway toward the fellowship hall.

"Wait," Pastor Ellen called. "Let me announce you before you walk inside."

"Announce us?" Cindy looked at Drew. "Why would she announce us?"

"I don't know." Drew shrugged.

Pastor Ellen stepped through the door and said, "It is my honor to present Mr. and Mrs. Drew Collins."

Then a chorus of claps erupted from inside the hall.

"Who's here?" Cindy asked.

"I have no idea," Drew said.

He led Cindy into the hall and found a group of friends from church applauding while standing around a table. On it was a three-tiered wedding cake adorned with a topper featuring a bride and groom, along with plastic wineglasses, plates, and napkins. Someone snapped a photo with a camera.

"I hope it's okay that I invited some of your friends from church to help us celebrate today," Pastor Ellen said.

"That was very thoughtful of you," Drew said as appreciation whipped through him. "Thank you so much."

He turned to Cindy, and her smile widened as she squeezed his hand. Her beautiful face glowed with pure elation, and his heart warmed. This wedding was a dream come true, and he was so grateful for his church family. He pulled on her hand, towing her to him.

"I'm so thankful you married me," he whispered.

"I am too. I'm excited to be Mrs. Drew Collins. Thank you for asking me to be your wife." She traced his jawline with the tip of her finger. "Today is perfect."

"Toast!" someone called.

A woman from the church started handing out plastic wineglasses filled with sparkling cider.

Drew turned to Pastor Ellen. "I don't have a best man. Am I supposed to make the toast?"

"No." Pastor Ellen pointed toward her husband, who stood by the cake. "I took care of that for you."

"Good morning," Grayson said, and everyone repeated it back to him. "I'm honored to stand before you today to toast Mr. and Mrs. Collins." He held up his glass. "I've known Drew since he started attending here, and Ellen and I have always thought he's a fine young man. We're delighted he met Cindy and that they're now starting their new life together. I'd like to wish them happiness, love, and a house full of children."

Grayson lifted his glass higher. "Here's to Drew and Cindy."

"Hear, hear!" a few people called.

Drew turned to Cindy beside him and held up his glass. "To us."

"To us," she echoed, her eyes sparkling as her smile brightened like the afternoon sun.

They intertwined their arms and then sipped the sweet cider. A camera flashed again.

"Let's cut the cake," someone else called.

Drew looked at Cindy. "The tradition is that we cut the cake and feed it to each other. Do you want to do it?"

She gave a little laugh and shrugged. "Sure."

Drew moved to the cake, cut a piece, and then held it up to her. She took a bite, and everyone cheered. She cut a piece for Drew to take a bite, and when he did the small crowd of well-wishers cheered again. Drew savored the delectable white cake with almond flavoring. Then one of the women cut the rest of the cake and handed out pieces.

"This turned out beautifully," Cindy said as they ate their cake. "I'm so honored and excited that our church family wanted to celebrate with us."

"I am too. It truly is the perfect wedding." Drew looked over at Pastor Ellen as she joined them. "Thank you for everything."

"Yes," Cindy said. "Thank you. This was more than I could have ever imagined. I'm so happy we were able to celebrate our new life with friends."

"You're welcome." Pastor Ellen smiled. "I couldn't let your wedding pass without a celebration."

Drew smiled, pushing away the feeling that Cindy would one day look back and grieve her family's abandonment on such a special occasion.

. . .

"Everything was wonderful," Cindy said as Drew parked the pickup truck in their driveway later that afternoon.

"It was." He pointed to the stack of envelopes in her lap. "I can't believe they gave us gifts too."

"I know. This is so generous." She smiled over at him. "The man who took photos said he's going to email them to you. I guess you can get them printed, right?"

"Right. I can make a little wedding album for us to remember today."

"I would love that." Cindy felt her smile fade as the reality of what she had to do settled over her.

"What's wrong?" Drew touched her hand.

"We still have to go get my things from *mei dat's haus*." She looked toward the road. "It's going to be difficult."

"No, it won't." He pushed open his door. "Let me get out of this suit, and then we'll go do it."

She remained in the truck as he started toward the house.

He reached the porch and then spun to face her. "Aren't you coming inside?"

"*Ya.*" She pushed the door open, and a mixture of excitement and anxiety bogged down her steps as she made her way to the porch of what was now her home.

He unlocked the door, and Bruce bounded toward them, barking and wagging his tail as he walked in circles around them.

She leaned over to pet Bruce and then yelped as Drew swept her into his arms.

"What are you doing?" she squeaked through her giggles.

"I'm carrying you over the threshold. That's what new

husbands are supposed to do with their wives." He pulled the door open, stepped over the threshold, and then set her on her feet as she giggled again. "Welcome home, Mrs. Collins."

"Thank you." She leaned against his chest, and he kissed her, sending an explosion of fire through her veins.

He studied her and then stepped back. "Let me go get changed. We'll get your things, and then we can celebrate our new life."

As he disappeared into the back bedroom, Cindy set the stack of greeting cards filled with checks and gift cards on the kitchen table and then glanced around the house. Excitement danced in her chest. This was real. It was happening! This was now her home.

Drew appeared behind her dressed in jeans and a black T-shirt. "Are you ready?"

Cindy folded her hands. "I guess so."

"Come on. We'll get your things and then get you settled. I'll be with you the entire time." He took her hands in his.

She pulled strength from the feel of his warm skin against hers. She could do anything with Drew by her side.

. . .

Cindy stepped into the kitchen with Drew standing close behind her. Her heart began to race when she found her father, Florence, Jamie, and Sarah Jane all sitting at the table.

"What are you doing here?" *Dat*'s voice bellowed as he seemed to point his furious glare at Drew.

"We're here for my things," Cindy said, her voice sounding more confident than she felt. "We were married this morning."

Dat grunted as Jamie, Florence, and Sarah Jane studied the kitchen table with downcast eyes.

"Come on. Everything is boxed up and ready to go." Cindy took Drew's hand in hers and walked past her family to the stairs.

They climbed the steps together and entered her bedroom, where the sea of boxes waited for them.

She turned to Drew and touched his chest. "I'm sure they aren't going to help us. We'll just do the best we can to load them up quickly and then get out of here."

"I understand." He touched her shoulder and seemed to look deep into her eyes. "Are you all right?"

"*Ya.*" She nodded. "Let's just get my things and leave."

"Right." Drew grabbed two boxes, balanced one on top of the other, and started for the stairs.

Cindy followed behind him with another box. They hurried through the kitchen, where her family still sat at the table, ignoring them. They made ten trips up and down the stairs before her boxes, bags, sewing machine, and sewing table and chair were all loaded in the back of Drew's truck.

Cindy looked at the house and hugged her arms to her chest.

"Talk to me." Drew's breath was warm on her ear as he stood behind her.

"I was just hoping they would at least say good-bye." She hated the trembling thread of sadness in her voice.

"I can tell they love you and that they'll miss you, but I'm sorry they can't express how they feel." He wrapped his arms around her waist and pulled her to him. "I'm here for you. You can tell me how you feel, and I'll listen. I'll be the shoulder you can cry on anytime."

She looked up at him. "Thank you."

"You're welcome, Mrs. Collins."

She laughed and then spun toward him. "Let's go home."

"Yes." He smiled. "*Our* home."

She climbed into the truck, and they made the short trip back to his house.

Later, after she'd put the last box into the bedroom she planned to make a sewing room, she sat down and touched her machine. Confusion bit at her heels. She had Drew now, but she was still floating between two worlds—the Amish and the *English*.

"Hey."

She looked up at her handsome husband as he leaned against the doorframe.

"What's going on in that pretty head of yours?"

"I'm confused." She gestured toward her dress. "I don't know how to dress. I can't imagine giving up my prayer covering because it's part of who I am and part of my history. I don't know if I should stop using the Amish words I'm used to saying, or not. I'm not Amish now, but I still have parts of me that feel Amish. I'm your wife, but you're not Amish, and I'm not quite *English*. Who am I now? Where do I fit into this world?"

He stepped into the room and sat down on a stool beside her. "You're Cindy Emma Collins, and you're my wife." He took her hands in his. "You should dress any way that makes you feel comfortable. You should use any words you'd like . . . but if you speak Pennsylvania Dutch, you're not allowed to mutter words behind my back that I don't understand."

She laughed. "I promise I'll translate unless I'm angry with you."

"That's perfect." He stood and lifted her to her feet. "We don't have to figure all this out right now. We'll figure it out as we go along." He placed his hands on either side of her face. "All I know is I'm the happiest man on the planet because you're my wife, and forever starts right now."

Drew leaned down and gently touched his lips to hers, making heat thrum through her veins. He deepened the kiss, sending her senses spinning.

Then he picked her up and carried her to the master bedroom.

When Bruce barked and raced after them, Drew shushed him and shooed him away before setting her down and shutting the door.

Drew turned toward her, and the intensity in his blue eyes sent more heat into her veins.

"I love you, Cindy." His voice was low as he wrapped his arms around her waist. "I love you with all my heart."

"I love you too."

He leaned down, and his lips crashed into hers. Her heart hammered in her chest as she looped her arms around his neck and pulled him in closer.

He deepened the kiss, and her body flushed with pure pleasure. She closed her eyes and savored the feel of his mouth against hers as passion exploded around them like summer lightning. She felt her body relax as she enjoyed the love pouring from her new husband.

This was where her heart belonged. Her home was here with Drew.

CHAPTER 25

"Happy Thanksgiving," Drew said as he sat across from Cindy at their kitchen table a month later.

"Happy Thanksgiving," she sang in response as she scooped a pile of mashed potatoes onto her plate.

When he looked at the other food she'd prepared—turkey and stuffing, green bean casserole, and egg noodles—his stomach growled with delight.

"Everything looks and smells amazing. Thank you," he told her.

"You're welcome."

"Are Gertrude and Ervin stopping by later?" he asked.

"No." She lifted her glass of water. "They're visiting cousins out in Strasburg. They won't be back until later this evening." She set her glass on the table and then sliced her canned cranberry sauce before popping some into her mouth.

"Cindy." He reached over and touched her hand. "How do you feel? This is your first holiday without your family."

"I'm okay." She looked up at him. Her expression remained serene, yet he didn't doubt her true feelings. "I keep thinking my father or my sisters will come surprise me. They haven't stopped by once." She sighed. "It's as if I never existed. I knew this was going to happen, but I kept thinking maybe they would accept my decision despite the community rules once I was married and out of the house."

"I'm sorry." He gave her hand a gentle squeeze. "I'm sure they miss you just as much as you miss them." A long rope of guilt coiled in his gut and tightened, the guilt that had never gone away. "Would you like to go visit them? I'll go with you."

"No." She shook her head. "If they can't come to see me, then why should I go see them?"

"Is there anything I can do?"

She looked over at him, and her lips twitched. "You can tell me this is the best turkey you've ever had."

He grinned. "That I can do, because it's the truth."

She gave a little laugh and then scooped a forkful of mashed potatoes into her mouth.

While they ate, Drew racked his brain for a solution that would take away her pain. The past month had been wonderful as he and Cindy had settled into a routine. He attended classes and worked on the farm while she sewed for customers— almost all of them non-Amish—cooked, and kept their household running.

They were a couple, a team, and he cherished every moment with her, but he still felt guilty for what their marriage was doing to her. Although she put forth a brave face, he knew she missed her family, and he yearned to help repair the rift he'd created for all the Riehls.

When they'd finished their Thanksgiving dinner, he helped carry the leftover food and dishes to the kitchen sink.

"Why don't you go rest?" he asked as he began to fill the sink with hot water.

"What?" She turned toward him, her pretty nose wrinkled and her brow furrowed.

"You go rest, and I'll wash the dishes."

"No." She gestured around the kitchen, littered with dirtied pans and platters. "You're not going to clean this up yourself. It's not right."

"I don't mind. You did all the work of making the meal." He scraped a plate and then dropped it into the water where he'd already added soap.

"But you took care of Ervin's animals and the milking this morning. That's work too." She made a dismissive gesture. "I've got this. You go sit on the sofa and work on your school project."

He wrapped his arms around her waist and pulled her close. "How about we compromise and work together? And then we can work on that puzzle we started earlier this week. I can do schoolwork later."

She smiled up at him. "I'll agree to that."

"Good." As he kissed the top of her head, Drew wondered what he would do if his wife ever regretted marrying him. If she didn't experience some level of reconciliation with her family soon, how could she not?

. . .

Later that evening, Cindy climbed into bed beside Drew and pulled the covers up to her neck as she snuggled down with her back facing him. She yawned and adjusted her pillow as all the work and preparation for the Thanksgiving meal caught up with her, sucking her strength and leaving exhaustion in its place.

While she and Drew had worked on their puzzle together and then later rested on the sofa this afternoon, she'd imagined her family gathered at her father's house, enjoying the holiday with the people they loved most. She had hoped a few of them would stop by later to wish her and Drew a happy Thanksgiving. But they hadn't.

Had they even thought of her? Had anyone mentioned her name or wondered how she was doing?

Sadness welled up in her chest, but she breathed past it. She loved her life with Drew, and her family's decision to forget her wouldn't ruin that.

Drew rolled over and wrapped his arms around her waist before pulling her against him. "Happy Thanksgiving."

"Happy Thanksgiving," she whispered back through the dark.

"Thank you for an amazing meal." His breath was warm on her neck.

"You're welcome." She closed her eyes.

He held her close and kissed her cheek. Soon his breathing changed, and his body relaxed. He'd fallen asleep.

Her thoughts turned back to her family. Laura would be having her baby in a few weeks. Would anyone let her know when her baby was born? Would she be invited over to see the little one?

Cindy squeezed her eyes shut as a prayer filled her mind.

God, I miss my family, and I long to have them in my life. I love Drew, and I'm happy with him, but I've realized how much I need my family too. Please bring them back to me. Please soften their hearts toward Drew and me. Help us all be a family together.

She listened to her husband's breathing and hoped sleep would soon take her too.

. . .

Drew stepped out of Ervin's barn the following morning and mopped sweat from his brow. While he'd fed the animals and mucked the stalls, he recalled the guilt he'd felt during their

Thanksgiving meal yesterday. He loved his wife deeply, and he knew how close she'd been with her siblings and father. Drew had single-handedly ruined her relationship with the most important people in her life when he married her. He still feared someday she would regret marrying him, and for her sake, he almost regretted proposing to her. Perhaps she would have been better off without him.

He rubbed the stubble on his chin as he looked out toward the street. He couldn't shake the feeling that he could do something to bridge the great chasm their marriage had caused between Cindy and her family. But what?

When an idea struck, he started walking down the driveway. He hoped Cindy was busy working on one of her projects in the sewing room and wouldn't peek out the window to see him leaving.

Drew made his way to the street and then to her father's driveway. Apprehension tightened the muscles in his back as he continued toward the house.

When Jamie emerged from the barn, Drew sighed with relief. He'd hoped to have a chance to talk to Jamie and not Vernon, reasoning Jamie might be more apt to listen to him.

Jamie met his gaze and froze, his expression blank. He glanced toward his father's house and then started down the path toward him.

"Good morning," Drew called, hoping to keep his voice even despite his growing feelings of resentment toward the Riehl family. "I was hoping to talk to you for a few minutes."

"Is my sister all right?" Jamie asked, concern written on his face.

"Yes and no." Drew folded his arms over his zippered sweatshirt.

"What do you mean?"

Drew tilted his head. "We're happy together and we're building a good life. But I know she misses her family. Have any of you considered that she might want to see you? *Need* to see you?"

Jamie shook his head. "She made the choice to leave the community, and that means we can't include her the way we used to."

"Come on, Jamie. Just for one minute consider what would have happened if you'd fallen in love with Kayla and she wasn't Amish. How would you feel if you were torn between your wife and your family? Wouldn't it hurt if your siblings turned their backs on you?"

Jamie blew out a deep sigh and glanced toward his father's house again, and then he leveled his gaze with Drew's. "Look, we do miss her. Laura and Mark were just talking about her yesterday during Thanksgiving dinner. They said our family isn't complete without her. Laura cried. But *Dat* . . ."

"Cindy feels the same way without all of you. She keeps hoping some of you will come visit her." Drew took a step toward him. "Can't you try to make your father understand it's acceptable to see Cindy occasionally? Maybe you and Kayla could come over for supper or something."

Jamie cringed. "I don't know. My father follows the bishop's rules."

"You're the oldest. You must have some influence in your family. Just try to talk to him. Tell him Cindy misses you all and you miss her. See if you can come to some sort of compromise."

"All right." Jamie nodded. "I'll see what I can do."

"Thank you!" Drew shook his hand as hope took seed in his soul. "That's all I ask." He started down the driveway with a spring in his step.

"Drew!"

Drew spun to face him.

"Remember what I said earlier. If you joined the church, we could all be a family."

Drew felt his jaw set. "I'll keep that in mind, but I don't think that's what Cindy wants."

Jamie shrugged. "It would solve a lot of problems, and it would bring us all together."

"I understand." Drew waved and then hurried down the driveway as he asked God to help Jamie convince his father to reach out to Cindy—and show her he still loved her.

. . .

Cindy shivered and hugged her coat to her chest as she stepped into the grocery store and grabbed a shopping cart nearly two weeks later. When December made its appearance in Lancaster County, it brought winter temperatures.

She steered the cart down the aisle with spices as she pulled her shopping list from her pocket. She was looking for cinnamon when she heard someone call her name.

Cindy smiled as Priscilla steered her cart over to her. "Priscilla!" She stepped around her own cart and hugged her. "How are you?"

"I'm well." Priscilla touched Cindy's arm. "You look great. How are you?"

"*Gut.*" Questions swarmed Cindy's mind. "How are Ethan and Annie and Adam?"

"They're all great." Priscilla's smile was warm. "The *zwilling-bopplin* are getting so big. They're with *mei mamm* today because it's so difficult for me to shop with them."

Tears filled Cindy's eyes as she pictured her niece and nephews. "I miss them."

Priscilla opened her mouth, but then closed it.

"What?" Cindy asked. "Is everyone all right?"

"*Ya.*" Priscilla's smile faded. "Laura had her *boppli* last week."

"She did?" Disappointment and anger stirred in Cindy's belly. "Why didn't anyone tell me?"

"I don't know." Priscilla touched Cindy's arm. "I wanted to, but Mark insisted I shouldn't."

The hurt boiled over, and Cindy wiped away tears. "What did she have?"

"A *bu.* They named him Allen Junior. Allen is so *froh.* He finally has his *sohn.*" Priscilla rubbed Cindy's arm. "I knew you'd want to know, but you know how it is."

Pain squeezed at Cindy's heart, and she tried to breathe past it. Had Gertrude known and not told her? No, she couldn't believe that. She and Ervin were the one Amish couple who hadn't treated her as though she were shunned.

"How are you doing? How's Drew?" Priscilla asked.

"We're *gut.*" Cindy tried to smile, but it felt more like a grimace. "I just miss everyone. I thought maybe *Dat* would reach out to me, but it's as though I never existed."

"No." Priscilla shook her head. "We all miss you. It's just that we're bound by the rules of the community. We'll always love you. You're our *schweschder.*" She looked toward the end of the aisle. "I need to go. My driver will be here soon. You take care."

"*Ya.* You too. Tell the *zwillingbopplin* and Ethan that I love them. Mark too." Cindy hugged her again, and her heart broke. She was missing so much.

. . .

Cindy put the last of the groceries into a cabinet as her conversation with Priscilla rolled through her mind. She'd kept her disappointment and hurt to herself as she and Drew had driven back to the house and as he helped her carry the bags into the house. But the conversation had lingered in the back of her mind, taunting her.

"So." Drew appeared and leaned on the counter beside her. "It's my night to cook. What do you want for supper?"

"Whatever you want to make." Cindy set the container of cinnamon in the cabinet with the rest of the spices.

"Did something happen today?" Drew touched her arm. "You've been quiet since we left the grocery store."

She turned to face him. "I ran into Priscilla there. She told me the family all miss me, but she also said Laura had her baby last week. No one bothered to tell me." Her lips trembled, but she forced back tears.

"Oh no." Drew pulled her against his chest and rubbed her back. "I'm so sorry. I had hoped my talk with Jamie would change things."

"What?" She stepped back from him and stared. "You talked to Jamie?"

"Yeah." Drew frowned.

"When?"

"The day after Thanksgiving." He rested his hip against the counter. "I asked him to try to convince your father to at least let some of the family visit you."

"Why didn't you tell me?" She searched his eyes for an explanation. "I thought we decided not to keep secrets from each other. You promised me."

"I'm sorry I kept this from you, but I didn't want you to be disappointed if my effort didn't help." His shoulders hunched.

"I'm sorry it didn't work." He brightened a bit. "Jamie did say Laura and Mark both talked about you on Thanksgiving. Laura especially missed you. She cried. I should have told you that sooner."

"She did?" But then she shook her head. "None of this is your fault, and you didn't do anything wrong. I'm glad I wasn't completely forgotten that day. But I still don't understand how they can turn their backs on me. Laura said she wanted me to be part of her baby's life, but she couldn't even call me to tell me she and Allen have a son."

"Come here." Drew pulled her against him once again. "Laura must feel stuck because of the rules."

She spoke into his chest. "But she's my sister. The rules shouldn't matter to her."

"I'm sorry your family is still hurting you." He kissed the top of her prayer covering. "You must wish we'd never married. If I hadn't proposed to you, you wouldn't be missing out on things like your new nephew. I ruined your life." The regret in his voice was palpable.

"No." She looked up at him. "I never regret that. You're the greatest blessing in my life." She stood on her tiptoes and kissed him. "Don't forget that."

"I'm so grateful you think so." Then he pulled her closer for a hug.

. . .

Later that evening, Cindy slipped into the bathroom and locked the door. She pulled the package out of her purse and read the instructions. Then she opened the package and lifted the lid on the commode.

Cindy held her breath as she followed the instructions and then stared down at the stick. When the second blue line appeared, she bit back a squeal. This was the best news she could have!

It would be difficult, but she'd wait to surprise Drew with her news on Christmas Day—the best Christmas gift ever!

CHAPTER 26

Drew looked out from the barn's double doorway a week later as an Amish woman he didn't recognize got out of a van and walked up the driveway toward his house. He smiled and waved, and she returned the gesture before mounting the porch steps and knocking on the front door.

When Cindy appeared, he took in her beautiful smile as she welcomed the guest. She was the loveliest woman he'd ever known. Some days he had a difficult time believing she was his wife.

They'd been married for nearly two months, and every day he prayed that God would reveal a way for her family to welcome her back. He longed for the day her father would appear at their door with a smile and a hug for his youngest child, reuniting the Riehl family and making Cindy feel important to them again.

Until then, was his love enough?

. . .

"How are you, Lydia?" Cindy asked the Amish woman as she stepped into her house.

"I'm well." Lydia smiled. "Were you able to repair my quilt?"

"*Ya*, of course." She motioned for Lydia to follow her into her sewing room. "I have it back here. I finished all the stitching and then remade the hem." She took the lone star-patterned quilt out of her stack of sewing projects and held it up for Lydia to see. "What do you think?"

"Oh, Cindy. You're still the best seamstress I know. You're just as *gut* as your *mamm* was." Lydia ran her hand over the quilt.

Cindy's smile faded at the mention of her mother, but she was grateful for the compliment. "*Danki.*"

Lydia handed her a stack of bills. "It's perfect." She took the quilt and then seemed to study Cindy, her brown eyes making her self-conscious. "You married an *Englisher*, but you still dress like an Amish person. Why is that?"

Cindy ran her fingers over her apron. "I guess it's because I'm comfortable in these clothes. Drew said I can dress any way I want, and this is how I choose to dress."

"If you're still Amish in your heart, then maybe you should reconsider why you left the church."

Cindy stared at Lydia, her mouth gaping at her words. What was she saying? That she should leave Drew?

"I saw your *schweschder* last week. Do you know she had a *sohn*?"

"I heard."

"He's adorable. They named him after his *dat*." Lydia tilted her head. "You must miss them so. It had to be difficult to leave them after losing your *mamm* the way you did."

"It was." Cindy suddenly felt as if she'd swallowed a pail full of rusty nails.

"You look as if you long to be Amish, though. That doesn't make much sense. Why would you marry an *Englisher* if you consider yourself Amish?"

Cindy opened her mouth to speak, but then she closed it again. What could she say that would make any difference?

"Well, I must be going. My driver has to take me to a few more places. *Danki* for saving my quilt." Lydia gave her a little wave. "Take care."

Cindy followed Lydia to the door and then watched her climb into her driver's van and leave. Then she put on a sweater and hurried to Gertrude's house, where she knocked on the back door.

"Hi, Cindy." Gertrude opened her door wider and unlatched the outer door as well. "How are you?"

"Do you have time to talk?"

"Of course. Come in out of the cold. I just heated water for tea." Gertrude gestured for her to enter the house.

"I can help." Cindy walked into the kitchen and retrieved two mugs from the cabinet where she knew Gertrude kept them, along with sweetener. She was so grateful Gertrude and Ervin treated her the same way they treated Drew. They were risking the bishop's displeasure if he found out.

Gertrude brought two filled teacups and then a container of cookies to the table, and they both sat down.

"Is there something you want to tell me?" Gertrude said before lifting an oatmeal raisin cookie toward her lips.

"I'm expecting," Cindy said.

"Oh!" Gertrude lowered the cookie and touched her hand. "What a blessing! What did Drew say when you told him?"

"I haven't told him yet. I want to make it a Christmas surprise since Christmas is only a week away."

"Oh, that is *wunderbaar*." Gertrude placed one palm on her chest. "He will be so *froh*. I bet he'll cry. Have you figured out how you're going to surprise him?"

"I have a few ideas, but I haven't worked them out yet."

Gertrude clicked her tongue. "What an exciting time. Your first *boppli*."

Cindy looked down at her cup of tea as sadness filled her chest. "I just don't know how to have a *boppli* without my family." Then she shared how Laura hadn't told her about her baby and how hurt she was to be left out. "I feel so lost sometimes. I love Drew, and I don't regret marrying him. But being joyful is hard when I can't share news like this with my family. Even if I tell them, they won't respond in any meaningful way."

"*Ach*, I'm so sorry." Gertrude shook her head. "You and Drew have Ervin and me. We're here for you whenever you need someone."

"*Danki.*" Cindy sipped her tea as Lydia's words echoed in her mind. Was Cindy Amish in her heart? If that were true, then why had she never felt ready to be baptized?

"Is there something else you'd like to discuss?" Gertrude asked.

Cindy looked deep into her friend's eyes. "Do you think it's *narrisch* that I still dress Amish even though I married an *Englisher*?"

Gertrude blinked, and then she lifted another cookie from the container. "I don't think it's *narrisch*, but it is unusual."

"Do you think it's wrong that I dress Amish?"

Gertrude's smile was warm. "Why would I think it's wrong? If that's how you feel comfortable, then it's okay." She studied Cindy. "Are you doubting yourself?"

She shared what Lydia said to her, and Gertrude waved off the comments.

"Lydia Smoker likes to hear herself talk. Don't worry about

what she says." Gertrude pushed the container toward Cindy. "Have a *kichli* before I eat them all."

. . .

"Merry Christmas." Drew set a large package wrapped in bright red paper decorated with candy canes in front of Cindy.

"Oh my goodness! Thank you." She ripped the package open and gasped when she found a large sewing basket, complete with several little storage compartments. "This is perfect!"

"I thought you might like one since you were complaining that you needed to organize your sewing room the other day." He sat down next to her on the sofa. "But if you don't like this one, we can take it back and exchange it."

"I love it!" She kissed his cheek. "Thank you." Then she set a small wrapped package in his hand. "This is one of your gifts." Her heart seemed to flip as he turned the box over in his hand.

"Thank you." He unwrapped the small box and then took off the lid. A gasp escaped his mouth as he lifted a yellow baby bootie she'd crocheted last week.

He turned to her, his blue eyes wide. "You're-you're-you're—"

"*Ya.*" She nodded, and he wrapped his arms around her. She laughed as he kissed her all over her face. "I guess this means you're happy."

"I'm ecstatic!" He kissed her on the lips and then grinned as he touched her abdomen. "How long have you known?"

"I took a test a week ago, but I had suspected for a while. I think I'm due in late July or early August. I have an appointment with a doctor next week to find out for sure." She touched his cheek. "Will you go with me?"

"Of course." He pulled her against his chest. "I'm so happy. I've always wanted a family. This is the best Christmas gift ever."

She rested her cheek against his shoulder as thoughts of her *dat* and siblings filled her mind. She imagined Laura's first Christmas with her new son, as well as her other siblings sharing Christmas morning with their children.

"Penny for your thoughts." Drew's voice rumbled in his chest as she kept her cheek on his shoulder.

"I want to tell at least Laura about our baby, but I don't know how. I'm still disappointed and hurt that she hasn't contacted me, but I miss her anyway."

He kissed her head. "I know you miss her. Maybe you should try reaching out to your family. Priscilla told you they miss you."

She pulled away from him. "I don't know how to do it."

"We'll think of a way." He pulled her against him once again. "Right now, let's just enjoy each other and our first Christmas together as husband and wife."

She closed her eyes and breathed in his familiar scent as she imagined her child growing inside of her. She prayed their baby would grow up healthy and happy despite a world without grandparents, cousins, and aunts and uncles to love. But the thought left her feeling more empty than hopeful.

. . .

Drew stepped into the cold and shivered as he zipped his coat and walked out to the barn to care for the animals. The late December wind sliced through his clothes and bit at his skin.

He hurried into the barn and jumped with a start when he found Ervin standing by the horse stalls.

"Ervin," he called. "Good morning!"

"Good morning." Ervin smiled at him. "How was your Christmas yesterday?"

"It was nice." Warmth spread through Drew as he recalled the romantic day he'd spent with his beautiful wife.

After she shared the news of her pregnancy, they curled up together on the sofa, sipping hot chocolate and opening the rest of their gifts. They spent the remainder of the day snuggling, talking, and planning for their baby. He was so happy he couldn't stop smiling.

"Maybe more than nice? You look like you had a truly special day." A grin turned up Ervin's lips. "I'm glad to see it. The first Christmas is always a special one."

"It was." Drew leaned on a horse stall. Cindy said Gertrude had kept her secret since last week, even from Ervin, but there was no reason not to tell him now. "Cindy told me we're expecting."

Ervin looked a little taken aback, but then he said, "Really?" Ervin clapped Drew on the back. "That's *wunderbaar* news! I'm so *froh* for you."

"Thank you so much." Drew shook his head. "I had hoped it would happen, but I didn't expect it so quickly. It's a true blessing."

"*Ya*, a baby always is."

Drew's smile faltered. "I just hope I can be the father our child needs and deserves."

Ervin squeezed his shoulder. "We all worry about that, but God leads us. Besides, Cindy will guide you too. Just pray about it."

Drew looked at Ervin. "I don't know how we'll make it without any family, though. It's just the two of us, and that will be a struggle."

"You'll be just fine. Besides, you're here with us. Gertrude and I can be surrogate grandparents. We'll help you with anything you need."

Drew felt his heart swell with appreciation for Ervin. He'd always appreciated Ervin and Gertrude's kindness toward him. Not only were they his employers, but they had become like family when he needed some most. He admired how they had accepted him even though he wasn't Amish, and they hadn't turned their back on Cindy when she married him. But Drew had always wanted an extended family like Jamie and Mark had.

"Thank you." Drew fingered the door of the stall. "But Cindy's family means everything to her. Do you think there's a chance Vernon might change his mind and want to be a part of her life again—especially when he learns about the baby?"

Ervin nodded. "*Ya*, I do. My son never joined the church, but just in the past few years, Gertrude and I have started talking to him again. It's taken us a while, but we're rebuilding our relationship. I believe that, with God, all things are possible. Just keep praying about it."

"I will." Drew smiled as renewed hope filled him. "So are you here to help with chores?"

"I am," Ervin said. "Put me to work."

CHAPTER 27

"You really think this will work?" Cindy hated the quaver of fear and longing in her voice as they walked up the path to her father's house the next day.

"Yes, I do." Drew pressed his hand to her lower back, and the gesture filled her with much-needed confidence. "How can your father resist a visit if you show up with his favorite pie?"

"Right." She glanced down at the lemon meringue creation in her hands, the sweet aroma making her stomach gurgle. "This is *Mamm*'s recipe. His absolute favorite."

"Like I said, how can he possibly resist?" Drew took her arm, stopping her. "Not just the pie, but you? He hasn't seen you in two months. He must miss you. You're his youngest child." He touched her cheek. "And you're glowing."

She felt a blush rising into her cheeks.

"Are you going to tell him?"

She shook her head. "No, we don't talk about things like that."

He raised an eyebrow. "Why not? It's the best kind of news."

"It's just how our culture is. Pregnancy is private." She knew Ervin must have felt a little embarrassed when Drew told him they were expecting, but she put that aside and looked up toward the porch. "We should go before I lose my nerve."

"Right." He took an exaggerated breath. "Deep breath. You've got this. I believe in you."

"Thank you." Her heart swelled with love for her husband. "You always have faith in me."

"That's my job." He pointed toward the door. "Now go."

Cindy plastered a nervous smile on her face as she climbed the back steps and reached for the doorknob.

Then she stopped. She didn't live in this house anymore, and she'd been all but shunned. Did she have the right to simply walk in like a member of the family? She froze in place as confusion surfaced.

"What's wrong?" Drew stood at the bottom of the steps.

"I'm not sure if I should knock or just walk in." She held up the pie. "What should I do?"

"Well, why don't you—"

The back door opened, and Sarah Jane appeared, her brow furrowed. "Cindy? What are you doing here?"

"I have a gift for *mei dat*." Cindy held up the pie. "Is he home?"

"*Ya.*" Sarah Jane looked past Cindy and then disappeared into the mudroom.

Cindy tapped her foot and glanced across the pasture toward Jamie's house. Were Calvin and Alice playing in the family room? Had they grown taller since she last saw them? Was Alice talking yet?

"Cindy?" *Dat* cracked open the storm door. He seemed older somehow, with more lines on his forehead and around his eyes. Had her leaving aged him?

"I brought you a gift." She held out the pie. "It's lemon meringue. It's *Mamm*'s recipe, your favorite."

Dat looked down at the pie and then up at her again. His blue eyes seemed to hold confusion and pain.

"It's for you." She nodded to the pie. "Please take it." She held her breath as her heart started to crack. *Please, please take the pie. Please forgive me. Please love me. Please tell me I'm still your daughter.*

Holding the door open with one foot, *Dat* reached for the pie and took it into his hands. "*Danki.* But why did you bake this for me?"

"Because I miss you." Her voice sounded foreign to her—too high and shaky. "I've been thinking of you, and Drew thought it would be nice if I brought you something you'd like."

Dat looked past her, and his eyes narrowed.

"Hi, Vernon." Drew spoke boldly despite her father's murderous glare.

"Could we come in and visit for a while?" Cindy asked. "We won't stay long."

Dat looked at her again, and his glare softened. "I don't think that's a *gut* idea."

"Why not?" She heard desperation seep into her voice.

"You know why not, Cindy." *Dat* sighed as if the weight of the world sat on his shoulders. "You chose to leave and marry an outsider."

"We haven't spoken in two months," she pleaded with him. "Don't you miss me?"

"You should go," *Dat* said. "*Danki* for the pie."

"I'm your *dochder,* your youngest *kind.* How can you send me away like *I'm* an outsider?"

"You are an outsider now, Cindy." *Dat* looked past her. "Ever since you married him. You knew this would happen, but you did it anyway. And it did no good for your husband to ask Jamie to convince me to break our rules. Goodbye."

Dat started to close the door, and she stuck her foot between it and the doorframe.

"Why didn't anyone tell me Laura had her *boppli*?" she demanded. "Didn't anyone think I'd want to know?"

"You left, Cindy," *Dat* said.

"But I'm still your *dochder* and Laura's *schweschder*." Her voice rose. "I missed you on Thanksgiving and Christmas. Don't I matter? Don't you wonder if I'm well? I'm right next door." She pointed toward the Lapps' farm. "I'm not in Europe or Africa. You could come see how I am. Don't you care at all?"

Dat's expression remained stony, but she spotted a flicker of emotion in his eyes.

She forced words past the thickness expanding in her throat. "What would *Mamm* say if she knew how you're treating me?"

When she felt hands on her shoulders, she jumped.

"That's enough." Drew's voice was calm and soothing next to her ear. "You're getting too upset. We should go."

She looked up at her husband. "But I need to tell him how I feel."

"This was a mistake, and I'm sorry." Drew looked at *Dat*. "Someday you're going to realize you've made a huge mistake, Vernon, and it might be too late to repair your relationship with your youngest child." He steered Cindy down the porch steps and toward his truck. "We need to go."

Cindy climbed into the passenger seat and covered her face with her hands as tears burned behind her eyelids.

"I'm so sorry. My expectations were too high." Drew touched her arm. "Why don't we go see Priscilla? She's always been nice to you."

Cindy pulled a tissue from her pocket and wiped her eyes and nose. "I don't think I could take another rejection today."

"Priscilla is different." He turned the key, and the truck roared to life. "Let's give her and Mark a chance to talk to us."

He asked Cindy how to get to her brother's house, and she gave him directions.

Ten minutes later, they pulled into the driveway, and when the Allgyer's Belgian and Dutch Harness Horses sign came into view, her stomach dropped. What if Mark and Priscilla sent her away too? Priscilla might have changed her mind about visits like this—or Mark might have changed it for her.

She choked back a sob.

Drew drove his truck up the driveway and stopped by the path that led to the house Mark built last year. Although he and Priscilla had started their marriage living in the two-bedroom *daadihaus* on her father's property, Mark had saved enough money to build her a two-story, five-bedroom brick house with a sweeping porch and a spacious kitchen.

Priscilla told Cindy she would've been happy in a small home, but Mark was determined to give Priscilla only the best. Cindy suspected they would fill the home with more children and a lot of love.

"Let's go see your brother," Drew said as he pushed his door open.

Cindy watched him start up the path with determination. She climbed out of the truck and caught up with him at the front door, where Drew knocked.

The door swung open, and Priscilla appeared with Ethan standing behind her. "Cindy. Drew. How are you?"

"Hi, *Aenti* Cindy!" Ethan pushed open the storm door and joined them on the porch. He gave her a hug that warmed the coldness in her chest.

"It's so *gut* to see you, Ethan," Cindy said before looking at Priscilla. "Did you mean it when you said Drew and I would always receive a welcome at your door?"

"Of course." Priscilla took a step back and gestured for them to come in. "It's so *gut* to see you."

Drew stepped into the foyer and glanced around the large family room. "Wow. This house is amazing."

"Thank you." Priscilla seemed a little sheepish. "Mark designed it."

Mark came around the corner, and his blue eyes widened. "Cindy. What are you doing here?"

"I wanted to see family, and Priscilla told me Drew and I would always be welcome in your home." Cindy placed her hand on Drew's arm. "Are you going to throw us out?"

"No." Priscilla's voice was almost forceful. "You're family, and you're welcome here."

"Right." Mark nodded, and his Adam's apple bobbed.

Cindy let out a breath in relief.

"Come into the kitchen, and I'll make some tea." Priscilla turned to Ethan. "Would you please grab that chocolate cake I baked yesterday?"

"*Ya, Mamm.*" Ethan left the room.

"Mark." Drew turned to her brother. "Could I speak to you alone?"

Mark pointed toward the front door. "We could walk outside."

"Perfect." Drew touched Cindy's arm. "I'll be back." He leaned down. "Everything will be fine. I promise you." Then he kissed her cheek before heading outside with Mark, who'd lifted a coat from a hook by the door.

Cindy stepped into the kitchen, where Priscilla placed the kettle on the burner and Ethan set a chocolate cake on the table.

Priscilla turned to Ethan. "Would you please go check on the *zwillingbopplin* and then go read a book in your room? I need to talk to your *aenti* in private."

"*Ya.*" Ethan touched Cindy's hand. "See you soon, *Aenti* Cindy."

Cindy's heart seemed to turn over in her chest. "Bye for now, Ethan."

Then her nephew disappeared, and soon his footfalls echoed in the stairwell.

"He's such a *gut bu*," Cindy said.

"I know." Priscilla smiled. "I don't know what I'd do without him. He's a tremendous help with the *zwillingbopplin*." She pointed to the table. "Have a seat. I'll bring our tea."

"Do you want help?"

"No." Priscilla waved off the suggestion and took two mugs and some tea bags from a cabinet. "Tell me what brought you here today out of the blue."

"I've missed you all so much, so Drew suggested I try visiting *mei dat*. I baked his favorite pie and took it to him just before we came here." Cindy took a deep, shuddering breath. "He took the pie, but he refused to invite me in or visit with me. I was so upset that Drew suggested we come here. You've been so supportive of me through all of this."

"*Ach.* I'm so sorry." Priscilla shook her head. "I know your *dat* hurt you."

"He broke my heart."

The kettle whistled, and Priscilla poured water into the cups and then carried them to the table. She retrieved a knife, two forks, and two plates before bringing them to the table as well. Then she cut two pieces of cake.

They ate in continued silence for a few moments, but when Cindy felt her emotions bubble up, they came rushing out.

"I told *Dat* I missed all of you on Thanksgiving and Christmas, and I asked him if I mattered. He didn't answer. I can't tell you how much that hurts." Cindy stared down at the cake. "What I didn't tell him is that I'm expecting, due in late July or early August."

"Oh, Cindy." Priscilla clapped her hands. "What a blessing."

"Danki." Cindy looked at her. "I wish my other family members could celebrate with me too."

Priscilla clicked her tongue. "I'll work on Mark. Maybe I can talk him into speaking to Jamie and Laura."

"Drew told me he spoke to Jamie the day after Thanksgiving. He was upset that no one had come to see me since our wedding, and Jamie agreed to try talking to *Dat.* But Drew's efforts didn't change anything. That was obvious when *Dat* rejected me today and made it clear Jamie had failed."

"Keep praying." Priscilla squeezed Cindy's forearm. "You remember how horrible *mei dat* was to me, right?"

Cindy nodded.

"Well, through prayer, he's changed quite a bit. Our relationship isn't perfect, but it's definitely better. You can't give up hope. God is our great healer and comforter, and he can soften anyone's heart."

Cindy nodded. *"Danki,* Priscilla. I'm so grateful to call you *mei schweschder."*

Priscilla smiled. "And I'm grateful for you too."

As Cindy took another bite of the sweet, delicious cake, she longed for Laura to be there with them.

. . .

Mark kicked a stone with the toe of his boot as he and Drew stood in the driveway. "I can't believe *mei dat* was that cold to Cindy after not seeing her for two months."

"I know. She's devastated." Drew leaned back on the fender of his truck and gazed toward Mark's house. "She's missed you all so much. She tries to act strong, but it's really tearing her apart. I was hoping maybe you could help us."

"How?" Mark looked over at him. "You already said Jamie tried."

"Maybe you could talk to your other siblings, and then the three of you could talk to your father all together. Remind him that Cindy's still family even though she isn't Amish anymore."

Mark rubbed his light-brown beard and frowned. "I'll try, but I can't make you any promises. I think *mei dat* is getting pressure from the bishop."

"What do you mean?"

"I saw the bishop talking to him at church last month. When I asked about it, *Dat* said the bishop wanted to make sure we were treating Cindy like an outsider. He said we can't let her think she can marry an *Englisher* and still be a member of the community." Mark shook his head. "I know you think we're all ridiculous, but it's our way of life."

"It just doesn't make sense to me. You should cherish each other for all the days you have left together. You've experienced loss like I have, and it's the worst kind of pain."

"Look, Drew," Mark began, "I'll do my best. I miss my little sister, and I want her to be a part of my family's life. I'll speak to Laura and Jamie and see if we can talk some sense into *Dat*, but I can't promise any miracles."

"Thank you." Drew shook his hand. "That's all I can ask for."

"*Gut.*" Mark rubbed his hands together. "I believe my wife is sharing a chocolate cake she made for me, so I'd like to grab a piece before it's all gone. What do you say we go inside and get some for ourselves?"

As they walked up the porch steps, Drew grasped the little bit of new hope that seemed to take root in his heart. He was sure Cindy had been telling Priscilla about the baby, and if Priscilla told Mark, maybe he'd have even more incentive to do whatever he could for Cindy.

CHAPTER 28

Cindy touched her hand to her abdomen as a cramp gripped her. She dropped a breakfast plate into the sink and sucked in a breath, then grabbed on to the kitchen counter and bent at the waist as another horrific pain sliced through her middle.

What was happening?

She rushed to the bathroom and gasped when she found she was bleeding. Panic seized her heart and her chest.

"Drew!" she called. "Drew!"

"Yeah?" he yelled from somewhere in the house.

"Something is wrong," she yelled back.

"What?" His voice sounded from outside the bathroom door. "What's going on?" He sounded as panicked as she felt.

"I'm bleeding. I think something's wrong with the baby. I need to go to the hospital."

Icy fingers of dread gripped her windpipe and squeezed, blocking more words as tears streamed down her cheeks.

Am I losing my baby?

Please, God! Please save my baby! Please don't take this child before I have a chance to hold it in my arms!

"Cindy, I'm going to warm up the truck, and then I'll grab your coat and come back for you. I'll be right back."

"Hurry!" Grateful, she took down the clothes she'd just

hung on the back of the door, intending to bathe before a trip to town for supplies. She did her best to clean herself up and prepare for the ride to the hospital, gathering the towels they might need. Then she sat down on the edge of the bathtub, gasping with each pain.

This was a nightmare. How could this happen? Had she done something to cause her pregnancy to fail? Where was Drew?

"Cindy!" Drew's voice was close to the door again. "The truck wouldn't start at first, but it's running now. Can I come in?"

She stood and pushed the bathroom door open. Drew's handsome face was twisted with worry.

"Can you walk?"

"I-I think so."

"Let me help you." He held out his hand. "Let's get you to the hospital."

She let Drew help her pull on her winter coat, and then he held on to her as they made their way out the front door.

Cindy shivered in the late January cold and leaned against the porch post. She glanced out at the frozen grass and up at the clear blue sky that seemed to mock her as fear ran through her like a roaring river. The pickup truck hummed in the driveway.

Please, God. Please protect our baby.

"You stay inside, buddy," Drew told Bruce as he closed and locked the front door. "We'll be back soon. You guard the house."

Then he took her hand and helped her climb down the steps and into the truck.

Cindy stared out the window as Drew drove. She continued praying for their baby as dread surrounded her heart.

. . .

"Mrs. Collins." The doctor stood next to her hospital bed and touched Cindy's arm a few hours later. "I'm very sorry to tell you you've suffered a miscarriage."

She curled up in a ball as tears blurred her vision and dripped down her hot cheeks. Her worst nightmare had come true. When she closed her eyes, she felt as if she were spinning in a black abyss.

She'd lost her mother and then her family. Now she'd lost her baby. What else would she lose in this life?

"It's really over, Dr. Ross?" Drew's voice sounded like it was a million miles away, even though he stood next to her bed with his warm hand gripping hers.

"I'm sorry, Mr. Collins, but unfortunately, yes. The ultrasound showed the fetus is gone. Parents usually ask why, but most miscarriages just happen, usually for no reason we can detect."

Drew made a strangled sound in his throat, and when Cindy opened her eyes, she saw him wipe his.

"We'd like to keep Mrs. Collins here for a few hours for observation, just to be sure she'll be all right."

"I understand." Drew's voice was soft and thick.

"Let me know if you need anything," the doctor said. "And I'm truly sorry for your loss."

"Thank you, Dr. Ross." Drew's voice was weak, as if he were on the verge of shedding more tears.

Footsteps sounded, and then a door opened and closed.

"Cindy." Drew's voice was soft against her ear. "I'm here." He moved his fingers over her back, making circles and sending waves of warmth through her. "We'll get through this. When the doctor says it's safe, we can try again. We're young."

Another flood of tears overcame Cindy as the hurt weighed heavily on her heart.

"Cindy." He sniffed and touched her shoulder. "What are you feeling? Don't keep all your sadness inside. Let me help you."

"I want Laura," she whispered between sobs. "I need Laura."

Her sister had suffered two miscarriages. Laura would be able to help her through this. She could relate to how she felt. Laura would hold her hand and be a comfort to her.

But it had been almost a month since they'd visited Priscilla and Mark. Drew had asked Mark to help repair the great chasm separating her from her family, but none of her siblings had called or stopped by, and now she needed her family more than ever.

She hugged her arms to her chest and let grief take hold.

"Calm down." Drew sounded frantic. "I'll try to reach Laura."

"She won't come." Cindy looked up at Drew, and the pain in his red, puffy eyes compounded hers. "She doesn't care. None of my family cares about me anymore."

"That's not true." Drew shook his head. "I refuse to believe that."

"If they cared, they would have come to see us by now." Cindy rolled onto her side, facing away from him. "We're all alone."

"No, we're not." Drew placed one palm on her back. "I'm going to call Laura. I'll ask her to come. I'll be right back."

She closed her eyes, praying for relief from the anguish that racked her body and soul.

. . .

Drew's shoulders slumped as he nearly stumbled down the hospital hallway. He wiped away the tears that had continued to fall ever since the doctor told them the news. Cindy had lost their baby.

He needed to find a place to sit down and collect his thoughts. He didn't want to reach out to Laura and have Cindy witness the rejection that might follow. He found a chair in the hallway a few doors down from Cindy's room, and he flopped into it.

A hot mixture of agony and heartbreak washed through him as he looked down at his phone and tried to recall the name of Allen's business. It had the words "carriage shop" in it. What was it?

He held his phone to his forehead, trying to hold back more tears. The anguish on Cindy's face was too much for him. He longed to take away her pain. Losing the baby was a tragedy no one could have prevented, but her family's rejection was his fault. He was a failure as a husband.

Focus, Drew! Focus! Call Laura and then get back to your wife! She needs you!

He racked his brain once more, and then it came to him— the Bird-in-Hand Carriage Shop. Of course!

He searched the internet on his phone for the number and then dialed. After six rings, Allen's voice rang through the phone. It was his voice mail. "You've reached the Bird-in-Hand Carriage Shop. We restore, repair, and sell buggies. The shop is open Monday through Friday, eight to five, and Saturdays, eight to noon. Please leave a message, and I will call you back as soon as I can. Thank you."

After the beep, Drew began to speak, doing his best to keep his voice steady.

"Allen," Drew said. "This is Drew, Cindy's husband. I need to reach Laura." He shoved his free hand through his hair while staring down at the tile floor, not caring if the Amish didn't speak about "these things." Maybe they did, but what did it matter now? "I'm at the hospital with Cindy. She's suffered a miscarriage, and she really wants to see Laura. She needs her."

He paused and took a deep breath. "If Laura could find it in her heart to see her, it would mean a lot. We're going to be at the hospital for a few more hours, and then we should be home this evening. Please pass this message on to Laura. If you want to call me, here's my cell phone number." He recited the number. "I hope to hear from you soon. Thanks. Bye."

He disconnected the call and then pulled up Mark and Priscilla's farm number, stored in his contacts.

When he got their voice mail, too, he waited for the beep.

"This message is for Mark," Drew said. "This is Drew. I'm at the hospital with Cindy. She's suffered a miscarriage and could use the support of her family. I hope you can find it in your heart to come and see her. I expect we'll be home in a few hours, but you're welcome to come to the hospital too. It would mean a lot to both of us to know you care." Then he left his cell phone number. "I hope to talk to you soon. Thank you. Bye."

He disconnected the call and then stared at his phone as he started to pray.

God, please help us. We need to feel your love and comfort right now. Heal our hearts as we go through this loss, but also please bring Cindy's family back to her. She needs all the love and support she can get right now. So do I. Thank you.

Then he stood and walked back into Cindy's room. When

he found her sleeping, he sat down in the chair by the bed to wait for the doctor to discharge her.

He closed his eyes and leaned back, allowing his head to smack against the Sheetrock behind him. He listened to Cindy's soft breathing as he continued to beg God for the help they so desperately needed. Only God could heal the rift in the Riehl family, and he was certain prayer was their only hope.

. . .

"Here you go." Drew handed Cindy a mug of warm tea as she sat propped up on the sofa in their family room. He sat down on the coffee table across from her and rubbed Bruce's ear as he smiled at her. "What else can I get you?"

"Nothing. Thanks. This is perfect." She studied his smile as she sipped from the mug. He'd received a call on his cell phone earlier, and she'd hoped it was Laura, returning the call Drew left on Allen's voice mail. But when she'd questioned it, he insisted it was a wrong number. Still, he seemed to have something up his sleeve. She wondered if he'd left a message for Gertrude to come by, but they didn't seem to be home.

"How's the tea?" he asked, and then he looked out the window—again.

"Delicious. What are you looking for? You keep peering outside."

"Nothing." He stood and arranged her blanket so it covered her feet. "Do you want something else? Maybe another blanket?"

"Drew." She touched his hand. "What's going on with you?"

"I love you." He touched her cheek. "We're going to make it

through this. Trust me. Please." He kissed the top of her head and headed into the kitchen.

Cindy cupped the mug in her hands and tried to hold back another rush of tears. She'd been home for more than an hour, but her thoughts were still stuck on the doctor's words. The child who had been growing inside of her was gone. Their hope for bringing a baby into the world next summer had evaporated, and her prayer of giving Drew a family had been dashed.

Bruce whined and then moved closer to the sofa.

"Hi, Bruce." Cindy rubbed his ear. "How are you, buddy?"

Suddenly the warm aroma of coffee filled her senses, and she heard the belching and hissing of Drew's coffeemaker.

"Why are you making coffee?" she called.

"Why not?" His answer was so simple. What was going on?

When Cindy heard the *clip-clop* of horse hooves and the whirring of buggy wheels, she turned toward the window. A horse and buggy headed up the driveway, the late afternoon sun low behind it.

"I wonder where Gertrude and Ervin have been," she muttered to herself.

A second horse and buggy followed, and then a third. Her heart seemed to flip-flop.

"Are Gertrude and Ervin expecting company?" she asked.

"I don't think so." Drew appeared in the family room. "But we are."

"What?" She stared at him. "What's going on?"

"Look again, Cindy." He pointed to the window.

She turned toward the window, and then happy tears filled her eyes as she spotted Laura, Mark, and their families climbing out of their buggies.

"What did you do?" she asked Drew.

"You know I left a message for Allen, but I also left a message for Mark. Then a little while ago, Mark called me. Yes, I lied and said it was a wrong number, but I think you'll forgive me."

Drew opened the front door and waved. "Hello there. How are you?" He turned to Cindy as she shifted on the sofa. "Stay there. I'll get some folding chairs from Ervin's barn."

Cindy's hands trembled as she set her mug on the coffee table, and then she touched her prayer covering to make sure it was straight. She peeked out the window again and tears streamed down her face. Her father, Florence, Sarah Jane, Jamie, and Jamie's family were all walking up the driveway.

"Everyone is here?" she asked as shock filled her.

"Yes. Everyone is here to see you. I'll be right back. Come on, Bruce! Come with me, buddy." Drew stepped out onto the porch and Bruce followed, his collar tinkling as he walked.

"Mark, hello! Would you please help me get some chairs?" Drew's voice sounded from the porch.

The front door opened, and Laura stepped in carrying a baby in a car seat.

"Cindy!" Laura exclaimed as she crossed the room. She set the car seat with the sleeping baby on the floor and then leaned down and hugged Cindy.

"Laura." Cindy looped her arms around her sister's neck and held on to her as if her life depended on it. Tears flowed down her cheeks as she buried her face in Laura's shoulder and sobbed.

"*Ach*, I'm so sorry, *mei liewe*. I'm sorry for everything," Laura whispered. "I'm sorry I haven't been here for you. I'm sorry you lost the *boppli*. I'm sorry for hurting you."

"I'm so relieved you're here." Cindy worked to control her

emotions as voices filled the family room. "I'm so glad you came."

"Allen got Drew's message and told me right away. Then Mark called and said Drew had called him too." Laura pulled back and handed Cindy a tissue from the end table. "Then Mark called Jamie, and I called *Dat*. We all wanted to come as soon as we heard. Mark called to coordinate what time to be here with Drew." Laura gestured to her nieces and nephews behind her. "So we're all here."

"And we brought food." Mollie held up a cake plate.

"We brought a *lot* of food," Kayla chimed in as she, Sarah Jane, and Florence headed to the kitchen, each of them carrying a dish.

"Thank you," Cindy said as happiness bubbled up inside her. Her family was here! What a wonderful answer to her prayers!

Laura seemed to hesitate a moment, but then she asked, "Would you like to meet your new nephew?" She unhooked the car seat and picked up the sleeping baby.

"Of course," Cindy said, realizing Laura must have thought she might not be ready. But as Laura handed her the precious boy, she was only grateful for this blessing in her sister's life. "Oh my goodness. He is so *schee*."

"*Danki*." Laura leaned down. "This is Allen Junior."

"That's what I heard." Cindy looked down at the baby as renewed tears flooded her eyes. "Why didn't you call me when he was born?"

"I'm so sorry." Laura's eyes misted over. "I wanted to call you, and I should have. I was just so confused. I felt like you chose Drew over the rest of us."

"No. I would never do that." Cindy shook her head. "I wanted to have all of you in my life. I still do."

"I know. I'm sorry." Laura wiped her eyes with a tissue. "Will you forgive me?"

"Of course I will." Cindy touched her new nephew's little hand, and an inevitable bittersweet feeling overcame her. Would she ever have a baby of her own?

"Don't give up hope," Laura whispered as if reading her thoughts. "I believe you'll have one. It will just come in God's time."

"I know." Cindy gave her a watery smile.

"*Mamm*!" Catherine screeched as Allen carried her into the house.

"Shh, Catherine." Laura held out her arms, and Allen handed her their middle child.

"Oh, she's grown so big." Cindy touched Catherine's hand.

"I have too." Mollie appeared beside her. "*Onkel* Mark says I'm going to be taller than *mei mamm*, but I told him everyone is."

"That's not nice," Laura said, and everyone laughed.

Allen touched Laura's arm. "I need to go help with the chairs. Can you handle the *kinner*?"

"I'll help her," Mollie said. "I'm a *gut* helper."

"*Ya*, you are." Allen touched her nose. "I'll be right back."

"Why don't you go see if your *aentis* need help in the kitchen?" Laura told Mollie. "*Aenti* Cindy and I will take care of Catherine and Junior, okay?"

"*Ya, Mamm*." Mollie turned to Cindy and kissed her cheek. "I hope you feel better." Then she scampered into the kitchen.

Cindy smiled as she watched her sweet niece hurry off to assist with the food. Laura pulled a chair over to the sofa and sat down beside Cindy.

Priscilla and Ethan maneuvered a double stroller through

the front door, and then *Dat* followed them in. Cindy's chest constricted as he came near.

Her lower lip trembled as she looked up at him. "Hi, *Dat*."

"Hi." He pulled another chair over and sat across from her. "How do you feel?"

She looked down at Allen Junior and touched his little cheek. "I'm *bedauerlich*."

"I'm so sorry." He touched her arm. "We're all sorry for your loss. And I'm sorry for rejecting you. When Jamie told us what happened, I finally let God break through my wall of anger and resentment, even my heartbreak. I knew you needed us, and the truth is we'll always need you, Cindy—no matter what. You're *mei dochder*, and you always will be. *Ich liebe dich.* I never stopped loving you."

He paused before taking her hand. "Please forgive me. I'm the one who insisted the family follow the rules, even when they all started to have reservations and miss you so much— Florence and Sarah Jane too. But this rule doesn't work for our family. We love each other too much."

His words were music to her ears, and they sent a deluge of tears to her eyes.

"*Danki*," Cindy said. "Of course I forgive you."

"We have chairs," Drew announced as he and her brothers appeared in the house. "We all can sit now."

Drew, Jamie, Allen, and Mark arranged the chairs around the family room, and soon conversations floated throughout the house. Cindy smiled and laughed as she caught up with her siblings, nieces, and nephews.

Soon Florence, Kayla, and Mollie were serving their bountiful dishes—macaroni and cheese, hamburger pie casserole, tuna casserole, and chicken alfredo and pasta casserole. Then

Mollie and Kayla carried out platters of chocolate chip, peanut butter, and almond cookies. The conversations and eating continued into the evening.

At one point she saw *Dat* motion Drew to the corner where the puzzle table sat. She couldn't hear them, but she could see *Dat* doing most of the talking. Then Drew held out his hand and the two men shook as Florence joined them. In another moment or two, she saw her stepmother touch Drew's arm.

A few more tears dripped down Cindy's cheeks.

When her nieces and nephews grew cranky, their parents started packing them up to take them home.

Mark and his family were the first to leave. Cindy stood and kissed Ethan, Annie, and Adam good-bye before Priscilla and Mark took them out to their buggy. Mark and Priscilla promised to see her soon.

Jamie and Kayla left next, and Cindy thanked them for coming, saying she hoped to see them and their children soon as well.

"We need to get going too." Laura hugged Cindy. "It was so *gut* to see you, but I'm sorry for the circumstances."

"*Danki.*" Cindy gave her one last squeeze. "You were the first person I wanted to see."

"I'll visit you soon." Laura's eyes were determined. "We won't lose touch again."

"I'll hold you to that." Cindy leaned down and hugged Mollie.

"I will too." Mollie smiled. "I want to see you soon." She turned to Drew. "*Gut nacht, Onkel* Drew!"

"Good night, Mollie." Drew grinned as Mollie hugged his legs.

Mollie looked up at him and tilted her head. "We need to teach you some Pennsylvania *Dietsch* words."

Cindy's heart melted as everyone laughed. Even her nieces and nephews were accepting Drew as part of the family. This was indeed an answer to prayer she'd hoped for!

"Gut nacht." Cindy kissed Junior and Catherine before they headed out into the cold January night.

"We want you to come for supper on Sunday," Florence said as she and *Dat* walked to the door. "We want you to come for supper *every* Sunday if that works for you and Drew."

"Really?" Cindy hugged her arms to her middle as she divided a look between Florence and *Dat*.

"Ya, really." *Dat* hugged her. "We want you to be part of the family—both you and Drew."

"Danki, Dat." She rested her head on his shoulder as he put his arm around her. "This is what I'd hoped for."

"I know. I'm sorry it took me so long to get here," *Dat* said.

"So we'll see you Sunday?" Florence asked as she pulled on her coat.

When they were once again alone, Drew sidled up to Cindy and gently pulled her against his side.

"Thank you for bringing my family back to me," Cindy said as she looked up at him. "You're the best husband I could ever ask for."

"No, not really." He shook his head. "I'm the reason they pulled away from you."

"But you brought them back." She touched his cheek. "Don't blame yourself for how they pulled away. I realized something tonight, something I should have accepted long ago instead of simply blaming. That's what Amish are supposed to do when someone leaves. But you encouraged them to visit me anyway when I needed them most, and God used that to break down the walls we'd all constructed in our disappointment and pain."

He nodded. "I love how your community reaches out to someone in need, even those who aren't blood relatives, or even Amish. I've never experienced that before. I'm so excited to be a part of your family."

Warmth filled her as if God were wrapping her in his arms. "This is how it's supposed to be. We're meant to be together, and I'm so grateful."

"So am I. God answered our prayers." He leaned down and kissed her, sending contentment and love rippling through body and soul.

CHAPTER 29

Cindy sang along with the hymn as she sat next to Drew at church. She glanced up at him and he winked at her, sending her insides fluttering on the wings of a thousand butterflies.

She smiled to herself as she reflected on how the past month had flown by. After suffering the miscarriage, she found herself in a renewed relationship with her family. As Florence had promised, she'd invited Cindy and Drew to join them for dinner every Sunday for the past month. Cindy had enjoyed getting reacquainted with her family, especially with her nieces and nephews.

Today she and Drew would go home to rest after church and then head to her father's house at five. She could hardly wait to see her nieces and nephews and talk to her brothers and sisters. Sometimes they were all too busy to see each other during the week, but their Sunday meal together made an enormous difference in Cindy's life.

Although she still grieved the loss of their child, she felt happier than she had in years. The doctor had told her to allow her body to heal another month, and then she and Drew could try again. She prayed for children, and she hoped they would come—in God's time.

Pastor Ellen called for the prayers, and Drew flipped down the padded kneeler under the pew in front of them. Cindy knelt beside him and bowed her head as Pastor Ellen began to read the prayers to the congregation.

Cindy closed her eyes and opened her heart to God. For the first time in years, she felt a renewed faith in him. It was as if she had suddenly let go of the pain and doubt her mother's loss had caused her. She felt God's love surrounding her as she prayed for Drew and her family, and happiness rippled through her veins. She felt restored and almost reborn in her faith.

Cindy finally realized she had pulled away from God and her church when her mother died. But he hadn't pulled away from her. He'd been there all along. Drew said he accepted God's will after his parents died, and it was time for her to do the same, even if she might never understand why God made all the choices he did.

Her thoughts moved to her family, and she imagined them worshipping in a barn on this Sunday morning. She prayed for her former congregation, and a smile turned up her lips.

While she enjoyed the community church and the congregation, her heart suddenly felt drawn to her Amish life. She missed her former church district, and for the first time in her life, she thought perhaps she really did belong there—with Drew. But after everything he'd been through for her sake, how could she ask her husband to abandon his *English* life?

God, I finally understand that you've been with my every step. I'm sorry for pushing you away, as well as my church and family, and I thank you for bringing Drew into my life. He helped me see you were here all along, and he's one of your greatest blessings to me. But now that I have my family back, I'm confused. I think I feel the call of the Amish church, but I don't see how I can go back now. I can't expect Drew to abandon the life he's accustomed to living just for me. What should I do, Lord?

Do I belong in the Amish church? Does Drew? Please guide my heart.

Cindy went through the motions of the rest of the service and then held Drew's hand as they walked out to his truck when the service was over. She shivered against the February wind as she climbed onto the bench seat beside him.

"It was a nice service, wasn't it?" Drew gave her a sideways glance as he steered through the parking lot and onto the main road.

"*Ya*, it was." Cindy looked out the window in search of buggies heading home from church. Where was the service held today? No one in her family had mentioned hosting it.

"Is something bothering you?"

"Huh?" Cindy turned toward Drew as he slowed to a stop at a red light. "I'm sorry. What did you say?"

He lifted an eyebrow. "You're awfully distracted. Do you want to talk about what has you preoccupied?"

Cindy chewed her lower lip as the sound of the blasting truck heater filled the silence between them. "I was just wondering where my family is worshipping today since the families within the district take turns hosting church in either their home or their barn."

"I remember that." Drew nodded as he steered the truck through the intersection after the light turned green. "You can ask them when we go to your father's house for supper tonight."

"Right." She fingered the hem of her black winter coat.

"Is there something else on your mind?" He peered over at her.

"*Ya*, there is, actually." She took a deep breath. "I realized something today while we were praying. I told you I doubted God's will, but now I know the real problem was that I pulled away from him when my mother died. You've shown me his love was there all along. You didn't lose faith in God when you suffered loss, and your example has helped me renew my faith in him."

Drew steered the truck into the parking lot of a strip mall, parked in the back of the lot, and then turned to face her, taking her hands in his. "But I'm the reason you lost your family."

"Stop saying that." She cupped her hand to his cheek. "You're the reason I've found a renewed faith not only in God, but in my community. I was lost for so long when my mother died, but now I've found my way back."

He clicked his tongue as his eyes sparkled. "I love you so much."

"I love you too." The question that filled her mind during church echoed once again. "How would you feel about joining the Amish church?"

He blinked as if trying to comprehend her words. "Did you just ask me to join the Amish church?"

"*Ya*, I guess that's what I'm really saying." Her voice was tiny, resembling that of a young child who might be in trouble.

He pursed his lips and rubbed his chin as he studied her. "So you said you never were comfortable joining the Amish church, especially after your mother died because you thought no one in your community really understood the depth of your grief. Then you were willing to leave the church to marry me. But now, four months after our wedding, you think you want to go back to the church?"

"*Ya*, I do." Her words were confident, along with her love for her community. "I feel as if all the pieces of my heart are back intact. But I would never try to force you to do something you don't want to do. If you don't want to join the church, then we won't."

"Cindy, I'm really surprised by this. I don't know what to say."

"I know it seems sudden." She held up her hands. "I've just realized so much since the miscarriage. I now understand that my family experienced the same loss I did when my mother died, grieved just as much, but my grief overwhelmed my ability to see that."

She took his hand. "You're the love of my life, and I'm certain God brought us together. He sent you to me not only to love me, but to show me how wrong I was about pulling away from him. Now I'm ready to be baptized and become a faithful member of the Amish church, but I can do it only with you at my side. You're my partner. You're my life. Will you think and pray about it?"

"Yes, I will." He kissed her. "Let's go home."

. . .

Cindy's words about wanting to join the Amish church echoed in Drew's mind as he drove the rest of the way home, confused. Just before he turned right onto Beechdale Road, he spotted a line of horses and buggies heading in the opposite direction.

"Someone must have hosted church at the other end of the street," Cindy said.

He parked the truck in the driveway and pushed his door open. When he climbed out, he met her at the front of the truck and took her hand in his.

As they walked up to the front door of the house, he took in her appearance. She wore the traditional Amish dress of a prayer covering and a plain purple dress and black apron. He'd never once seen her dress in jeans or a fancy dress. Perhaps she'd never let go of her Amish roots at all.

He began to consider their few months as husband and wife. She'd never once turned on his television or asked to use his laptop. He'd never seen her use the microwave or his cell phone. She always asked Gertrude if she could use her phone in the barn when she needed to make a call. Not once could he remember her being excited about trying something new from the *English* world.

Could he possibly convert to the Amish religion with her? Would they even accept him?

He unlocked the door, stepped inside, and looked around his house. They couldn't stay here if they converted. It had electricity and other modern conveniences. Where would they live? Would they have to leave the Lapps' farm?

"Drew?" She walked up behind him and touched his arm. "Are you all right?"

"Yeah." He smiled at her. "I was just thinking about lunch." He stepped into the kitchen. "What are you in the mood for?"

"I don't know. Surprise me." She disappeared into the bedroom.

As Drew searched the refrigerator for something to eat, he realized he needed someone to talk to, and he knew who would help him. He'd wait until Cindy went to take her usual Sunday afternoon nap, and then he'd go seek advice.

. . .

An hour later, Drew knocked on Ervin's back door. As he waited for the older man to answer, he stretched his neck against the mounting tension.

"Drew," Ervin said when he opened the door. "How are you?"

"I'm well. I was wondering if we could talk."

"*Ya*, of course." Ervin motioned for Drew to come in. "Gertrude is visiting a neighbor."

Drew followed him through the mudroom and into the large kitchen.

"Would you like some coffee?" Ervin motioned to the percolator. "It's fresh."

"That would be wonderful. Thank you."

Ervin poured two mugs of coffee, and then they sat down at the table across from each other. "What's bothering you, *sohn*?"

Drew stared down at the dark-brown liquid in his mug and tried to corral his questions. Finally, he looked up into Ervin's curious brown eyes. "What would it take for me to become Amish?"

Ervin's eyes widened. "Why are you asking?"

"I just want to know." Drew gripped his mug.

"You'd have to meet with the bishop, who would assess if your heart and your reasons seem to be pure." Ervin sprinkled sugar into his mug as he spoke. "Most likely, the bishop would tell you you'd have to live like an Amish person for a year. That would mean giving up your truck, your schooling, your electricity, your cellular phone, your computer, and anything else considered worldly."

Ervin pointed to Drew's chest. "You'd have to dress like an Amish person, so Cindy would have to make you new clothes."

"Right." Drew rubbed his hand over his face. Was he strong enough to give up all the worldly things he'd known?

Drew only wanted to make Cindy happy. Besides, he'd finally have a family and a community of his own. His heart warmed. Yes, maybe this was where he and Cindy belonged.

"What's this about, Drew?" Ervin asked. "You need to be honest with me, because this doesn't seem like something you'd want to do."

Drew took another sip of coffee and then leveled his gaze with Ervin's. "Cindy told me that for the first time in her life, she feels ready to make the commitment to the Amish church. She asked me if I would consider joining the church with her. I'm just confused. I never expected her to ask me to be Amish."

Ervin was silent for a few moments, fingering his beard as he studied Drew.

Drew felt itchy under the older man's examination. "Please just tell me what you're thinking."

"Well, I think your heart and your reasons need to be pure if you're going to join the church. You can't do it just for Cindy, no matter how much you love her." Ervin took a long drink of coffee. "You said Cindy hasn't felt ready to be baptized until now. You shouldn't join the church until you feel a true and honest call to be baptized either. It's not something you join like a club at school."

"I understand that."

"You should pray about it. Ask God to talk to your heart, and then do whatever you feel is right."

Drew considered this. "How will I know if I hear his call?"

Ervin tapped his chest. "You'll know in here."

Drew nodded. How he appreciated the meaningful talks he shared with Ervin. He thought again that, in just a short period of time, Ervin and Gertrude had become like family. If Drew and Cindy were Amish, they would have more people in the community like them to cherish. His heart swelled at the thought.

Drew and Ervin finished their coffee while discussing some

of the chores Drew needed to accomplish around the farm. Then Drew stood and shook Ervin's hand. "Thank you for this talk. I'm going to go check on the animals before I head back to the house."

Ervin smiled at him. "You have a *gut* head on your shoulders, *sohn*. I'm certain you'll find the right answers if you just open your heart to God."

How Drew enjoyed hearing Ervin call him "son."

Drew shivered as he walked outside and down the path to the barn. He stepped inside and started toward the horse stalls.

When he reached them, he stopped and closed his eyes. Then he began to pray.

Lord, I want to be the husband Cindy deserves, and I want to make her happy for the rest of her life. I feel as if becoming Amish might be the right path for me, but I'm not sure. I know I'd have to give up a lot, and I also want to do it for the right reasons, just as Ervin said. Please lead me down the right path for Cindy and me. I need your help.

As he ended the prayer, he suddenly felt as if tender arms wrapped around him. He smiled as he looked up at the ceiling above him.

"Thank you," he whispered. "I'm listening."

CHAPTER 30

Drew whistled as he walked out to his truck Friday morning. He unlocked the passenger side door and tossed his backpack in before looking toward the Lapps' house.

"Drew! Drew!" Gertrude was rushing down the back-porch steps. "We need help! I think Ervin is having a heart attack. He has chest pains, and he says he feels dizzy. I know you have class today, but would you please take us to the hospital?"

"Of course!" Panic gripped Drew. "Yes, we'll go right now. Do you need help getting him out to the truck?"

"What's going on?" Cindy came running out the front door of their house, her blue eyes wide.

"Gertrude thinks Ervin is having a heart attack." Drew worked to keep his words even despite his flaring worry.

"*Ach* no!" Cindy cupped her hand to her mouth. "You go to the hospital. I'll run to *Dat*'s and get a ride there with his driver. We'll let the community know what's going on."

"Thank you." Drew turned to Gertrude. "Let's get Ervin into the truck fast."

"I'm praying, Gertrude!" Cindy called after them.

Drew hurried up the Lapps' porch steps, his heart thumping and his mind begging God to protect his friend.

. . .

Drew sat in the waiting room at the hospital and stared at the television set a few hours later. Gertrude sat beside him, wringing her hands.

"I'm sure everything will be fine," Drew told her for probably the hundredth time. "We got him here quickly, and he was talking and joking in the truck."

"*Ya*." Gertrude's focus was on the television set, but she didn't seem to be absorbing what was on it. She was most likely praying and thinking of her husband.

"Gertrude!" Cindy strode across the waiting room, followed by Vernon and Florence. "How is he?" She sat down beside Gertrude and took her hand.

"The last I heard, he had a mild heart attack, but they're running more tests. He might need surgery." Gertrude's lower lip trembled, and Florence pulled a wad of clean tissues from her pocket and handed them to her. "I was so scared this morning. Drew was our savior. I'm so grateful God brought him to us." She turned to Drew. "I don't know how long I would've had to wait for a ride if you hadn't been there."

"I'm just grateful I was there to help," Drew said.

Other members of the community came in and gathered around them, peppering Gertrude with questions. Drew found Jamie and Mark in the knot of people, along with other Amish folks he didn't recognize.

Cindy stood and motioned for Drew to follow her to an empty corner of the room.

"How is she?" Cindy asked when they were alone. "How is she really?"

"She's worried sick, and I can't blame her." He touched her arm. "I was the same way when we were here not too long ago."

"I know." Her face clouded with a frown.

Drew took in the large group of people ministering to Gertrude, and his heart swelled with appreciation. "Who did you call?"

"I ran and told *Dat* and Jamie, and then Florence started calling people. The word spread from there." Cindy leaned her head against his arm. "I'm so grateful for my family and friends. It would be horrible for Gertrude to sit here alone and worry, you know?"

"I knew the Amish are willing to help anyone in need, but are they always like this when someone is sick?"

She laughed. "Wait until you see the parade of people bringing food to Gertrude when she goes home."

"Really? Like your family did when you came home from the hospital?"

"Really. Just like that." She nodded. "The Amish know how to take care of their own. It's like having a giant family."

"Wow." Drew stilled as her words washed over him. "Do you think we could attend the service this week?"

Her eyes widened. "You want to go to an Amish service?"

"Yeah." He nodded. "I want to see what it's like."

"Okay. My family's church district is off this week, meaning there isn't a service. But we could go to a service in another district."

"I'd like that."

"I would too. I'll talk to Walter and Nellie and see where their church district is meeting on Sunday." She squeezed his hand. "Thank you for considering joining the church with me. It means more than you know."

Once again he felt that warmth wrapping around his heart. Was this an answer from God? No, it couldn't be that obvious.

But maybe it could.

. . .

Drew and Cindy sat on folding chairs at the back of the Zook family's barn Sunday morning in Gordonville. Cindy had contacted her stepbrother, Walter, about joining their district's service, making him promise not to tell anyone in the family that she and Drew were considering joining the church. He agreed, mostly because he didn't want to get anyone's hopes up.

The bishop sat at the front of the barn and spoke in Pennsylvania *Dietsch* while the congregation listened with what seemed like rapt attention. He turned to Cindy, and her expression was serene as she, too, focused on the bishop. Then she met his gaze and took his hand in hers before treating him to a warm, beautiful smile that sent his pulse galloping.

Still holding her hand, Drew turned back to the bishop. While he couldn't understand the language, he still felt God's presence in the barn, guiding his heart and his thoughts. Could this be his new community? Could he become a member of this extended family with Cindy at his side to guide him toward understanding their culture and customs?

His wife tapped his arm, and he leaned down to hear her whisper. "I'd teach you the language. It wouldn't be long before you'd understand what the ministers and bishop are saying."

It was as if she could read his thoughts. Or maybe she could feel his apprehension. He nodded, and she squeezed his hand once again.

"I promise," she whispered. When she returned her attention to the bishop, he closed his eyes. *Lead me, Lord. I won't be able to make this decision on my own.*

. . .

"What did you think of the service?" Cindy asked as they drove home in his pickup truck. She held her breath, awaiting his response. Would he decide not to join the church? If so, could she handle that decision?

"It was definitely different from what I'm used to." He gave her a sideways glance. "No music. No altar. No English."

"Was it too different?" Her chest constricted as he stared at the road ahead.

"No." He shook his head. "I think I could get used to it." He smiled at her. "Are you worried I'm going to tell you no?"

"Maybe." She gave him a half shrug. "But it's okay if you decide not to join. I'll support whatever you feel is right."

"I told you I'd think about it and pray about it, and I promise you I will. I'm not sure yet, but I promise I'll give you an answer soon."

"Why don't you talk to Pastor Ellen about it?"

He slowed to a stop at a red light and turned toward her. "You think that would help?"

"Ya, I do." Cindy nodded. "Tell her how you're feeling about the decision to convert and discuss it with her. She was a great help to me when we asked her to marry us."

"You're right." He rubbed her arm. "I think that's a great idea. I'll call her tomorrow."

"Good." Cindy felt her shoulders relax. Pastor Ellen would help lead Drew to the right decision, and Cindy would support whatever choice her husband made.

. . .

Drew sank down into a chair across from Pastor Ellen's desk Wednesday morning. "I appreciate your taking the time to meet with me today. I've been wrestling with a decision for over a week now, and you were such a great help when Cindy and I decided to get married."

"I'm always happy when people reach out to me when they need someone to talk to. So what's on your mind?" She rested her forearms on the desk.

"Cindy asked me if I would consider joining the Amish church."

"Really?" Pastor Ellen's eyes widened. "How do you feel about that?"

"Well, I like the idea since the Amish community is like an extended family, which I've never had. You know I was an only child, and when my parents died, my aunt raised me. Once she passed away, I was alone, and I was envious of Cindy's family when I met her. I could tell how close she is to her father and siblings. They pulled away from her when she married me, but as I shared with you before, we've repaired that rift.

"She told me after we attended service here last week that she finally feels the call of the Amish church and she wants to be baptized, but we'd have to join the church together. She said she'll respect my decision, but she truly would love it if we did. I've been thinking about it and praying about it, and we attended an Amish service on Sunday."

"How did you feel about the service?"

Drew rubbed his chin as he considered his response. "I could feel God's presence there, but I couldn't understand what the bishop was saying. Cindy said she'll teach me the language."

"But did you feel welcome at the service?"

"I did." Drew rested his right ankle on his left knee. "Her stepbrother Walter and his family welcomed us, and I think I would feel like a part of the congregation if we joined Cindy's district."

"Would you miss worshipping here?" She gestured around her office.

He heaved a heavy sigh. "Yes, I think I would. I grew up in a church similar to this one, but it would be like a new beginning for Cindy and me. I'd have the family I always wanted, and Cindy would be able to go back to the community where she was born."

"But would you be giving up too much?" Pastor Ellen sat back in her chair. "If you convert only to make her happy, you could wind up resenting your decision and eventually resenting her."

Drew considered Pastor Ellen's point. Would he resent Cindy? He shook his head. "I don't think so."

"Why not?"

"Because I can see myself assimilating into the Amish culture. When I close my eyes, I see visions of raising Amish children with her. I can see myself owning a horse and buggy and taking our family to services. I can almost feel it to the depth of my bones."

Pastor Ellen smiled. "I think you might have already made up your mind."

Drew pressed his lips together.

"You seem hesitant." Pastor Ellen tilted her head. "What are you afraid of?"

"I'm not sure." He looked down at his lap. "Maybe I'm afraid the community might not accept me completely since I wasn't born into the culture."

"But Cindy said they would, right? And you got that feeling from her stepbrother too?"

He nodded, and she smiled.

"I think you already have your answer, but pray about it again. I'll be praying *for* you."

He stood and shook her hand. "I appreciate your time. It's helped to talk this through with someone."

"I'm here anytime you need me."

"Thank you," Drew said, and then he left.

Pastor Ellen's words filtered through his mind as he drove home. When he steered into the Lapps' driveway, he spotted a group of Amish women delivering food to Gertrude and Ervin.

For the past few days, the parade of Amish people, as Cindy had called it, hadn't stopped visiting the Lapps. They seemed to come by like clockwork—arriving every afternoon with whatever Ervin was allowed to eat—and then some. They were as reliable as the rising of the sun, as his aunt used to say.

Drew was grateful to hear Ervin's condition was improving. He'd had surgery to clear a blocked artery, and he was already feeling better. He would have to start physical therapy soon, but Gertrude said he already felt like he had more energy than he'd had in months.

As he made his way to his porch, he pondered his conversation with Pastor Ellen once again. He considered the service he'd attended and felt the question twirl through him. Should he and Cindy be baptized together and join the Amish church?

He looked over at Ervin's house again. If they joined the church, he, Cindy, and their future children would be part of this wonderful community, this supportive extended family. Was this what Drew wanted? Was this what God wanted for Cindy and him?

He looked up at the sky as a resounding *Yes!* echoed in his mind. Excitement rippled through him.

He stepped into the house and was greeted by both his dog

and the chatter of the sewing machine. After hanging his coat on a peg by the front door, he rubbed Bruce's ear and then walked into the back bedroom, where Cindy sat with her head down, concentrating on a sewing project. Her tongue stuck out and she looked adorable as all her focus was trained on what looked like a blanket.

He sat down on the stool across from her and waited for the machine to stop.

When she looked up, she gasped.

"I hate it when you scare me!" She swatted him with her hand and then laughed. "How was your meeting with Pastor Ellen?"

"It was good. We had a nice talk."

"And . . . ?" Her beautiful face looked hopeful.

He sucked in a deep breath and then just blurted it out. "I've thought about it and I've prayed about it. My answer to you is yes. I would like to be baptized in the Amish church with you by my side."

She stared at him for a moment, and then her eyes opened wide and she gave a little squeal. "Do you mean it?"

"Of course I do. I wouldn't joke about something this serious."

"You know what you'll have to give up, right?" Her questions came out in a rush. She pointed to the light fixtures around them. "We'd have to move out of here. And you'd have to stop going to school and sell your truck. And you'd have to—"

"I know, I know." He leaned forward and took her hands in his. "I know what I'll have to give up. When I spoke to Ervin about it, he said we'd have to meet with the bishop and probably live like Amish folks for a year before we can join. So it won't be a quick process, but I believe that's where God wants me. I've prayed about it, and his answer came loud and clear."

"So you're certain?" Her beautiful eyes seemed to sparkle.

"Yeah." He rubbed his chin. "At first, I considered it because I wanted to make you happy, and then because I realized the Amish community is like one big family, and I want that. Those are still important to me, but the most important thing is that I believe God wants me to be a part of the community and the church. And I want that with you."

She launched herself into his arms and rested her face against his shoulder. "I love you, Drew."

"I love you too." He leaned down, and when he kissed her, he felt a calmness cover his heart.

This was where he belonged. This was where God wanted him to be.

. . .

Drew knocked on the Lapps' back door the following morning. He looked over at Cindy and she smiled at him as they waited.

"Good morning," Gertrude said when she opened the door and then smiled. "What are you two doing here?"

"We're on our way to meet with John Smucker, but we want to know if you need anything," Drew explained.

"Why are you going to meet with the bishop?" Gertrude asked.

"We're going to join the church together," Drew said.

Gertrude gasped, and her eyes lit up. "That's *wunderbaar!*"

"Who's at the door?" Ervin called from inside the house.

"It's Drew and Cindy," Gertrude called back. "You have to hear their news." She beckoned them to come in.

Drew and Cindy followed her into the kitchen, where Ervin sat at the table eating a bowl of cereal.

"How are you feeling?" Cindy asked.

"I'm doing better. *Danki.*" Ervin wiped his beard with a paper napkin. "So what's your news?"

"We're going to join the church," Cindy announced. "We're on our way to meet with the bishop."

"Is that so?" Ervin focused on Drew.

"It is." Drew threaded his fingers with Cindy's. "I prayed about it, and the answer seemed more and more clear every time I asked God to lead me. We attended an Amish church service on Sunday and then I visited with my pastor yesterday. I discussed it with Cindy yesterday, and we're ready to take the next step."

Ervin looked at his wife. "This is the answer we were praying for, too, isn't it?"

"*Ya.* I'm sure it is." Gertrude seemed to be asking him a question with her eyes, and he nodded.

"Tell them," he said.

Gertrude took a step toward them. "If John agrees to your joining the church, and I'm sure he will, we want to give you the farm."

"What?" they said at the same time.

"We've been thinking of giving it up for a while, and my heart attack seems to be a direct sign it's time for a smaller house," Ervin added. "Our *sohn* doesn't want the farm, and he doesn't expect us to sell it. He's doing very well in his career. So we decided to find a young Amish couple to take this place, and here you are. We'll remove the electricity from the smaller house and move in there. You two can have this *haus* and the farm as long as you let us live in the smaller house."

"There's plenty of room for your family to grow," Gertrude said. "There's a bedroom downstairs and three more upstairs. I think it's perfect for you."

Drew felt stunned, and when he looked at Cindy's face, he knew she did too.

Then she grabbed Drew's bicep and looked up at him. "What do you think?"

"I'm a little overwhelmed." Drew looked at Ervin. "Are you sure?"

"I'm absolutely positive, *sohn*." The older man nodded. "We'll be honored to give you the farm."

"We'll be honored to preserve it for you." Drew shook his hand as a wide smile broke out on his lips. "Thank you. We'll take good care of it. What a gift."

Cindy hugged Gertrude and then looked at Ervin. "*Ya*, thank you so much."

"You're welcome." Ervin gave them a broad smile. "I'll find someone to come remove the electricity. You be sure to tell John we're working on that, and we'll have it done as soon as possible. He'll want to know how soon you plan to live Amish. We can work out when we switch houses too."

Drew smiled as his thoughts spun. "This is such a tremendous blessing. I'm so grateful God led me to this farm and this life."

This was happening! If the bishop agreed, he was going to be Amish—and a dairy farmer too!

CHAPTER 31

Cindy's heart felt as if it might beat out of her chest as Drew steered his truck into the bishop's driveway. John Smucker and his wife, Naomi, were retired and lived in the *daadihaus* behind the main farmhouse on their family's dairy farm. They expected him to be home this early in the morning, even if he had errands somewhere.

"Are you ready for this?" Drew asked as the truck tires crunched their way up the rock driveway.

"*Ya*, I am." She looked at him. "Are you?"

"With you by my side, I think I can accomplish anything."

She smiled. "I feel the same way."

Drew parked his truck at the top of the driveway, and then they climbed out. This conversation would be life-changing, and a mixture of excitement and anxiety surged through Cindy as they strode up the path to the porch.

Her pulse thudded as she climbed the steps and knocked on the door. Drew stood directly behind her, his body heat mixing with hers. He rested his hand on her shoulder, and it gave her strength and courage.

The door swung open, and Naomi, John's wife, smiled at her. "Cindy. What a surprise." She looked behind Cindy, and her smile faltered. "Hello."

"Hi, Naomi." Cindy made a sweeping gesture between Naomi

and Drew. "This is my husband, Drew. We were wondering if we could speak with John."

"Oh. Was he expecting you?" Naomi's gaze bounced between them.

"No," Drew chimed in. "But does he have a few minutes to talk?"

"*Ya*, of course." Naomi motioned for them to enter. "Please have a seat. I'll tell him you're here."

Cindy stepped into the small cottage and stopped to scan the room, finding a small sitting area with a sofa, two wing chairs, two end tables with propane lamps, and a coffee table. Drew stood beside her.

"Cindy." John stepped into the family room, his expression seeming hesitant yet polite. And formal.

"Hi, John." Cindy gestured at Drew, who held out his hand. "This is my husband, Drew. We'd like to speak with you."

"Hello . . . Drew." The men shook hands, and then John gestured toward the sofa. "Please sit down."

Cindy sank next to Drew, and John sat down on a chair across from them.

"What brings you here today?" John said as he folded his hands in his lap. Still no smile.

Cindy looked at Drew, thinking he must also have noticed the bishop wasn't exactly happy to see them, and he nodded for her to continue. "We've been doing a lot of thinking and praying, and we want to be baptized. I know it's unusual for someone to leave the church, marry an *Englisher*, and then want to come back. But we both believe this is the path we're meant to follow."

She paused when she saw the bishop's eyebrows rise slightly, but then plunged ahead with what was in her heart. "The truth is, after *mei mamm* died, I felt even more disconnected from my family and the church than I had before. When I met Drew, I felt like I'd finally found my home, and I've learned a lot from him." She smiled at Drew and then looked back at the bishop. "Drew has faced tremendous loss in his own life, but he never lost faith in God. He's helped me find a renewed faith."

She entwined her fingers with Drew's. John had leaned forward, as though he was hanging on her every word. "We're building a life together, but even though we attended Drew's church, I've realized that my heart belongs to the Amish community. I needed to renew my faith in God to realize I've belonged in the Amish church all along. I've prayed about it, and I feel God leading me back home. I'm ready to be baptized into the faith, and I'm ready to commit my life to the church."

John nodded slowly, then looked at Drew as he leaned back in his chair. "What about you? What makes you feel you should be Amish?"

"I lost my parents when I was young, and then last year my aunt who raised me passed away. I've always longed for a family." Drew looked at Cindy. "Cindy is my family, but I've admired the Amish community for a long time. I work for Ervin and Gertrude Lapp, and I've always appreciated how they included me as a part of their family."

He looked at John again. "When Cindy asked me if I would consider joining the church with her, I began praying and asking God if I should join. We attended an Amish service together this past Sunday in her stepbrother's district, and then I went to talk to my own pastor, who supports me in this decision. When I asked God again, his answer came loud and clear. He's guiding me here as well."

"We know this is unusual, but we feel in our hearts that we should be Amish," Cindy said.

"Are you certain your reasons are pure?" John asked.

"Yes," they answered in unison.

John studied them both. "I heard you were living with Ervin and Gertrude Lapp. Is that right?"

"That's true," Cindy said. "We're living in the small house they built for their *sohn*."

"That house has electricity, right?"

Cindy nodded, but John spoke again before she could mention Ervin and Gertrude's plan.

"If you've been living like *Englishers*, then you'd have to live like Amish folks for a year before I can let you join a baptism class. That means you need to live without all the modern conveniences—"

"We understand," Drew said, interrupting him. "Ervin and Gertrude just told us they want to give us their farm. They're going to remove the electricity from the little house and move in there. Then we'll move into their farmhouse and take over the farm."

"That's very generous of them," John said.

"We're immensely grateful," Cindy added.

"And you'll have to give up your truck," John told Drew.

"I plan to advertise it right away. As soon as I sell it, I'll buy a horse and buggy. I'll also stop attending college classes." He looked at Cindy. "And I need you to make me new clothes."

"I'll do that." Cindy squeezed Drew's hand.

"What does your *dat* think?" John asked her.

"He doesn't know yet," Cindy said. "I've been praying about it for a couple of weeks, and I wanted to speak with you first. We'll go see my family after we leave here."

The bishop rubbed his beard and was silent for a moment. "You need to be sure, Cindy. You truly believe God put this decision in your heart?"

"Absolutely," Cindy said, emphasizing the word. "I could never have decided this without his guidance."

"And what about you, Drew?" the bishop asked.

"Yes," Drew said. "I have prayed over and over about this, and when I think of becoming Amish, I feel as if God has wrapped me in his love. That feels like a yes to me."

Cindy gasped as tears streamed down her face. "That's beautiful."

"It's the truth," Drew said with a rasp in his voice.

"I believe you." John pointed between them. "You're ready to shed all your *Englisher* ways immediately?"

"Yes," Drew said. "Ervin and I are going to find someone to take the electricity out of the house as soon as possible." He glanced at Cindy once again. "I'll start wearing Amish clothes as soon as Cindy has them ready, and we'll be in church with our district. I'm ready to make a full commitment to this community and to my new life right away, and I'll be ready for my instruction in the spring, if you'll accept us into the class."

Cindy held her breath, her body thrumming as they awaited John's decision.

John touched his beard once again, and then a smile broke out on his face. "I'm thrilled to hear you both have made this decision. If all goes as planned, you'll be baptized with the other young people in our district next fall."

"Oh, *danki*!" Cindy clapped her hands together. "I'm so grateful." Jumping up, she shook John's hand with vigor. "I'm so thankful. I appreciate your time." Then she turned to Drew and hugged him.

"Thank you for inviting me into your community." Drew kissed her cheek and then shook John's hand.

John chuckled. "Go tell your *dat*, Cindy. He's going to be thrilled."

Cindy took Drew's hand and they said good-bye to John and Naomi before they practically ran to Drew's truck.

. . .

"Cindy! Drew," Florence said when she opened the back door. "Please come in. What a nice surprise. We just sat down for lunch."

"Thank you." Cindy's body trembled with excitement as she followed Florence into the kitchen, where *Dat* and Sarah Jane were eating sandwiches. "Hello." She gave a little wave.

"*Wie geht's?*" *Dat* said. "We weren't expecting you."

"Hi," Drew said.

"We have an announcement." Cindy looked up at Drew, and he winked at her, giving her the courage to move on.

"Oh!" Florence covered her mouth with her hand. "So soon?"

"No, it's not what you think." Cindy felt a blush coming. "It's something else, and I think you'll be pleased." She took a deep breath. "Drew and I just met with the bishop."

"What?" *Dat* stood, his eyes rounding and shimmering.

"We're going to join the church." Cindy's throat felt thick with emotion. "We've both been praying about it, and we realized we belong in this community. In the past few weeks, I've felt the church calling me."

"God has been calling me here too," Drew said.

"Oh, Cindy!" *Dat* crossed the kitchen and pulled her into a tight hug. "This is the best news I've ever heard. I'm so *froh*."

He whispered the words into her ear. "Your *mamm* would be so *froh* to hear this too. *Danki*, Cindy. *Danki* so much."

As Cindy held on to her father, something inside released and tears flowed. She was home! God had called her and her husband back home.

"This is so wonderful!" Florence exclaimed. "Sarah Jane, call everyone! Let's celebrate!"

Dat released her and wiped his eyes. Then he shook Drew's hand. "Welcome to our community, *sohn*."

Cindy wiped more tears when she heard her father call her husband "son." Drew was fully accepted into her family.

"I'm so *froh*," Florence said as she hugged her.

"I am too." Sarah Jane hugged her next. "I'll go call everyone." She disappeared through the mudroom.

"Sit!" Florence ordered. "I'll get plates, and you can make yourselves some sandwiches."

Cindy and Drew sat down with her father and explained their plan for the coming months. They also told him they were going to take over the Lapps' farm.

Dat wiped his eyes as he listened to the story. Happiness came off him in waves, and Cindy's heart swelled with elation. For the first time in years, she felt like a true part of her family.

Later, her siblings and their families came by to celebrate their news. They all spent the evening talking, laughing, and eating together. Cindy watched in awe as her brothers talked with Drew as if he were already a member of the church. Drew looked like he belonged with her family, and it warmed her from the inside out.

By the end of the evening, Cindy was exhausted, and her face hurt from smiling. She hugged everyone before she and Drew headed home.

When Drew parked his pickup truck in the driveway, he turned off the engine and then angled his body toward hers.

"I had a great time tonight," he said.

"I did too. I'm so excited about our new life in the church."

"I am too." He blew out a sigh. "We still have a lot to do." He tapped the dashboard. "I need to advertise the truck, and then I need to buy a horse from Mark and a buggy from Allen."

Cindy pointed to her chest. "And I need to teach you how to guide a horse."

He laughed. "That's right. You have a lot to teach me. You need to start Pennsylvania Dutch lessons right away. I guess some German ones too."

"I will." She touched his cheek and smiled. "And you'll need to grow a beard."

"I can do that." He reached over and pulled her to him. "I'm so happy right now. I already feel like a part of the community."

"I do too." She looked up at him. "Thank you for helping me find my way home."

As Drew brushed his lips against hers, she felt her body relax. Then she rested her head on his shoulder and silently thanked God. He'd led her to Drew, and then he'd guided her back to the Amish community and Drew to a new home.

EPILOGUE

Cindy held her baby girl against her chest as she exited her father's barn and walked toward the main house. The sweet September breeze kissed her cheeks and made the ties to her prayer covering bounce off her shoulders.

"You're finally a member," Laura said as she gave her a side hug. "I know you've been counting down to this day."

"I have." Cindy looked down at her six-month-old daughter and smiled. "I'm so grateful that Drew and I will raise Emalyn and her future siblings in the church."

"I am too," Priscilla said as she came up behind her with Kayla at her side.

"Welcome back to the community," Kayla told her.

"*Danki*," Cindy said.

It had been nearly eighteen months since she and Drew had moved into the Lapps' house and taken over their farm. Drew had adjusted well to the Amish lifestyle, learning the language, beliefs, and customs as if he had been born into the faith. Drew also enjoyed the hard work of running the dairy farm.

As Drew and Cindy fell into their new lifestyle, Emalyn became their miracle, and they prayed that God would bless them with more children when he saw fit.

Cindy made her way into *Dat*'s family room, where she set the diaper bag on the sofa and began to change Emalyn's diaper. The voices of women in the community sounded in the kitchen as they prepared to serve the noon meal.

"Cindy." Drew came up behind her and kissed her cheek. "I was looking for you."

She smiled down at Emalyn as she finished putting the new diaper on her. "Say hi to your *dat*. Say hi!"

Emalyn gurgled and kicked her legs, and Cindy and Drew laughed in response.

Drew touched Emalyn's little leg. "With her beautiful blue eyes and blond hair, she's just as *schee* as you are."

"*Danki*." Cindy looked up at him. He looked handsome in his Sunday black and white and his beard. "How does it feel to be a church member?"

"Like I've finally come home." He kissed her cheek. "*Danki* for inviting me into your family."

Her eyes burned just a little. "I'm so grateful God brought you to me."

"Me too." Drew held out his arms, and she handed him Emalyn. He kissed the baby and then grinned at Cindy. "Let's go see our family."

Together, they walked outside, where her nieces and nephews played on the elaborate swing set her father and brothers had built for them.

"Before you know it, Emalyn will be on there too," Drew said as he patted the baby's back.

"*Ya*, she will."

When she turned, she spotted a cow trotting out of the pasture toward the street. "Look! It's Cucumber! She's on the loose again!"

"Oh no. That *narrisch* cow!" Drew shook his head and laughed.

"We love that *narrisch* cow." She looked up at Drew. "We have a cow named Cucumber to thank for bringing us together. You know what they say," she began. "The Lord works in mysterious ways."

"*Ya*, he does."

"Cucumber!" Jamie called, running after the cow with Mark in tow. *"Hoi! Hoi!"*

"That *gegisch* cow," *Dat* muttered as he approached Cindy and Drew.

"I think Jamie needs to padlock that gate," Drew said.

"Welcome to our community, *sohn*," *Dat* said as he shook Drew's hand, and then he kissed Cindy's cheek. "I'm so glad you're back."

"I am too." Cindy smiled at her father. They were a family, and she and Drew finally belonged to the community.

As the two men talked, Cindy touched the cross necklace she kept hidden under her dress. She was so grateful for the path God had set for her and Drew, and as she looked around at her family and community, she realized she'd never felt so welcome.

DISCUSSION QUESTIONS

1. When Cindy left the Amish church to marry Drew, she believed she'd never go back. By the end of the book, she's realized the Amish community is her true home. What do you think caused her to change her point of view throughout the story?

2. Priscilla is Cindy's closest confidante when Cindy finds herself falling in love with Drew. While the rest of the Riehl family turned against Cindy, Priscilla told her she would always be welcome at her home. Why do you think Priscilla accepted Cindy's decision to marry Drew more readily than the rest of the Riehl family?

3. Cindy suffers a miscarriage and yearns to talk to Laura since she experienced two miscarriages of her own. Could you relate to Cindy and her experience? If you feel comfortable doing so, share this with the group.

4. Drew is searching for a family and a home after losing his parents and then the aunt who raised him. When he and Cindy decide to join the Amish church, he finally feels he's found his true home. What do you think drew him to the Amish church?

5. Laura feels guilty for staying away from Cindy when she comes to see Cindy after the miscarriage. Why do you

think Laura stayed away from Cindy after she married Drew? What do you think made Laura change her point of view about her relationship with her sister after Cindy's miscarriage?

6. Vernon refuses to talk to Cindy after she chooses to leave the Amish church and marry Drew. Close to the end of the story, he comes back to Cindy and asks for her forgiveness. What do you think made him realize he'd been wrong to disown Cindy?

7. Florence and Sarah Jane both try to convince Cindy to join the church and find a nice Amish man to marry instead of pursuing a relationship with Drew. Have you ever had a friend or family member who insisted they knew what was best for you? If so, how did you handle that person? How did the situation turn out?

8. Which character did you identify with the most? Which character seemed to carry the most emotional stake in the story? Was it Cindy, Drew, or someone else?

9. Cindy is still grieving her mother's death even after seven years. Think of a time when you felt lost and alone. Where did you find your strength? What Bible verses helped?

10. What did you know about the Amish before reading this book? What did you learn?

ACKNOWLEDGMENTS

As always, I'm thankful for my loving family, including my mother, Lola Goebelbecker; my husband, Joe; and my sons, Zac and Matt. I'm blessed to have such an awesome and amazing family that puts up with me when I'm stressed out on a book deadline.

Special thanks to my mother and my dear friend Becky Biddy, who graciously read the draft of this book to check for typos. Becky—I'm sure you ran out of a few dispensers of tape flags on this one! Also, thank you, Becky, for your daily notes of encouragement. Your friendship is a blessing!

I'm also grateful to my special Amish friend, who patiently answers my endless stream of questions. I'm especially thankful she generously shared the story that inspired this book.

Thank you to my wonderful church family at Morning Star Lutheran in Matthews, North Carolina, for your encouragement, prayers, love, and friendship. You all mean so much to my family and me.

Thank you to Zac Weikal and the fabulous members of my Bakery Bunch! I'm so thankful for your friendship and your excitement about my books. You all are amazing!

To my agent, Natasha Kern—I can't thank you enough for your guidance, advice, and friendship. You are a tremendous blessing in my life.

Thank you to my amazing editor, Jocelyn Bailey, for your

friendship and guidance. I appreciate how you push me to dig deeper with each book and improve my writing. I've learned so much from you, and I look forward to our future projects together. I also cherish our fun emails and text messages. You are a delight!

I'm grateful to editor Jean Bloom, who helped me polish and refine the story. Jean, you are a master at connecting the dots and filling in the gaps. I'm so thankful that we can continue to work together!

I'm grateful to each and every person at HarperCollins Christian Publishing who helped make this book a reality.

To my readers—thank you for choosing my novels. My books are a blessing in my life for many reasons, including the special friendships I've formed with my readers. Thank you for your email messages, Facebook notes, and letters.

Thank you most of all to God—for giving me the inspiration and the words to glorify You. I'm grateful and humbled You've chosen this path for me.

THE AMISH HOMESTEAD SERIES

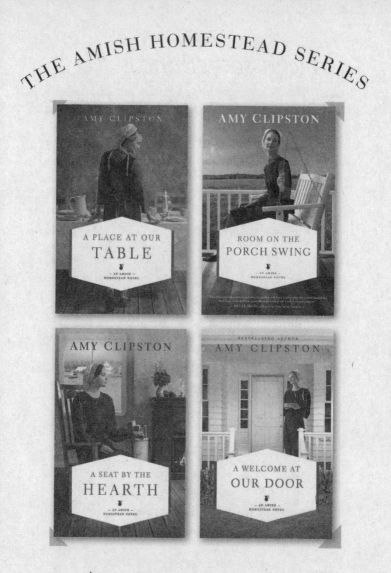

Need something sweet?
Pick up *An Amish Picnic!*

DON'T MISS OTHER BOOKS BY AMY CLIPSTON IN THE AMISH HEIRLOOM SERIES!

Available in print, e-book, and audio.

Check out
AN AMISH HOMECOMING
for more stories by your favorite authors!

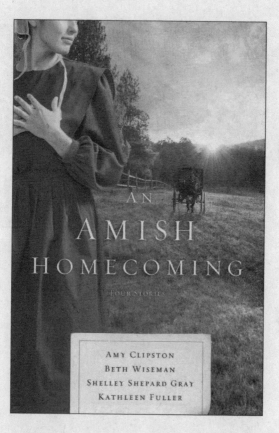

Available in print and as an e-book

Enjoy these Amish collections for every season!

AVAILABLE IN PRINT AND E-BOOK